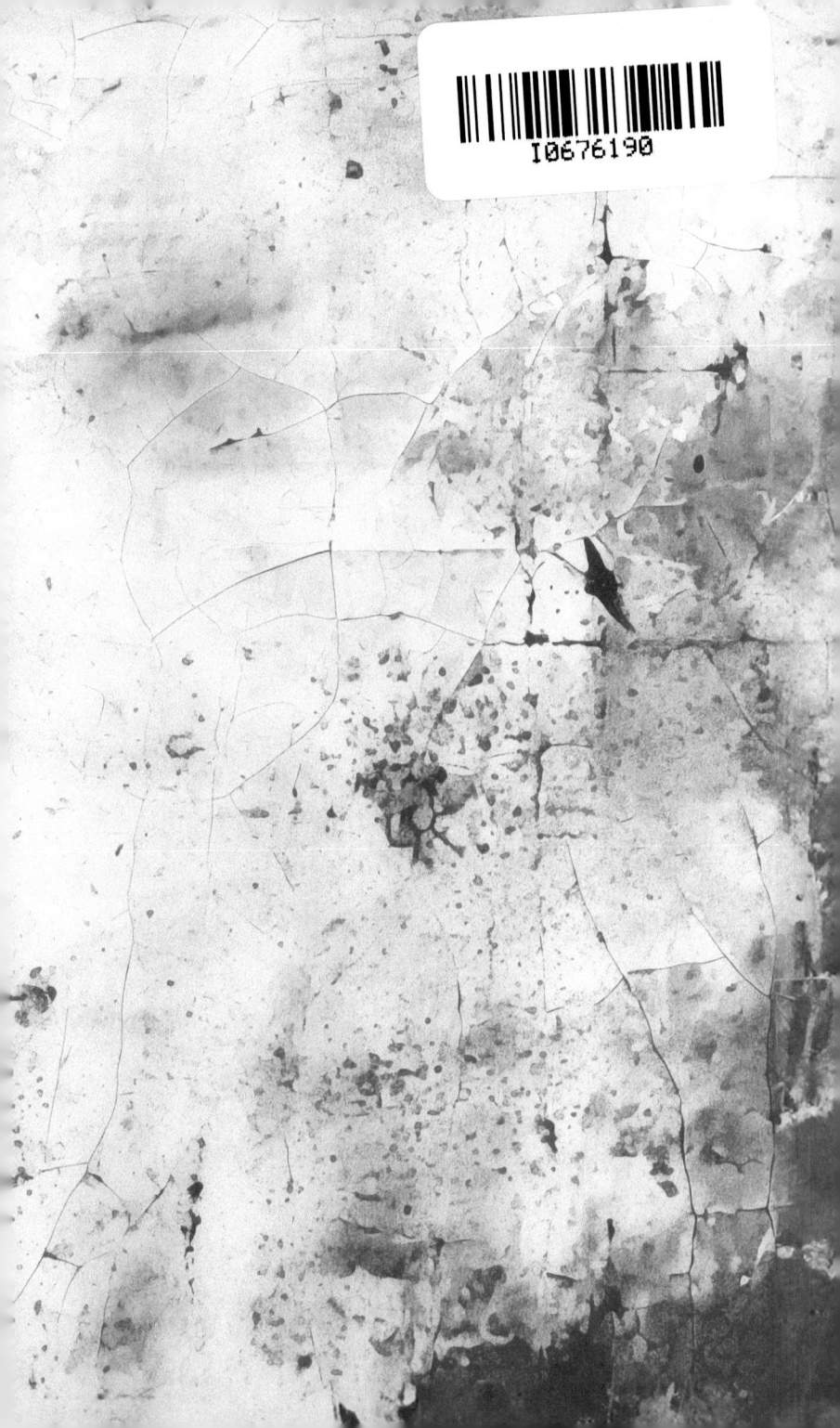

ELLIS KROSS · DALIVIA PLAUT · P.B. JACOBI

BLACK FANGS
MOTORCYCLE
CLUB AND OTHER STORIES

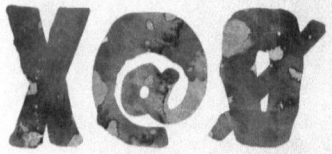

First Edition, November 2025
Stories by Ellis Kross, Dalivia Plaut, P.B. Jacobi
Edited by Sidonie Lailler
Copyright © 2025 Ellis Kross, P.B. Jacobi, Dalivia Plaut

PUBLISHED BY X@Ø

ISBN: 979-8-9919643-1-9
Black Fangs Motorcycle Club and Other Stories
I. Title. Horror. Thriller

ISBN: 979-8-9919643-1-9 pbk.

Book Design by Izzy
Cover artwork by Inna Sinano

Printed in the United States
10 9 8 7 6 5 4 3 2 1

CONTENTS

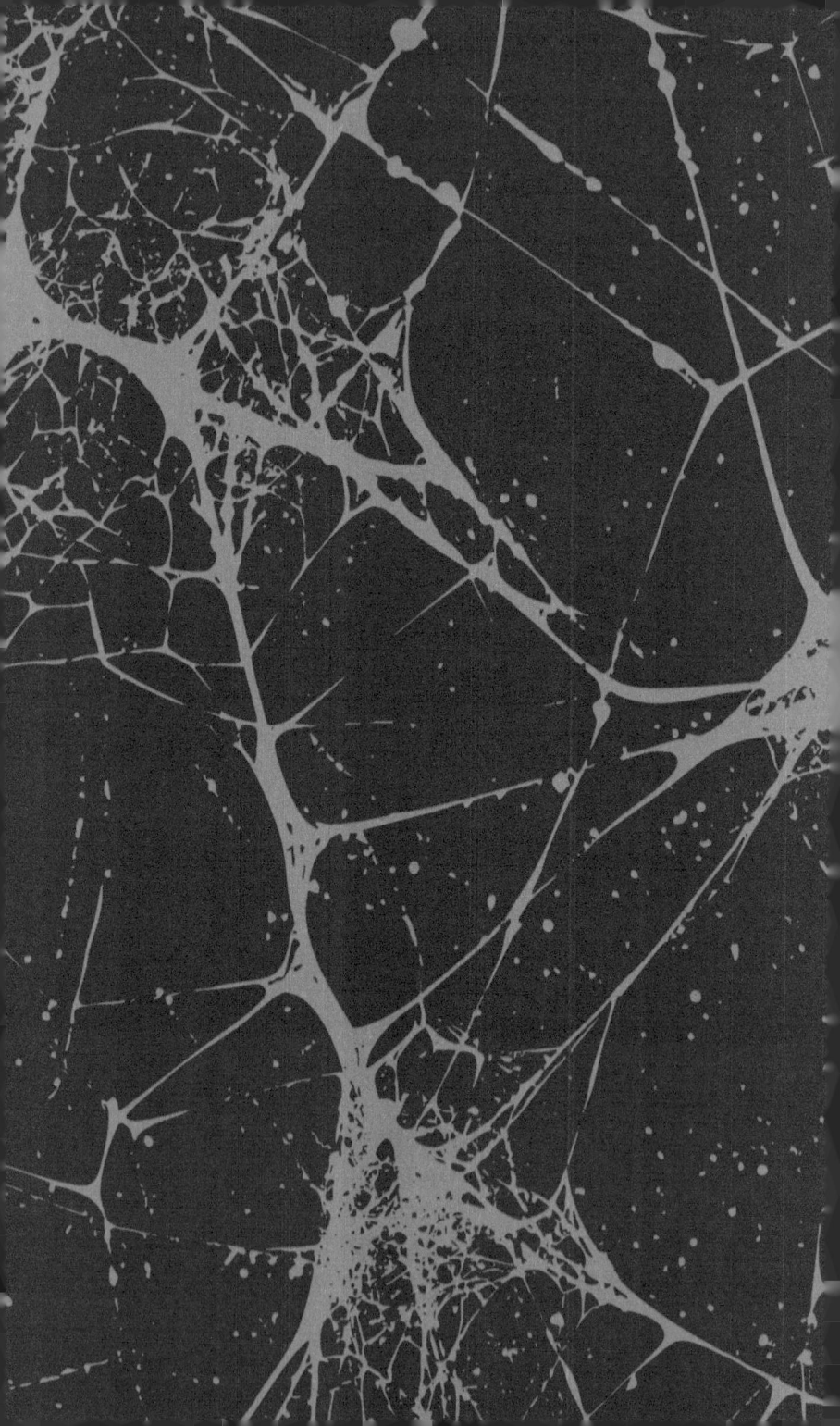

BLACK FANGS MOTORCYCLE CLUB AND OTHER STORIES

X@Ø

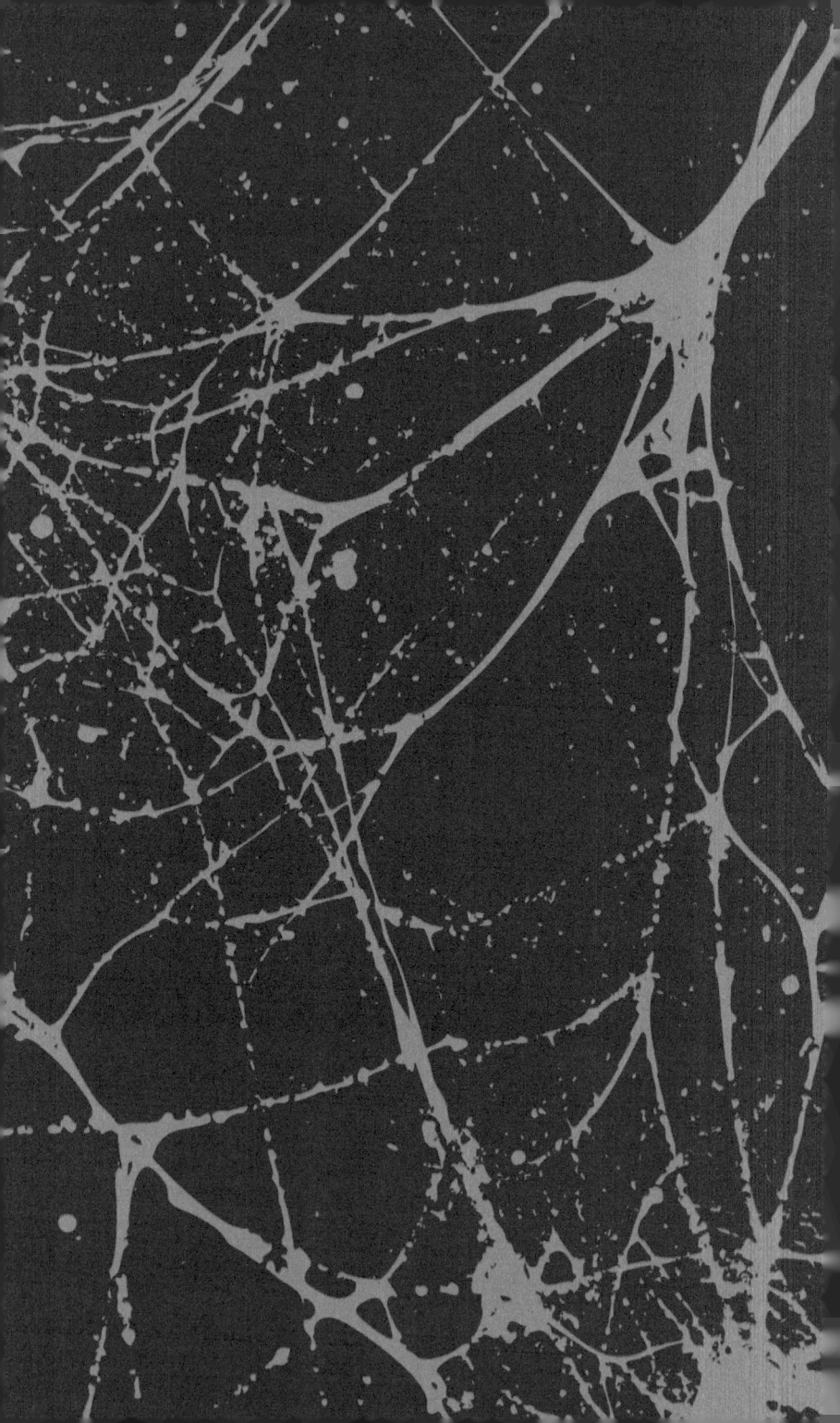

DIFFERENT seasons tick by like seconds before my eyes. The minute hand climbs closer to eleven, standing bare, embroiled, and magnanimous. Needle and *thread*, the holy receptacles of past voices, weave through one season to the next, prophesying, monopolizing, and sowing seeds of the darkest of all spells: my index finger closes in on His inevitable hour.

Now kiss me, deep and dark, caress my *nefarious ballad*.

What a cruel and untimely prelude.

The charred remains of a soot-covered field, once consumed by fire.

Enter *The Dumpster*:

McKenzie Horrorwich recoils in disgust as the projectile of vomit catches part of the salmon colored blouse by Flos that her Conehead girlfriends were admiring earlier during that oppressive summer night, but I'm way too wired and wasted to fend or fight,

(The nuclear winter leaves me shaking)

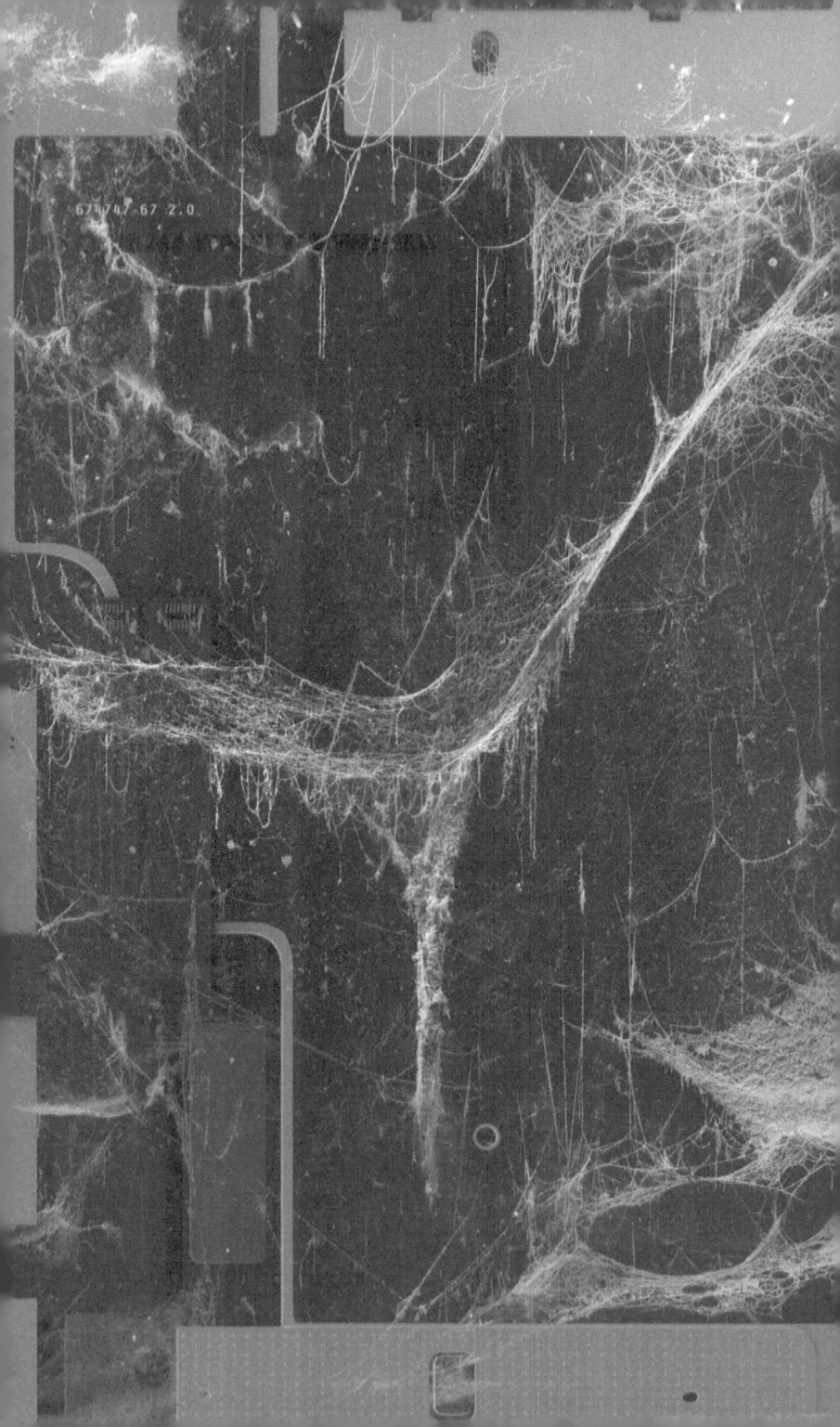

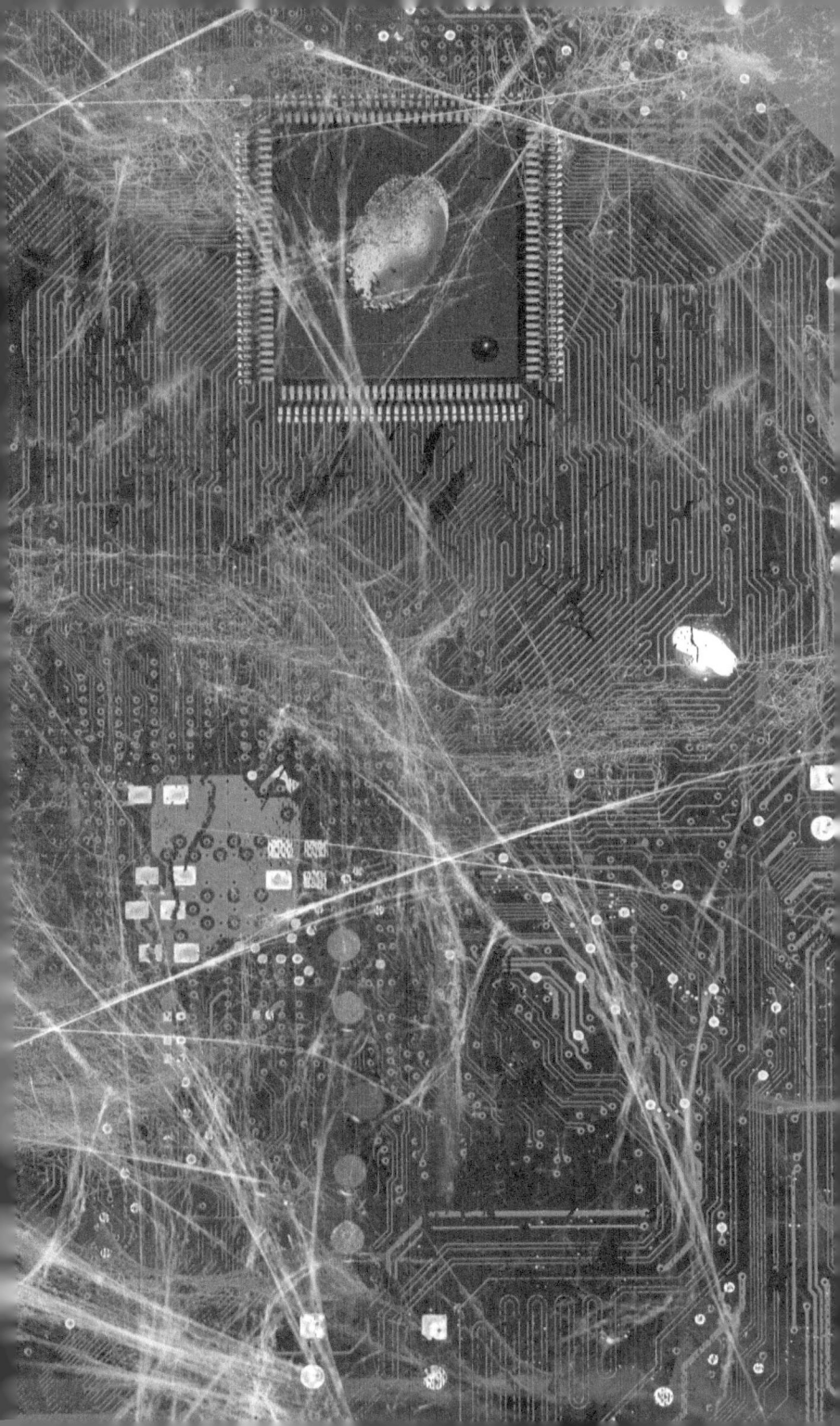

my father raises a chapped leather belt above his head and pre-pares to strike me down, like Zeus holding a bolt of lightning, after I take blame for accidentally destroying his miniature model of the Niña and as he's about to whip me until I'm red and raw, his bloodshot eyes light up with tiny flames cast from a re-flection of the fireplace,

(Late spring uncoils a knot in my gut)

Stella's face flushes as she checks the text on her smartphone while slipping a fork of saucy chicken Alfredo into her mouth, yet somehow I'm so damn enthralled by her cover-girl-like allure to determine whether it's the food that's causing her to react with the nudge of a partial smile or the unfolding mystery behind the glow of her phone (the wolf inside me howls into a deep, dark valley); *Amelia wakes up in the dead of night, aggressively rolls out of bed, and blindly staggers her way to the bathroom and as the pale light cast from a full* Strawberry Moon *basks over her body, the outgoing woman, whom I once eternally adored despite our many differences, ideologically and politically, is peeling apart at the seams and looks more and more like a sorry stranger, her undefined shape deformed and decayed, parts of her body bumpy and bloated, like a swamp creature, her natural beauty, both internal and external, misplaced and forgotten,*

(Only does autumn seem so familiar to me now)

Wynona's corpse rests inside a fancy casket that a dead-faced funeral home employee sold to my mother, who (many spells ago) *lets loose her trademark laugh, one that has plagued my teen ears, with yet another wet-voiced man behind her bedroom door, but as I stand, head tight and feverish, at the end of the dark hall-way, the rectangular light of the doorway outlining the closed bedroom door reminds me of a gateway to a much darker di-mension where only demons parade; a red-faced Francis pokes his head from the bed sheets while Riley doesn't budge an inch from her side of the bed, once* my side of the bed, *as she crosses her arms over her saggy breasts and stares at me as if I'm worse than earth-scum, just a dried-up, hardened blob of gum wedged between the worn tread of a shoe, and all I wish to do right* "Now" *is burn their perfect little world to the ground.*

A life of many roads diverged into a stage full of repeat O' fenders.

One avenue left untraveled.

Purged by fire.

But is it the fire I desire?

Shattered glass falls like snowflakes from a starless sky, covering a barren, rubble-ridden ground around me. Thousands of smoldering ambers release snake-like hisses. Elevators of stem ascend above me.

That nag of uncertainty triumphs into the blaring of a delayed *ringing* sound, *greeting* me, *engulfing* me, *becoming* me. Yet, despite the violent welcoming, the ringing remains tucked away underneath the eternal hum of life, soft yet present like a subdued soundtrack curated by the designated life-jockeys who brace space and time. Those dog days of summer, nevermore.

— Demi "Dimzy" Ruffiano
EPITAPH: *"These lemons are rotten."*

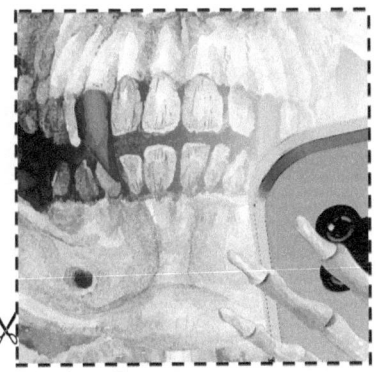

BLACK FANGS
MOTORCYCLE CLUB *

AT 9:03 AM Pacific Time on August 9th of 2018, I entered the main offices of Key Light Studios to pitch a movie idea for Hollywood studio executive, Frank Waters, aka "The Hit Maker," who heard from a close friend of a brother's girlfriend's hairdresser's cousin's partner's dog walker's mailman's sister's dentist's son's friend's father that this new kid on the block was developing a modern spin on an old legend, one that dated all the way back to early Greek mythology, however, wasn't first introduced to America cinema until the year 1941 in the horror film, *The Wolf Man*, which was produced, as well as directed by George Waggner and written by Curt Siodmak.

The receptionist, Cerby, told me that Mr. Waters was currently tied up at the moment and would be right with her and in the meantime, to take a seat in a chair. Cerby commented on the silver snakehead cane that I was using to assist my walk, which prompted a tight-lip smile from me and then a cordial response of informing Cerby of the boating accident I was involved in last year.

Before Cerby could further inquire about the recent injury, both doors to Mr. Waters' office swung open.

Cerby escorted me into Mr. Waters' office.

After a short introduction, I pitched the idea to Mr. Waters, a story editor, as well as two producers, who were eager to hear my new take on ole Wolfy.

Here was how it went down:

INTERIOR. . . A stale dimly lit hospital room.

We open with CLOSE UP of the profile of a sweaty, pasty, skeletal face of a Hispanic woman lying in a hospital bed. The lashes along her dopey eyelids fluttering like the wings of a housefly inside cavernous eye sockets. Her frail, feverish body hooked up to machines.

Her name: GWEN LOPEZ, wife of GRANT WILSON[A] – strong, stern, and black, masonry who repairs monuments in Washington, D.C. – a mother of two sons, 18, CHARLEMAGNE "CHARLES," and ARMANI "ARMY," a war veteran who recently returned home from Afghanistan.

The three family members huddle around GWEN as she slips away, taking her final breaths. The haunting sound of a flatline draws out underneath FADING blackness.

We CUT to the town of WILDWOOD[B], Maryland, which lies north of Baltimore: Shots of the annual "<u>Summer of Gold Festival</u>" taking place on MAIN STREET[C]. The festival commemorates former slave and local legend, JULIUS S. HAMMER[D].

Driving past overcrowded streets, we see drunken townspeople dressed as the jerrybuilt knight, HAMMER[E]; items of gold-colored memorabilia, T-shirts, hats, coffee mugs; lastly, locals wearing costumes of their own versions of The Wildwood Beast. Like Halloween during summertime[F].

The WILSON family, GRANT, CHARLES, and ARMY[G], who's accompanying the two in order to help with the transition, ride in a MOOVIN' USA truck[H], carrying their possessions from their bungalow in D.C. to Grant's father's countryside home, which he had refinished before his passing. Restarting their lives in a small town, GRANT and his two sons remain positive about the fresh start, except for the youngest CHARLES, who has taken the loss of his mother the hardest and doesn't see eye to eye with his father, who, like CHARLES, also had issues with his late father, MARLEY.

The conflict begins with CHARLES, who, after misplacing his mother's box of vintage paperbacks and timeless record collections which he suspects GRANT donated to a non-profit organization before the move, has an argument with his father, who considers himself to be a realist, not an idealist, and isn't fond of frivolous possessions. Frustrated by his father's inability to accept his passion for music and storytelling, which go hand-in-hand like peanut butter and jelly, CHARLES sneaks out of the house later that night and wanders into town where The <u>Summer of Gold Festival</u> is wrapping up.

After a scuffle breaks out between the bike gangs, THUNDER STREET SOLDIERS[J] and BLACK FANGS MOTORCYCLE CLUB, or the BFF (*Black Fucking Fangs*), which make up 8 members with their bikes varying from mopeds to 4 wheelers to dirt bikes to crotch rockets, all of whom are passing through Wildwood and taking part in local festivities, as well as paying their respects to the Wildwood Beast before a "group hunt," CHARLES accidentally trips the pursuer, a STREET SOLDIER, who's chasing after a BFF, resulting in him falling into the street where he gets sideswiped by a drunk driver. Temporarily dazed by the blow, the bald-headed SOLDIER hobbles away, ultimately leading to the rescue of an essential member of the club.

That member: SASHA, one of two females, as well as the youngest of the CLUB, even though she looks much older than CHARLES, is forever in CHARLES'S debt for his quick thinking and bravery. In return, FINGER, runt and prankster of BFF, hands him a souvenir – a butterfly knife – that fell from the SOLDIER'S pocket during the collision. SASHA asks CHARLES to join them in a night ride. CHARLES declines at first, but after being pressured by other members, accepts the invite.

CHARLES rides on the back of SASHA'S 4 wheeler. The two follow BFF deep into the woods where CHARLES ends up getting plastered with the other members by a campfire.

Encouraged by BFF, CHARLES, total lightweight who can't hold his liquor, hooks up with SASHA[K] and after passing out, has a horrific nightmare of a pack of BLACK WEREWOLVES hunting down a deer in the moonlit woods, killing it, then picking it apart by the campfire[L].

The next morning, CHARLES wakes in his own bed and is unaware of how he made it back home in one piece and doesn't remember a thing about the night before, except for thinking that he might've gotten lucky with some girl named SASHA. With the one-night-stand on his mind, he helps his father and brother unpack boxes but spends most of the day in the bathroom, sick to his stomach.

CHARLES'S new neighbor RICK^M stops by the house. CHARLES is suspicious of the neighbor and believes him to be a CONSPIRACY THEORIST based on his paranoia of the government. Plus, he's a "flip phone" kind of guy. Which, to CHARLES, is the first of many red flags.

As CHARLES skips dinner and heads to bed early, he hears the choking sounds of a muffler outside the house. He checks the window, only to spot a STRANGE MAN on a bike idling across the street. The bike is similar, if not, same as the bikes that the THUNDER STREET SOLDIERS rode. CHARLES immediately assumes the bike gang has sent a SCOUT to find out where he lives and starts to feel as if, by helping out BFF, he has put not only himself, but also his father and brother in danger. The BIKER rides away once he notices CHARLES watching him from behind the upstairs window.

In fear of retaliation, CHARLES sneaks out of the house that night and borrows his father's car and drives to the edge of the woods where, on foot, he walks to the campsite from last night in hopes of tracking down BFF and asking them for their protection. The campsite is deserted; however, CHARLES comes across a trail of blood on the ground. He follows the blood to the mutilated corpse of an animal. Possibly a deer?

FLASHES of last night's nightmare piece together: the carnage, the flesh, the blood, the feast by campfire.

Still hungover, CHARLES sleeps in late the next morning and wakes up determined to locate BFF.

CHARLES runs into RICK, who's blasting to HEAVY METAL MUSIC while cleaning his rifles, in the garage next door. RICK invites CHARLES over to his house and after several minutes of talking to CHARLES and observing his current health, suspects CHARLES'S life may be in jeopardy. RICK shares a theory with CHARLES that the United States government has created a way to depopulate the country by infecting women with a deadly virus. While RICK rambles on and on about theories, CHARLES comes across a glaring sword, which is made of pure silver, mounted on a wall. Intrigued by the sword, he further inquires about RICK'S background but before CHARLES receives any answers or proof of evidence to back these wild conspiracies, ARMY stops by to tell CHARLES he is needed back at the house.

Frustrated by their elusiveness, CHARLES catches a break in the BFF's whereabouts while combing through photos posted on social media.

He spots the same BFF DECAL that he saw on one of the BFF's dirt bikes hanging from a sign behind the window of a shady-looking bar located on River Run Street, which CHARLES maps to Baltimore[N].

With a photo discovered on the Internet driving his pursuit, CHARLES tracks down BFF inside THE LUNAR LOUNGE where two of the eight members win in a bet based on CHARLES'S unexpected yet timely visit. Without any knowledge of the situation, except for the suspicion of the mysterious biker from what CHARLES believes to be THUNDER STREET who was sent to spy on him, he informs BFF of the bike gang's plans to kill him for injuring one of the SOLDIERS. BFF's are skeptical of CHARLES'S suspicions but willing to protect him. TREY, leader of BFF, comes up with a proposal for CHARLES. He will initiate CHARLES into the club but only on one condition: In order to become a member of BFF, CHARLES must drive to a town in the Chesapeake Bay area to recover a briefcase full of "Z's" or "ZIG-ZAG," a new drug[O] on the street manufactured by BFF, from a man named DT; the drugs were stolen from TREY at a party.

Desperate to prove himself worthy, CHARLES takes up the offer and drives with club member, BANKS, to the house in Chesapeake Bay. At DT's house a shootout ensues, leaving CHARLES stuck in the cross-fire. Once more, CHARLES rescues a member of the BFF club, who is struck by a bullet. CHARLES protects BANKS and ends up killing DT with his own gun in self-defense.

After acquiring the Z, CHARLES and BANKS speed away and evade local police; however, during the getaway, not only does a witness write down the license plate of Charles's father's car, but CHARLES is also caught speeding through photo-enforced red light. CHARLES and BANKS return stolen drugs to TREY, who rewards CHARLES with bump of ZIG-ZAG.

High off the drug, CHARLES is invited to go on a GROUP HUNT with BFF where the leader, TREY, will reveal why CHARLES hasn't felt like himself lately.

When asked to kill a local gang member in the city, CHARLES refuses and immediately regrets having started any relationship with SASHA or BFF. CHARLES manages to escape BFF before the GROUP HUNT. But TREY knows CHARLES will return once he finds out _WHAT_ he has become.

On DAY 3 after CHARLES hooked up with SASHA the lingering hangover from days ago intensifies, thus resulting in CHARLES becoming violently ill. After spending the entire day in bed, GRANT drives CHARLES to a hospital where he is admitted for observation.

In his fever dreams, CHARLES has a FLASHBACK of the day that his mother died. CHARLES recalls bumping into a TALL, LANKY MAN in the hallway. He was holding a bouquet of flowers in his black-gloved hand. While drifting in and out of consciousness, CHARLES removes the IV cord from his arm and escapes from the hospital and seeks out the darkest nook in the parking deck where he undergoes the slowly agonizing, grotesque transformation from MAN TO WEREWOLF!

The next morning after CHARLES'S transformation he wakes up in a pool of blood surrounded by a dozen of maimed and mangled bodies. THUNDER STREET SOLIDER BIKERS, their girlfriends and boyfriends, all dead inside an abandoned airport hanger.

In CHARLES'S bloody hand, he clutches the same butterfly knife, which was given to him as a souvenir, or some may see it as a "TROPHY" for CHARLES helping out BFF.

Using his incredibly enhanced senses, CHARLES gathered the scent off the handle of the knife to track down that NAZI BIKER, which led him to the SOLDIERS' HANGOUT. The rest of CHARLES'S memories are lost on the other side of midnight. Before he can fill in the gaps, TREY hits him in the back of the head with the butt of a pistol and before leaving the hanger, orders the rest of BFF to collect the Soldiers' high-end motorcycles, mostly choppers, and place them in the back of a truck.

Like the previous nightmares, CHARLES witnesses FLASHES of violence behind the darkness of his eyelids. FLASHES of his two hairy, clawed hands digging into flesh, tearing apart flesh, or breaking, snapping, and pulling off limbs like the legs of a crab.

As CHARLES comes to inside the back of THE LUNAR LOUNGE, TREY and SASHA and the rest of BFF are ALL circled around CHARLES. Impressed by CHARLES'S willingness to take matters into his own hands, TREY shows CHARLES a news report on TV, what they're calling "THE MASSACRE IN RAVENS EDGE." Altogether sixteen people found dead inside the airport hanger, all said to be killed by "wild animals."

TREY corrects the reporter by stating it was only ONE wild animal – singular, not plural – and that CHARLES, being that animal, had already beaten BFF to the punch before the club could make sure a

THUNDER STREET SOLDIER never laid a hand on a BLACK FANG ever again.

Baffled by recent events, CHARLES still doesn't believe he was responsible for The Massacre, even though he has memories of brutally murdering SOLDIERS.

TREY escorts CHARLES to a garage behind the LOUNGE and shows him a recent score of choppers, which will be put to good use and stripped for parts. CHARLES recognizes one of the choppers and says it was the same one he saw outside his house. TREY suspects that the person watching CHARLES *wasn't* a member of the STREET SOLDIERS.

BUT SOMEONE FAR WORSE...

This is where we reveal that the BLACK FUCKING FANGS are not only a motorcycle club, but also a PACK OF WEREWOLVES, who share the bloodline of the legendary WILDWOOD BEAST.

ELLIPSO, the other female, as well as the oldest member of BFF, being ALPHA female and TREY, ALPHA male. TREY briefly explains to CHARLES that he has been turned into a WEREWOLF, which comes with endless power, super senses, and longevity. SASHA, daughter of ELLIPSO, a FULL BREED female unlike the four others in BFF, Banks included, who are HALF-BREEDS, and FINGER, like SASHA, is FULL BREED, but not nearly dominant enough to take over as the pack, is next in line to become the alpha female since ELLIPSO is too old to bear pups, making SASHA <u>essential</u> to the survival of their sacred bloodline.

Overwhelmed by the latest discovery, CHARLES leaves THE LUNAR LOUNGE; however, after CHARLES manages to track down RICK inside a big-box store in an attempt to debunk TREY'S *wild story*, learns that he's wanted by authorities for questioning in the death of the ZIG-ZAG THIEF, DARRELL TWINE or "DT," found shot inside riverside home.

RICK, clearly understanding CHARLES'S predicament, refers him to a friend, VIETNAM VETERAN who can provide shelter for the time being, until RICK can relay information back to GRANT and inform him of his son's dire situation[P].

Riding on a stolen crotch rocket, CHARLES is pulled over by police before he reaches the Vet's house.

CHARLES evades DEPUTIES but crashes motorcycle. Having not sustained any life threatening injuries, CHARLES is then taken into custody where two detectives from Baltimore, DETECTIVE SMITHEN^Q and BOYLE, pay a visit to the SHERIFF'S OFFICE where CHARLES is being held. SMITHEN and HIS PARTNER have a chat with CHARLES, who doesn't give them any information about the BFF.

Frustrated by CHARLES'S lack of cooperation, SMITHEN informs him about the person he was seen with, JONATHAN BANKS, who, according to SMITHEN, is bad news and has a warrant out for his arrest after he struck a patron in the head with a beer bottle, leaving the patron blind in one eye. The DETECTIVES have witnesses who saw CHARLES and BANKS fleeing the crime scene, as well as footage captured by a street camera showing CHARLES running a red light several miles from TWINE'S RESIDENCE.

Before CHARLES is escorted from the interrogation room to his holding cell, SMITHEN has one of his FORENSIC INVESTIGATORS collect evidence from underneath CHARLES'S fingernails, which will later be used to link CHARLES'S involvement to THE MASSACRE IN RAVENS EDGE.

While spending a night in jail, CHARLES wakes up to a blood-curdling scream coming from the SHERIFF'S OFFICE^R. The power to SHERIFF'S OFFICE is cut, leaving entire building pitch black. One after another, armed DEPUTIES are yanked up into ceiling by WEREWOLVES. Muffled gunshots RING out above ceiling panels before DEPUTIES' screams are silenced. A full-on ambush! The PACK plunges through the ceiling while flashes of gunfire pepper the darkness. Members of BFF leap through glass cubicles, turning over desks for cover, paper and utensils and debris clouding the air, as each WEREWOLF dodges gunfire – the bullets that hit them have little to no effect – then each WEREWOLF tears each DEPUTY to shreds until only one remains: a ROOKIE DEPUTY who stands guard with a shotgun in hand in front of the holding cells.

TREY, in full transformative state, kills the ROOKIE, thus freeing CHARLES from his cell.

Outside the SHERIFF'S OFFICE, we find GRANT and elder son, ARMY, who have been camped in a car and watching over CHARLES throughout the night. ARMY is carrying a pistol loaded with SILVER BULLETS, whereas GRANT is holding RICK'S SILVER SWORD. RICK is positioned along a distant hilltop with a RIFLE and waiting to take a perfect shot at members of BFF.

RICK fires a shot a TREY, striking him in the arm; however, TREY bites off his arm before the silver can spread through the rest of his body. This allows enough time for CHARLES to break free from the PACK and seek cover while ARMY unloads on BANKS, putting TWO BULLETS in the chest, one in the head. Killing BANKS. One down, seven to go.

ARMY reloads and fires at a fleeting FINGER but only grazes him in the leg. Other WEREWOLVES retreat into the woods while TREY and ELLIPSO stay behind. RICK, who has TREY in his crosshairs, fires another shot at TREY. RICK misses TREY, who, in return, charges at GRANT...

With the backside of his massive paw, TREY strikes GRANT and causes the sword to fall from his grip. ARMY unloads on TREY; however, TREY dodges each bullet and rams ARMY with his shoulder. The blow sends ARMY flying across the parking lot, which results in him landing on a metal post, which spears into ARMY'S abdomen. GRANT rushes to the sword on the ground. TREY, whose intention was to only incapacitate CHARLES'S family, is left with no other choice than to kill CHARLES'S FATHER before he reaches the sword in order to protect the bloodline.

At a distance, RICK readies himself to take a shot at TREY. Right before RICK pulls the trigger, FINGER attacks RICK from behind, killing him with a fatal bite around the neck, decapitating him.

TREY charges at a dazed GRANT, and in the nick of time, CHARLES, who's partly transformed, grabs the sword and rolls underneath TREY'S attack and stabs TREY in the back. TREY then reverts back to his human self. The silver running through his blood like poison. TREY dies from the stab wound, forcing ELLIPSO to flee into the woods since she is no match for a younger, stronger, and fully transformed WEREWOLF LIKE CHARLES.

Startled by his son's moans, GRANT hurries over to ARMY, who eventually dies from his injury. A shrinking-eyed GRANT turns to CHARLES and blames him for ARMY'S death.

GRANT calls DETECTIVE SMITHEN, leaving a guilty CHARLES with no other choice than to run away.

With the assistance of FEDERAL AGENTS, the POLICE from neighboring towns arrive at the deadly scene, including DETECTIVE SMITHEN, who, after receiving GRANT'S statement, makes sure GRANT is escorted to his house, safely. SMITHEN drives away[5].

Later that night, as DEPUTIES watch over GRANT'S HOUSE, CHARLES, who has transformed back into his human form, sneaks into his bedroom window without being spotted by DEPUTIES; however, he's *not* alone. Remaining members of BFF follow CHARLES back to his home. CHARLES confronts GRANT, tempted to turn CHARLES into the authorities.

More worried about his safety, DETECTIVE SMITHEN decides to return to GRANT'S house.

As CHARLES hides in a closet, GRANT welcomes the DETECTIVE into the house. They hear a commotion outside. The two DEPUTIES, who were watching the house from their car, have been torn to shreds by WEREWOLVES. Both are dead.

While rushing back into the house, DETECTIVE SMITHEN is attacked by LUPE, one of the half-breeds of BFF. The DETECTIVE fires a few rounds at LUPE, but, as we've learned before, regular bullets have NO EFFECT on a WEREWOLF. LUPE moves closer for the final kill. CHARLES, after transformation, bursts from the closet, storms out of the house, and attacks LUPE, kills LUPE, thus saving DETECTIVE SMITHEN from death.

As other WEREWOLVES circle the house and create a perimeter, one steps forward to challenge CHARLES: the alpha female ELLIPSO, who has a bone to pick with CHARLES. ELLIPSO pounces on CHARLES while CHARLES is tending to SMITHEN and GRANT and temporarily knocks the wind out of him.

Coming to CHARLES'S rescue is the Lone Wolf, SLIM, a former member of BFF, the one who was parked outside the house the day after CHARLES met BFF. SLIM has a similar slender build as ELLIPSO; however, after a vicious fight takes place in front of the house, SLIM prevails as victor. With the alpha female dead, the rest of the PACK retreats into the woods. The only injury sustained to the LONE WOLF is a scratch along the face. CHARLES doesn't recognize SLIM but is eternally grateful for its help. SLIM walks away on the neighborhood street; the LONE WOLF fades into the night darkness.

As days pass, we learn that DETECTIVE SMITHEN closes CHARLES'S case, freeing him of any guilt by ruling TWINE'S DEATH as a suicide, as well as destroying the DNA results from CHARLES'S fingernails.

Which came back as a match to the blood of the victims discovered in the hanger. His father GRANT takes the blame for TREY ROLLINS'S death, which is proved to be an act of self-defense.

After the media storm tapers off in Wildwood, CHARLES visits the cemetery and pays respects to his brother's grave when a WOMANLY MAN approaches him from behind. The wavy, longhaired individual removes his bike helmet, revealing a scar on the side of his face, which has been covered up with makeup. The individual is the LONE WOLF, SLIM, who saved CHARLES the night BFF freed him from jail. CHARLES recognizes SLIM'S face from the hospital on the day GWEN passed away. THE STRANGE MAN HOLDING A BOUQUET OF FLOWERS. A man, who, as revealed, is "DIFFERENT" from the other members of the PACK^T.

In this discovery, SLIM confesses to CHARLES that he was responsible for getting GWEN sick and has been working his way up to apologizing for what happened to GWEN^U. SLIM reveals he's working for a pharmaceutical company, who has used his blood^V to create a trial vaccine that will help cure and prevent anyone else from getting sick or dying, like GWEN, and that TREY was going to betray his daughter SASHA by handing her over to the company in order to further study the WEREWOLF VIRUS^W. For the exchange, TREY, who already froze his sperm for the company, was promised vast sums of money. SLIM asks an enraged CHARLES if he loves SASHA^X and is willing to protect her; and if so, he will tell the company that she's dead and not worth pursuing. After once more confessing his love for GWEN, who was his first and only love, as well as admitting his shame for allowing her to die by his hands, SLIM then pulls out a knife from his pocket and CUTS OUT HIS FANGS and hands them over CHARLES^Y.

Bloody-mouth and fang-less, SLIM places a vial carrying the VACCINE on ARMY'S headstone. Before leaving the cemetery, CHARLES warns SLIM to leave SASHA alone and if he, she, or they, should ever come near SASHA, then there will be hell to pay. SLIM understands the message loud and clear and rides away^Z.

After CHARLES leaves the cemetery, he rides into Baltimore where he stops by THE LUNAR LOUNGE in plans of running away with SASHA; but the bar is closed and marked off with yellow caution tape. The remaining members of BFF had already packed up and moved out before the police raided the place.

Estranged from his father after ARMY'S death, CHARLES returns home and before entering, stops by the front porch where GRANT is repairing a window, which was destroyed during the attack. CHARLES asks his father if he needs a hand with anything – which, to GRANT, is another way of CHARLES finally accepting and acknowledging what has happened and making a subtle attempt at his first steps in apologizing for his reckless behavior. Either way, it's a good place to start.

We close with CHARLES waiting in the bathroom before making a decision to dump the vaccine in the toilet. Then rummaging through storage boxes in the garage until he digs out two boxes, one of GWEN'S crinkled paperbacks, ranging from science fiction to horror, and then the other, GWEN'S impressive record collection, both buried underneath GRANT'S dusty golf bag.

Surprised by the discovery, CHARLES hauls the boxes of goodies to his bedroom where he sorts through his mother's vast collection of 70's albums, including THE TEMPTATIONS' Sky's The Limit album, the song Just My Imagination (Running Away With Me) immediately coming to mind. In a child-like wonder, CHARLES shuffles through more records, recalling jams from certain LPs, including "Supernatural Thing, Pt. 1" by BEN E. KING, "When Will I See You Again" by THE THREE DEGREES from the self-titled album, "Drowning In The Sea Of Love" by JOE SIMON, or "Thin Line Between Love and Hate" by THE PERSUADERS. It's a toss up between SLY & THE FAMILY STONE'S There's a Riot Goin' On or BILL WITHERS' Just As I Am. He settles on BILL WITHERS, carefully places the vinyl on a record player, then drops the needle. The song "Ain't No Sunshine" starts to play.

As a droopy-shouldered, pensive-faced CHARLES sits along the edge of his bed listening to WITHERS sing about heartbreak, we. . .

FADE TO BLACK.

"So, what do you think?"

Mr. Waters remained quiet with his chin rested against his hand.

"There is potential here," he said, thinking and leaning forward over his desk. "*What if* we turned it into a revenge story instead and we remove the part where Charles becomes one of these werewolves through, as you pointed out, sexual intercourse, and have him be bit instead. It makes more sense, don't you think? The viewers don't want to be introduced to new facets of a monster that has been around for ages. Some would deem it an insult."

"But it's *not* a revenge story."

"Well, make it one," Waters didn't suggest, but demanded. "Let's have our Wilson family move to the small town under the false pretense of restarting their lives after a tragedy when, in fact, the father figure, Grant, a strong black male—who I can see Denzel playing—tracks down the werewolf who killed his wife to the town of Wildwood and behind his sons' backs, starts his campaign of vengeance."

"Instead of *Black Fangs Motorcycle Club*, why don't we name it *Rare Breed*? Could bring in a more diverse cast to play the bikers. As for the Slim character, man oh man!" the producer said ecstatically, repositioning himself in the chair, "we can really ruffle some feathers there—of course, in a good way. Talk about a marketer's wet dream!"

"Or *Strange Animal*? I like the sound of that."

"Is Slim supposed to be like a freak of nature? A mutation in the gene pool—"

"I don't think you should use that terminology anymore, Mr. Waters."

"What? Freak—"

"Sir, please, it'd be wise not to."

"Well, why not?"

As the four rattled off new ideas for the story, I stormed up to Waters' desk, removed the sword from my cane, and made one lightning fast stroke in the air. Then inserted the sword back into the disguised sheath before Waters or the others had a chance to react. With both eyes and mouth gaping open like a yawn, Waters' head lazily topples forward and falls from a perfect red line along his neck. Streaks of blood squirt upward like a perforated hose from his headless neck, leaving the other three speechless.

One of the producers, Martin, finally chimes in: "If you're going to make it in this business, sweetie, you're gonna have to learn how to take criticism."

The other producer stood from his chair and said in a trembling voice, "I liked it."

One by one, the other two joined.

"You don't know how long I've been waiting for somebody to do that," the story editor said with a sigh of relief. "The man is like a human recycling bin."

Martin asked me, "Say, Liv, do you have any other material that isn't a throwback or a reimagining of a certain character. Don't get me wrong," he said abruptly, as though he was trying to correct himself. "We like the story—"

"Love it," the story editor said, bobbing his sweaty head.

"And we're ready to be in the Plaut Business. But what else do you got for us?"

Where to begin?

I grinned.

"I have one or two you might be interested in," I said and picked up Waters' lifeless body from the chair and tossed him on the floor and then sat down in his place.

Lastly, with a flicking motion, I pushed Waters' bloody, severed head from the top of the desk with the backside of my fingers.

The others waited in anticipation.

"Ready?"

And they all nodded like good children.

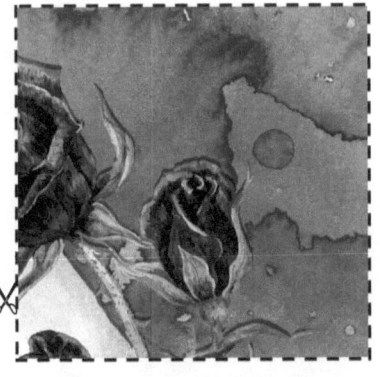

THE ROOSTER AND THE SERPENT OF THE MIDNIGHT SUN (♌, THE STORY FORMERLY KNOWN AS LEO)

ANOTHER dead body for Detective Tulip.

Unlike the last victim, a male.

The back of the head, like the others, caved in like a sinkhole.

Shards, chips, and crumbs of skull combined with pulpy gray matter.

An eerily similar modus operandi, or what the baggy-eyed sleuth calls "MO."

Daddi's own signature.

Raw and boiling violent.

The body left stripped bare, clothes missing.

Head shaped like a bowl from where it was bashed in with a meat tenderizer.

Lastly, a large chicken egg left at the scene of crime.

Painted red with the victim's blood.

This one's blood is dark and brownish-black, old.

"Been dead for a good forty-eight hours," coroner Mike Poole says while he snaps photographs of the corpse laying facedown

in the dirt with the contents inside his head exposed for the outside world to see.

Poole kneels down, closely examines similar marks created by blunt force trauma, and based off the previous victim's wounds, a one Diana True, a known white collar criminal in charge of running a well-orchestrated state-wide racket that involved telemarketer and IRS scams, expresses himself with an educated yet strictly theoretical statement that the murderer was *not* a copycat but **Daddi** himself.

The coroner claims the kill has **Daddi** written all over it: A square-like pattern of multiple indentations on the skin, as well as parts of brain tissue.

Autographed in mint condition for Lead Detective Raymond Tulip, as well as his fresh-off-the-street informant turned beat cop turned undercover narcotic officer turned full time crime solver for the Major Crimes Division, Detective Dallas Fawn, who both work the scene with heavy shoulders and heavy minds.

"Now he's just playing games," Tulip says, as he carefully stalks around the victim's body. He nods at his partner, "Find anything unusual?"

"There's *nothing* usual about any of this," Fawn says, less than upbeat.

Tulip plants himself next to the corpse and rests his hands along his hips.

Another coroner snaps a photo of a darkly painted egg hidden inside the crevice of a missing brick along the side of the building.

Tulip runs his fingers along the scruff of his five o'clock shadow as an alternate way of scratching his noggin.

"What, Raymond?"

"Usually, he'll hide the body," Tulip says, surveying the muddy, trashy landscape. The body positioned in a way for anybody to see, especially drivers on the highway overlooking the rundown neighborhood, for instance, a passerby, Stanley McGovern, who was on his way to work early this morning when he spotted the pale shape. Even a couple of drivers have pulled off the highway to see the workings of what TV people have branded as "The Jonesy Town Beater." "This time," he says, drawing his attention toward the egg, "it's the opposite. Why?"

Fawn suggests, "Like you said: could be messing with us."

"Or rushed. A'lot easier to hide an egg than it is a body."

"Sure."

Tulip asks Fawn, "How about any witnesses?"

Reading from a notepad, Fawn replies, "The clerk, who runs the Fill 'Em Up across the street, says he saw a woman sulking around last night. Says she looked like a working girl."

"Well, a prostitute didn't do this," Tulip says.

"But maybe she had something to do with it?"

"Doubt it."

Fawn shakes his head from his partner's stubbornness.

"All I'm saying is we keep an open mind, Raymond," Fawn says.

Poole smirks from the remark, whether or not Fawn meant to make a pun.

Tulip ignores the remark and while examining the corpse below, says to his partner, "If you are right, Dallas, then our guy's evolving."

Fawn asks, "How so?"

Tulip looks up from the corpse, makes direct eye contact with Fawn, and says to him, "He's building his own congregation."

From a distance, a car alarm blares out over the street ambience!

Detectives and coroners acknowledge the disturbance.

Tulip leans underneath the yellow caution tape wrapped around the back section of the rust-covered textile factory and ambles to the edge of the building.

On the street in front are several ACTION NEWS vans, as well as a swarm of reporters, cameramen, and pedestrians, who form a large crowd outside the police barricades. The cops set up a tight perimeter on both sides of the street, preventing any reporters or onlookers from stepping foot inside the crime scene.

One of the cops pops open the hood of a noisy car, the one that a reporter had bumped into, and removes the wire from the battery, shutting off the alarm.

Tulip glances over his shoulder; Fawn approaches from behind.

"Looks like one of your boys couldn't keep his mouth shut."

Fawn says optimistically, "And you've been a detective for how many years, Raymond? When're you ever going to learn: If you play 'em correctly, the News can work to your advantage."

Tulip's eyes shrink in annoyance.

He shrugs off the "rookie" comment.

If you only knew how a parasite worked.

⚓

THE reporter from WXYZ Channel 9 News stands outside police barricades near the abandoned textile factory of what used to be called Klark and Son's Textiles. Now, like most of the buildings on the North End of Jonesy Town, it's just a brick building on the verge of collapse. A place to get high and have unprotected sex or, in this instance, commit murder. The reporter, without knowing any details of the case except for the ones given to her by the commissioner like, for example, "*the body found behind a textile factory*," or the victim being "*white*" and a "*male*"—for the News, names don't matter, only pigmentation and gender titles, especially when concocting a storyline—suggests the killing may be the work of, ready for it, "The Jonesy Town Beater."

Absolutely no such evidence supports the reporter's claims; however, she throws it out there anyway to "warn" viewers.

But everybody knows *warn* is just another word for *scare*.

⚓

DRIVING away from the crime scene, Tulip and Fawn don't speak a single word to one another. Most of the ride the two keep to themselves until Fawn receives the call from the police station saying that a man, a *white male* named Jerry Neufeld, was reported missing a few minutes ago. Jerry's wife, named Storie, was deeply concerned about her husband and how he didn't return home from work last night.

The detectives stop by the Neufeld's household to have a chat with Storie but after matching the photos of John Doe from the crime scene on Fawn's iPad to the photos of Jerry Neufeld, determine that their John Doe has a name and his name is Jerry Neufeld.

When Fawn asks Storie if she thinks Jerry might've been with another person last night (the working girl), she hesitates and tells the detectives that she and her husband are going through what she calls a "rough patch."

Which isn't a definite "yes" or "no" answer.

But another way of saying "He's only human."

⚓

BACK at the station, after Storie identified the body at the morgue, the detectives sit on the information regarding the latest murder and dig up the goods or whatever dirt they can find on the latest victim, Jerry Neufeld, his lifestyle, his habits, his pornography, and lastly, career, which, according to Storie, as well as a brand new 4,000 square-foot house Jerry recently bought for his wife, was, in her own words, undergoing "a surprising resurgence." The killing, as well as the planting of the egg, draws similar parallels to The Jonesy Town Beater or "Ｄａｄｄｉ," as the detectives call him, spelled with an "i," *not* a "y," which Tulip believes favors the killer's narcissism; however, if Fawn's preconceived notion proves correct, Tulip and his latest theory on Ｄａｄｄｉ branching out and using more players in his sick twisted game—"evolving," as he'd say—would contradict the whole "There's no 'i' in team" expression.

Tulip stands in front of a wall of notes, evidence, photos, suspects, even victims where each item or memorabilia is strategically pinned and mounted on corkboard.

"Jerry Neufeld," Tulip says and pins a photo of Jerry next to the other victims on the corkboard. Thirteen of them, Jerry making fourteen, all found in or around Jonesy Town. All immortalized by the hands of a monster whose story will be dissected or taught in universities, whose face will share similar popularity—and disdain—as Santa Clause, or glorified and dramatized over in documentaries or even gloated about in pseudo-bestsellers by relevance-seeking, lazy Susans whose attempts to exploit America's thirst for scandal, murder, and vengeance ultimately become, in itself, a mockumentary.

The first victim was twenty-four year post-grad Geoff Salem, who was working part-time at an automobile accessories store called Royal Rims. The surveillance camera, as seen in the grainy photos on the corkboard, captured footage of a masculine figure dressed in all black grabbing Salem on his way from work after closing up shop, striking him over the dome with what Tulip believes to be a billy club, knocking him unconscious, then carrying his lifeless body to a stolen Ford Taurus, and driving away into the darkness of night. Salem later found in a shallow grave near an old rail yard with a black—once red—egg placed on top of the mound of dirt.

From there, the killer built a soapbox made out of dead bodies and started to fine-tune his voice.

Sending out letters, like the ones posted on the corkboard, to the two detectives working the case, addressing them to the "dicks" in charge.

An excerpt of a nursery rhyme here and there, like, for instance, the nursery rhyme, *A-Tisket, A-Tasket,* written in a letter, which was sent to Tulip and Fawn before the body of Courtney Husk, who had a rap sheet about as thick as a high school textbook, her crimes mostly involving theft, was found in the sewers, a blood-covered egg placed on top of a manhole covering in front of a local diner, The Basket, or *Baa, Baa, Black Sheep* around the time Evin Sarge, a highly sought out contractor who was known to pay employees below minimum wage and often overcharged and ripped off the vulnerable, mostly the elderly, was found stuffed inside a dog house in the backyard of a forlorn house in the projects, the bloody egg set on the stringy WELCOME mat on the front porch, or *Ring a Ring o' Roses*, which was discovered on Tulip's desk the same day Wylie Blaylock, the mayor's assistant, was found inside one of the containers inside the morgue, the red egg first spotted on the bedding around the rose tree in front of the morgue by one of the coroners, which was, by far, the closest one to home, which led to an internal investigation, or, don't forget, the nursery rhyme *Hickory Dickory Dock*, which was sent to the detectives days before the *Ring a Ring o' Roses* letter, however, the body of Jeremiah Forsythia wasn't discovered until one week later inside the bedroom closet of the Charles Armistead's House, a historical eighteenth century museum, which is maintained weekly by curator, as well as property manager, Patty Levelle. Levelle was the one who discovered Forsythia, a financial advisor who owns three houses, one in Jonesy Town, which was the town he was born in, one in

Manhattan, and another one in the Caribbean island St. Barts. As far as the bloody egg, a local discovered it cracked open and sitting "over easy" directly below the Jonesy Town's Clock Tower, which was built by the architect Charles Armistead himself in the 1700's. The detectives believe **Daddi** had placed the egg under the old clock and either a storm or a curious bird knocked it over. Nonetheless, each one of the victims' injuries was consistent: their heads were bashed in.

For a while, after one of the detectives in the department leaked a story about the *Ring a Ring o' Roses* letter around the time of Blaylock's death, Fawn overheard that the media hounds were floating around the idea of branding the killer as "The Nursery Rhyme Killer."

But Tulip guessed a killer with the words *nursery rhyme* to describe his rituals wasn't "shocking" enough.

When it came to throwing around brands or labels, Tulip knew that the media was better off being as blunt as possible.

"Beater" had more shock value than its other contenders.

As far as these letters that were sent to the detectives, each one was written in similar handwriting of a child and more than likely, done so with the left hand.

Daddi is right handed, as the coroners pointed out based on the angle of each blow to the victims' heads—and most definitely "male," Tulip suggests, and quite muscular too, based on the sheer force of the bludgeoning, as well as the pulverization of the victims' heads or, in some instances, like Thomas Fickle, a con artist playing the part of a plastic surgeon who was swindling his patients by injecting them with fake Botox, what's left of them.

Tulip stares long and hard at Neufeld's photo, which Storie had given them. It was taken three years ago in front of his yacht in Stone Lakes, only a few miles up the coast from South Beach. Except for **Daddi's** first victim, Salem, like most of **Daddi's** other victims, Neufeld was well-off and living the comfortable life, a former CEO of one of largest banana brands in the country, who ended up moving from a cozy penthouse in New York City to the countryside outside Jonesy Town, only to later start up his own food truck business—booming, by the way—called The Pink Taco. He first started out with a couple of food trucks stationed around the city (in front of the coliseum, next to the central business district, or outside gymnasiums) before he franchised out and had a fleet of trucks up and down the East Coast. The food and service was ★ ★ ★ ★ ★'s based on paid-for reviews on Yummy, a site where customers review and rate restaurants; however, the gimmick was pink-colored hard shell tacos—a trick Jingle Jerry learned while working in the banana business; in fact, it was his idea to put those catchy stickers on bananas such as "Brain Food" or "Super-Power."

As discussed by both detectives, according to his wife, Storie, every now and then, Neufeld would go through these spells where he'd stay out late at night, then he'd come home stinking of Top Shelf whiskey and Coffin Nails.

Alone and drunk.

His lips wearing a different shade of color.

"You're starting to see a pattern here, aren't you?" Tulip asks his partner who kicks back his feet on the corner of the desk while skimming through the folder of two victims ago, the twelfth victim, Deter Gage, the snake oil salesman who made millions from selling supposed cures for The Plague on the Internet when, in fact, it was a combination of vitamins. "Like I've been saying, our guy here is becoming more righteous."

"What's the theme?" asks Fawn.

"Simple," Tulip says. "Theft. Whether it be property theft," Tulip says while pointing at a photo of the victim, Marcy Brown, "or bribery." Tulip points at the photo of victim, Cordon Renaldo. "Or, just straight up stealing." He points at the photo of Courtney Husk, a common thief.

"Well, I'll tip my hat off to him," another detective teases. "He's making our job much easier."

Neither Tulip nor Fawn falls for the joke.

Fawn stands from the seat and walks toward a photo gallery of suspects who are pinned and mounted on the other side of the corkboard: first one being a drug dealer, Mikhail Kuznetsov, a twenty-nine-year-old burnout who sold illegal substances such as meth and Mexican heroine to minors, happened to be in the vicinity where the body of Tito Bowly, a known counterfeiter who ran into the wrong side of **Daddi's** meat tenderizer, was discovered when he was caught red-handed slinging dope to fifteen-year-olds behind the Burger Hut parking lot and ended up open-firing on the two detectives, hitting Tulip in the thigh, just inches away from one of his main arteries, which resulted in the detective walking with a slight limp. Kuznetsov's ugly mug replaced a photo of the owner of the arcade Legends, Howie Donem, who had his fair share of run-ins with the law, most importantly, twelve years ago when he was one of the main suspects who was accused of murdering his roommate, Ashley "Twitchy" Twiddle, an independent video game designer, or "DEV," recognized for two games, one the critically-acclaimed game called *Reign of Lexis Evidicus*—"ROLE," as fans call it—and the other, a cult indie game, *Crackhead*, which follows the R-Rated adventures of a homeless junkie who navigates through urban decay and the fallout of bad policy while at the same time struggles for his own survival after witnessing a crime committed by a member of an underground syndicate who has more power than the leaders elected to clean up a morally and structurally declining city. The cult game was created four years after Twitchy went off the radar while the fans of ROLE—"Vidis," as they were known as—launched a year-long campaign for Twitchy to make a sequel to ROLE; however, Twitchy defied expectations and "went back to his roots" with *Crackhead*. Only two months after the game was released, Twitchy was found in his apartment beaten to death with a baseball bat. Police believed it to be a robbery, since most of Twitchy's belongings were stolen. Donem was let go once Los Angeles Detectives confirmed that he was in Vegas on the night of Twitchy's murder. Like Kuznetsov, Donem was apprehended a couple of miles from the site of a dead body; however, instead of slinging dope, he was found sleeping in his car on private property by one of the officers who responded to a report of disturbance where the caller described "a man screaming." Cops also found the *Bhagavad-Gita* in Donem's possession. Donem's excuse was that his birthday was yesterday, July 21st—Donem was found on the 22nd—and he claimed he had one too many to drink the night before. Tulip and Fawn didn't have any evidence on Donem to link him to the murder of Geoff Salem.

The more **Daddi** killed, the more potential and credible suspects came forward and Donem fell to the bottom of the pool until eventually being replaced and forgotten.

Another suspect was a con artist, Talor Creek; another a pedophile (based on **Daddi's** attire, Tulip believes **Daddi** used to be an altar boy for The Church and shares resentment for priests—it could also be why their killer refers to himself as **Daddi** and not Father); another being a seventy-two year old man with thin wavy white hair dressed in a flashy orange suit from the 1980's who was brought in for questioning after Hazel, the wife of one of the previous victims, Deter Gage, spotted, as she quoted, that "tacky-looking" suit while driving through town, but then after being pressed hard by both Tulip and Fawn, the older man verified, by a way of receipt, that he bought the suit at a thrift shop Vintage USA, which later proved Fawn's theory correct that **Daddi** was pawning off the victims' clothes or according to Tulip, just getting rid of evidence; another suspect, a professional sketch of a *Easter Bunny* (it's fair to say the boys at the station have a sense of humor); then of course, lastly, their prime suspect, **Daddi** himself, who remains at the very top of the pyramid along with a giant question mark. A photo of a still, a sharper silhouette of **Daddi** himself, captured by an ATM camera. As described by several key witnesses, **Daddi** dresses in a black priest outfit and has a fairly heavy built and according to forensics, is physically strong.

To the left of the suspect pool is a photo of not the actual weapon but a replica of the weapon: a stainless steel meat tenderizer, which he uses to make brain soup from the eleven-pound part that rests on top of the human body.

While the detectives continue to breakdown the recent conversation with Storie, the telephone rings. On the third ring, Fawn answers, "Major Crimes."

Only listening to a few words from the caller, Fawn moves his eyes from the desk and plants them on Tulip, who acknowledges his partner's slack expression.

Fawn scribbles a couple of notes, as well as the caller's contact information, including phone number and address, on whatever piece of paper he can find and gives several head nods and "yes, ma'ams" before hanging up.

"That was a friend of our working girl," Fawn says to Tulip, then reads from his notes. "Her name is Glitter. She said a woman by the name of Bonnie Stover had a job last night in the vicinity where Neufeld's body was found. She said her friend,

Bonnie, is not returning her calls. She says that, as soon as she heard the report on the News, she knew Bonnie was in trouble."

Tulip grabs his coat and tells another detective to put an "APB" on this Bonnie Stover. For now, he wants to have a more in-depth conversation with "Glitter."

"See," Fawn says, gathering his notes, "Told you."

"Told me *what*?"

"Told you the News can come in handy."

Tulip ignores the comment and heads straight for the exit while Fawn grabs his stuff and follows.

⚓

WHILE Tulip and Fawn are talking with Stover's fellow associate, Glitter, inside an dimly lit parking deck since her "*cane-wielding*" pimp Hell Jay wouldn't be pleased if he heard one of his girls was talking with the cops, Fawn receives a call on the recent APB. A couple of cops have beaten the detectives to the punch and tracked down Bonnie Stover, or "Bonnie Busty," as Glitter calls her, hanging outside Devil's Den, a seedy club well known for attracting working girls, and is now waiting in a holding cell.

Before leaving Glitter, the detectives acquire a tidbit of information on their guy (Daddi) and that he paid triple the amount for Bonnie's services.

When pressed by Tulip, Glitter informed him that the dead man on the boob tube wasn't Bonnie's client last night. It was, as she says, some "weirdo priest."

⚓

TULIP and Fawn use an old tactic of letting Bonnie sweat a little before barging in on her. Every now and then, Fawn enters the interrogation room and asks Bonnie if she needs anything, like water or coffee. Just enough distraction to interrupt the story that she's developing inside her head.

Finally, once the detectives enter the interrogation room, Tulip makes a note of Bonnie's brittle hands, as well as her long skull-painted fingernails, which, after close study, he rules out Bonnie as their killer. Tulip knew that there was no way a person with those hands could do the damage that Daddi inflicted on his victims.

Once the interrogation begins, it doesn't take long for Bonnie to crack under the pressure. With black mascara running down her face, she explains to the two detectives that she was paid to hook up with another man, that man being "Jerry Neufeld," whom she met at a bar a couple of blocks from the site where his body was found. Based on her intuition, as well as past experiences with men, in particular, a hubby with a short and stubby who couldn't "pitch a tent if he had a face full of tits and ass," the client was one of those types who "liked to watch." Possibly homosexual. Or, even possibly played on both teams. She didn't get a good look at the client's face, the one who paid her enough money to get the hell out of Jonesy Town—which Bonnie was planning on doing once she gathered the nerve—but she, like the other witnesses, described him as being a big man, heavyset, not fat but more so thick and muscular, was around 6' 3" even with the noticeable slouch of shoulders, dressed in a priest's outfit— the details, based on their inconclusiveness thus far in the case, especially a priest outfit, were not once shared or leaked to the press, so Tulip knew there was no way she would've known about Daddi's description through the News—however, one detail stood out the most to Bonnie; to Tulip, a new detail.

"*A ring*," she says, "it was strange."

"Like a wedding band?"

"No," Bonnie says. "It was more like one of those rings a kid would wear."

"Last time I checked, a ring wasn't on the top of a kid's Christmas list."

"I mean, like the college kids," Bonnie says, impatiently. "Kind of goth, kind of hip and trendy. All I know is that it had a face on it."

"A face?"

⚓

ONCE Poole finishes with the autopsy of Jerry Neufeld, Tulip and Fawn are immediately notified about the coroner's "shocking" discovery.

"Found inside Neufeld's stomach," Poole says, as he holds up a severed fingertip for the two detectives. "Looks like your guy force-fed the finger down the victim's throat before he. . . " Poole points at the gaping hole in the backside of Neufeld's head, ". . . you know, did his thang."

Poole hands the bag with the finger to Tulip.

"You run any prints?"

"Sure did," Poole says and takes a couple of beats before facing Tulip with a worried expression. "The finger belongs to a man named Edward Hopkins."

The name sends a ripple of nausea through Tulip's belly.

"Edward Hopkins?"

Fawn asks Tulip, "You know him?"

"No," he says, sighing, "but I know his brother."

"You're not talking about Jonathan Hopkins, are you? The man who's serving life behind bars for murdering his wife and two children?"

"Yeah," Tulip says, as he can barely utter the name's name. "That Jonathan Hopkins."

Tulip glances at Poole, who, in return, shares a similar look as Tulip as if the two know something that Fawn either doesn't know or will never understand; and by their unified silence, they hope to keep it that way.

⚓

WITH a warrant to search the property, Tulip and Fawn arrive at Edward Hopkins' household with dozens of police officers.

Cops give Hopkins a verbal warning right before breaking down the door and storming inside.

Hopkins is not home—well, not *all* of Hopkins.

On the kitchen countertop, Tulip comes across a red plastic Eastern egg under an envelope addressed "Raymond Tulip."

With a glove, Tulip opens the envelope with a switchblade and pulls out the letter inside, which reads in child-like handwriting "*It's what's on the inside that matters.*"

Fawn orders Tulip not to open the red Easter egg.

But Tulip doesn't listen.

Instead, Tulip gives the red Easter egg a shake.

"There's something inside," he says, listening closely.

He carefully pops open the red Easter egg, releasing a foul stench.

Grimacing, he pulls away the top half of the egg and in the other half, finds a bloody eyeball sitting inside.

"Like you said, Ray," Fawn says with mild disgust, "he's evolving."

"Or devolving," Tulip says to himself.

⚓

EXTREMELY exhausted after spending weeks following up on leads in a case that seems to never end yet continues to spiral 'round and 'round like a vicious never-ending loop, Tulip arrives at his ranch-style house located in the older district of the city, Freeman Park.

As they normally are when Tulip returns home after a hard day's work, both his wife, Sara, and his nine-year-old child, Luke, are already sleeping. He finds a note on the countertop saying there's dinner in the oven. He opens the oven and finds a plate covered in foil: a chicken breast with a side of mashed potatoes and green beans, all cold.

Tulip takes a bite of the cold chicken and ends up tossing the rest of the food in the trash.

On a twisted empty stomach, Tulip heads straight to bed where Sara is half-asleep. She doesn't bother acknowledging her husband when she smells the sour waft of cigarette smoke from his clothes blow her way or when she feels the dip in the other side of the mattress seesawing downward from her husband's weight; instead, she lies with her back turned and says to the silhouette of her husband who has spent the last few weeks walking through graveyards that it'd be in his best interest to take tomorrow off, which was Good Friday. Tulip isn't the least religious like Sara, who can do a good verbal smiting whenever she gets fired up by the Holy Ghost, yet he's quite the opposite; however, he knows how much the day means to her. The day completely slips his mind, not Good Friday, but the date, the 2nd of April. Tomorrow marks a three-year anniversary of Luke being cancer-free, a day which he refers to as his "Sick Day." Usually, on the 2nd of April, the father and son would spend the entire day together. Last year, Tulip took Luke to the water park.

The year before: Play-A-Round. Sara tells Tulip he's been talking about his father taking him to Legends—"Practically won't shut up about it," Sara says but Tulip hasn't built up the strength to tell her he can't take his son and that he's too busy chasing down a serial killer.

When these thoughts cross Tulip's mind, Jonathan Hopkins pops in his mind. *How does* **Daddi** *know my history with Johnny Hopkins? Or, it can all be coincidence? That family is nothing but trouble. And what about the eye? What does it mean? Is* **Daddi** *watching me?* Worse, *does* **Daddi** *know what I did to ole Johnny?*

After Tulip removes his coat and shoes, he leaves the bedroom and stops by Luke's room at the end of the hallway. He's sound asleep in his green caterpillar bed. Clearly by the way Luke's ankles hang over the hump of the caterpillar, he's outgrown the bed and the conversation of buying Luke a brand new bed has come up once over breakfast and usually, depending on what mood Sara is in, whenever topics, such as buying new stuff, come up a second time, Tulip is often dragged into shopping, mostly during a weekend where he'd rather play golf opposed to spending a Saturday splurging his paycheck away on new, temporary stuff that's going to be tossed away in a couple of years.

Eyes closed, Luke readjusts positions from his father's presence.

He pulls up the insect blanket over Luke's curled body, tucks him in, kisses him on the forehead, and tells him goodnight.

"Don't let the bed bugs bite."

As he heads out, he notices a comic book on Luke's nightstand.

He picks it up and reads the title: "*The Adventures of Humpty Dumpty.*"

Immediately, the **Daddi** case comes to mind and washes away any lingering thought of Hopkins.

For the rest of the night, he can't stop thinking about **Daddi** and that prostitute, Bonnie Stover.

Is **Daddi** *getting sloppy or is Bonnie just another distraction?*

⚓

THE very next morning, after only catching an hour or two of decent shuteye, Tulip is awakened by the sounds of Sara aggressively prepping her hair in the bathroom. From the way Sara tosses the comb against the countertop or closes the drawers or stomps through the bedroom with more weight on her heels—and not to mention, last night, Sara practically hanging off the edge of her side of the bed and keeping her distance from her husband as if he was contagious with The Plague—Tulip realizes his answer last night or *lack* of answer to her question regarding Luke's "Sick Day" has rolled over to the next day and every little action Sara makes, every little yet big noise, every flex of the muscle, is all done with poise and purpose and meant to do what she does best whenever he leaves her in the dark, which is to get a rise out of him.

Tulip rises all right; in fact, he rolls out of bed, one side of his hair all jacked up from having slept awkwardly on a folded pillow.

"He's waiting. . . " Sara says, as soon as she acknowledges an upright sack of bones that is her husband. She paces toward the closet and grabs an outfit for the day.

"Sara," Tulip says, clearing his throat, "would you just stop, huh? You know I'm up to my neck with work. I promise once the case is over I'll take a week off and take Luke wherever he wants to go—"

"You know how much this day means to him, Ray," Sara says, standing in front of the closet while sorting through blouses.

"I can't, Sara," he pleads, "not today."

"If you're not going to take him," Sara says and grabs her outfit, "then you're going to tell him. I'm done playing the messenger of bad news."

Before Tulip has a chance to respond to Sara, she storms out of the bedroom with her outfit in hand.

Tulip checks the clock on the nightstand.

"7:37," it reads.

Normally, if he's not up by six, Sara wakes him.

The sight of the time causes Tulip to cringe with anger; however, the anger is spread out, rather than consolidated. Partly anger with his wife for always getting on his back and riding him, especially during moments when the job somehow finds a way to follow him home. Partly anger with Luke for inaudibly and mostly inadvertently putting pressure on his old man about these "Sick Days," which makes no sense, and should be called

"Better Days." Partly anger with Fawn for not being able to understand what it's like raising a child while hunting bad guys. Most of the hot anger, however, that seed germinating deep inside Tulip's fiery gut, stems from **Daddi**, who, as of late, has become a giant strain on Tulip and his family.

After Tulip dresses for work, he heads downstairs where Luke is sitting at the kitchen table with a bowl of soggy Dragon Puffs in front of him.

The cereal untouched, for he's too busy doodling with crayons.

Tulip walks up behind his son, who has become estranged, and tells him good morning; however, Luke remains quiet *as always* and continues to doodle as if his old man is a ghost who speaks in boos.

Sara, all dressed now, follows in and pours herself a cup of coffee and acts as though she's minding her own business when, in fact, Tulip knows she's eavesdropping over Tulip's excuse as to why he can't take a day or even half a day off work and spend time with their son, whom she commonly referred to with her bookclub friends as a miracle.

Intrigued by the usage of the red crayon, Tulip leans over Luke.

With the red crayon, Luke fills in an oval, not circle, inside what looks like a dark cave.

"What's this you're drawing?" he asks while pointing at the round red oval on the piece of paper.

"An Easter egg," Luke finally says and doesn't blink an eye nor does he look up at his father when he speaks.

Tulip leans upward and glares at his wife, who has her back turned to Tulip.

As anger boils up inside Tulip from the notion alone of Sara allowing Luke to rummage through his case files or watch the reports on the News, he redirects his attention to Luke and finds the job eating away at him.

He studies the drawing: a red Easter egg lying inside a hole or a dark cave; three black stick figures standing outside the cave; and in the distance, a greenish-purple blob-looking creature with tentacles and claws.

"Where did you see this, Luke?" Tulip asks more seriously.

The tone in her husband's voice prompts Sara to acknowledge Tulip.

Luke doesn't respond.

"Luke," Tulip says, "I'm asking you a question."

"That's enough, Ray. . . " Sara says, the frustration more pronounced in her voice.

She sets down the coffee mug on the counter.

"Answer me, Luke," Tulip says.

"In a game," Luke says, finally looking up at his father.

His face like a puppy dog that recently made a boo-boo.

"A game?"

With heavy eyes, Luke nods.

"What kind of game?"

"It's an arcade game."

"Are you going to tell him, Ray?" Sara asks, crossing her arms over her chest as she shifts her weight to one side of her body.

Tulip turns toward his wife and then rotates back around at Luke.

"An arcade game," he says, "at this place. . . "

"*Legends*," Sara fills in the rest of her husband's thought.

"Right," he says. "Legends. Well," he says, thinking, "what are you waiting for? Get ready and I'll take you. What do you say?"

Luke's eyes swell, his face lights up.

"Really?"

"Really, really," Tulip says and glances over at his wife.

Sara appears shocked by her husband's response; however, knowing the case he's been working on for the past weeks and the details of all the violent murders reported on the News, she doubts whether Luke's father Ray is the one who's going to take their son to Legends or Detective Tulip.

At this point, she can't tell the fucking difference anymore.

⚜

ONCE Tulip and his son arrive at the arcade a quarter till nine o'clock, except for a several families, mostly grandparents acting as babysitters for their grandchildren, Legends isn't nearly as packed as it is on the weekends.

Next to the entranceway, Tulip walks past a round glass vending machine, "A Nest of Secret Treasures," filled with hundreds of various colored Easter eggs, all of which contain mysterious prizes. For only a dollar, the user can unlock one of these prizes inside the egg. It's not the actual machine, however, that strikes him as odd. It's the color of each egg. Tons of colors, Tulip sees, greens, blues, and yellows, and every color along the spectrum; yet, the only color that seems to be missing is the color red.

Curious, Tulip walks closer to the vending machine and finds a couple of red eggs buried in the bottom of the glass pod. He supposes that maybe they're more hidden in the bottom. Tulip stops himself from thinking and for a moment, forces himself to leave the job at the office.

"Wanna give it try?"

Tulip nods at his son, who, in return, shakes his head and appears as though he has absolutely no interest in the eggs.

Before heading into the main arcade section, the two play a couple of games, the first one being Whack-A-Mole and the second, Skee-Ball, which used to be a favorite of Tulip's whether or not he'd like to admit it.

Finally, after realizing Luke isn't having much fun playing the kind of games his father enjoyed when he was his age—but mostly not making it so damn obvious to Luke that one of the main reasons he brought Luke to Legends is based on that suspicious drawing—Tulip hands Luke a handful of quarters and tells him to go have fun.

Without hovering over Luke, unlike Sara, Tulip grabs a cup of watered-down coffee from the concession stand and watches his son head straight toward his *favorite* arcade, which is already occupied by three other kids a few years older than Luke. Between the ages of ten and fourteen, Tulip guesses.

Tulip pays for the coffee and checks on Luke, who's waiting in line to play a game that he wouldn't stop talking about in the car.

That game is. . .

THE HUNT FOR THE RED EASTER EGG

Similar to Luke's drawing, the "egg" in the title is the color red.

The three frustrated kids in front of Luke struggle to beat the final stage in the game, which, as Luke breathlessly explains to his father, involves a ragtag team of space cowboys, as tough as leather, including: leader, Nefarious Ballad, or "Nef," former astronaut turned galaxy explorer who'd make Crimson Cowboy look like a two-dimensional cardboard cutout; Dudley, "Dud," a marine who acts as a comic relief for the group, finding any opportunity to slip in a "dick joke" or reference, went AWOL, labeled deserter; "Tatta Babba," leader and combat specialist of the now extinct Twelve Tribes on Mars, exiled from his planet after a mutiny against the GGA (General Galactic Allegiance); "Port-a-Bot," an overused, outdated, obsolete android that still operates up to par and performs basic functions for its human allies; and then lastly, "Brid," a headstrong bounty hunter who, after a deadly civil war, fled a totalitarian governed Earth before it became Post-Earth, a wasteland of a rock where very little life forms survived The Final War and left forever cursed by a plague of endless century-long storms. Barely making it out alive, Brid spent the past two decades coasting through the stars in search of God.

Three, or better yet, three and a half characters Nef, Dud, Brid, and the upper torso of a partly functional Port-a-Bot, which Nef carries in his backpack, stand in front of a giant egg, the one in the game's title, also referred to as "Queen Alien's Egg," which happens to be the color red.

Coincidence or not, Tulip is more than intrigued.

The goal, according to Luke, who speaks about the game with an enthusiasm that Tulip has never seen before, in fact, Tulip believes that his son talking about the game is probably the most words he's ever spoken to his old man, is to find a way inside the egg without *cracking* it open. Whenever you, player Nef, cracks open the egg, as seen played out multiple times on the greasy fingerprint-covered screen, the Queen, "*Mommi* (yes, spelled exactly like that)," as the monster alien is called, awakes from her deep slumber and appears out of nowhere and violently tears the team to shreds and according to Luke, basically consumes *every* living thing in her path.

Then, it's Game Over, Man.

Try Again?

After four times of trying but failing, the kid slams his fists against the arcade and shouts out, "Forget this fucking shit!"

"The game's too smart for you, huh?" another one teases.

Then, the other kid chimes in: "Screw these puzzle games. Let's play a first person shooter."

The kid leaves, so too does his two other friends.

Luke steps forward and stands in front of the now open game. He slides in a quarter and starts from the very beginning of the game with a crash landing of the main character, Nef, on the planet Ozloft-451. From there, Nef battles hostile life forms in hopes of locating a repairman who can fix his spaceship. This is where Nef stumbles across the marine, Dud, who conceals his insecurity and disavowed cowardliness with jokes. The two don't get along at first, especially Dud having what Nef would refer to as a "potty" mouth—constantly referring to jokes about God, like one about when it rains acid, it's "(Nef's) God taking a piss," or whenever there's a cosmic light storm, it's "(Nef's) God throwing a hissy fit"—and it's not until Nef finds Dud's snow globe, which falls out of a backpack, that Nef starts to loosen up to Dud. With a swarm of nectirines, which would make quills on a porcupine look like peach fuzz, close in on their tail, Dud shares a touching story about his daughter, Julie, whom he hasn't seen in years since The Final War; in fact, the snow globe is a gift for his daughter. Inside is a figurine of a man's head, his hair untidy and wild, and when shook, releases dandruff like snow from the man's hair and covers a farm-like landscape— somewhere in the conversation, there is a joke about Nef's God scratching His head.

Surprisingly enough, for a game intended for teens, the game has many religious—and political undertones (Dud cracks a joke and draws analogy to "Mommi" and "Evil Capitalism"—as well as deeply conflicted characters who are struggling to discover faith and meaning in a faithless, meaningless universe presented to the detective in *The Hunt For The Red Easter Egg* where each one of these characters is constantly being attacked by much greater—and higher—forces.

Tulip sips from his coffee as though he's dragging on a ciga-rette and watches Luke storm his way through each of the twelve levels, starting with the formation of Nef's team or trekking through rough terrain where space whales float above and ending with the final level where they reach the Queen's egg, which, according to ancient ruins and past lore, is meant to bring about "*Salvation of The Upright* (Man)."

Impressed by Luke's wits and strategy, Tulip grabs another coffee and rushes back to the arcade game where his son contemplates his next move to defeat the Queen.

A two-headed snake slithers past one of the characters.

Tulip points at the scene and asks Luke, who appears unflappable by the outside world, "You just see that? I must be seeing things. . . "

"That's J," Luke says shortly.

"J?" Tulip says and shrugs. "Okay. . . So, who's J?"

Luke shushes his father as he tries to figure out how to beat the puzzle.

Tulip stands back and lets his son, in a way, play the role of detective.

I now see who he takes after and it's certainly not his mother.

Luke uses Nef to crack open the egg.

Thick black ooze pours from the opening in the egg and drowns Nef.

Game over.

Two lives remaining.

Luke starts at the last checkpoint and tries yet again. He uses a ladder in the dropdown Inventory, accessing BACKPACK + TOOLBELT menu, climbs up the egg in an attempt to enter the egg from the top—perhaps it's not an egg but more so a hatch—and cracks open the top of the egg without all that black ooze gushing out, which killed him the first time around.

A few seconds later Mommi comes rushing in, grabs Nef, and eats him like a snack.

Game over.

One life remaining.

"You got this," Tulip says with encouragement.

Respawning at the last checkpoint, he thinks harder about the next move before exhausting his last life.

"If you crack open the egg, you die," Luke says, drifting off in thought.

He doesn't think for too long before he realizes the final boss, "Mommi," like the levels prior, such as Level 4 where he had to combine different devices in his BACKPACK to open the invisible door of the Rook Chamber, is a puzzle.

Luke pulls down the TOOLBELT menu and grabs Zeus's Bolt, a magnifying glass-like intensifier contraption, which allows players to increase the size of objects; however, Luke has no intention to use the magnifying part of the contraption, rather the opposite.

From his BACKPACK he uses the "time crystal switch," which, when combined with the ZB, grants players exactly thirteen seconds of uninterruptible free rein, either forward in time or backward in time. He sets the switch in the forward position. Once the time crystal is attached to Zeus's Bolt, from his TOOLBELT, Luke attaches a winder engine, which can reverse the function of certain contraptions and when combines with Zeus's Bolt, will, finger-crossed, reverse the magnifying process, thus shrinking objects. He only has two bolts. He first tries it on J, who slithers by Dud's feet. J is shrunken down to the size of a worm!

"It worked!" Luke shouts out.

"What worked?" asks Tulip, stumped by how his son was able to jerry built such a contraption.

"Now," Luke says, "I use the Zeus Bolt on the egg—"

"Yeah? Then what?"

"Then, I eat it."

Nef points Zeus's Bolt at the massive red egg and zaps it with a bolt, shrinking it down to the size of a chicken's egg. With the joystick, Luke controls Nef to walk over to the egg and presses the "A" button once he arrives at the egg.

Nef stuffs the egg inside his mouth.

Swallows it whole with a cartoonish *gah-gulp*.

"Now what?"

"Just wait. . . "

The two wait for thirteen seconds and once the time crystal wears off, the egg returns back to normal size.

Nef is gone.

Swallowed and now trapped inside the egg!?!

"Is that it? Where'd your guy go?"

"He's inside the egg," Luke says.

The game plays a time lapse of the egg with a distant sun going up and down, up and down, up and down, until finally it's time for the egg to hatch.

First, a claw protrudes from the egg, its crack appearing like a dent in a windshield.

Smiling from ear to ear, Luke watches the alien finally emerge; however, it's not like Mommi's offspring. It's part Nef-part Alien.

As Mommi recognizes the abomination of her youngling, the Alien Nef turns on its mother and destroys Mommi, thus allowing the other members of Nef's team, Dud, Brid, and the mutilated android, Port-a-Bot, to survive and escape the danger, leaving behind Alien Nef to start a new race on the hostile Alien planet.

The end credits roll.

Tulip reads the name of the creator, "Humpty Dumpty."

The game ends.

Overwhelmed with the elation of sweet victory, Luke enters his initials "LIT" into the top of the scoreboard.

Tulip notices those same initials "LIT" toward the bottom of the scoreboard with a slower time.

He ignores the thought of his son already beating the game once before and pats him on the back.

"Way to go, Luke," Tulip says, his voice fading from the very thought of the game's concept, the righteous undertones, as well as its stark parallels to the case he's been stressing over.

Tulip can't even remember the last time he's seen his son filled with so much joy. He wouldn't be lying if he said the same about himself.

But there's a dark cloud in the distance.

And it's approaching fast.

And building.

So many clouds.

Like a bad storm.

⚓

TULIP and his son talk about the victory over a slice of greasy pepperoni pizza for lunch.

Afterwards, he walks his son over to the prize stand. Luke has enough tokens to buy a ridiculous clown horn with the whoopie cushion (yes, Tulip definitely does *not* look forward to hearing Luke making fart noises with a horn on the drive back home, but he doesn't want to ruin his son's high from earlier), the same one he's been eyeing ever since they stepped foot into Legends.

Stepping forward through the curtains and greeting the father and son behind the glass case of prizes is a well-built man with a thinly shaved beard.

Immediately, Tulip recognizes the man, whom his son calls "Howie."

By the way Luke talks about the game with Howie, who sounds as if he has beaten the game in his sleep, it doesn't take long for Tulip to piece the puzzle together.

"Mr. Donem," Tulip says to Howie, who also recognizes the detective.

Howie clears his throat.

"Detective Tulip, correct?"

"That's right," he says and reaches out his hand to shake Howie's.

The two shake hands, Howie's having a firmer, manlier grip over Tulip.

It's what he's wearing, or in this case, what he's not wearing that sets off the detective's suspicion. He notices the pale outline of a ring on Howie's ring finger; however, it doesn't look like the traditional wedding band.

"So, how's the case going so far?" Howie asks and releases his hand over the brief macho "my-grip-is-stronger-than-yours" introduction.

"I'm sure you've heard about it on the News."

"Yes," he says. "I'm pulling for you, Detective. I hope you catch the guy."

"Whoever said it was a guy I'm looking for?" asks Tulip.

Stumbling with words, Howie says, "Well, I just assumed it was a guy. . . "

"Just messing with you," Tulip says, relieving tension between the two.

"So you two were playing *The Hunt For The Red Easter Egg,*" Howie says to both Tulip and his son.

"Yes," Tulip says and closely watches Howie's reaction. "Interesting game. You wouldn't happen to know the creator of the game—"

"You're talking about Humpty Dumpty."

"That's right," he says.

"The *elusive* Humpty Dumpty."

"You know this person?"

"I don't," Howie says. "But I've heard rumors about him."

"What kind of rumors?"

"For starters, it's the only game he created," he says. "According to Game Facts, only twelve arcades were ever made. One of the eleven resides right here in Legends. Something, huh?"

"Too bad he didn't capitalize off the game," Tulip says. "In today's world he could make a lot of money with a concept like that."

"For someone like Humpty Dumpty, it's clearly not about the money. . . "

"What's it about?" asks Tulip.

"If it was me, I'd say it's about exclusivity."

"Exclusivity, huh?"

"That is if *I* was Humpty Dumpty," he says casually and almost playfully.

The tingle of a hunch creeps into Tulip's gut, a tightness rising in his chest.

"How'd that work out," he says with keen focus, "you obtaining such an exclusive game?"

He says with a twinkle in his eye, "I know a guy who knows a guy who has a cousin who knows a guy. That's usually how it works, right?"

Tulip nods at the vast spread of arcade games.

"You must know your games, huh?"

"I dabble here and there."

"So," Tulip says, interrupting more tension and awkwardness, "you know my son here Luke?"

"Of course, I do. Little dude practically lives here."

"One day I'm going to create my own game," Luke says.

"I bet," Tulip says, then turns to Howie. "But I'm sure it takes a lot of hard work, right?"

"Heard it took Humpty Dumpty six years to complete *The Hunt*."

Tulip is tempted to ask Howie if he has any kids, but he remembers he asked him the last time they spoke.

"So," he says and sighs before the detective can ask him any other questions, which, to Howie, seemed on the horizon, "what do you want, little dude?"

Luke points at the clown horn.

"You got it," he says to Luke.

With a hint of a grin curling into the side of his face, Howie glances at Tulip. Then fetches the horn for Luke.

"So, how long have you owned this place?" Tulip asks, as if he's warming up to Howie and slowly easing into those *obvious* questions.

"Thought I mentioned it to you already," Howie says. Tulip doesn't respond. Howie hands the horn to Luke, who, in returns, hands Howie the correct amount of tokens. "Ten years this October," he looks around and with an overwhelming sense of pride, admires his own establishment. "This place," he says, holding his hands up, "*this is my sanctuary.*"

⚓

TULIP parts ways with Howie, but in the back of his mind he knows this isn't the last time he'll see the man's face.

Tulip walks Luke to the car and warns him not to be honking that thing (as in the clown horn) in the car.

Once inside, Tulip asks Luke about Howie and that ghost of a "ring."

"What do you mean *ring*?"

Tulip holds up his hand and shows Luke the wedding band on his finger.

"You know," he says, "ring."

Luke thinks for a moment.

"Yeah," he says. "He does. But it doesn't look like that."

"What does it look like? It wouldn't have a face on it, would it?"

Luke thinks more.

"Nef," he says. "It's a ring with Nef's face after his transformation."

"Like the one in the game? The *alien*?"

Struggling to face his father, Luke hesitantly bobs his head up and down and hangs his head as if he committed a shameful act.

As the fun of the day wears off and is replaced by the pressure of the job, Tulip starts up the car, then switches off the ignition. Tulip looks around the parking lot for a parent. He finds one, a woman in her late forties, whose leaving Legends with her two sons. Tulip tells Luke to follow him.

They leave the car.

Tulip asks the woman, who's about to drive off, if she can watch his son until his mother arrives.

The woman, at first, refuses; then he shows her the badge and tells her it's an emergency.

She agrees.

Tulip says the mother will be coming to pick up the son shortly.

In the meantime, Luke hangs out with the woman's two boys while his father calls his mom and without answering any of the questions as to why she should drop what she's doing (which is shopping for new books to discuss at her bookclub with a friend), tells her to drive herself to Legends to pick up their son. "And hurry," he demands.

Just in case his hunch is right, Tulip unbuttons his shoulder holster.

He enters Legends and heads directly to the stand.

Howie isn't there.

Tulip stops an employee and asks her if she's seen Howie.

She points behind the curtains and says he went to the back.

Tulip brandishes a badge for the employee and tells her to get everybody out of here and to do so as quietly as possible and not to make a scene.

The employee doesn't question Tulip. Instead, she does what he tells her and rounds up the gamers, parents, and grandparents alike.

While the employee escorts people from the front and side exits, Tulip walks through the beaded curtain into a dark "Employees Only" room, which looks like a garage with rows and rows of out of order arcade machines.

In the corner of his eye, Tulip spots a dark figure dashing to the shadows.

"Mr. Donem?"

As Tulip walks past one of the arcades, he removes the gun from his holster.

In the reflection of one of the screens, he spots a large figure, Howie, looming closer.

The beaded curtain opens, giving way to light.

Luke is standing at the opening.

In a distance, he hears the voice of the woman, whom he told to watch over his son, calling out to the boy.

The flickering glint of a stainless steel meat tenderizer glares against the arcade, forcing Tulip to face Howie who's towering directly behind him and rearing back his right arm, ready to strike down on Tulip's head.

Tulip reacts and fires a gunshot, striking Howie in the shoulder.

Howie manages to catch Tulip in the forehead with the side of the tenderizer, causing Tulip to fall backward.

Dazed, Tulip stumbles and trips over his own feet.

Howie runs to the EXIT and flees from Legends while Tulip slowly stands to his feet and checks on Luke to make sure he's okay. Luke is cowering behind the wall and is okay but more so confused as to why Howie would hurt his father.

The woman arrives, only to find Tulip bleeding badly from the forehead.

Tulip tells the woman to call the police.

The woman pulls out her phone and doesn't waste anytime calling police.

Tulip kisses his boy and tells him he loves him and gives the woman a second chance to watch over his son while he chases after Howie.

All Tulip can think about is the hunt.

A part of Tulip wishes he was stuck in a video game right now, like the same one Luke was playing, and that he could defeat the final boss with only the strategic usage and combinations of buttons and the reactive maneuvers of a joystick.

But another part of him just enjoys the *thrill* of the hunt.

And that part makes the risk of dying all the more meaningful.

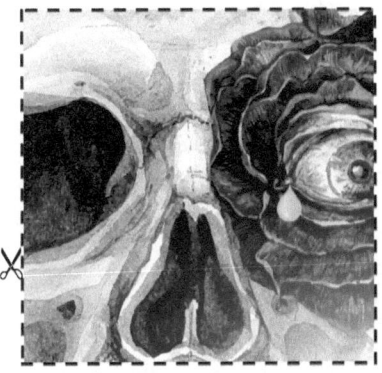

THE RUSE

FORECASTERS *blew it again*, Cain thought.
  Amazing how they get paid money to predict the weather.
  It's a good thing I brought out Baby.
Should hold them accountable.
But *then again. . .*

The car he brooded about in sarcasm was a 1970 Firebird—his "Baby," as he called it whenever he wasn't in the presence of other people. His own personal *love affair.* The mistress who whispered engine purrs and guttural revs like sweet nothings in his ears.

As the wind picked up, the vintage car took quite a beating from debris, including small pebbles and twigs, all whipped in the air by a strong band of rain from Hurricane Luke, which was *forecasted* to make a sharp turn due east along the tip of the Florida panhandle but, at the eleventh hour, a weakened high pressure system allowed the storm, currently barreling through Louisiana as a CAT 1 hurricane, to head north and continue its destructive path.

Floods.
Leveled houses.
Debris strewed everywhere.
Downed power lines.

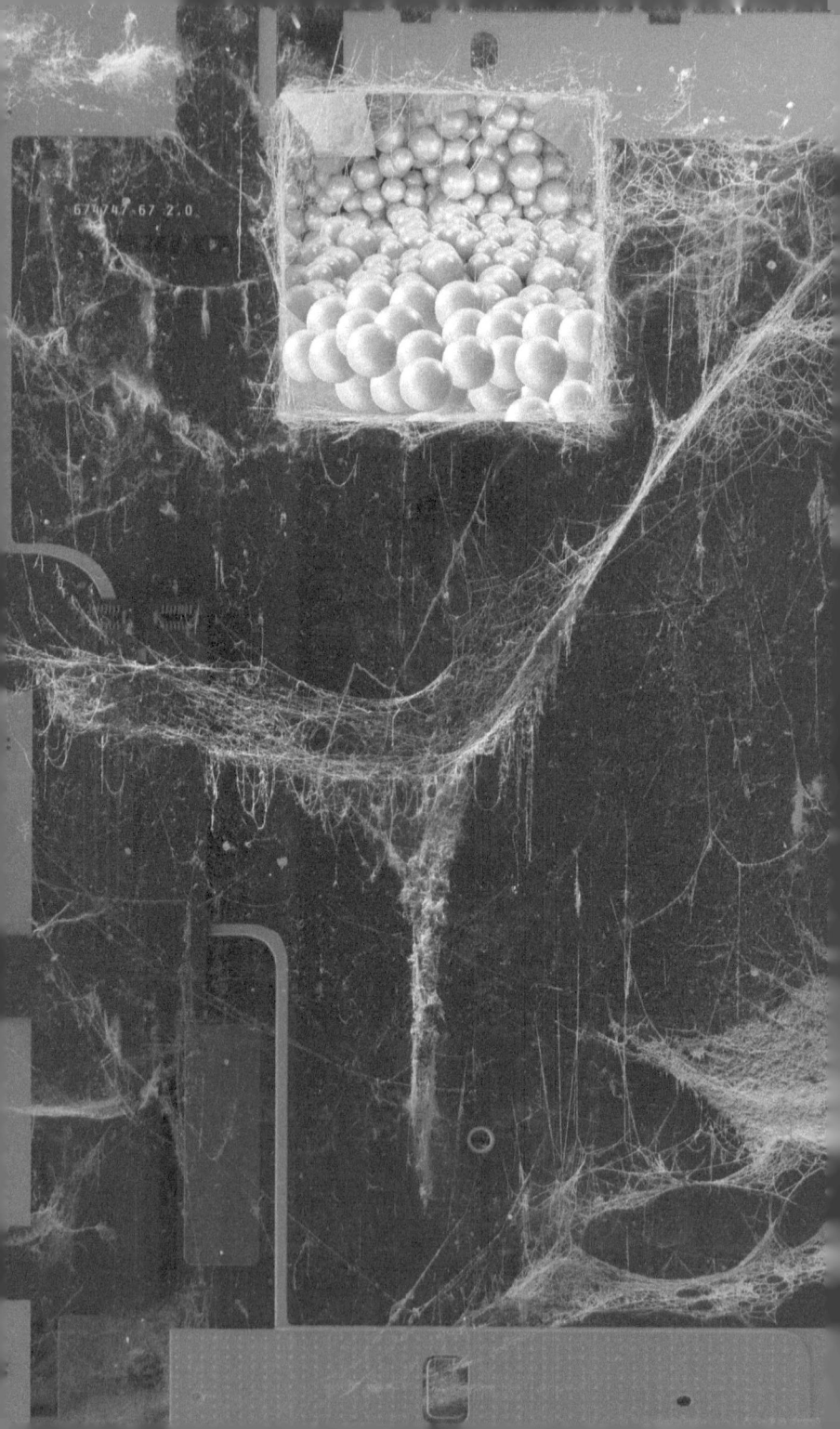

One last retort by Mother Nature herself before Old Man Winter's inevitable arrival.

I should've seen the storm coming from a mile away.

Most importantly, I *should've felt it coming.*

In disgust, Cain cut off Bob's voice on the radio station.

Man won't shut up about Luke.

As the wind intensified with a tremendous howl, Cain wiped the steam from the foggy windshield, which left behind a clear, curved streak on the glass, and watched the gale of wind chew through the NEW AGE GOSPEL billboard from its steel support beams. The tattered billboard nearly disintegrated as it tumbled across a desolate highway. The furious burst sent tiny projectiles into the air at bullet-speed.

Cain suddenly ducked underneath the dashboard as debris came shooting over the front end of the black Firebird—his "Baby." The torn debris skipped like a saucer over the flame decal on the hood, leaving behind a few dents, as well as deep key-like scratches.

Sheets of hard rain continued to pound against the sides of the Firebird, arousing Cain into a state of urgency. And anxiety.

A lightning bolt flashed behind him, startling him.

If I knew it was gonna be *this* bad, I would've taken my another baby, old "Buddy," a beat-up Chevy, which he used to haul around building materials, as well as junk that he dropped off at the dump; however, time was of the essence.

Thunder choked the gray sky. A bone *crunching* sound of a tree trunk ripping from its roots soon followed. Cain checked the rear view mirror, only to witness a large oak tree uproot and then topple onto the street behind him. The tree was a massive thing that appeared as if it had survived many generations of violent storms like Luke, even worser than Luke.

Growing more frantic with each passing second, he peered over his shoulder to make sure his weary eyes hadn't deceived him.

The road was impassable.

Cain inched the Firebird forward through the murky floodwater but soon realized the water was way too high and like the road behind him, the road home was completely impassable.

What I'd do to have one of them airboats, Cain thought, *like the one Okie used in the swamps.*

He desperately looked for another way out but found none. He stared at his bare ring finger and rolled his thumb over the pale imprint, the sight of which inspired him to not only push forward and find another way out of this godforsaken mess, but to also remember Show Low, as well as the mission at hand and what waited for him once the mission was done. It'd be like "icing on the cake," Cain told, in fact, convinced himself before he set out on this wild journey—his own reward for making things *right* again.

To Cain's right was a way out, a dark, ominous stretch of road called Nede Drive, which didn't appear flooded.

Cain rolled down the passenger window, leaned over the center console, and squinted hard through a gray wall of rain and chaos as if, by doing so, he was able to spot phantoms.

The two-lane road was surrounded by woods, backwoods-kind of sketchy, covered in leaves and broken tree branches.

But it *was* passable.

Cain had no other option.

He made a right-hand turn and while exercising the most extreme caution, proceeded down the dark road.

After about a quarter of a mile in, he received a message on his pager.

Of *all* times to be needed, Cain thought to himself.

He unclipped the pager from his belt buckle and read the phone number first, which was Hogan's number, as well as the code sent to him: "9-1-1."

"What is it this time?" Cain asked himself.

He remembered explicably telling Hogan that he was going to be out of the office for a few days, not working on his new house but instead taking personal time off, and if he needed any counseling, Hogan could reach out to James, a former counselor who was retired but every now and then helped out Cain whenever he was in a jam. During their last sit-down, he specifically told Hogan to contact the phone number that he provided.

At the end of the road, Cain reached a dead end. There was no sign, no nothing, only the woods whispering foreign languages.

Despite the looming dread, he felt as if he was on the right path. Cain checked his surroundings and, as before, weighed what little options he had before and around him.

His mind was flooded by a stream of heavy doubts surging like a raging river.

He began to grow hopeless and worried, like he-was-in-the-shit kind of worried, and he didn't know why nor could he explain why but a part of him felt betrayed. He was hit by a sudden dizzy spell. The uncomfortable tightness caused by panic crept inside his body like a warm hand tiptoeing its way up his chest.

In a dizzying spiral, he spotted a tilted mailbox swaying in the wind like a loose tooth ready to be plucked free. Next in his desperate attempt to find refuge, he spotted a gravel driveway, like the road, winding. He traced the *path* up to what appeared to be a two-story house; however, Cain couldn't quite tell for the hard rain was coming down sideways.

As Cain turned away, a soft-yellow light suddenly switched on inside the house.

Curious, he leaned over the passenger seat and rolled down the window for a closer look.

Behind the lit window slouched the frail-looking silhouette of what looked like an older person—a woman, from its shape. Cain certainly didn't want to impose. But as those doubts continued to pour in, he thought to himself, *what other choice do I have?*

Caught in a terrible state of indecisiveness, he *finally* decided to turn the car around. Cain drove back the same way he came and hoped—even prayed, which was something Cain hadn't done since his ugly divorce—to brave it through the floodwaters.

A quarter of a mile in, the road was blocked.

Like the road before, a tree with a trunk twice the size of a telephone pole had fallen across the entire length of the road, as well as the waterlogged grass that ran toward the edge of the woods, making it impossible to pass.

He could see the highway not too far ahead. It was right there. Not even the length of a football field.

The wind started to pick up more violently this time, gusts ranging from sixty to eighty miles per hour.

Tree branches smacked the side of his car, leaving behind long cracks in the windows.

Cain was *out* of options.

The house, he thought.

It was calling to him.

More decisively, Cain put the car in reverse, turned around, and drove back to the house.

The driveway was protected by an archway of trees; and at the very end, many tire tracks jutted out toward an outhouse behind the two-story house where in the backyard stood an angelic-like sculpture meshed with twisted branches and swollen roots, which Cain initially mistook as a playground. He didn't put much thought into the strange sculpture for the rain was coming down harder now.

Cain shut off the vehicle and before counting down "1-2-3," the sudden thought of the mission momentarily left him in a sickening state. That ache in his gut, that lurch, pulling him in two different directions, two fates. He pushed the feeling aside and ran out into the storm with his jeans jacket worn over his head like a hood and hurried to the rear of the car where he popped open the trunk.

Temporarily shielded from the rain, Cain glanced at the leather briefcase covered with smears of dirt next to a shovel, which appeared as if it had been recently used from the clumps of hardened mud on the edge of the blade, as well as a pair of scissors, a rusty handsaw, then, finally, a navy blue duffle bag packed with clothes.

Lightning flickered all around him.

Thunder immediately followed, choking the black sky above.

Cain closed the trunk, left his things, and sprinted to the porch. The back of his heel slipped on the slick and stringy goo of pumpkin guts splattered all over the porch steps. He suddenly threw his arms out in his best impersonation of the drunken twist, recovered, and then foolishly rebalanced himself as he grabbed hold of a wobbly railing.

Like the house, the porch was unkept, furniture worn, molded, and dry-rotted. Planks of wood bent upward along the floor like dog-ears on paper. Gusts of wind blew forth a putrid odor coming from a dead garden along the side of the house.

Next to an overturned wicker bench rested an old, shabby pink doll with black flat buttons for eyes. One of the buttons—the left one—was missing from its spotty-brown face.

While Cain waited under the overhang and found himself shivering from a sudden drop in temperature, he couldn't help but notice the pumpkins scattered throughout the front yard.

Retired jack o' lanterns, mishandled and misshaped. Most of them, like the one on the steps—or what was left of it—with carved-out faces caved in and squashed from the harsh winds.

Expecting trick-or-treaters all the way out here, thought Cain.

He scoured the street, searching for neighbors but was unable to find any.

Pushing aside the strangeness of the situation, he rang the doorbell.

He felt a sudden pinprick against the tip of his index finger in what he thought was a rogue current of electricity.

Cain recoiled, then waggled his hand, then voiced his pain.

Nobody answered, only the random drumming of shutters banging against the moldy siding.

In great need of shelter, Cain resorted to pounding on the door, like one of those movie-cops with a short fuse.

The door *squeaked* open after the third pound.

Cain was greeted by a potent aroma coming from a strange root or herb, which appeared like a wrung and wrinkled egg-plant dangling above the doorway. He found himself taking a step back and squeezing his face from the horrible odor.

A woman with a small stature finally stepped forward from the shadows and answered the door.

Cain straightened up. He guessed she was well over a hundred and incapable of common tasks most wouldn't have a problem carrying out, like opening up a pickle jar or climbing a flight of stairs or composing email messages. The more Cain thought about it, he figured the petite old lady didn't own a computer or, better, probably hadn't even heard of AOL. And, if so, she'd probably think it was a *slang* word or secret code kids were using nowadays. Her gray face was as coarse as a baseball glove that had been left in an attic for decades and the sunken parts of her skull were lost in the lively shadows of a dimly lit foyer. Both her eyes were lit like silver marbles in those dark sockets.

Cain heard a *click* from behind the wall!

A porch light switched on directly above him.

Squinting, Cain's eyes soon adjusted to the light.

The strange woman was cast in more comforting light.

Temporary relief washed over Cain.

The woman appeared at least twenty years younger than the dim lighting had first suggested. She was a rather sweet-looking lady, grandmotherly, not sickly, the kind you wouldn't mind baking you a warm pineapple upside-down cake. She was wearing a salmon-colored sleeping gown with a yellow floral pattern, which matched her fluffy cat slippers.

"Can I help you?" asked the woman, her voice as delicate and innocent as a child's.

"Thank God," Cain said, more relieved. "Don't mean to disturb you, ma'am, but I've caught myself in a jam. I was. . . " Lightning struck close by, the clap of thunder that followed soon after causing Cain to flinch, ". . . I was on my way home when the storm hit. All the roads are flooded."

"On the way home?" said the woman as if she had caught Cain in a lie. "All the way out here?"

Cain backtracked.

"Again, I don't mean to disturb you, but I have nowhere else to go—"

"Are you injured?" she asked.

"No," Cain said, as his body shrunk with defense. "I'm okay." With his shoulders curled tightly into his body, he braced himself from a gust of wind the same way a wide receiver would brace for an open-field tackle. "If it's no trouble, I was hoping I could take shelter here until the storm passes. I assure you I don't mean any trouble, ma'am. If you don't mind, I could even wait here on the porch until the storm passes. . . if it's okay with you." Cain pulled out the wallet from his back pocket and showed her cash—he only had six dollars—and said with lesser urgency, "I have money."

"That's ridiculous." She waved Cain inside. "Come inside."

"You sure?"

"Yes," she said, as if she could use the company. "Of course."

The woman stepped aside.

Gladly, Cain entered.

"Cain Brindle," he introduced himself.

"*Sorrel* Mayfair," the woman said, the first name spoken with a different, more foreign tongue.

She closed the door behind Cain.

More at ease, Cain followed Sorrel into a dusty living room that looked like any other normal living room occupied by what was best known as an older person, not an *old* person. She had picture frames strategically placed on various tabletops around the room. She owned a small TV set, which was hidden in the far corner of the room opposite of a fireplace. The TV looked as if the last time it was turned on was July 20, 1969.

Sorrel pointed to a dilapidated couch. The appearance alone of the couch made his skin itch. She instructed Cain to make himself at home; however, Cain decided to stand.

She insisted yet again.

Finally, Cain sat but did so on the very edge of the couch almost as if he was trying to hover over it.

"Would you care for some tea while you wait for the storm to pass?"

"Yes," Cain said. "Please. If it's no trouble. . . "

"Not one bit."

Sorrel disappeared into the kitchen.

Cain heard the sound of a faucet running.

From the kitchen, Sorrel asked him, "So, Cain Brindle, you live around here?"

"I live up in Moorestown," he said.

"You're a long way from home. What's brings you all the way out here?"

Cain didn't think too much about the question.

"My ex wife lives about an hour or so from here," he said naturally. "I was actually picking up my daughter for the weekend."

There was a slight pause between question and answer.

"Daughter, huh?" She poked her head from the kitchen as Cain stopped roaming around the living room to rotate his body toward the kitchen where he witnessed Sorrel staring at him with a smirk on her face. He was somewhat startled by Sorrel's look—and worried. As before, he didn't put much stock into it. Cain figured that his ugly mug was the only face she had seen in days, perhaps even weeks or months. With a creeping suspicion, he looked around the cobwebs along the ceiling. Maybe even *years*.

"How old?" asked Sorrel.

"Five."

"Don't you just love 'em at that age?"

"I swear," he said with a telling remorse buried deep in his eyes, "she gets bigger and bigger each time I see her."

Once more, Sorrel disappeared into the kitchen.

Cain couldn't resist snooping around the living room. He noticed a particular picture frame above the fireplace. A photo of a man, woman, and child, possibly a girl—he couldn't tell for the hat and crew cut and boyish clothes—posing on a bridge along Grandfather Mountain. Except for the hairdo, Cain couldn't identify the child for its face was missing and nothing remained of the face but a warped smoky oval.

Same went for the man and woman.

Their faces, burned out with what looked like a flame, gone.

Cain's nostrils twitched.

He smelled a waft of smoke.

Curious, he leaned forward and sniffed the picture frame. The smoke wasn't coming from the picture, Cain realized. Instead, the smell was coming from *his* clothes. He pulled up the collar of his shirt and brought it closer to his face, then took a whiff of the material. His shirt smelled of ambers.

As panic crept back in, Cain came across a memorial card for an eighty-three year old fellow named "*Bob Mayfair*." The date of his death was August 21, 1979, which, if Cain's math was correct, was around nineteen years ago. Mr. Mayfair was survived by his wife, *Sorrel Dubois* Mayfair. He searched for children, even grandchildren, particularly a girl, in the memorial card but couldn't find any.

"So, you have any children, Ms. Sorrel?" Cain asked, trying to take his mind off the strong smell.

A soft yet raspy voice from behind: *Save yourself.*

Cain snapped to the voice and saw Sorrel standing at the edge of the kitchen.

She was staring blankly at Cain.

"Excuse me."

"Sugar," said Sorrel, her brow rising. "Do you take sugar?"

"Ah. . . yes. Sugar's fine."

A sudden flicker of lightning startled Cain. He braced himself for the clap of thunder but instead, received a deafening boom!

"Sounds like she's directly over us," she said as, like before, she disappeared into the kitchen.

She?

"Yeah," Cain said anxiously. "Guess so."

All of a sudden he felt the pager weighing heavily along his hip.

"May I use your phone?" asked Cain.

"Absolutely." Once more, she poked her head from the kitchen. "I reckon your *baby* must be worried sick about you," she said and pointed at a beige telephone sitting on the table next to the couch.

The woman's words, more importantly, that one word, cut right through Cain and left him frozen.

"No," he drawled. "It's a patient of mine."

With a patronizing tone, she said to Cain, "Patient, huh? You a doctor?"

"No. . . " he said, shrugging off Sorrel's previous remark. "I'm a substance abuse counselor."

"So what's that exactly?" asked Sorrel.

"I help those who are chemically dependent."

"Chemically dependent?" asked Sorrel, her tone heavy with bitterness.

The tone alone of Sorrel's voice captured Cain's interest and in that moment, he could actually hear what she wanted to say to him; however, he had a feeling, well, more like an intuition, that if Sorrel had gotten to know Cain for a little bit longer, say, once the ice was broken, she'd start speaking her mind.

"You mean, drugs?"

"Yes," Cain said patiently. "Correct. I counsel people who are struggling with addictions, like drugs and alcohol."

"Interesting line of work," she said and once more, disappeared into the kitchen.

Cain picked up the phone and called Hogan.

Clearly, as soon as Hogan answered the call, Cain recognized a sick desperation in Hogan's trembling voice. Hogan used to drink like a fish and smoke like a chimney, mostly weed and cigarettes, not always in that order, until one day when he was as high as a Coloradoan hiker he fell down a flight of stairs and broke his leg, or what the doctors called a "compound fracture." Most say the worst kind of fracture. Hogan's drink of choice was Bourbon before he nearly lost his leg. Now, after dealing with the lingering pain of a past injury, Hogan became hooked on a brand new drug of choice: Oxys. He popped them in his mouth the same way a person with acid reflux popped breath mints. On top of that, he started to mix the booze with the pills.

Before Cain had a chance to reassure Hogan that the urge to use again would soon pass like the clouds, the phone went dead.

"Hogan?"

Cain checked the receiver.

The dial tone.

Nothing. Only silence.

He hung up the phone and walked over to the window, peered out, and another flicker of lightning brought out the strange figure that he had witnessed during his dash through the thunderstorm. At first, he thought it was a playground, as first suspected.

He peered closer, both of his eyes adjusting to the darkness.

With the tension building, he waited for another flash of lightning to reveal the strange structure for what it truly was.

Lightning struck!

He realized the playground was *not* a playground. It appeared as if it was a religious totem of some kind with a jagged-looking cross or emblem suspended directly above it.

Dark cloaked figures, small, like children, were circling around the massive structure. He thought he saw several of them bowing down to it in creepy, cult-like fashion.

He waited for yet another lightning strike.

On cue, lightning struck again.

Cain peered closer.

The cloaked figures were gone.

All of a sudden, Cain was overcome by a similar dizzy spell as before.

Sorrel said coldly, "Phone trouble?"

"May I use your restroom?" Cain asked twice.

"Down the hallway, first door on the right," Sorrel said with her back turned to Cain.

He paused from the sound of Sorrel's voice. It sounded different, more of a European accent unlike its original Southern drawl, as words like *hallway* and *door* rolled off her tongue.

German?

Cain thought more about the accent as he located the bathroom down the hallway, first door on the right.

He locked the door behind him. He didn't know exactly why he decided to lock the bathroom door—maybe it was instinct—but he did observe a change in Sorrel, in her look, in her manner and attitude, a particular coldness, as if that first initial warm welcome had started to wear off and now her true face was emerging.

How could the old bag know?

Regardless of the mountain of evidence, he was convinced that a lie wasn't necessarily a lie if you think it's true.

You can tell a lie a million times before. . .

A rush of blood ran through Cain's body.

In an overflowing sink were romance novels submerged in what looked like floodwater.

With his index finger and thumb shaped like pincers, he singled out one paperback, *The Quiet Storm*, carefully gripped it by the top right-hand corner as if he was a detective handling a key piece of evidence, and lifted it from the murky water. He spun around the soggy paperback and skimmed over the summary on the back.

Words like *hurricane* and *hunger* immediately leaped at him.

Except for the whole weirdness of the situation, like books being soaked in water like dirty clothes, Cain didn't think too much about Sorrel's poor taste in literature—or "smut."

Unruffled, he placed the paperback back into the sink.

After all, it was just a book.

Cain squared himself in front of the surprisingly clean toilet and raised the pink-carpeted lid.

As he was relieving himself, he stopped mid-stream.

In the bowl was a gold wedding band.

Intrigued, he zipped up his pants and scooped out the ring with the toilet brush.

His eyes lit up with surprise as the ring slid back into the toilet bowel.

He didn't know when or where he had heard that accent before, but he knew the particular tongue and the way words loosely rolled off it.

"*French*," he said to himself.

The lights went out followed by a dying hum!

The entire room went pitch black. . .

Cautiously, Cain exited the bathroom.

To the right of him he could hear *tick, tick, tick* of a grandfather clock. Then, nothing. No ticking. The clock went dead.

"*Sorrel?*"

Cain blindly made his way down the hallway, using his hands in front of him to safely guide him to the window in the kitchen. The rolling sound of water, as well as the flickering light from outside which cast barely enough light into the kitchen, helped Cain locate the pot of boiling water.

"Sorrel?" said Cain. "You here?"

He heard a playful yet familiar sound of a girl's giggle coming from the darkness of the living room. He turned toward the sound but couldn't make out his surroundings for it was way too dark to see anything, not even his own hand inches in front of him, and the only light came from the pale flickers of lightning.

"Sorrel?" Cain said and strangely, laughed to himself at the absurdity of a situation that he could've avoided. "Where'd you go?"

The water was starting to bubble over, the cast iron hissing like a snake from where droplets splashed over the hot surface.

With the damp corner of his jacket, Cain removed the hot pot from the stove but ended up burning his hand.

He dropped the pot, boiling hot water splashing everywhere.

"Shit!" Then, yelled out, "Sorrel! Where are you?"

Cain switched off the gas.

The fire would not recede.

Instead, a flame leaped upward, singeing his eyebrows.

The flame caught the wooden shelf above and slowly spread throughout one half of the kitchen. The fire cut through the darkness and shed more light onto *things* that dared to be brought forward. However, Cain never turned to acknowledge the eerily gray and scar-covered face of an old decrepit woman looming in the dark shadows of the kitchen doorway.

Cain heard another giggle, this time followed by a beat of footsteps racing through the darkness.

He ignored the fire, ignored the flames licking up the wall, and followed the sound of giggles, innocent as they may be, yet, again, so familiar. The giggling led Cain to a basement at the end of the hallway. He stood at the top of the smoky landing, unsure whether or not to enter. Strobe light-flickers of lightning flashed throughout the basement, highlighting warped and lanky reflections moving along a mirror-like floor like specters. Once more, he turned to a much tamer fire in the kitchen. Then, as he turned back around, he swore he saw the floor moving below as if the floor itself, like that sneaky darkness, was a living entity.

With his heart pounding harder and faster, he paused, glanced down at the ghostly pale imprint on his bare ring finger, and decided to push forward.

Exercising the utmost caution, he inched his way down a flight of creaky wooden stairs.

The basement was flooded up to Cain's shins.

He pushed forward.

Once more, he called out to Sorrel but encountered someone whom he least expected.

As Cain rounded a dilapidated brick pillar, he found a little girl with streaky bleach blonde hair staring at those flashes of lightning behind the basement window. She was wearing a dress and standing ankle-deep in murky water.

He peered closer in his sleepy gape and rubbed his eyes to make sure they weren't fooling him. He soon realized that not only was the floral pattern the same as the one on the old woman's sleeping gown, but the color was also the same. A pinkish-yellow.

Carefully, he cleared his throat, hoping to grab the young girl's attention. She didn't move a muscle. She appeared as if she was caught in a trance as she stared up at the small basement window.

As Cain stood a few feet behind the girl, he tried to think back to the conversation he shared with Sorrel but couldn't remember if she had spoken or even mentioned anything to him about a granddaughter, even a son or daughter for that matter. He thought about the picture frame, the one with the missing faces.

Burned away.

He thought about his other "Baby," his Evelyn.

"You must be Sorrel's granddaughter," said Cain.

The girl rotated around.

A flash of lightning illuminated her lifeless face.

Cain gasped.

"Evelyn? Is that you?"

"I'm scared, daddy," the girl whined.

Cain hurried over to his daughter—or a girl who could've easily passed as his daughter. He studied her pale face.

It was *her*, his Evelyn.

Overcome with jubilation, Cain stepped forward.

"Evelyn," Cain said and hugged his daughter, "where have you been? How in the world did you get here—"

"I dunno," she said over his shoulder. "I'm scared."

"Don't be, Evy," Cain said, as he stroked the back of her head. "Daddy's here now. Daddy's here."

As he embraced his daughter, he ran his hand over her blonde hair, gently stroking it.

Clumps of stringy wet hair stuck to the palm of his hand as well as the spaces between each finger. He tore off a handful of hair as soon as he removed his hand from the back of Evy's head.

Shocked by the discovery, he stared at the hair in his hand and then a section of his daughter's gray-like skin, which was exposed along on the top of her head. Even the smell of her hair, her skin, her whole body reeked of decay.

A sudden terror came over him. Cain soon realized that he wasn't hugging his daughter, *his Baby*, his *Evelyn*. Her skin was as rough as bark and as knobby as a tree trunk.

He slowly pulled himself from what used to be his daughter and found himself clinging onto the leg of something unmistakably inhuman. His horror-stricken eyes traced the wide scaly leg to a demonic winged beast towering at least seven feet above, its mouth stretched open, its serrated teeth dripping with ropes of drool.

From the top of the landing, Sorrel shrieked at the great beast below, "Bon appétit!"

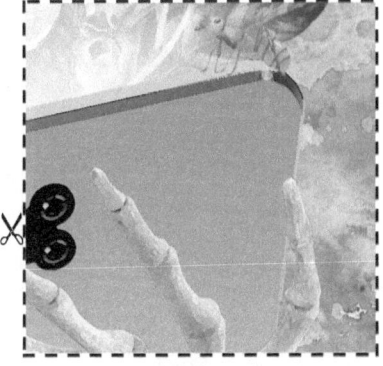

DARK AND BLOATED

WINNIE carelessly stuffed the March issue of the magazine, *Bon Appétit*, inside an already-crowded glove compartment filled with old receipts, napkins from various fast-food restaurants, as well as a car manual that was bound by a leather casing. She slammed the flimsy door shut with an extra oomph as if she was making a sound point and delved back into her smartphone.

For the third time in a row, her boyfriend, Gideon, spotted the dark billboard on the side of Interstate 15. Yet, not a single word, an utter, or exclamation was voiced by Winnie, who uncomfortably sat next to him in the passenger seat.

Without making any erratic movements, Gideon gradually increased the speed of the Bronco.

As his girlfriend scrolled from one headline to another on her smartphone, Gideon shot a glance at her through the corner of his eye and attempted to work a wicked kind of mind job on her, like he was mentally and forcibly willing Winnie to keep those beautiful little eyeballs glued to the screen of the phone and maybe, somehow, by sheer luck—or magic—he'd drive past the billboard without her noticing for she was too occupied and

mad-props to her Silicon Valley overlords, *distracted* by a news feed filled with articles of rage bait and political pimping.

Gideon glanced up at the approaching billboard.

The weathered caption underneath the aimlessly flying bed sheet ghosts read in an offset Rosewood font:

GHOST WORLD

"*It's settled*," Winnie said gleefully next to him while pointing at the passing billboard, a black and off-orange Halloween-esque display with sketches of wavy, white ghosts that stood out against the backdrop of a sun-baked desert. "We're officially stopping."

"Wait—what?" He briefly took his eyes from the road and glared at his girlfriend. "Winnie, baby, we haven't even gotten out of Cal-i-for-nia."

"That's three times," Winnie said, jabbing him on the arm. "We had a bet, remember?"

The scowl fell from his face.

"You know how much farther of a drive we've got?"

Winnie checked the GPS on her phone, which Gideon referred to as her "dumbphone."

"According to Maps, exactly two thousand and two hundred and eighty-one miles with an estimated time of thirty-five—"

"Please don't tell me," he said, trying to ignore the last part, the hours.

"But at the speed you're driving, I doubt we even make it there."

"Hey, not funny."

"You're going to get us pulled over, Giddy. You think tacking another speeding ticket on your record is going to help you get into Conway Coal's stunt driving school?"

More defensively, Gideon said, "CC doesn't look at his drivers' records—"

"I'm talking about money," she said, more practically. "You won't be able to afford going to that man's school after having to fork out the money to pay for all those tickets."

"You're starting to sound like your mom. You know that, right?"

Winnie gave Gideon that "don't-go-there" look, which was accompanied by no words but only soon-to-be words.

"I've driving the speed limit, baby," Gideon said.

She checked her phone once more.

"The speed limit is fifty-five," she said emotionlessly.

"Thought it was seventy," he said, glancing down at the needle climbing well past the 70 mark along the speedometer.

He eased his foot off the gas pedal, reducing the speed to 65 mph.

"Gideon," Winnie said, louder, "we made a bet."

"The hell we did—"

"Giddy, nah-uh, don't do that," she said, her tone sharpening. "You know I've been looking forward to this for a while now."

"Yeah, you won't stop talking about it."

"Hey, you dragged my ass to see that superhero movie last week."

"Baby, I thought you liked *The Synchronizer*."

Winnie didn't respond as quickly as Gideon desired.

"Serious?"

"What can I say?" Winnie shrugged, a hint of a smirk creeping over one side of her face. "I'm good at acting."

"You're unbelievable," Gideon said to Winnie, "we're definitely not stopping now."

"Don't you need to stretch your legs?"

"I'll stretch them somewhere else," he said, finishing a previous thought, "Besides, I don't trust any place that advertises drawings of folks dressed in white cloaks."

"Why not?"

"Can you guess what word I'm thinking of right now," he said, "in fact, three words, and they all start with the letter K?"

"You really just went there, huh?"

"Yup."

"Do I need to explain why people dress up in white bed sheets and pretend to be ghosts?"

"A'ight, Black Buffy, *enlighten* me."

"Well, back in the day before people were buried in coffins or cremated, their dead bodies were wrapped in white cloth called a 'burial shroud.' Some believe it all started with western European cultures—"

"Of course."

Gideon laughed to himself.

"Don't be like that, Gideon," Winnie said. "Can I finish my story or what?"

Gideon ceased laughing and listened, somewhat.

"It started somewhere between the 1400's and 1700's but some believe that it started all the way back to Christ, who—ready?—was also wrapped in white cloth after he died on the cross."

"Is that a fact?"

Winnie rolled her eyes at Gideon and held them on him.

Gideon innocently shrugged.

"What?"

"Story goes that thieves would dress up in white bed sheets and pretend to be the decease who have risen from their graves in order to scare people to death—figuratively speaking. The thieves would then *capitalize* on the opportunity and steal money from the people, who were probably so frightened that they couldn't even move. I mean. . . we're talking about a time when horror movies didn't exist."

"Not a bad gimmick," Gideon said, impressed. "But back then, folks didn't need to watch horror movies. They lived them. Of all people, you should know."

Winnie said profoundly, "History is always violent because we only chose to tell the violent parts."

She flashed her tight and recently "did" brows at Gideon, who paused and told Winnie quickly and shortly as if he was ripping off a band-aid, "I told Zahara we'd be there by Friday. The last shit I'd want to do is upset her again, Winnie, especially, you know, with how I left things with her. I mean, hell, I haven't seen the woman in over six years!"

Winnie hung her head; and all of a sudden, she turned as quiet as a mouse.

"Don't do that," he said, acknowledging the excitement deflating from Winnie. He glanced down at the gas gauge. "I got a quarter of a tank left. You really want to get stuck all the way out in Death Valley?"

The fraction of silence was a good enough answer for Gideon.

He trailed off, "That's what I thought. . . "

In return, Winnie noisily used her phone's GPS to track down the nearest gas station located eight miles away from Ghost World.

As soon as she held up the phone to Gideon, he knew it was a poor and incredibly "outdated" excuse.

"Nice try," she said. "Just admit it. You don't wanna go."

"Yes," Gideon finally said. "You got me. I don't want to go. Now I'm starting to regret what I said earlier. Maybe we should've flown."

Winnie completely ignored what he said about flying, instead of driving, and focused on his previous comments.

"So," she said, her tone drawn out and indicating a prologue to a fight, "I can go along with whatever you want to do and when it comes to me and what I wanna do, you start showing an attitude—"

"You know what? Fine," Gideon said, holding up his hands in surrender. "You win." He changed lanes and veered into the slow lane, since the theme park was only a few miles up ahead. "And by the way," he said bitterly, "I'm not taking you to see *The Synchronizer Part 2*."

Without showing it, Winnie was—but would never admit it—grinning inside.

"Thank the Lord," she wanted to say but didn't.

△

THEY crossed the state line of Nevada and drove about ten miles along a two lane highway until reaching La Valhalla, an ittybitty town which looked like a greasy smudge of a booger on Winnie's GPS.

The town had a Main Street, which was about a length of a bowling lane with only two rundown, façade-less restaurants and a Super Duper Store that sat alone in a small valley and was partially cloaked in the late morning shadows cast from a range of mountains.

Winnie could care less about La Valhalla for she was engulfed by a video on her phone.

"What you watching?" asked Gideon.

She clicked on a lined-out speaker button on the bottom corner of the screen, turning off the mute feature. She then increased the speaker's volume to its max, which was barely loud enough for Gideon to hear.

She showed Gideon, who briefly took his eyes off the road to check out the promo video for "Ghost World," which was located in the neighboring town of La Valhalla called Blackwater, a once bustling mine town with the population of a goose's egg.

The video explained the many interactive features of the theme park, all made available through the downloadable app, G.W.I. (Ghost World Interaction), which used "augmented reality," a trending technology similar to virtual reality, however, instead of an entirely virtual world, it allowed its users to experience each interaction with ghosts of Ghost World through computer generated input strictly set in "real world" environments. Downloading the G.W.I. app on a smartphone wasn't required, but it was strongly encouraged, in fact, recommended in order to experience the theme park the way it was intended. What was also recommended but *not* required were AR headsets or smartglasses, which was said to give the guests a fuller, much richer, as well as "hands-free" interactive experience.

Winnie didn't even think twice. She downloaded the app on her smartphone; and by the time they finally arrived at Ghost World, the download was complete. Before opening G.W.I., Winnie allowed the app to access her "location" through GPS; otherwise, the app wouldn't work properly.

Gideon parked the car in a half full gravel parking lot in front of the old, rundown ghost town of Blackwater, which, from the outside, looked like the dozens of other ghost towns across America that Winnie had, prior to the trip, researched on her phone; however, none of them compared to Ghost World—at least, not on paper—considering most of them were basically tours or walk-throughs, *not* fully immersive interactive experiences, mostly guided by dopey high school graduates who were trying to earn a quick buck in order to pay for recreational drugs—or "college."

"Least there are other people here," Gideon said, surprisingly relieved by the sight of other tourists. He looked twice at a family of tourists, counted at least six or seven of them exiting from a camper and waddling like ducks toward the front entrance of the park. He noticed a couple of them putting on smartglasses before entry into Ghost World.

As Gideon and Winnie stepped out of the vehicle, Winnie held the phone up to her face. She touched the bed sheet ghost icon on the screen, resulting in red curtains to spread open.

"Anything?"

"It's all black and white," she said, scanning the front of the ghost town with her phone. "Grainy," she added, "like an old silent film."

"Lemme see," Gideon said.

She gave him only a peek but suggested he download the app on his phone.

As they made their way to the entrance, he downloaded the G.W.I. app after witnessing how much fun Winnie was having with the different filters available to her on the app; however, once the download was complete and he started to play around with the filters, he wished he'd charged up the phone before their arrival. The battery was getting low and about to reach that red area with only 13% left of usage, and he knew the app would only drain up the rest of the battery so he tried to conserve as much power as possible by closing the phone whenever he wasn't using it but even that, he soon learned as he made his way closer to Ghost World, would be quite a feat.

The preset filter was black and white; however, there were three other filters: "*negative*," which darkened everything and turned day into night, and made people appear a gray and midnight bluish color, "*infrared*," which pretty much spoke for itself, and finally, "*hellscape*," which piqued Gideon's interest the most. The filters allowed tourists to uncover more secrets and side-quests once inside Ghost World than one could only discover in the standard and recommended "black and white" or as it was called, "ghostly filter."

Once the app was downloaded, Gideon immediately aimed the camera at the front entranceway of the theme park and turned on the "hellscape" filter.

The screen switched to blood red.

Somewhat amused by the app's features, Gideon held his hand in front of the camera lens of his phone and through the app's special filter, witnessed, not his own hand, but a dark shadow of a hand on the screen. Gideon turned the phone's camera toward

Winnie, who appeared like a blurry silhouette standing before him.

"Holy shit!" he cried out. "You're a shadow!"

"A shadow, huh?"

Even the other tourists filing into the theme park through what appeared to be a train, which acted like a wall or perimeter, were like these gangly shadows. The landscape, Gideon noticed as he pulled the phone from his face and then up again, then down, then up, comparing both his reality, an empty ticket booth in front of a rusty train and behind the train, the distant wooden building tops of an abandoned town, and then, the nightmarish filter that displayed a smoky, hilly, barren landscape washed in blood red, including the once smooth, glassy blue sky.

Gideon showed Winnie the hellscape filter.

She decided to turn it on but only briefly for she wasn't as amused as Gideon; in fact, she was disturbed by it.

As Gideon changed the filter to the recommended one, they arrived at the entranceway where they were given a list of three options: $5 for one hour; $20 for three hours; and $50 for the "paranormal package." Winnie was dying to try that third option, but she knew there was only so much convincing she could do before getting on Gideon's nerves; and the last thing she wanted to do right now was push her luck.

Before Winnie could convey the pros, *not* the cons, of blowing half their food money on the paranormal package, Gideon was already pulling out the ten-dollar bill from his pocket. He slid the wrinkled bill into the cash insert, but the bill shot back out, forcing him to straighten out the bill along the edge of the booth before carefully walking it back into the insert where a cartoonish sound of a trembling, softly spoken "boo-eww" noise came from what he believed to be a speaker followed by the two one-hour passes dropping into a slot in front of the ticket booth, which, after Winnie pointed the phone at the booth, wasn't empty.

Gideon reached into the glass case and grabbed the two passes.

"Look, Giddy!" she said to Gideon, who pointed the phone at the booth.

Behind the black and white filter was a startling bed sheet ghost *hovering* inside the booth.

They heard yet another sound, similar to the last, coming from the ghost inside the booth; however, this time it seemed to be coming from Winnie's phone.

She turned up the volume on her phone, but it was already maxed out.

More boos.

The app, she realized, also made sounds, which accompanied the visuals.

Gideon's phone, however, was outdated, a third gen that was on its last dying leg, partially cracked screen from where he had dropped it dozens of times.

"Phone's speaker is busted," Gideon said to Winnie and then himself. "That sucks. . . "

With a shrug of her shoulders, Winnie said spitefully, "Too bad."

Gideon ignored Winnie and once more, scanned the ghost who was pointing toward the entranceway. Gideon managed to catch a peek of the ghost's hand underneath the white bed sheet. The hand was one of a man's covered with disease.

Which, Gideon didn't think much at first, at least not until he stepped inside the dark tunnel.

Above the sign read:

You are now entering the town of. . .

BLACKWATER, NEVADA

Aiming the phone's camera at the sign, the lettering, despite the dangling "L" in the name "Blackwater" or perhaps "Backwater," appeared much different than what Gideon read *not* using the filter.

On the phone's screen read the words:

Welcome to. . .

GHOST WORLD

Gideon used G.W.I. to read the sign, where, through the app's filter, each letter was unsteadily hovering up and down in a similar movement to the bed sheet ghost inside the ticket booth.

They exited the dusty tunnel, which, turns out, was a railroad car attached to an old train.

Gideon removed the phone from his face and witnessed Ghost World without the app.

Along the dusty, tumbleweed-infested dirt road of "Dead Street, U.S.A" were other tourists of all shapes and sizes interacting with ghosts in the app; however, from Gideon's perspective, the tourists appeared as though they were interacting with air, like motioning to or playing with certain attractions that, in reality, didn't exist or holding up invisible objects in their hands.

Once he returned to the app, he saw tourists either talking to ghosts, dancing with ghosts, fighting with ghosts, or even, like in the old Wild West days, shooting ghosts with "ghost guns," which, in reality, looked no different than a tourist pointing one's finger at would-be an outlaw, bending one's thumb (the hammer of a revolver), and recoiling one's hand as though one was a cowboy or cowgirl.

"If these folks only knew how ridiculous they look," he said to Winnie, who was left in awe by Ghost World.

He pointed out that most of the tourists were wearing smartglasses, which, after he thought more about it, seemed like the best and most comfortable device to use inside the theme park, considering his arm was starting to grow sore from holding the phone to his face while exploring Ghost World; every now and then, he had to alternate hands.

As soon as Winnie agreed with Gideon's complaints, she came across a general merchant called "Barrel of Bones." Unlike most, if not everything inside the park, the gifts and memorabilia inside the store were real.

Positioned on a display case at the front of the store were smartglasses, like the ones Gideon saw the tourists wearing.

He saw the price tag. He even looked at it through the filter to make sure his eyes weren't deceiving him.

"Oh," Gideon said sarcastically while showing Winnie the smartglasses, "no big deal. They're only five hundred dollars. Whatta freakin' rip off? Wonder if they'll let us borrow—"

"Doubt it," Winnie said and proceeded down Dead Street, U.S.A.

On the app were several what looked like miners standing next to the Undertaker. One of these possible miners was lying on the ground, his body covered in mud and soot. Both of his arms were missing. He appeared dead. The other possible miners, them too covered in debris, were standing over his body, mourning.

Gideon pointed the phone elsewhere and scanned other abandoned buildings, which, on the app, were thriving with ghosts, including the Holy Fountain Saloon with billiards next to a hotel, Dead Inn, as well as a meat market, a blacksmith, a barber shop, a carpenter, a bank, a restaurant, the sign "Baths" hanging over a tub of bathtubs, which, in reality, were splattered with brown stains, a sheriff, a tailor, county offices, and then, finally, a drug store, all of these places both occupied by the quick, the living, or the dead.

Winnie and Gideon stopped behind a small crowd in front of an open theatre on an old wooden stage where, in the app, a cloth banner read:

SPIRITS AT SUNDOWN

Gideon pulled his phone from his face, only to find an empty stage. Then, he looked on his phone's screen where five actors, Dark and Bloated, Dark being one man, while Bloated being quadruplets, were performing the play, *The Mousetrap*, written by the popular whodunit author, Agatha Christie, whose most notable works included the novel, *And Then They Were None*, which was later turned into a play, *Death on the Nile*, also, play based on novel, and *Spider's Web*, also, a play, and other novels like *The A.B.C. Murders* and *Murder on the Orient Express*. Altogether there were eight characters in the play, *The Mousetrap*; Dark playing two of the characters, one Detective Sergeant Trotter and another, a voice on the radio, and then three of the four Bloated quadruplets playing two characters each.

Toward the end of the play, once when the role-players were about to reveal the identity of the murderer, the play suddenly ended, thus causing a small crowd of other actors—*not tourists,* as Gideon first suspected—who were standing in the front of the stage with weaved baskets of tomatoes, to respond with an over-reaction of vile disapproval. The actors reached into the baskets, handed out tomatoes to their colleagues, and altogether, started pelted the role-players on the stage with tomatoes. A wave of "boos" rattled over the speaker of Winnie's phone.

One of the tourists watching the play bumped elbows with his wife and accidentally spilled a to-go cup of black coffee on his son's pants, which resulted in a brief scene.

Distracted by the commotion, Gideon glanced over the screen of his phone to check out the tourists. While the wife was bark-ing orders, the father grabbed his son, who was throwing a hissy fit, and together, the two searched for the nearest restroom to clean up the mess.

Gideon brought his eyes back to his phone.

Neither he nor Winnie could tell if the violent display was part of the act or if this was how, during that time period—which, if Gideon had to guess, would've been around 1883, as the EST. sign stated above the beer gardens—audience members con-veyed their message to actors and showed them how they truly felt about their performances with the soft, gooey punch of a tomato.

Either way, Gideon thought out loud, "Must've sucked being an actor back in the day."

But, then again, how is it any different than today?

"Tell me about it," Winnie said, as the curtains closed and the play ended.

As the crowd of tourists moved on to other attractions, like a knife fight between a black clad executioner known as The Guil-lotine and The Butcher From La Valhalla Falls or visiting the local barber for a straight-razor shave—a fun and at the same time, chilling experience where the barber, Easy-Ezra, who hap-pened to be a drunk with hands as shaky as a alcoholic during withdrawal, would often cut too close to a tourist's neck, causing the tourist to bleed out, of course, on the app, *not* in real life, but the sight of augmented blood for most tourists was quite star-tling—Winnie pointed out the tailor, "Cutting and Fitting," where behind the storefront window were manikins dressed in clothing one would wear during the Wild West.

A couple of tourists were inside trying on Colonial Prairie dresses and other formal wear. Several male tourists trying on cowboy hats.

Gideon pulled down the phone for a moment and glanced at the store, or what was now as a dusty, termite-infested building that looked as if it was about to collapse.

"Your niece would really get a kick out of this place, you think?"

"I dunno, Giddy," Winnie said hesitantly while scanning Dead Street, U.S.A, with her phone. "It may be a little too traumatic for Jendayi. You know how she can be. You saw how she was with Nay Nay just the other day."

"What? Hypersensitive and manipulative?" he suggested but more so stated. "I'll admit, though, her *Auntie Indie*," Gideon said, referring to Winnie as a name that was given to her by Jendayi after she discovered her auntie's profound love of Independent music, "isn't as gullible as her sister to take Jendayi's bait."

Winnie rolled her eyes at Gideon.

"All I'm saying is that her getting out more and exploring the world would do her a lot of good. She can't live on the Internet forever."

"She's twelve, Gideon," Winnie said. "That's what they do. I was the same way when I was her age. Trust me. Once she goes off on her own and gets a taste of the real world, she'll realize the world doesn't revolve around her."

"Knowing Jendayi, she'd try to cancel this place."

"What do you mean?"

Gideon pointed the phone at an empty porch where, in the app, a sheriff was securing the heads and arms of criminals inside pillories, wooden devices used for public humiliation. The sheriff's way of warning any criminal or scoundrel who dared to show his or her face in the town of Blackwater.

"Pretty harsh, don't you think?"

"Of course, it's harsh," Winnie said. "Wasn't that the whole point?"

"Nothing really has changed, though, if you really think about it," he said to Winnie and studied the expressions on the faces of those being punished. He held down the "Home" and "Power" button on his phone, capturing a screenshot of the criminal's face. He wrote the hashtag, #Canceled?, below the image and thought about posting it on his MyCircle page. Instead, Gideon showed the image to Winnie. "Same shit, right? Just a different medium."

"You may have a point, Giddy, *but* you can't cancel history."

Winnie directed her attention back to the storefront.

"No freakin' way I'm going in there," Gideon said and continued to walk down Dead Street, U.S.A.

"It's sort of like a video game," Winnie said, scrolling through pages of various outfits or "skins" on Ghost World's website. "Says here you can create your very own character using various skins and wherever you go inside the park, that skin will be seen through the G.W.I. app."

"Yeah," Gideon said, "and I'm sure it costs money too."

She read the price underneath each skin but didn't give Gideon a response.

As Gideon raised the phone back up to his face, his finger accidentally hit the infrared filter.

He aimed the phone around the street and all of a sudden, witnessed what appeared to be the thermal image of a young boy with a long and jagged scar running diagonally across his face darting across the screen and coming inches away from running into him. Strangely, for a moment, he somehow felt the boy's presence, like something actually grazed his sleeve. Gideon told himself it was a gust of wind; nonetheless, startled, he glanced down at his sleeve but didn't see anything, including a tourist who might've touched him. When his eyes returned to the phone, he saw the same scar-faced boy yet again, this time running into an alleyway.

Once more, he pulled down the phone and didn't see the boy.

He changed from the infrared filter to the black and white filter.

But the boy had already disappeared into the alley.

"You just see that?" Gideon asked Winnie.

"See what?"

Winnie was too focused on those ghost dresses and skins displayed inside the store.

"Nothing," Gideon finally said and followed Winnie toward the store.

As he walked past the front window, he was startled by yet another ghost.

In the reflection of the window was a clergyman missing part of his face, the other part badly lacerated and plagued by infection and covered with maggots that were crawling over the open wounds. His right arm looked as if it had been bitten off or, more like, chewed off, possibly like the miner before, and he also had deep claw marks over his neck and chest—three of them, Gideon counted.

Startled once more, Gideon rotated around, his phone drawn before him.

There, he witnessed the same clergyman, not injured, walking by.

Holding a Holy Bible in his hand, he nodded hello to Gideon and went on his way.

Gideon peered closer at the book and realized it wasn't a Bible but something else. On the front cover was a gilded, emboldened dotted circle.

Winnie leaned over Gideon's shoulder and said jokingly, "You checking out that whore?"

"Wait—what?"

"That's what they used to call 'em back then. Who is she?"

A group of these "whores," as Winnie called them, were standing outside the parlor behind the saloon.

"Get outta here," Gideon said, lowering the phone.

"You wanna go in or not?" Winnie asked, motioning toward the store. "We don't have to buy anything. . . "

"Nah," he said and looked around. "You go. I gotta use the head."

"Sure you do," Winnie said, smirking.

"Quit playing."

"A'ight," she said, looking at Gideon strangely. "I think I saw a sign somewhere around here—"

"I'm sure I'll find one."

"A'ight."

While Winnie went inside the store, Gideon searched for a restroom.

Something wasn't quite right here, he knew, as he stood still and watched his girlfriend gladly mosey around the dead space of the store and occasionally eyeball a certain outfit or sample the clothing by holding it upward. To Gideon, she, as well as the other tourists inside the store, looked like mime artists. He moved his eyes away from Winnie and scoured the dusty street for a restroom sign, both with his eyes and then the G.W.I. filter, but couldn't find any.

He came across the same dark and narrow alley where the boy entered.

More curious and at the same time, cautious, he held the phone before his face and peered into the screen, hoping to find clarity, and fingers crossed, a sign, not only a restroom sign—he really did have to take a piss—but also any kind of sign that would help give him a sense of reassurance and mend his fractured sanity.

He switched through the different filters on the app, starting with the negative filter.

"Creepy," he said, staring at the ghost rats covered in a pale blue light scurrying along the edges of the walls.

Finally, he switched to the hellscape filter.

The screen washed over with red.

Buildings disappeared.

Clouds of thick smoke wiped across the screen like a stocked loop.

Once the smoke cleared, a lanky figure appeared. He or she or it was dressed in a black cloak standing on top of a distant rolling hill.

Alone.

And watching.

He lowered the phone from his face and before him was the same dark, narrow alleyway, empty.

"Yeah," he said, glancing at the strange figure in the phone, "let's not use that filter again."

He decided to switch back to the recommended filter; then proceeded through the alleyway, this time using his own trusting eyes to guide him.

Halfway through, he heard the distant sounds of a motor.

As he made his way to the end of the alleyway, he heard a spike in the sound and realized it was the sound of a blower.

While rounding the corner of the alleyway, Gideon noticed three claw marks, massive in size, at least ten feet long and three feet wide, running along the side of the building top.

Walking but not looking ahead of himself, a dark figure appeared in the corner of his eye and once he looked down to gather his surroundings, Gideon suddenly bumped shoulders with the same man from earlier, the man with the coffee; holding the man's hand was his son, no older than ten years old, now with a dried coffee stain on his pant leg.

Gideon found an old wooden sign dangled above them. On it were the words MEN and WOMEN.

Gideon was first to apologize.

Then, the other man followed: "No problem," he said and glanced at the restroom door closing behind him. "Kind of a strange place to stick a restroom, don't you think?"

Gideon was left without words.

"Jim," the man said abruptly before Gideon could find his words and reached out his hand for Gideon to shake, "Jim Wagner." He pointed at the boy, who was holding his hand. "This is my son, Tyler."

"Sup Tyler," Gideon replied.

"Hey."

"I'm Gideon," he said and shook Jim Wagner's hand.

"You were saying?"

For a moment, Gideon lost his train of thought.

Then, the word *strange* came back to him.

"Yeah, right," he said, "everything about this place is strange."

"I can't get enough of it," Jim Wagner said enthusiastically. "So, where you from?"

"Los Angeles," Gideon said.

"The City of Angels."

"And you?"

"Punuckette, Minnesota," Jim Wagner said.

"Minnesota, huh? That's pretty far away."

"It's a twenty-seven hour drive," he said, "not including all the rest stops, but it's totally worth it. Every year, I take the family on road trips across the country. For a while now, I've been *dying* to check out this place."

Jim Wagner laughed at the pun; however, Gideon didn't get the joke, at least not until Jim Wagner asked Gideon how he heard about Ghost World.

"Girlfriend," Gideon said with slight hesitation. "She's sort of into this kind of creepy stuff."

"So, where you two headed?"

"West Virginia, actually."

"And I thought I had a long drive. . . "

Jim Wagner laughed again.

Gideon tried to.

"So what part of West Virginia?"

"Loganson."

"Oh yeah? Have you ever been there before?"

"Once," Gideon said, "when I was a kid visiting my grandfather. I don't remember much, though."

"That's cool. I have an old college buddy who lives in Charleston."

"Right on," Gideon trailed off and motioned toward the restroom behind Jim Wagner. "If you would excuse me. . . "

"Of course," Jim Wagner said, stepping aside. "When you got to go, you got to go! Nice to meet you, Gideon."

"Likewise," Gideon said, walking toward the restroom.

The two walked away.

"Friendly people," Gideon mumbled to himself.

As he was about to enter the restroom, he stopped and out of mere curiosity, looked back at Jim Wagner and his son, Tyler, through the G.W.I. app.

The two were dressed in the costumes, "skins," as they were called. The father, Jim Wagner, was wearing a Guillotine skin while his son, Tyler, was wearing The Butcher From La Valhalla Falls.

More skeptical now, Gideon held the phone in front of his hand, his arm, then his shirt and then scanned the rest of his attire. As expected, he was still wearing the same clothes. A part of him was relieved, yet another part disappointed.

As he surveyed the area using the app, he came across an overturned wagon sitting near a couple of boulders along the edge of the desert.

He removed the phone from his face to make sure the wagon was real.

It was.

As Gideon raised the phone back up to his face, he witnessed that same scar-faced boy from earlier poking his head from the side of the wagon.

Surprisingly, he made eye contact with Gideon.

Once more, Gideon lowered the phone from his face.

The boy was *neither* there nor real, he concluded, for the boy was only part of the app. And yet, he could see Gideon!

The boy ran away.

On a whim, Gideon decided to hold it in, as in his piss, and followed the boy.

Keeping the phone close to his face to track the boy yet far enough away to watch where he stepped, he ended up at the front of a cave.

The boy eventually disappeared inside the darkness of the cave.

"*Great*," he said, weighing his options.

He could check on Winnie and watch her try on various skins.

Which sounded as boring as watching paint dry.

Or, the option before him, the mystery and possibly, Gideon thought, unlocking the secrets of Ghost World.

"The hell with it," Gideon said and made his way toward the cave, which he soon realized was a mine.

Scattered on the ground were wheelbarrows and pickaxes used for mining. A wooden frame was positioned along the rocky walls and ceiling in order to prevent the cave from collapsing.

Gideon wasn't quite sure of the range of the G.W.I., but clearly, based on the black and white filter he was peering through, the app *still* worked.

Which, Gideon knew, meant only one thing: He was *still* inside Ghost World.

Up ahead, outside the app, he caught a glimpse of an object on the ground.

Below, he noticed, were two sets of footprints, one of a larger shoe, possibly the shoe of a grown man, and the other, smaller tracks, those of a child or even a woman.

The closer Gideon approached the object the more disorganized and scattered the tracks had become. They didn't bare any unified direction; instead, they indicated a possible scuffle of some sorts.

He walked up to the object, which was an AR headset, and picked it up. The headset was partially cracked.

Gideon ran his finger across what looked like a streak of blood along the side of the headset.

Curious, Gideon put on the AR headset, which was already set to the recommended filter; however, the left side of the screen had a spider web-like fracture, obscuring part of his vision.

He proceeded farther into the cave.

Not too far away from where he found the headset, he came across a man lying on the ground, a tourist Gideon soon realized once he removed the AR headset from his head.

"You okay, man?" asked Gideon, as he kneeled down to check on the man's condition.

The side of his forehead was red and swollen. He had a deep gash, as well, from where he was struck in the head by a rock. The rock, Gideon saw, was covered in the man's blood. Gideon could only assume that he tripped and fell on the rock. *But how would the AR headset wound up closer to the entrance of the cave?*

Gideon lightly patted the man's face.

"You awake?"

No response from the man.

He checked for a pulse on the side of man's neck and barely found one.

All of a sudden, he heard a noise coming from the internal speaker of the AR headset—or so he thought.

He pushed on, using the AR headset more vigilantly.

The ceiling of the cave became lower, forcing Gideon to walk in a crouching stance; the pathway grew significantly tight before the cave declined sharply into a deep, dark hollow; the sandy ground covered in real human bones.

Having suffered from claustrophobia as a child, Gideon was tempted to turn back around before the cave become too tight to pass; however, his curiosity compelled him to push forward.

He used the flashlight of his phone to shine over a pile of skulls; however, the flashlight, he knew, would drain the rest of the power left in his phone.

As Gideon stood to his feet, he witnessed that same boy from earlier standing close enough to identify his face. The boy's eyes, however, were glowing like a cat in the darkness.

Gideon's phone went dark, then, finally, died.

He drew his eyes back to the scar-faced boy whose eyes were strangely rising upward and appeared as if he was being lifted by an elevator.

Using the AR headset, he switched to the negative filter and saw, not a boy, but rather a much taller man who had taken the boy's place.

That man was the actor, Dark.

Gideon stepped closer for a better look and more eyes appeared behind Dark, precisely four sets of eyes, altogether making eight eyes. The eyes were attached to four bodies, each one belonging to the quadruplets known as Bloated.

After switching filters back to the recommended one, Gideon witnessed the five actors, Dark and Bloated, take a step away from Gideon until they were bathing in darkness. Their glowing eyes, however, remained, then started to multiply! Ten eyes doubled and turned into twenty eyes, twenty eyes tripled and turned into sixty eyes, sixty eyes turned into hundreds of eyes!

Once more, Gideon heard that guttural sound, this time coming directly from the growing creature before him.

A phlegmy exhale released from the creature's mouth, its stinky breath sending a cloud of dust at Gideon and forcing him to shield his nose.

Bracing himself, he switched filters one last time, from black and white to the negative filter.

Before Gideon sat a massive stumpy creature, which nearly took up the entire space of the tunnel. Its body was round and froggy with many rolls of excess fat underneath its chin and sides of its neck, its skin as coarse and rugged as the desert itself; however, its face, in particular, its skeletal structure was similar to that of a Gila monster, sharp and pointy, although its deep and black, glowy, cosmic-colored eyes were vast and promoted trance-like states to any onlooker who dared gaze into the abyss.

Below the gargantuan cave dweller were two curling hands slowly raking up ground with its razor sharp talons the size of the arms on an excavator, which left behind shallow trenches in the parched earth.

Carefully, Gideon removed the AR headset from his head and peered into the dusty darkness where thousands of eyes lit up the cave like a night sky full of Chinese lanterns.

Another cloud of dust was blown at Gideon, forcing him to gradually take a step backward.

As those eyes grew brighter and vaster, Gideon continued to backpedal until he finally made a run for it.

Neither stopping nor looking back, Gideon sprinted the same way he came in; however, not once did he ever feel as though he was being chased. But there was still the idea that the *thing* was still behind him, hungry and pursuing.

Gideon could see sunlight reflecting off the walls, rays spearing through and bringing more relief.

He reached the spot where he came across an unconscious man, who was lying on the ground. The man was no longer there; in fact, he could see more tracks leaving the cave, newer tracks that weren't like normal footprints; yet they were wavy and serpentine-like and appeared as if he had been dragged out of the cave or, maybe, Gideon thought, somehow, the man managed to crawl out on his own.

As Gideon approached the exit of the cave, he decided to put on the headset one last time.

Using the negative filter, he scanned the cave behind him but saw no creature chasing after him. He rotated back around and the blood rushed through his veins from the presence of a slender, blue-skinned woman standing only feet away from him. Staring at him.

He changed the filter back to the recommended one and before him stood not a blue-skinned woman but a paler woman, weak and trembling.

"I didn't mean to startle you, mister. . . "

Gideon was tempted to remove the AR headset, but the olive-skinned woman with wiry blonde hair dressed in a forest green prairie dress was incredibly attractive and he couldn't help but gawk at her. The bottom part of the dress was partially torn, revealing her leg, mostly knee and thigh.

"You didn't," Gideon said, taking his eyes off her thigh. "I'm Gideon."

"Lottie Hart," she said.

"Lottie? Lovely name."

"It was my grandmother's," Lottie said with a heavy pause. "Listen, Gideon, I don't mean to bother you, but. . . Springwood is in danger."

"Springwood?" asked Gideon.

"That's the town where I'm from," Lottie said. "For the past three days, we have been terrorized by the great beast whom many in the town have called 'The Void' for its endless appetite.

So far, this beast, The Void, has already taken out half the towns-people, and I'm afraid, Gideon," she said, as she stepped closer, "if someone doesn't stop it, then it'll spread to other towns and destroy them. Please, Gideon. I'm begging you. We desperately need your help. . . "

"Why my help? I'm just a driver—"

Lottie stepped even closer to Gideon and was now standing only a couple of feet away.

Gideon heard more footsteps, even when Lottie wasn't walking.

Which, for a moment, Gideon thought maybe something was wrong with the speaker of the AR headset. Perhaps the damage suffered to the side of the headset created a delay in sound.

Lottie's skin darkened a shade, her once green eyes darkened as well, and now she had brown eyes.

Gideon gave a light tap to the side of the headset.

When Lottie spoke to Gideon, he heard the sound of Winnie's voice: "Thank, God! I've been looking everywhere for you," said Lottie.

"You have?"

"Yes," she said, still in Winnie's voice. "Are you okay?"

"Yeah," he said. "But. . . "

"Gideon?"

"I can't help you, Lottie," he said. "Sorry. I wouldn't know where to begin."

"Giddy," Lottie said, Winnie's voice louder and more pro-nounced, "who in the hell are you talking to?"

As two faces doubled over one another, moving back and forth from Lottie's face to Winnie's face, he removed the AR headset and witnessed Winnie, with her arms planted on the sides of her hips, staring at Gideon in a state of utter confusion.

"Winnie?"

Winnie drawled, "Yeah. . . Who were you talking to?"

"Nothing—I mean, nobody."

"Where did you get that thing?" asked Winnie, as she pointed at the headset.

"This," Gideon said, looking down at the headset. "Found it."

All of a sudden, Gideon heard the same guttural, beastly sound that he heard when entering the cave.

"What was that?" asked Winnie.

"You heard it too?"

"Yeah," Winnie said and slowly raised her phone up to her face.

Her eyes widened.

On the screen, Winnie saw a large blob of a figure materializing but couldn't make much sense of it.

Gideon rotated his shoulder and with his own eyes, witnessed hundreds and thousands of eyes glowing in the cave darkness.

"I don't like this," Winnie said, lowering the phone from her face.

She, too, not only recognized those eyes manifesting in the darkness, but she also felt the presence of something greater than them slowly approaching.

Gideon grabbed Winnie's hand, and together, they ran out of the cave.

They didn't bother checking out the rest of the theme park.

The two went straight to Gideon's Bronco.

"What was that thing?" asked Winnie, as Gideon drove away from the town of Blackwater.

"Dunno," he said, as he was still somewhat freaked out by the recent encounter with what he believe to be The Void, "*but* whatever it was, it was big."

"A bear maybe?"

"Nah," Gideon said, leaving Blackwater. "It was much bigger than a bear."

Winnie grabbed the AR headset on the dashboard and looked it over.

"Least we got ourselves a souvenir."

As Winnie was about to put on the headset, Gideon snatched it from her hand at the very last second.

"Don't do that," he said.

"Why not?"

"It's defective," he said.

"It is?"

"Yeah," he said. "I tried to use it, but all I could see was static."

"Static, huh?"

"Yeah." He glanced over at Winnie and shrugged. "What can I say? It must have broke after I dropped it."

"Okay," Winnie said and placed the AR headset aside.

Gideon decided to fuel up at the nearest station located in the town of Schilling, since the next one was at least thirteen miles away.

After Gideon filled up the tank and waited in the car as Winnie paid for gas, as well as a couple of drinks and snacks for the road, he grabbed his dead phone from his pocket and attempted to switch it on but received a flashing battery icon. He grabbed the charging adapter from the glove compartment and plugged it into the phone. With his mind racing and wondering as he turned his eyes toward the AR headset on the dashboard, he couldn't resist putting it on.

Surprisingly, once the headset was secured to Gideon's head, the G.W.I. app still functioned properly, even though he was miles away from Ghost World.

As Gideon surveyed the black and white surroundings around him, he drew his eyes toward the rear view mirror where he nearly jumped out of his seat after witnessing Lottie, who was quietly and patiently sitting in the backseat.

"What the hell are you doing in my car?" asked Gideon.

"Please, Gideon," she begged. "Springwood will be no more if we don't stop The Void. I know where I can find us weapons. Lots of them. My cousin, Belle, keeps a stash in the well."

"No," Gideon exclaimed. "I told you I can't help you!"

He heard the cowbell above the convenient store ring out.

As Winnie exited the store, Gideon removed the AR headset.

Before Winnie arrived at the car, he exited the Bronco and buried the headset underneath a pile of trash in the closest trashcan next to the gas pump, and then he hurried back to the vehicle and got inside.

"All set?" asked Gideon, as Winnie sat in the passenger seat.

"They were all out of vanilla," she said, holding up the *Gauntlet* bar. "So, I got you dark chocolate instead."

"Thanks," he said depressingly.

"Be happy, Giddy," she said. "It was either that, or some strange meat on a stick. The clerk said it was pork, but it didn't look like any pork I've ever seen."

"You ready?"

"Let's hit the road," Winnie said, as Gideon drove off.

No more than three miles of driving down the highway, they rode past a sign that read, of all places, "Springwood."

Gideon couldn't help but acknowledge the road sign and the story that Lottie had told him.

"Springwood," he said, thinking. "Say, why don't we stop and take a break?"

"But Gideon, we just stopped."

"I'm getting hungry, aren't you?"

"That's why I bought the snacks."

"I could eat some *real* food," he said, holding up the *Gauntlet* bar. "Besides, I've heard a lot of good things about Spring-wood."

"Never heard of it," Winnie said and researched the town's name in a search engine on her phone. "Says here," according to a travel website, Trip Facts, "they have a lot of restaurants, anything you want, really. Plus," Winnie said, shooting a lustful glance at Gideon, "they have a Red Velvet store."

"Red Velvet, huh?"

Winnie continued to scroll through the many images of Springwood, including luxurious shopping malls, designer stores, high-end restaurants, bakeries, all-you-can-eat buffets, multiplex movie theatres, bowling alleys, laser tag, a fun center with bumper cars, arcade, and miniature golf, then a par 3 golf course, as well as a scenic manmade lake surrounded by a park with basketball and tennis courts and walking trails. "Yeah," Winnie said casually. "I'm down to clown. *But* what about the drive?"

As the next exit for Springwood approached, Gideon shrugged and said, "We have plenty of time. We're ahead of schedule, right?"

She closed the web browser on her phone and as she was about to open the Foodie app, Gideon noticed the G.W.I. app on the home screen and a number "1" inside the red circle along the corner of the app, which indicated either a message or a notification.

As she clicked on links to various restaurants and read the reviews, as well as the descriptions of each one, Gideon snatched the phone from her hand and said, "And no phones."

"Wait—what? What you doing, Gideon? Cut it out, will you?"

She reached over the center console and tried to grab the phone from her boyfriend's hand.

"Hold up a sec," Gideon said, blocking her hand with his shoulder. "Hear me out—"

"Give it back. . . "

"Let's make a deal, huh?"

"Quit fooling around, Gideon."

"The deal: Let's see how long you can go without a phone."

"That's absurd, Gideon."

"Really, how so?"

"Gideon, we need the phone to get to your mother's house. What are we going to use: a map?"

"I know the way."

"You do?"

He thought about "the way" and realized how much he didn't know the way.

"Okay," he said, switching off Winnie's phone. "You can turn it on when we leave Springwood."

"I can turn on my phone whenever I damn well please," she said critically.

"No phones in Springwood," he said, more seriously. "Let's enjoy it the old way."

"The old way?"

"Gideon, you're starting to sound like my daddy—" she paused, "—Hold up for a sec." She grinned. "That place has you bugged out, doesn't it?"

"What place?"

"Ghost World."

"No," Gideon immediately said.

"Giddy, I'm serious. Would you hand over my phone? I'm not going to ask you again."

"No."

Winnie studied Gideon's face, the seriousness.

"A'ight," she blurted out. "Geez. You win. No phones in Springwood. Got it. *But* you'll give it back as soon as we leave?"

"Of course I will." Gideon focused on the road before him. "Relax," he said and readjusted himself in the driver's seat.

"I am relaxed," Winnie said unsteadily. "Maybe you're the one who needs to relax."

The two didn't speak a word to one another until they reached the once small town now densely populated and very active city of Springwood.

By then, their eyes and ears were doing most of the talking and listening and taking in as much of the atmosphere as possible.

Words and thoughts eventually followed without any interferences or distractions of Winnie's phone.

For Gideon, it was an invigorating but mostly good time.

Maybe the best of times.

He and Winnie together.

And yet, whenever the thought of Lottie Hart came to mind, maybe the worst of times.

But Gideon leaned more toward the good, opposed to the latter.

Or at least, he tried to.

"GO TELL IT TO THE DEVIL"/
THESE BAGS OF BONES
AIN'T FOR SALE

LOUNGING in a navy blue recliner stained and speckled with the aftermath of late night drunk-eating, Baby watches the final showdown between hard-nosed detective, Raymond Tulip, and his elusive "White Whale" in *Go Tell It To The Devil*, a mystery-thriller loosely based on the short story, *The Rooster and The Serpent of The Midnight Sun*, which is set in the present day, not 1995, like in the film, more specifically, on the eighth day of April.

In the scene, the character, a sweaty, blood-soaked, wrung-out Detective Tulip backs the priest, intoxicated with both disbelief and amusement from the old dog's ambition, against the corner of a wall. He picks up his service-issued pistol from the sweaty tile floor. With a sore arm, Tulip aims the barrel of the pistol at the giggling priest's head.

Disguised in the priest's outfit is Howie Donem or "Daddi," the name he uses whenever addressing himself in the nursery rhymes containing clues to the location of a latest kill, or after Tulip discovers the creator's name when his son beats a thought-provoking video arcade game *The Hunt For The Red Easter Egg*, which not only inspired, but also acted as the template, as well as

a warped, overly symbolic confession for Donem and his me-
thodical, self-righteously driven spree of murder, "Humpty
Dumpty."

With his back sliding against the bloodstained wall, Donem
falls to the floor. His giggles cut short as he spits out a rope of
clotted blood from his mouth. He winces slightly in pain. Even
the wince itself draws more waves of pain, mainly in the center
of his face, mainly his swollen nose, which is as crooked as a
Texas tombstone from where Tulip repeatedly punched Donem
in the face.

Tulip now cocks the hammer of the pistol.

"Don't you want to hear why I did all them lowlifes?" says
Donem.

Swallowing the words, Tulip clenches his teeth in rage.

"Whether or not you or your buddies in the FBI choose to
believe me, Ray—can I call you, Ray?" he says heavily while
breathing in and out from his mouth for the airways in his nose
are jammed up like a dam with blood and bone.

Underneath a scowl, Tulip grinds his teeth from the very
thought of the FBI sticking their shitty noses in *his* case and according to the previous scenes involving Tulip and his Captain
which took place the day before he and Donem's "run in" at the
arcade, inevitably taking over *his* case.

"After everything we've both been through, it only seems fair
that we address each other on a first name basis, am I right?"

Tulip readjusts the grip around the pistol; finger ready to pull
the trigger.

"*Fate* led you to me, Ray. All of those people—those cruel and
self-absorbed leeches who sucked out the marrow of life and
ruined it for those of us who were simply trying to find our
footing in this cancerous, ashtray of an existence—you and I
both know they weren't worthy of living—"

"And what? You were doing me a favor, right?"

"I weeded out the greed to create a more humble, a more sus-
tainable world where ideas aren't stolen. They're *shared*. Call it
what you will: God's work, or me doing the job that nobody else
will, like you Detective Tulip. Years from now when people
look back at what I did—*what I'm doing*—they will be in complete awe by my audacity and with a sense of newfound grati-

tude—which is something you, Ray, need to work on—they will carry on my legacy."

A bead of sweat rolls down the side of Tulip's face like a slug.

He tightens his grip, trigger finger trembling.

"Let me ask you something, Detective Tulip, you want to know why I really killed Ashley Twiddle—"

A dead pause.

Followed by a blaring gunshot!

The bullet hits Donem right between the eyes.

Donem's head whips back, as the rest of his body lifelessly flops to the floor.

"Go tell it to the devil," Tulip says, the smoke of the pistol clouding over his vacant-eyed expression.

The TV screen goes dark.

End credits roll.

In that taut silence, Baby suddenly bursts out laughing.

"*Go tell it to the devil*," he recites Tulip's words.

Still laughing from the slick one-liner.

According to the Behind the Scenes footage, the final scene was shot on the very last day of filming right before production called it a wrap. In the industry, the shot referred to as the "martini shot," the last scene shot before the end of the day, or in this case, the end of a thirty-seven day-long shoot. Having only filmed *Go Tell It To The Devil*, which ran under the working title, *Easterland*, in such a short amount of time, the film crew considered it to be one of the longest shoots they've ever been on. Filled with weather delays and endless periods of being at Mother Nature's mercy where days lasted as long as eighteen hours, all to squeeze in the final shot, that "martini shot" before their deadline, director Elijah Burgher, known for pushing his actors to the brink of insanity, worried that he would have to ask the studio for more money. Normally, since most films are shot out of sequence based on the production's tight and volatile schedule instead of following the exact timeline, from beginning to end, of the film, especially for a production which filmed mostly on a set location, Burgher was fortunate enough to shoot the last scene of the film on the last day of the production—and you can certainly see the pain and exhaustion on Tulip (played by actor Alfonzo Hovels), as well as his face when he delivers the final line of the movie. Hovels said the line at least thirteen times, using different variations, before nailing it for Burgher.

Baby pushes forward the lever on the left side of the recliner, which folds the footrest back underneath the seat. He springs forward and stands up and along his bouncy walk through the lobby to fetch himself another beer from the kitchen just to the right of the check-in desk, continues to recite that one-liner and does so in the various masculine voices of a rugged gunslinger, each one dropping an octave and sounding more dark and deadly.

"*Go tell it to the devil*," he says more deeply as he peels off the last beer from the sixer of Coleman's Classics in the fridge.

He tosses the plastic in the garbage. Cracks open the beer.

Then makes his way back into the living room where the credits end.

Another scene appears on the TV screen.

A post-credit scene.

In the scene, Tulip, after putting one in Donem's word processor, inches over to Donem's lifeless body.

In a state of relief, he looms over the former murderer and as he's about to kneel down to check his pulse, Donem leaps up at Tulip.

Tulip reacts by stepping back and firing four shots into Donem's chest.

Finally, as Donem's chest deflates like a balloon and releases what Tulip perceives to be a death rattle in the back of his throat, Tulip spots an object hanging from Donem's pocket. He kneels down, this time without any surprises and theatrics, and picks up a bloody rosary from the floor. The Wi-Fi connection weakens, images on the screen, in particular, the rosary, fuzzy and heavily pixilated. Before the inevitable is about to happen—Baby can sense it coming—Tulip pockets the rosary.

As the exhausted, injured, relieved detective is about to walk away from the locker room showers, capping off the film, it happens. . .

The scene freezes.

While in mid-slurp, Baby receives that loading circle again on the TV screen.

Spinning away like a merry-go-round.

Laughing at Baby.

Baby gives the TV a more than aggressive love-tap.

Baby's wife, Judy "Beatrice," the other "B" in B&B, stops dusting the furniture and calls out from one of the guest rooms to the left of the lobby, "You get them snowflakes again?"

"Nah," Baby says. "Worse. The Circle of Death."

"You need to call the cable company already and have 'em come out here to look at it—"

"It ain't cable. It's the Internet."

"What's the difference?"

"What in the hell are they gonna do. . . " Baby says, trailing off.

The stream eventually cuts to black.

"Piece of fucking shit," he seethes and bangs his palm against the side of the TV, as if it's the TV's fault.

Three times this week when Baby was either half way through a TV show or like with *Go Tell It To The Devil,* at the end of a movie, he'd receive that dreadful spinning wheel on the screen.

Just an hour ago when he was watching a couple of DIY videos on "How to Make a French Drain," hoping to fix the standing-water problem along the side of the hotel, the signal was strong and robust.

No lag.

No pixilation.

No bullshit.

And now, Spin City.

"Whatever happened to a good ole DVD?" Baby asks himself, as, eventually, he turns off the TV. "Now, we're stuck with this streaming shit that don't work half the goddamn time. No wonder we're losing guests. . . "

While sipping from his Coleman's Classic, Baby hears the *ring* of a doorbell!

With his face a shade paler, he slowly brings the beer from his face.

More alert, Baby sets the beer aside, walks to the monitor behind the check-in desk, and according to the surveillance camera positioned over the front entrance, sees nobody there.

Thinking maybe the person is standing out of the camera's view—or worse, a person who doesn't want to be seen by the camera—Baby creeps to the front door anyway.

He listens closely for a car engine or a person but doesn't hear a peep outside. He rechecks today's schedule behind the check-in, making sure there weren't any last-minute reservations for today. Not a single one on the list. Before answering, he checks the window on the door but doesn't see anybody, including possible guests, and for a moment, he thinks maybe he heard the sound on TV. But then again, the TV is off. And Baby is a hundred percent positive that he heard the doorbell.

Cautiously, he cracks open the door. Nobody on the front porch. He takes a couple of steps from the porch and looks around the front lawn, but he doesn't see anybody. He looks up at the three-story house, inspecting it for possible damages. Last year, one of the guests thought it'd be fun to climb on the roof and gaze up at the stars in the middle of the night. A few days later after the family checked out, Baby heard a loud thud against the siding of the house and when he went to check on the noise, he found part of the gutter dangling from the roof like a broken limb. Till this day, he believes it was from that one guest, that little pothead, who loosened the gutter while he was climbing up on the roof to "stargaze." He doesn't have proof, except for a comment made by the kid's friend while eavesdropping over their conversation, but Baby has suspicion, and usually, nine out of ten times, Baby's suspicions come true.

Baby walks back inside and just as he takes a couple of steps toward the living room, the doorbell rings yet again!

Frustrated now, Baby storms toward the door, opens it, and like before, finds nobody behind the door.

"What the heck. . . "

Baby looks around the front porch, then, out of shits and giggles, decides to push the doorbell button himself.

The doorbell works just fine.

A thought suddenly comes to mind.

Maybe it was the wind. . .

Wind, especially a strong gust, wouldn't seem so unlikely but would certainly make some kind of sense—that is, *if it were windy.*

On the contrary, the air is still, silent, and not so much as a breeze can be felt in the air.

Baby is left perplexed, as he walks back inside the house.

Halfway toward the living room, he decides to check out the doorbell box on the side of the hallway wall.

"Baby, you gonna answer the door or what?" Judy asks from the kitchen.

More determined to get down to the bottom of the doorbell issue, he doesn't answer neither Judy nor the front door.

She fires yet again at Baby yet stops in mid-complaint while walking past the garbage can. With her index finger and thumb, she picks out the six-pack rings, or the "yokes," as referred to by the industry, and holds the plastic rings away from her body as if she's holding up a dead animal by the tail.

"What did I tell you about throwing away plastic?"

Again, Baby doesn't answer.

Too focused now, as he uses a stool to reach the doorbell cover box.

Frustrated with Baby's stubbornness, Judy noisily grabs a purple handled pair of scissors from the kitchen drawer and cuts the rings, which, according to her, act like nooses to the little duckies and fishys. Baby ignores his wife for she has been watching too many of those tearjerker infomercials about saving marine life from pollution and plastic waste. Graphic images of plastic wrapped around a seagull's neck or a dead beached fish appear right when "money" is mentioned. *"For only a dollar a day, 'you' can help save these helpless creatures."* Baby loves his wife dearly; however, she has a way—a "vulnerability," he'd call it—of being easily manipulated by swindlers. Like the scammers who send her suspicious links attached to her emails all the time. 20% off coupons. Spring sales. Half-off bottles of wine. He has to be one step ahead of Judy and delete the emails before she can click on them. To Baby, she's a fish who's aching to take the bait.

As Judy's cutting snippets of plastic in order to prevent it from snagging or strangling a fish that she's inevitably going to consume anyway, Baby opens the cover box and immediately flinches from the creature inside. He has seen plenty of cockroaches in his time, but this one is quite a horse.

The skittish cockroach taps on the coil spring inside, sounding off yet another *ring* of the doorbell.

"Jesus!" Baby shouts out and flicks away the cockroach with a finger. "You little devil, you! How'd the hell you get in there?"

Baby steps off the stool, scoops up the cockroach by using an *Infinity's End* magazine from the coffee table, and carries it to the toilet where he flushes it.

"What is it, Baby?" asks Judy.

"Cockroach," Baby says, watching the cockroach swirl around in circles.

He walks back into the living room.

"You say *cockroach*?"

"Yep."

"Eww," Judy pinches her nose and makes a face. "Should I call Carl again? We can't have cockroaches scaring off our guests. Bad enough we have a mouse problem—"

"We don't have a mouse problem, Judy. Okay?"

"By the way that reminds me: Mr. and Mrs. Fleck canceled."

"Who?"

"The couple coming up from Georgia," she says. "They canceled their reservation for tomorrow."

"Another one!" Baby says with brewing contempt. "What's up with people these days?"

"A good case of cold feet, I suppose."

"Cold feet?" Baby shakes his head in disgust. Words like *cold feet* don't exist in his vocabulary, except for maybe in the mornings during wintertime. "They not give you a reason?"

"Nope," she says shortly and then her voice trails off. "Who knows? Maybe something came up. . . "

She pulls out her phone as though she's ready to give Carl "The Bug Guy" a call and as she's scrolling through contacts, she receives a notification from her MyCircle feed. "You won't believe this, Baby," she drawls, the expression on her face stretched out like a yawn. She holds up the phone and shows Baby the HEADLINE of the news article from *GetUp Daily*. "*You're dead. . . "*

"What? Gimme that!" he attempts to snatch the phone from her hand but at the last second, she recoils.

Using her thumb to scroll through the page, Judy skims through the lengthy article and after reading two paragraphs of writing, which consist mostly of flowery language used by an amateur journalist who has mistaken a news story for the prologue of a true crime novel, finally arrives at the heart of the matter where she basically gives Baby the cliff notes version:

The body of a man named Baby Blue, *not* Judy's "Baby" but a thirty-three year old man who lives in Austin, Texas, who was recently dug out of the Rio Grande. According to the news story, "Mr. Blue had been missing for two weeks" and investigators are certain the body belongs to Baby Blue. So far, no signs of foul play, at least not external; however, it's too early in the investigation to rule out a homicide.

"Dead?"

"That's what it says," Judy says. "Don't feel so special now, huh?"

Baby gives Judy a look.

"And how many 'Judy Blues' you think are there wandering around? I can tell you this: More than just one—"

The doorbell *rings*, again, and leaves Baby looking like a ghost, again.

"What's going on with the ringer, Baby?" Judy asks, concerned.

"Are we expecting any guests today?"

"Not that I'm aware of," Judy says confidently.

Baby grabs the cover and thinking maybe another cockroach is still inside the cover box, inspects it carefully.

No cockroaches.

No draft from the AC.

Nothing.

Following the *ring* of the doorbell, Baby hears a *knock* at the door.

He places the cover back over the mount and carefully steps down from the stool. He stands still for a few seconds while staring at the looming shadow behind the front door. Eventually, the shadowy figure shrinks and fades.

He checks the living room window and spots a strange car parked across the street, the front end obscured from their hotel sign "B&B's B&B" in the front of the three-story, sixty-four year old house, but, again, no person. Baby looks twice at the car and after the second study, recognizes it.

"Honey," he says to Judy, "come over here and take a look." More briskly, she approaches the window. Takes a peek outside.

"Who is it, Baby?" she asks.

"Isn't that the same car that was following you the over day?"

Judy peers closer.

The car is a pale blue smartcar, SmartRide, a car, Baby once said, if you blink while passing it, you'd probably missed it.

"I think it is," she says, stepping away from the window.

Baby grabs an aluminum baseball bat from the hallway closet and after mentally counting to three, answers the front door.

Walking away on the front pathway is a darkly dressed man with dyed pale blue hair, which, surprisingly, matches the color of the SmartRide.

On the front porch steps is a clear case with a DVD inside. The words "**Play Me**" are written over the disc with a black Sharpie.

Baby picks up the DVD from the steps and says to the strange man, "Excuse me. Can I help you?"

The strange man hesitantly turns around, and Baby realizes it's no man but a boy. Probably around seventeen or eighteen or maybe older, he supposes, around that age between high school and college or those lost years of being "undecided." Having grown up with very few options to choose from like Army, Car Mechanic, or furthering his education in order to one day take over the Family Biz, none of which appealed to him, Baby certainly knows a thing or three about being undecided; however, after second study, he hones in on an age and ballparks a number much higher than his original guess. The young man's body is covered in tattoos. One, which pairs with the lightning bolt earring dangling from his left ear, is of a cryptic-looking, raggedy dressed, partly skeletal hand reaching up from his shoulder and collarbone and climbing along the side of his neck with a long and boney, pencil-like index finger inches away from touching the lobe of his ear, the end of the gnarly fingernail sparkling with the rays of a bright star. Another one, which Baby can only see part of, for it is concealed by the rest of his sleeve, is a garden filled with dozens of skulls. Another, an antique watch on the top of his hand, the time reading midnight. Another, the tiny symbol of an upside cross on the space between his knuckle and the middle joint of his middle finger.

Having recently turned forty-five and his vision starting to weaken, Baby can only recognize snippets of the other tattoos, like the end of a claw, a tooth, or part of a strange word—maybe Latin—or the handle of a dagger or the warped head of a doll-like figure or part of a pentagram symbol on his chest. Baby focuses elsewhere: his attire. Which is a loosely worn black leather jacket over what appears to be a silk weightless summer dress, which, surprisingly, matches the color of his hair. Along both wrists are metallic cuff-like bracelets. As for piercings, except for the one on his left ear, he has what is called an "erl," a straight barbell across the bridge of his nose. The horizontal bar is, of course, the same color as his hair. No surprise there.

"What is this?" Baby asks, holding up the DVD.

"You weren't supposed to see me, least not yet," the young man says shyly.

"Oh yeah? Why not? Who'r you supposed to be?" Baby asks, losing his patience with the young man.

He—or her, Baby can't quite tell which, for the feminine mannerisms he displays when he curls the side of his protruding jaw or both of his hands which hang lazily from his wrist like paws of a cat—doesn't answer any of Baby's questions.

Baby points his finger at the young strange man.

"Were you the one following my wife two days ago?"

The stranger doesn't answer.

"I'm gonna ask you one last time: 'Who are you?'"

"My name is. . . "

Baby tightens the grip around the handle of the baseball bat.

"My name is *Baby Blue*," the stranger says finally. "And I'm here to make a deal with you."

"Deal? Is this some kind of sick joke?"

"Not a joke, *Mr.* Blue," the stranger says, mocking the title, "Mr.," then nods at the house while, at the same time, taking control over the conversation with an upper-class arrogance that Baby has seen many times before when driving into the city and pretty much, tolerated—using a "Count to ten" method whenever pushed to his limits—and dealt with most of his adult life. "Please, may I come inside?"

"Let 'em in, Babe," Judy says from the inside. She folds her arms across her chest, leans up against the side of the doorway, and stares at the stranger as if he's a character from a carnival who's about to perform his act.

"Honey, go back inside—"

"No," she says, sharpening her gaze. "Let's hear what this *person* has to say."

Baby weighs his options.

Finally he lowers the bat, steps aside, and lets the strange man who calls himself "Baby Blue" inside B&B. Normally, except for the guests who receive first- class treatment, he tells any visitor, no matter who they are, including friends or family members, to take off their shoes—or in this case, the stranger's black shin-high boots—before entering the hotel. He doesn't with the stranger. Instead, he lets him inside, dirty boots and all.

Once the stranger is inside, Baby escorts the stranger to the lobby.

Baby and Judy stand to the side of the check-in desk while the stranger stands before them.

"So," Baby sighs, "what's this deal you're proposing?"

"I'm here to buy your name Baby Blue," he says, not batting an eyelash. "I'll pay you three million dollars in cash, but only on one condition: You will change your name from all of your re-cords: address, payments, credit cards, debit cards, social secu-rity, etc. Once all these changes are made and you live up to your end of the deal, then I'll send an associate of mine to hand deliver the cash to you."

Baby makes a noise from his mouth, not a laugh but, more or less, the sound one would make after being jabbed in the stom-ach.

Still left in awe by the remark, he turns toward his wife, Judy, who's equally amused by the stranger's deal.

"Can you believe this?" Baby asks Judy.

The stranger pulls out his smartphone and shows both Baby and Judy a selfie of himself posing in front of a mound of cash.

In the photo, the stranger is standing next to the cash and holding up the local newspaper *The Warthyme Observer*, which reads today's current date: "Thursday, April 22nd, 2021."

"How do I know that's not photoshopped?" Baby asks. "I've seen what you kids can do with your computer toys these days."

The stranger pulls out a stack of ten thousand dollars from his pocket and then tosses it to Baby.

Baby catches it.

The stack appears the same as the one of the many in the photo.

"There's more where that came from," the stranger says.

Baby runs his thumb along the corner of the many crisp hun-dred dollar bills. The notes pass by before him like a still of a cartoon. His eyes twirling in circles from all those hundreds. He hands the stack back to the stranger.

"Okay," Baby says, somewhat convinced. "Why?"

"You still don't know who I am, do you?"

Baby glances over at Judy, who appears more worried by the stranger's presence.

"Should I?"

"I am *the* Baby Blue," he says. "Internet sensation."

"Right," Baby says over the stranger. "I don't really go on the Internet. So, I wouldn't know what the hell you're talking about."

"According to *Topical*, I am considered the pioneer of the modern day Renaissance."

"*Topical*? What's that?"

"It's a magazine, Baby," says Judy, who's researching the multi-genre celebrity and all of his work on her phone. "Says here on Gumshoe that he's worth *billions* with a b."

Very trendy with the teens, she wants to say, but she doesn't want that noodle in her husband's head to start cooking with ideas.

Even the name Judy uses while addressing her husband causes the vacant expression on the stranger's face to crack with anger.

More composed, the stranger lets Judy do most of the convincing by combing through the many pages, the stories, the products, the gallery of photos of the so-called "celebrity" standing before them. Photos of the so-called celebrity posing with other so-called celebrities, including Terrance Pitty, all grown-up now, whom she used to watch all of the time with the kids when they were younger.

Judy reads the *Wikipedia* page on Baby Blue, *not* her Baby Blue, but the one staring vacantly at her husband.

According to the site, Baby Blue was born in Manhattan, New York, by the name Sebastian Ulysses Goldfinger. His parents are both successful. His father works as a management consultant for a private equity, venture capital, investment company, which has a reputation of buying failing companies. His mother is a socialite who operates a successful art gallery.

By the age of sixteen, Baby Blue became one of the most famous Tubers in the whole world—not Baby's Tube but the other Tube—making millions by explaining to young girls and boys how to properly apply lipstick and eyeliner. Now, at twenty-three, Baby Blue makes most of his bank off his clothing line, GLOSSY BOSS, as well as his own makeup brand. Not only is Baby Blue a fashionista, or *fashionisto*, if such a thing exists, but he's also a well known musician who has released four EPs—still working on a LP, which he plans to release by the summer—one of the singles ended up landing number one on the Billboard charts for three weeks in a row. He also released a short film, *Clamshell*, which received much praise at various film festivals across the world. He has plans to turn his short into a TV series—preferably one with eight episodes, of course, on one of the gazillion streaming platforms—which are currently in the works. Whenever Baby Blue's not making records and films and selling lipstick, he's running a podcast where he breaks down the latest trends and movie trailers.

"Well," Baby says finally while looking over the stranger who reeks of entitlement, "I ain't buying it. So, what? You got some fans, huh?"

"Over ten million," Judy reads Baby Blue's MyCircle page.

"Ten million, huh?"

"Three million dollars cash," the stranger says. "It's all yours if you do exactly what I've said."

"Can I even do that?" Baby asks Judy. "Change my name?"

"People change their name all the time," Judy says, looking over a photo of the celebrity's ten-foot tall golden statue of himself in front of a ten million dollar house in Nevada. "I mean, Baby, it's three million dollars. Just think about it for a second, with that kind of money, you can buy your own beer company and have 'em teleport fresh beer to you using your new teleportation device. Hell!" Judy says, trying to tame her sudden yet uncontrollable excitement. "We can sell the bed and breakfast, move down to Gregory's Island, and not have to work a single day in our lives. You won't even have to leave your recliner."

"I like buying my own beer," Baby says and once more, weighs his options.

He thinks about Judy's comment; however, what's bothering him the most is the name, *his* name, *his* family name, *his* very own birthright.

Baby tells Judy to grab the projector from the closet and meet him in the living room.

"But Baby. . . "

"Now, Judy," Baby says, more impatiently. "Please don't make me ask you twice."

Judy is slow to react.

"Get on a stick," Baby tells her, as he escorts the stranger into the living room and then points at the couch. He tells the stranger to have a seat.

The stranger refuses.

"This shouldn't take longer than it has to, Mr. Blue," he says. "We can settle this right now—"

"I wasn't asking you, *Baby*," Baby says.

The stranger takes a seat on the couch.

Eventually, Judy goes to the closet and rummages through a bunch of heavy black garbage bags stuffed full to the brim before busting out a carousel slide projector from the back of the closet. Accompanying the projector is a metal lunchbox of Dale the Tiger from the animated television show *Pluto's Vein*. Inside are old 35 mm slides. Judy blows and brushes away the dust from the projector and the container of slides, then returns to the living room where she places them both on the coffee table.

"And the photo albums," Baby says. "Grab them too."

Judy does as she is told—which is a first—and grabs armfuls of photo albums from the cabinets. Three of them, each one bound by cracked leather and as thick as tree stumps. She carries the albums to the coffee table where she sets them down next to the projector. While doing so, she catches a glimpse of the satanic pentagram tattoo on the stranger's chest. Part of the partially faded tattoo is starting to deteriorate, crumble, and peel away. Pieces of dried ink, like black shavings, pepper his skin and attach to curly chest hair.

Having two tattoos herself, both in indiscreet places where on occasion Baby may stumble across whenever making love to his wife, Judy recognizes the condition of the tattoo, most importantly, the cheapness of it, one resembling that of a sticker tattoo you'd win at Legends. It's been years since she took her two kids to the arcade. She remembers when Sapphire was around fourteen years old and she won one of those temporary peel-and-stick tattoos that lasted for a couple of days, the tattoo being a fairy, then the next day, when she couldn't find the tattoo on her arm or cheek, the area which Sapphire said she was going to use—she saw several of her friends wearing stickers on their face, too—she questioned Sapphire, who hesitantly pulled back her T-shirt and showed her mom the fairy tattoo, which she placed on the lower part of her back. Judy didn't have to further question where her daughter had seen other girls—in this case, grown women—with sticker tattoos in that particular area of the body. Judy has several friends, one of them being Claire, who proudly wore a tattoo of a butterfly on the lower part of her back and often times, regretted getting it on a location of her body for all the labels it brought, mostly one, the most common label: "Tramp Stamp."

Claire, like several of her other friends, are tattoo junkies obsessed with tattoos, despite those ridiculous labels, and she, Judy, knows exactly what a *real* tattoo looks like and the one on the stranger's chest is not it. *He could be no different than a businessman who puts on a suit and tie before heading to work? But instead of a suit and tie, well, yeah—got it. . .*

Judy doesn't say anything, at least not verbally; however, her mind does most of the talking as she makes eye contact with Baby and gives him the same worried expression she gave him earlier, the one before the word *money* was mentioned in the conversation.

More eager and enthused, Baby turns to the stranger and says, "You could've chosen any name in the world. But you chose Baby Blue. Why?"

The stranger shrugs.

"Because it's my favorite color," he says.

"Is that so?"

"Yes—" he says, tentative and unconfident.

"So, if you could, you would buy the color. Correct?"

The stranger shrugs again.

"That's the idea."

"I've heard plenty of crazy stories throughout my time but never have I heard one about a person wanting to buy a color. Now, it's your turn."

"My turn?"

"You ask me about *my* name."

"Well, after I pay you, it won't be your name anymore. It will be mine."

"Really?"

"Did I stutter?"

"Okay." Baby walks over to the projector and switches it on. "Judy, cut the lights. Will you?"

While Baby uses the blank wall as a screen, Judy turns off the lights, as well as closes the blinds.

"What are you doing?" asks the stranger.

"I'm going to tell you about the history of the Blue Family." He uses the remote control to change the first slide, which is a grainy photograph of his parents and younger brother posing for the camera next to a beat up station wagon in the driveway as they're packing and doing last minute prepping right before they embark on a summer camping trip to the Blue Ridge Mountains. "First," Baby says, "my father, Slate Blue, a well-respected optometrist who owned an eye care center in Jonesy Town, which was originally named after yours truly," he changes the slide to a photo of the exterior of the business, as well as his father standing next to the business sign with a trippy graphic of an eye, which is shaped like a window, "but was later changed to *Windows of the Soul* after my mother, Rosie," he changes yet another slide showing a photo of his camera-shy mother shielding her face with her hand while she's in the middle of painting in her basement studio, "gave birth to a second child, my brother, Electric Blue—it's fair to say my parents never outgrew the Sixties." He changes a slide, the next one a close up of a swollen, red-faced newborn baby resting peacefully in Rosie's arms. "Two years prior, on the 15th of March 1976, Rosie gave birth to—you're looking at him—a nine-ounce baby named Baby Blue. *The* Baby Blue."

The stranger tries to conceal the curvy grimace on his face, but his anger with the usage of his name, Baby, when he's not the only one being addressed by the name, is becoming more and more apparent to Baby and Judy.

Baby changes a slide to Baby himself, still a baby, in his grandfather's arms, the photo taken at his grandparent's house.

"In this photo," Baby says to the stranger, "you'll see my grandfather, a complicated man who went by the name Royal Blue. Royal was twenty-one years old when he stormed the beaches of Normandy to fight Nazis-Assholes. What were you doing at that age?"

The stranger replies bitterly, "I was making my first million, actually—"

"That's great," Baby says over the stranger as he proceeds with the presentation. "Royal was badly injured in combat. Shrapnel to his right leg." Another slide shows a photo of Royal with white bandages wrapped around the nub of a leg while lying in a hospital bed, French nurses and doctors gathered around his bedside, smiling for the camera. Baby says, "Royal's leg was amputated. Months later after Royal returned home, he said, quoting, '*my leg wasn't the only thing I left behind in France.*' Suffering from post-traumatic syndrome, or 'shell shock,' as they called it back then. . . " he changes the slide, next one showing a photo of Royal, his friend, Charles, who also fought in World War II, Charles's wife, Julie, and her friend, who, in the photo, was single at the time, ". . . eventually, Royal recovered. Met a woman named Violet, who went on to have a child with Royal in 1946 before she passed away from tuberculosis a few years after my father was born. From what I was told, Royal wasn't exactly a pleasant man to be around. According to my mother, he was extremely—how do I put this—neat and orderly. Very clean. Strict. Like the Nazi-Assholes he spent his youth killing." He asks, "What were you doing at the age of twenty-one? Right. Making your first million. Anyway," he ignores the stranger and proceeds with the presentation, "behind my grandfather's back, Violet compared her husband's strict behavior to that of the very monsters he fought, especially in the way he ran his household. Could be why my father was the complete opposite of my grandfather. Free spirited. A lover, *not* a fighter." He changes slides. On the slide is a photo of Royal and another woman. "While raising a child all on his own, Royal was left with the responsibility to take care of his sister, Azure, after she was involved in a cliff accident, leaving her disabled. Six years after Violet passed away, Royal met another woman, Lorene, who, my mother believes, helped rid that—that rage— that Royal had been holding onto for so many years, especially after he returned home from France. They were together for twenty-eight years before Royal died of a heart attack. Lorene died three months later. Even till this day, the cause of her death is unknown, but those who were close to her weren't surprised at all by her passing." Baby changes another slide, which shows a photo of a three-year-old Royal standing with his father, Baby's great grandfather. "Now, my great grandfather, Oxford Blue, the one here," Baby points, "standing with his son, my grandfather, Royal, was—"

"How much longer is thisss. . . " the stranger says with a sudden lisp that causes him to power through the question.

Baby stops and looks at the stranger funny and wonders why he keeps struggling to speak.

Finally, after watching the stranger's lips do awkward jumping jacks and for a moment, his teeth slide outward as though he's wearing dentures, he says, "You okay over there?"

"How much longer is *this* going to take?" he asks, his tone more pronounced and aggressive as he uncomfortably readjusts himself on the couch.

Clearly, convincing Baby isn't going to be as easy as he planned, and he—to be honest—doesn't know how much of the slideshow he can take.

"You in a rush or something?" Baby asks, more superiorly.

The stranger doesn't respond. Yet, he tilts his head to the side as though his patience, like water in a glass, is starting to tilt as well and eventually, empty.

"Oxford Blue was a—"

"Are you going to agree to the deal or not?"

"I'm almost finished," Baby says coldly over the stranger. "As I was saying before you interrupted me, my great grandfather, Oxford Blue, was a doctor in the small town of Deaver's Row. His father, my great, great grandfather, was an eccentric man named Cambridge Blue, an engineer said to be one of the most brilliant minds of the Nineteenth Century. Cambridge and his two sisters, Prussian and Sky. . . " Baby changes a slide. The next one shows a grainy, overly-exposed photo of the three strong-willed siblings, which was taken in the Serengeti: Cambridge, Prussian, and Sky, each one posing with hunting rifles either between their arms or plopped over their shoulders while standing over the bloody-faced carcass of a lion, ". . . were in charge of building a state-of-the-art railroad across the rugged landscape of Tanzania." He shows the stranger a slide with a photo of a river, which was taken at a distance, as well as another photo, a closer one, of a railroad track over what looks to be the same river. "Their most notable accomplishment: Blue Way, a hundred-meter long bridge, which runs over the Rufiji River, one of the largest rivers in East Africa. Their father, which would be my. . . " Baby stops and squints one eye while thinking, ". . . great, great, great grandfather, Ice-Blue, priest and son of the infamous *Midnight* Blue. . . " he changes yet another slide, arriving at the last one, the gory painting of a man being hung in the town square, the painting is said to be painted by artist Sir Peter Jurney ". . . a gunsmith from Pennsylvania, who was hung and later beheaded for committing an act of treason, after playing a key role in the Massacre of Thomas Port—"

"So, great," the stranger says more arrogantly, "you come from a family of psychopaths."

After the presentation, Baby decides to leave the slide up while taking a seat in the recliner.

The stranger leans forward and flips through the photo albums containing the photos of Baby Blue's family, staring with pages of Baby's own family, including his two children Sapphire and Cobalt, who are both away at college, one receiving his bachelor of science in Philadelphia, another on a full-ride scholarship to Florida State. Then, photos of Baby and his "baby" brother, Electric, as well as Electric's family, including his two children, Sapphire and Cobalt's cousins, Cyan and Ultramarine. Then, Baby and Electric's father, Slate, as well as his father before him and so forth.

As the stranger flips through heavy photo-riddled pages, each photo appears more and more aged, wilted, and faded.

"I barely know my family," the stranger says, leaning away from the coffee table. "For all I know, they all could've been crazy, like yours. So, *your name, three million dollars*, what's it going to be?"

After getting another closer look at the pentagram tattoo on the stranger's chest, as well as the slight bulge of what may be the handle of a gun protruding from his waistside, Judy recalls the story that she read just recently on her MyCircle feed. The one about another "Baby Blue" being found dead. She cautiously eases away from the couch. She shoots a glance at her husband, Baby, who has his hand over the right lever, *not* the left.

Baby's already counting in his head; in fact, he's well-past eleven.

All of a sudden, he yanks back on the lever, releasing a shot-gun from a hidden compartment along the side of the recliner.

In a swift motion, he grabs the shotgun and fires a shot *right* of the stranger's face!

Bits and pieces of cotton, fabric, and clouds of dust shoot up in the air. The stranger flinches violently, that blast leaving him partially deaf and dumb.

"Next one won't be as shy," Baby says, standing up while pumping the shotgun. He aims the barrel directly at the stranger's shocked face.

While Baby has the stranger in his crosshairs, Judy steps forward and reaches inside the stranger's jacket. She pulls out a yellow rubber ducky from his waistband.

"What the hell is this?" asks Judy.

"Whuut?"

The stranger struggles to hear Judy for his *left* ear is still ringing.

"I said, 'What the hell is this?'"

"That's my ducky," the stranger says, voice trembling.

"Ducky? How old are you? Three years old?"

Baby takes one of his two hands from the pump-action and waves at his wife to hand over the children's toy.

As Judy steps toward Baby, the rubber ducky changes shape and transforms into a hard cubical device with squishy, silicon-like bubbles.

Judy accidentally touches one of the bubbles, thus causing one of the cubes to jerk in her hand. She feels a zap on her palm, like a current of electricity giving her a shock. She drops the alien device and once landing on the floor, fires off a massive electric-ity-filled blast of a cloudy air. The force of the explosive shot is so strong and tremendous that it ends up knocking down the entire wall of the living room, rocking the foundation of the house.

In awe, Baby turns to the opening in the living room and can see the neighbor's house from a distance.

Neither Judy nor her husband, Baby, have any words to explain what kind of device—or *blaster*, Blue thinks—was capable of releasing such energy. The best Baby can describe the new technology is a weapon capable of producing—and harnessing—

the gale-force wind of a hurricane and when fired, resulting in a blast that can take out at least six people combined.

The stranger makes an attempt to flee but Baby puts him back in his place by sticking the barrel of the shotgun directly under his chin. He pulls him from the couch and escorts the stranger to the front door.

Judy opens the door for Baby, who, in return, positions the stranger in front of the doorway, his back facing Baby.

With the shotgun gripped in both hands, Baby rears back his leg and kicks the stranger directly in his derrière.

Firstly, the initial impact of the kick causes the stranger's smartphone to fling from his pocket; the phone bouncing and skipping along the front porch a couple of times before coming to rest.

(Baby will discover the phone on the very next day while sweeping the porch where, on the second attempt at trying to crack the password, he will unlock the *tourist's* phone by using the password "1-2-3-4," thus giving Baby access to more material for his new business venture)

Secondly, the impact of Baby's heel hurls the stranger over the porch steps and sends him flying through the air until, finally, he falls face first on the ground.

Standing sturdy and upright at the doorway, Baby says to the stranger in his most deepest, masculine, Oscar-worthy voice, *"These bones ain't for sale!"*

The stranger scurries back to his car and speeds away, leaving behind a piece of himself on the walkway—or a "souvenir."

Intrigued, Baby walks down to the walkway and picks up the mask of a face. He holds the fleshy layer of skin with five holes, two holes for eyes, two smaller holes for nostrils, then, finally, one larger hole for a mouth.

Speechless, Baby brings back his discovery to the house and shuts the door behind him. The impact of the door closing causes pieces of tile, wood, and drywall to fall from the massive opening in the foundation. One of pipes bursts open and water shoots out over the lawn in a fountain-like arch.

"What is it?" asks Judy.

"The hell if I know," Baby says, holding the mask loosely in his hands.

"Is that a mask?" Judy asks, looking down at the rubbery face in her husband's hands.

Baby responds in way of a shoulder shrug.

Judy walks over to the alien device, carefully picks it up, and shows it to her husband.

"Where'd he get this thing?"

Baby hangs his head in disbelief.

"Don't know, Honey," Baby says, as Judy carefully sets that strange device down on the coffee table.

Judy tends to Baby by rubbing his chest and reassuring him that the stranger, whoever he was, won't be coming back.

"You know, there's only one Baby Blue," she says while rubbing his chest. "You're my Baby Blue."

Baby looks down at his wife and smiles.

She notices a bulge forming in his pants.

"Impressive," Judy says, moving her hand down Baby's chest. "Let's say we add a new addition to the Blue Family. What do you say?"

"What about the damages to the house?" asks Baby.

Judy waves off the gaping hole where a wall once stood.

Not to mention, the busted pipe, which warrants their attention.

"Insurance will cover it," she says nonchalantly.

"Insurance? And what are we gonna tell 'em exactly?"

"I'm sure we'll come up with something," Judy says, still composed.

As Judy kisses Baby, Baby's eyes move away from Judy's face and turn to a glare in the corner of his eye. There, he notices the DVD on the coffee table.

Intrigued, Baby pulls himself from Judy and grabs the DVD.

"I wonder what's on the disc," he says, reading those words *"Play Me."*

"Does it matter, Baby?"

Judy kisses Baby on the neck; however, Baby, once more, pulls himself from Judy and focuses on the DVD.

"Just leave it be," Judy insists.

"We just turned down three million dollars, Honey," Baby says. "Maybe the TV version is a little more convincing than that sorry sack of potatoes who was once sitting on our couch."

Baby goes to the DVD player next to the TV and inserts the disc.

"Baby. . . "

"Just a peek," he says and plays the DVD.

The video starts out with the stranger known as Baby Blue filming himself in front of a mirror that covers the entire wall of an incredibly ritzy, golden-speckled penthouse suite. On the marble countertop is the same stack of cash—"three million dollars," he states for the camera. *The choice is yours, Mr. Blue. . . "*

He uses a counter clockwise wipe, like one used in cheap editing software to transition from one scene to the next.

The following scenes involve a series of stalker shots, which are mostly taken from a distance. The person behind the camera, more than likely, "Baby Blue," privately films his wife, Judy, while she's either leaving B&B or jogging through the neighborhood or attending a late morning yoga session in town or buying groceries or meeting her husband for an early dinner at Earl's Subs and Stuff or one, a much personal, intrusive shot showing the cameraman creeping up behind Judy and as she's checking for broken eggs while standing in the egg aisle of a grocery store, holding his gloved hand to the back of her head, his fingers coming inches away from touching her hair. At the very last second, he readjusts the camera and pulls out that same yellow rubber ducky from before, squeezes it, releasing a waft of air while making a high-pitch sound. Startled, Judy immediately rotates around while the stranger speed-walks away. She confronts another customer, who happened to be passing by with a buggy at the same time she felt someone blowing on her hair; but, of course, the stupefied customer acts as though he has absolutely no idea as to what Judy is claiming he did to her.

From behind, Judy says to Baby, "Just as I thought." Then, asks: "Should we go to the sheriff with this?"

Baby ignores Judy and continues to watch intently.

The scene cuts to a shot of Judy walking through town before entering a jewelry store called Greene's Jewelry.

We follow the stranger as he steps out of the car and films Judy while she's inside the jewelry store.

"Baby, can you turn it off already?" asks Judy, visibly upset by the DVD.

In the video, Judy distracts the owner, Samuel Greene. Mr. Greene walks off and while he heads to the back of the store, she reaches over the counter and grabs a silver necklace and then slips it into her cleavage.

Astonished by his wife's criminal behavior, Baby rotates around and gawks at Judy, who's clutching the necklace with the unicorn pendant over her chest.

"You still want to go to Sheriff Parker?"

In the video, she changes her mind about buying "another" item she was interested in, says goodbye to Mr. Greene, and leaves the store, stolen necklace and all.

"Baby," she says, "I'm going to return it."

"You're damn right you're going to return it," Baby says, the sides of his face clouding red with anger. "You know how much trouble you can be in if Sam finds out about this? Honey, I thought you were done with all this nonsense—"

"I am," she says. "I just. . . I wasn't myself. I'm sorry, Baby."

The video continues to play.

Baby faces the TV, which shows Judy walking down the sidewalk. The cameraman goes back to the car, the same SmartRide from earlier, enters the car, then the camera shakes and distorts a bit before transitioning to the next scene; however, something strange catches Baby's eye right before the video stops.

"You just see that?" Baby asks and rewinds the video.

He stops at the part where the stranger enters the car.

Then plays the video.

As he takes a seat behind the steering wheel, he leans over to the glove compartment. As the camera passes the rear view mirror, Baby gets a quick glimpse at the cameraman's face in the rear view mirror.

Baby pauses the video as soon as he sees part of a face in the mirror.

In the paused video is the reflection of the stranger's face covered in a dark hoody. He realizes it's the stranger from the pale bluish hair draped over his face; however, after closer inspection, he realizes the person behind the camera is *not* a person but something else.

"What the hell is that?" Judy asks with her voice drawn out.

The stranger's face is dark and scaly, creature-like. Its saucer-shaped eyes sit on the farthest corners of its face. Its many teeth, short and sharp like a piranha's.

"Maybe he's wearing a mask. . . "

Baby doesn't even have words, let alone, an answer to his wife's questions.

Judy stands behind Baby and rubs his back.

"Let's just forget this ever happen, huh?"

Baby plays the DVD and watches the rest of the video.

There, on the TV, both Baby and Judy see their own house, which they spent years remodeling. Their baby, a bed and breakfast called B&B's B&B. It's night outside, quiet; a spotlight shines over the sign in the front lawn. With the camera in hand, he approaches the house and using his other hand, pulls out a house key. He opens the front door with the key.

"How in the world did he get a key?" asks Baby.

Judy is just as confused as he is.

They continue to watch the video, which shows the stranger creeping through the dark house until arriving at Baby and Judy's bedroom. Using the light on the camera, he inches toward their bedside; and as Judy sleeps soundlessly, he holds a knife to her throat. On the other side of the bed, Baby rolls over, changing sleeping positions and passing gas while doing so. Baby knows getting caught farting on camera is the least of his worries. The video stops. The screen fills with static, or what Judy calls, TV "snow."

Baby turns off the TV and looks around the room, the chaos and destruction.

"We keep it the way it is," he says, drifting off in thought.

"Keep what the way it is?"

"*This*," Baby says. "Once word gets out and people find out what happened here today, they'll come in droves. We'll, of course, edit out the part with you at Sam's place."

"I said I was sorry, Baby."

"Just think about it, though: we can pay visitors to catch a glimpse of the *real* Baby Blue, the one hiding underneath the mask." He holds up the mask, or face, and shows it to Judy, who is too repulsed to even look at the thing. In reflection, Baby sets aside the soon-to-be framed attraction and walks toward the edge of the living room and leans through what used to be a wall, which is now shattered and strewed all over the lawn. "We'll leave everything the way it is. We'll even create side-stories and exaggerate your encounters with the *real* Baby Blue. Misadventures, hidden dangers, a thrilling car chase," his voice rises with exhilaration, "a daring escape!"

"Yeah, but don't we run a risk of being sued?" Judy asks, then tries to reason with her husband, who appears beyond reason. "We can't lie to people. . . I mean, I get it. We just went through quite an ordeal, Babe—"

"This man, whoever, *whatever* in the hell he is, just tried to blackmail us, Honey. You really think he's in any position to come at us for capitalizing on a situation. People do it all the time." He walks back to his wife and imagines the future of the bed and breakfast. "You'd agree people are visual creatures, right?"

Judy agrees with a hesitant nod of the head.

"B&B will become a tourist destination," Baby says. "We'll make a killing, Honey. Christmas. Spring break. Summer vacations—"

"A tourist attraction?"

"You saw the turnout this spring break—"

"We're always slow during the break." She pauses and stares at her husband, who's not batting an eyelash. "You're serious, aren't you?"

"I'm as serious as your Eggs Benedict, Honey," Baby says. "*This*," he emphasizes, "this might be the *thing* that gets us out of the financial rut we're in."

"*Temporary* financial rut," she corrects Baby.

"Then you agree, right? We do need to change our business? Think outside the box, yeah?"

Judy doesn't answer. Her answer, or lack of answer, is the answer.

"And you want to have another Blue?" He laughs at the thought of bringing another life into this world, especially one whom he can barely afford. His back hurts just by thinking about it. "I'll tell you this: We certainly can't have the government bailing us out again. Don't you think it's time for us to evolve with the times?"

"Don't *you* think you're getting ahead of yourself, Mr. Blue?" Judy asks and tries to calm Baby. "Let's go to bed. We'll talk more about this 'big idea' of yours tomorrow."

With a smirk creeping on her face, Judy holds out her hand; Blue grabs it.

Like a puppy dog, he follows Judy into the bedroom and before he closes the door behind him, he thinks to himself: *I'll be known as the guy who kicked ET's ass and lived to tell his story. Yeah*, Baby grins. *I'm going to be fucking famous.*

~~SAFECRACKER~~ C-WORD

AFTER Dalivia dismissed the producers from the office, she rummaged through each and every drawer inside what was once Waters' desk before it became *her* desk and discovered a pile of scripts in the bottom drawer, one being the screenplay, *"Cracker,"* which was based off the novella of a similar title, *Safecracker*.

She used her phone to research the novella on Gumshoe and found two novellas, the first one written by the author Ericka Barnes and the other one by Ellis Kross.

The screenplay was based on Ericka Barnes's version.

Based on her history with Ellis Kross, she was aware of the story; however, the first author, Barnes—or someone posing to be an author named Barnes—immediately grabbed her attention, not the author herself, but the name of the author, the name being one of the characters from Dalivia's very own story, *Send Us All Your Ghosts*, the third novella in the novel, *Possessed By Darkness*.

Intrigued by the story and at the same time, suspicious of the author's name, she purchased the ebook; and as soon as it downloaded onto her phone within a matter of seconds, she stood up from the desk, stepped over Waters' severed head, which was lying in a pool of blood, and began to read Ericka Barnes's novella, *Safecracker*:

AT exactly "7:53 PM," a lightning bolt rips through a heavy matted gray sky and zigzags toward a dense forest where it splits a shortleaf pine tree straight down the middle, like a serrated stainless steel blade cutting through the stalk of a cruciferous vegetable.

The tumbling smoky pine briefly catches fire before a downpour tames the rising flames and prevents any further damage to the fractured tree or its surrounding inhabitants.

The next morning, after the storm passes, a group of rugged lumberjacks returns to work, logging trees and then loading them onto trucks. By mistake, the split, partially burnt tree is mixed up with the other ones, which are then transported to the local mill where machines strip the bark from the logs and then clean the logs with recycled water. Next, the stripped, debugged logs are funneled into a wood chipper, which cuts the logs into tiny, manageable pieces. Eventually, after a chemical process, the wood chips are turned into a toothpaste-like pulp, the fibers, in return, are spread out, screened, as well as meshed, and any excess water is removed before the pulp is dried and formed into a thin sheet, thus creating newsprint.

Once the newsprint is finished, large rolls of paper are hauled into the back of delivery trucks and transported to a printing factory in Beauden, which uses its state-of-the-art printing press to produce newspapers for many of the surrounding counties, including New Folly County.

Among New Folly County is the town of Knob, home of 11, 737 residents who have developed a morbid interest in an unfolding, nationwide story, which, despite taking place on the other side of the country, feels very much close to home, especially for one of Knob's residents, who, over the past several weeks, has become the ass end of a sick joke.

THE very first feature of my wife that I fell in love with was that brilliant mind of hers, and how, regardless of an unwavering willingness to keep up with her youthfulness, she always had a witty response for whatever remark I directly or indirectly made to her. No matter what the context, she'd find a way to make me smile, even if I felt the climbing urge to strangle her to death.

At times, it felt as if her mind was so bright that its light somehow crept through the orifices of my head, highlighting each jagged thought inside it and displaying it on a projector screen for the entire world to see. She had the ability to read my mind based on a single expression on my face, and she wasn't the least bashful about expressing herself for she carried an endless list of original one-liners ready to be used given the opportunity and then crossed off, as if the words themselves were never to be repeated in the exact order they were spoken, but rather absorbed at the moment of their first arrival, like a drug, and any further usage of these words had all but expired beyond their shelf life.

The second feature was those sea green eyes, which, when we first met in the stuffy faculty room of Dornick College, appeared celestial, like they belonged to a rare species that was yet to be discovered by humans, and trying to remember what the eyes looked like before they began to dim and drag with grief, had become a feat so impossible that it wasn't even worth the attempt.

Once, those eyes were lights guiding me into a place where shadows ceased to exist.

Now, it's all see when I look at her.

The shadows.

I suppose it's the most asked question that manifests from every marriage: *At what point does the love for one another turn into so much hatred?*

Trying to find the exact moment in time is no different than capturing lightning in a bottle.

2

WHILE waiting for the train to pass, Rome waits on the other side of the railroad crossing where the tracks separate Knob from Reed Springs. Resting in the passenger seat to the right of him is his brother, three years his elder, reeking like a dive bar after last call, the odor alone so potent that even Rome catches a faint buzz.

The train eventually passes, thus causing the red lights to stop flashing. The bell stops. The crossing gate opens and straightens to an upright position, freeing up the two-lane road.

The train's wheels, which once drowned out the sound of his brother's snoring, fade into the early morning darkness.

As Rome proceeds across the bumpy tracks, a gang of bikers suddenly *roars* from behind!

Startled, Rome slows down and watches the rowdy gang vroom past.

In a glimpse, he catches one of the riders' ghostly faces, both his eyes appearing charged, as if he carries a tiny voltage of electricity inside them. The left eye, in particular, is intersected by a pinkish scar zigzagging down the left side of his face like a lightning bolt. He has greasy white hair, as well as a flowing frizzy white beard that trails behind his grayish face like a cape.

With one eye cracked open, his brother wakes from his drunken snooze-feast.

"Goddamn *Bolts*," he slurs, as he recognizes the sound of the gang's engines.

"Bolts?"

"White Lightning," his brother clarifies.

"You ever run into those assholes during your. . . *nightly* excursions?"

"Few times," he says, sitting up in the seat, "when I was out west."

"What are they doing all the way out here?" asks Rome.

"Beats me," his brother says.

"So, bolts, huh?"

"Yeah, also missing some fuckin' screws. Cultist whack jobs—"

"Well, if you run into them again, just be careful. They have numbers. *You don't.*"

He waves off Rome's comment and watches the first colors of dawn filling the dark sky, as Rome drives him home from jail.

After Rome drops his brother off at his apartment, he drives back to his house, which is located on the other side of Knob, and prepares himself for the upcoming workday.

By the time he returns home, the sun has already starting to creep over the horizon. Charley, who delivers the daily newspapers, tosses *The Hillside Messenger* in the front yard. While doing so, he waggles his hand as if being zapped and cries out, "Ouch!"

Paper cut is what Rome first assumes when he sees Charley nursing his finger as he rides away. After stepping out of the car, Rome waves at a fleeing Charley and says to the boy, who's around Jonathan's age, "Good morning."

Charley, in return, shakes off the sudden prick of pain and nods hello.

Rome reaches down and picks up the newspaper from the dewy lawn.

The sight of the name in the headline leaves him with an ache in his stomach.

Another victim, he tells himself.

He removes the rubberband from the newspaper and unrolls it and reads the headline to himself: "BOUCHARD LEADS PO-LICE TO VICTIM'S BODY."

The front door cracks open, pulling Rome from the article.

Gloria pokes her head from the crack of the door and says in a flat tone, "You're going to be late, Rom. . . "

Rome folds the newspaper and slips it underneath his armpit and with his shoulders deflated and his neck and posture as curved as a seahorse, ambles into the house where his family is eating breakfast.

Both of the kids, Jonathan, whose eight years old, going on nine, and Story, not his, instead Gloria's, sixteen years old and yet, acts as if she possesses more knowledge than a person thrice her age. Story's father is not in the picture, never was, physically, however, financially, his presence looms like a storm cloud. He works in pharmaceuticals, incredibly wealthy, nearly a quarter of his net worth has gone into child support, Story having enough money for ten different college educations.

Before a baggy-eyed Rome has a chance to pour himself a glance of orange juice, Gloria is already six inches deep in his ear, complaining about the man of the hour "Randle."

"He had one way too many, Gloria," Rome says in defense. "When you're intoxicated, you do things that you normally wouldn't do when you're sober—"

"When is the man ever sober?" asks Gloria.

"Enough, Gloria," Rome says, his patience sliding from his face.

"He spit on somebody," Gloria says in front of the two children at the kitchen table.

"Not in front of the kids," Rome says.

"They need to know the reasons why their uncle woke us up in the middle of the night. We can't continue to lie to them, Rome—"

"Is Uncle Randy going to prison?" asks Jonathan.

"No," Rome says. "But he will face the consequences for his actions."

"This has gone on for too long, Rome," Gloria says, moving from one chore, like cleaning the dishes, to another, like bagging up a peanut butter and jelly sandwich. "I've about had it with that man—"

"He's my brother, goddamn it," Rome says, raising his voice to a near shout. "And I'm not going to abandon him!"

Rome's tone causes Gloria to stop packing Jonathan's lunch box. She throws up her hands as if she's in no mood to fight and scurries from the kitchen.

From the kitchen table, Story says sarcastically, "Nice touch, *Román*."

Story doesn't bother to make eye contact with Rome, as she continues to scroll through her phone and nibble from a toasted English muffin with apple butter.

As Rome sips from the glass of orange juice, Jonathan glances up from a plate of scrambled eggs and says to his father, "You said a bad word."

Exhausted, Rome rubs Jonathan on the head and says, "I know I did. Sorry, kiddo."

Rome leaves the kitchen and checks their bedroom where Gloria is sitting on the edge of the bed and slipping her feet into a pair of slip-ons. She catches Rome in the corner of her eye.

"I can't do this right now, Rome," she says, annoyed by Rome's presence. "We're already late as it is and look at you, you aren't even dressed—"

"I'm going to have a long talk with Randle," he says.

"I'm sure that will help," she says, dismissive of Rome's remark. "Words won't do him the least amount of good. The man needs help."

"Like rehab?"

"Anything, Rome," she says. "We can't afford to bail him out of jail every time he goes on one of his violent benders. What does that make us, Rom?" She answers for him: "Enablers."

"From the police report, the guy was the aggressor—"

"Doesn't matter, Rome!" she says, her voice louder. "He assaulted a person."

As Gloria before, Rome throws up his hands like two white flags.

"You're right," he says.

"Of course, I'm right," she says, puts on her slip-ons, and before Rome can forgive himself for raising his voice earlier, marches out of the bedroom.

As Gloria drives the kids to school, Rome stays behind and gets dressed for work.

While he's removing the musty sweats, one of the pant legs snags along the backside of his ankle, causing him to stumble. In his hop-like dance, he finds the same newspaper from earlier this morning. He kicks off the sweats, unfolds the paper, and reads the latest development.

The name of the latest victim makes the draft of air even cooler along his bare legs.

There's a grainy low-resolution photo that was taken a month before her disappearance.

Her brown eyes, round jawline, brow, even the smile: Rome pictures her six years younger from what he remembered by shaving away premature crow's feet from the corners of her eyes. He snips off the baggy sag hanging below her cheeks.

As Rome mentally slims down the swollen face of a medicated woman, she looks incredibly familiar; in fact, she could pass as *his* Deborah. The thought alone terrorizes Rome to the point where he grabs the newspaper, races to the back patio outside, tosses it on the crusty grates of the charcoal grill, and then, finally, douses it with lighter fluid before setting it on fire with a match. Rome watches her face burn and slowly blacken until nothing remains of it but gray ash. He closes the lid of the charcoal grill, hoping it may bring him closure.

⊗

NOT everyday you wake up to find your name in the headlines.

You think she'd be more supportive and understanding, considering the recent revelations.

But then again, I'd be lying if I said it wasn't my first rodeo.

So far, there have been twenty-three victims and by the rate the FBI keeps pulling out corpses from the marshland on Eightball Island, the body count will be rounding fifty by the holiday season. 50. That's one body for each and every state of the United States. That's an entire beauty pageant. Minus three Jockstraps, that's an entire professional football team. Imagine all of those players on the sidelines, then picture young and attractive women, all of them ranging from the age of eighteen to forty-six, forty six being the oldest one who was discovered last week, and from what investigators gathered after an autopsy, one of his first victims. That's 50 people who had names, who once had parents or someone to provide for them, who went through all of the superficial nonsense that girls have been going through ever since the television created an image of exactly how they should look or dress or act. Despite their professions, most of the victims being Red Collars, I'm sure someone out there misses them: mothers, fathers, brothers, sisters, a past boyfriend—or girlfriend—close friends, even though, according to the statement by the FBI, he specifically targeted women who didn't have a social life nor friends or close relationships with family members; nonetheless, 50 people delivered into the world by women who once carried and nourished them (?) inside a womb. That's half of one hundred. No question, there won't be a short supply of topics for discussion while your relatives are slicing up turkey, that is if you don't burn down your house.

3

ROME arrives at Dornick College.

While walking to his building, he runs into Chuck Marlowe, an English professor who wears the same Corduroy that his grandfather sported when Chuck Number One was advocating widespread protests during the Vietnam War, Number One being a thoughtful and inspirational figure who adamantly pressed his body and mind against a system that only favored, at times, catered to those who gluttonously and greedily sucked the life force from the land, which nourished its providers, and demanded our political leaders be held accountable for their crimes against humanity.

"If it isn't *Mr. Far From So-So.*"

"Stop it," says Rome. "You too?"

The anger clouds over Rome's face.

"*Easy*, Rome," Chuck says amusedly, as he tries to calm Rome. "Getting you all riled up is like taking candy from a baby—"

"Not in the mood, Chuck."

Rome brushes off the nickname.

"Apologies."

"Everything has to have a nickname, doesn't it?" says Rome. "Last I heard the media was calling him 'Cordon *Bleu.*'"

"That's new to me—" the nickname suddenly dawns on Chuck, "—right," he says with a grin curling over one side of his face, "because of the weapon he uses or correctly, *used.*" His brow flickers with slight amusement. "How original. Bunch of good-for-nothings on the Web dug up some of his past videos, TV advertisements from his real estate company, when he was slinging multimillion-dollar mansions to overeducated snowbirds. Turns out that old sick bastard was as sweet as a fruit fly—" Chuck says from the corner of his mouth, "—the catch is that it was all a front. The man could've past as one helluva good actor."

"Those witches must be good for something. They caught your eye, didn't they *Professor*?"

"I suppose they do provide the service of gaining the algorithm to whet our own attraction to the *danse macabre.* Have you read about his latest victim?"

"No," Rome says, more short with Chuck.

"Looks like Gloria has been giving you a hard time, huh?"

"It's not just her, Chuck," Rome says, as Chuck keeps pace with him. "It's everyone. Everywhere I go I can't escape the fuckin' comments. I'm actually considering changing my name."

"Doesn't sound like you. You've worked too hard to throw it all away. For what? People expressing their First Amendment right?"

"I've been busting my ass to create a name for myself, my reputation. And then this asshole comes out of nowhere and puts everything that I worked for in jeopardy."

Chuck leans in closer.

"Ever think that he thought the same about *you*? With him being much older and all?"

"The man was completely irrelevant until his other life was exposed. Now, every time people hear my name, they immediately think of *that* shitbag."

"Well," Chuck brushes off Rome's grievances, "it's just people being people. Besides, how do you know what people think?"

"It's starting to wear on me, Chuck."

"Don't let it," Chuck says. "Have you looked in the mirror?"

Rome stops walking for a moment and glances at Chuck.

With a long expression on his face, he asks, "Why?"

"You look like you just crawled out of a toilet."

"Thanks," he says, more relieved by the superficiality of the professor's comment. "I didn't get much sleep. It's Randle. He's in trouble again. He also may need a lawyer."

"Geez. Ran just can't catch a break, can he? What is it this time—if you don't mind me asking?"

Rome waves off the incident.

"He got into it with some out-of-towner who was running off at the mouth."

"Your brother and his short fuse."

Rome sighs.

"I'm beginning to wonder if he even has a fuse anymore."

Chuck says more sympathetically, "I don't blame him. Seems like this entire town is growing by the minute—and not the good kind of growth, if you know what I mean. When in the hell did Knob start attracting rude, whiny, narcissistic city rats?"

"Shitty rats?"

"No," Chuck corrects. "*City* rats."

"City rats, huh?" Rome half-grins. "Well the door swings both ways, my friend."

A comfortable pause hovers over the conversation, as if both Rome and Chuck have an unspoken and amicable agreement on a sudden influx of new residents in Knob, most of them relocating from more condense areas of the country.

"Ever think about getting Ran some help?"

Rome stops again, this time facing Chuck.

He asks the professor, "How can you help someone who doesn't want your help?"

Chuck ruminates on the question.

Interrupted by the striking presence of one of his students, Melanie, Chuck's attention drifts away from Rome, both of his hazel eyes turning toward the passing senior. He follows the professor's eyes toward the senior, a twenty-two year old business major, who gives him the teasing, almost flirty look of a young woman begging for him to chase.

Even the smell emitted by her presence pulls him in like a spell.

As Melanie passes, Chuck leans closer to Rome.

"From what I've heard," he says with a lowered voice, "Melanie's become quite popular on the Web. But from what I've heard, she's known to give the fellas blue balls."

"Say it ain't so."

"In some way or another, I applaud them in how *out there* this generation has become."

"You sound jealous, Professor?"

"If only I had the guts they have when I was that age. . . "

"I don't wanna know," he says, waving off the very thought of a younger version of Chuck. "But then, you probably would've never gotten married."

"True and yet, despite all of Margaret's issues, I can't see myself with another woman."

"Makes you wonder why they're shoveling out so much money to be here."

"Is it me or do they all look the same these days?" asks Chuck.

"Who?" Rome says, dumbly.

"Not those narrow-minded cats," Chuck says, lowering his voice, "but the slutty types—The Melanies," Chuck emphasizes, redirecting his focus to the surrounding courtyard of the campus. "Look at 'em." Several more Melanie look-alikes appear before them, making their way to class. All dressed in similar, if not the same attire, only a varied in shade. The hair is worn in a similar manner as well. The style of makeup. Even the way each one walks to class. The speed, as well as the movement, a bottom-heavy gait, it's all the same. "It's almost as if they came straight off the assembly line. I'll tell you, my friend: They're completely unreachable."

"*Unreachable*?" says Rome. "So, they're not buying what you're trying to sell?"

"Conformity will be the downfall of society, my friend."

Rome nods at the wiry-haired, strung-out, homely-looking old hag with dyed green hair and wearing an authoritarian "INSERT HERE" symbol on her T-shirt underneath a holey cardigan, Ms. Goober, who hands out spoiled and smelly stink eyes to passing students with testicles and holds her glare on them, as if they're an abomination.

"You're starting to sound like one of them," he jokes.

Once more, a grin flickers over Chuck's face, this time pulling across each cheek.

"*Pah*-lease, Gonzo," Chuck says, his voice drawn out. "The day I start sounding like one of them is the day I forfeit my soul to Old Nick."

Rome and Chuck part ways and make their way to their classrooms.

Before his class begins, Rome wastes a few minutes on his phone, reading through theories on blogs about a serial killer, who each day is branded with a new nickname, Cordon Bleu, given the meat tenderizer he uses to bash in the heads of his victims, or Mr. Sow, a stage name that he earned for his uncanny ability to sell houses—the name derived from a TV advertisement for his company, Bouchard Reality, where in the showy Ad, the wonderful Mr. Sow himself magically appeared before the wishful couple of potential home buyers from a stock graphics effect with a swooshing glittery wipe. Sporting translucent clip-on wings behind the kind of casual attire that a weekend dad would wear during the early Eighties, the real estate agent planted magical seeds in the ground before waving around a wand and in the blink of an eye, the homebuyer's "Dream House" suddenly sprouted from the earth. Grainy stills of the Ad, in particular, the ones involving Mr. Sow and that goofy, wide marble-eyed gawk he made when first appearing from a tacky, low budget swoosh of glitter effect, have spread over the Internet, minimizing the seriousness of his horrific crimes, along with the tag line in the Ad of an out-of-pitch woman, who can't hit a note to save her life, singing: "Looking for a new home? *Plant your roots with Mr. Sow. He's got the magic touch to make your dreams grow! Mr. Sow, he's far from so-so."*

Frustrated beyond words by the sheer prevalence of the name, his birthright, his own name "Rome Bouchard" appearing everywhere he scrolls or clicks, Rome can no longer bring himself to read a single article—let alone, headline—or *thread* or post or blog about Mr. Sow, who, after decades of misleading authorities and avoiding arrest, is finally facing the chin music for his past crimes following a new break in a thirty-plus year long case.

Rome sets his phone on his desk and as he sits back in his chair and stews in his own steaming cauldron of thoughts, he returns to the phone and contemplates gumshoeing *her* name.

He remembers the time, just three years ago, when he had her in his class. All he can recall was that she was a completely different girl at the time and the three years at Dornick had transformed her into, not only a woman, but also a presence that couldn't be ignored.

It's not until he musters the courage to begin typing *her* name into the search bar that one of his students enters the classroom and halts any notion of giving into the urge, which leaves him perspired, flushed, and anxious, his heart palpitated, blood rushing through his plump and swollen veins, his insides feeling as though they're dying to burst from his flesh.

Standing outside his range of vision, the student says to Rome, "Hey, Mr. Bouchard?"

Rome immediately closes his phone.

The student is named Hoyt, good student, extremely attentive, has taken interest in Rome's past profession, once said he'd like to one day manage a golf course.

Rome greets Hoyt with a "Sup?" followed by a closed, shaky smile, as if he's carrying a bellyful of stinging bees in his stomach.

Once Hoyt takes a seat in the front of the classroom, Rome returns to his phone and deletes the three letters "M," "E," and "L" from the search bar and once more, closes the phone.

As the rest of the students file in and take their seats, they all want to talk about the elephant in the room.

With the latest victim gathering more public interest, Rome feels as if it's time to clear the air once and for all.

By lunchtime, Rome takes advantage of the free time between classes, walks to the other side of campus, and swings by Walker Coolidge Building where Gloria's art studio is located.

When Rome arrives, Gloria's in the middle of a sculpture class, observing and critiquing the unfinished work of her art students.

Instead of pulling his wife aside to talk with her, Rome stands by the doorway and watches her as she paces through the studio, occasionally providing feedback to her students' work.

Sensing a presence by the doorway, Gloria redirects her attention from one of her student's clay molding of a gnarly, curvaceous tree with human parts, the branches constructed with arms and legs, the trunk made out of dozens of various torsos, and then moves her eyes to the doorway where Rome is no longer standing.

"*Ms. Foster. . .* " the student says, waiting for a reply from Gloria.

Once more, the student calls out Gloria's name.

As he leans in closer to Gloria, she snaps from her trance and says to the student, "Sorry. I thought I saw someone at the door."

"What's the message. . . "

"Right," she says, returning to her original thought before the interruption, "The point being, Ian, not all art must convey a message. It's easy to box yourself inside a concept before allowing your mind to wander through various avenues of the work. It's in those moments, when we lose ourselves, that we discovery another, more deeper meaning. So, take risks. Be *spontaneous.*"

When both Gloria and Rome return home from work, they hardly speak to one another.

Most of the conversation during suppertime is tense and awkward. Their eight-year-old son, Jonathan, does most of the talking. The topic of discussion is centered on a punk kid in his class who's convinced Jonathan's family, in particular, his father, Rome, is associated with that mean evil old man in the papers, the same one behind bars, awaiting trial, who, each day, leads FBI to yet another new body. For the gazillionth time, Rome tells Jonathan that many people share the same name.

"Just because our names are the same it does *not* make us related," he emphasizes, as Gloria chugs the rest of the Chardonnay from the wine glass. "It's *coincidence*, that's all," he says and shoots a glance over at Gloria, who struggles to make eye contact with Rome.

At night, after Gloria goes to bed earlier than her usual ten o' clock time, Rome tucks Jonathan into bed first, and then, once the kiddo is settled in and dreaming about Deep Space and intergalactic voyagers, stops by Story's room to inform her of bedtime and with patience, instructs her to shut down all of her devices, more specifically, her phone. Nine times out of ten, Rome's demands are met with a rolling of the eyes or a mumble or grunt from a girl who grows more curious and defiant by the day.

After Rome leaves Story's room, he stops by his office and spends time in front of the computer, thinking about what Chuck had told him earlier that day, about one of their students.

"Melanie Faulkner," he types, as the image of his wife's face melts away after he imagines himself with a younger and tighter and more provocative woman.

Sure enough, the senior appears at the top of the search engine. Trending.

As the blood begins to race through his veins, Rome glances over his shoulder, making sure nobody is spying on him.

He finds the very first link at the top of the page: <u>Red Collar</u>, a pay-per-view-like subscription based web service that allows sex workers to create content.

Hesitant, Rome clicks on the link, which directs him to "Melanie's Melons" page where she has over two million followers. Rome does a double take at the number of followers. He thinks back to when he played on Tour. Even the premiere players, the big names, the elite athletes, the faces who constantly graced sports magazines, the ones who sports journalists would fawn over as if they were old high school sweethearts: except for one or two who broadened their brand by venturing away from the sport, none of these professional players, even those sponsored by well-known corporations, had as many admirers—and haters—as Melanie Melons.

Baffled, he scrolls through her page where she's posted dozens of videos, each one blurred out and only available through a paid subscription, either monthly or annually. One video in particular grabs Rome's eye and the video involves a watermelon.

Consumed by curiosity, Rome gumshoes Melanie's name, as well as the word "*watermelon*."

A video from a clickbait-riddled shady porn site appears.

He watches only twenty seconds of the video where in it Melanie is sitting on both her hands and knees, undressed, the camera aimed directly at her ass while she smashes a watermelon between her bare, muscular thighs. In those fifteen seconds, the watermelon bursts open and all of the pinkish pulp, watery juice, and black seeds inside dribble down her legs and pool on a red tarp underneath her body. She must've gone through dozens of watermelon, based on the pile of crushed melons lying in the far corner of the room. Her skin has a slight reddish hue and appears sticky from the way it pulls and peels along drier areas of the tarp.

Once the video ticks past the fifteen-second mark, the content goes from some weirdo-fetish niche, which, apparently based on the number of her subscribers, provides Melanie with a steady income, to incredibly erotic in nature, Melanie pulling out a bag of various tubular-shaped fruits, treating the juice as if it's lube.

As she's about to insert the fruit inside of her, Rome suddenly hears a *creak* from the hallway.

Rome closes the window; and before he puts the computer to sleep, he makes sure to clear the search history.

He even feels the sudden inclination to unplug the computer and toss it out the window. But the thought passes as swiftly as a click of a button, and Rome can't stop thinking about Melanie.

TURNS out that latest victim to be pulled from Eightball Island is the same Deborah Collins who I dated for a couple of years when I was attending Pepperidge University.

Last time I saw Deborah was two years before I turned pro. Details surrounding the incident are still somewhat hazy, but I remember that it had chilled me to the bone. She got too attached, and part of me felt guilty for allowing Deborah to get too close. At the time, I was immature and naive and hadn't quite yet explored the many dynamics of being involved with someone for such a long period of time, given both of us weren't officially a couple, but, more or less, friends with benefits. At that age, especially while attending college with girls who were eager and available, it felt as if a friendship was as temporary and short-lived as a trend that lost style over a couple of months. While juggling sports and education, which felt two-dimensional, surface-level, in one ear and temporarily retained for a test or essay and then out the other, I didn't have a lot of time for relationships; and as soon as I sniffed out how super-clingy Deborah had become, especially after at a frat party where she kept following me around as if she was a lost puppy, I wanted my space to concentrate on golf.

That night, after returning home from the frat party, we got into a heated argument. She had what her mother called an "episode." She struck me in the back of the head with an empty vodka bottle. If I hadn't thrown up my arms and ducked my head at the last second, the injury might've been more severe—at times, I wondered if a direct blow to the head would've killed me. But it didn't. The only injury was a knot on the side of my head, which, I knew, was as superficial as my college education. I contemplated calling the cops, not for my safety or peace of mind but Deborah's. She made threats about taking her own life. Her eyes were filled with rage and desperation. I was worried she might harm herself. Once her temper cooled, I went behind her back and called her parents, who supported me and frequently showed their faces at golf tournaments, and told them everything that happened. They informed me that it wasn't the first time for Deborah. A year before their daughter enrolled into Pepperidge, she had a break—a "bad episode"—and she threatened to cut off her father's head with a pair of gardening shears. The next morning, I drove her three hours back to her parent's house as if, in a way, I was shifting the responsibility over to Deborah's parents, as if she was some dog that had bit me and I was dropping her off at a shelter. I remember not sleeping that night. I remember I sat at her bedside that night, carefully watching her, studying her head, wondering what effect I had on her mind and what would it take to shatter a mind into thousands of bite sized pieces, only for those pieces to transgress beyond the scope of reality and become consumed by hellfire. I asked myself if it I had shattered her mind. Or, was it already shattered when I first met her and was this girl a temporary version with a fragile mind held together by duct tape?

According to the article in *The Hillside Messenger*, Deborah turned her life around after she graduated. Apparently, Deborah took a year off from school and finished the rest of her college curriculum online. After she graduated from Pepperidge, she worked at the hospital. Radiology. She chose a profession where she was able to peer into other people and see what they hid from society. Four years later, Deborah was reported missing while visiting a cousin who lived on the East Coast, you guess it, only an hour drive from Eightball Island.

Despite our history, if it weren't for Deborah, and how things ended between us, I probably wouldn't have met the artist known as Jubi-Lee, who was equally as disturbed as Deborah, but in all the good ways.

4

ROME stirs from the graphic image of beating Gloria to death with a meat tenderizer.

Both her arms are held upward in defensive positions, trying to shield each blow to her face.

As the strings of blood strip across Rome's face, he witnesses Deborah Collins lying before him, not Gloria.

She's older, though, a present version, more exhausted and worn down and battered by life, like what he imagines she'd look like if she were still alive: a woman who never married or had any children—even though, during the brief time Rome dated her, she *always* talked about having children—who never had any relationships, who never met the one, Mr. Right.

Rome suddenly wakes as soon as he strikes down on Deborah's face.

Both his eyes open, slow and steady, like a doll's eyes, one second blood and horror and the next, the blades of a ceiling fan outlined with a clumpy layer of gray dust.

The observation alone of dust rids away the violent images to the point where, even when he tries to remember them, they appear faint and faded, like the colors in a past memory.

Rome rolls over on his side where he finds Gloria lying with her back facing him.

He first notices the fresh bruises spotted around her neck, and then, second, red markings of fingers randomly patterned along the back of her ribcage and lower back.

Eventually, Gloria stirs and wakes, rolling around and facing Rome. The stress, once worn on her face, has vanished. The bags, gone. She has a glow about her. Rome is first to point out all of the bruises and markings on her body.

Left in a perpetual state of unease, Rome examines the injuries.

"That's not from me, is it?" Rome asks.

Gloria touches a sore area around the side of her neck.

She says, "Don't feel guilty."

Fragmented images from last night return, Rome striking Gloria and then Gloria forcing his hand, begging for the pain as if the pain itself aroused her. For Rome, attempting to access the images in their entirety, from start to finish, is like piecing together a timeline after being blackout drunk. The hangover from last night plays tricks on his mind, and each one of those markings on Gloria's body, feel as if they were made by the hand of someone else.

"I don't know what came over me," Rome says in a daze, "but I wasn't myself."

Gloria shrugs.

"I kind of liked it," she says with a light in her eyes.

"You did?"

"Reminds me of the time right before we had Jon—"

"Yeah, but I was never rough with you. Was I?"

She thinks, making an *mmm* sound behind her closed lips.

"Let's just say: The Old Rome was passionate. So. . . " she says, perking up, ". . . where's all of this rediscovered passion coming from, Rom? For the past several months, you've barely even acknowledged me."

Rome tells himself, even convinces himself that it's love, although what happened last night doesn't feel like love, but rather the opposite.

"I've just had a lot on my plate lately," Rome says, trailing off. "I think maybe what happened with my brother stirred up some emotion—"

"You're not Randle. Not even close." She jokes, "Actually, I often wonder if you two are related."

"Yeah, but I've been thinking a lot about *what if. . . *"

"What if what?"

"*What if* I'm starting to turn into him? Am I destined to become like him? Like our father?"

"Your brother is a lonely man," she says, running her hand over Rome's face. "You're not. You have me. You've had me the day you first made eye contact with me."

Rome strokes Gloria's hair, and the two make love in the morning daylight.

It's not until after they finish that Rome sees the extent of the markings from last night.

As Gloria rolls out of bed, he spots red marks all over her body.

The image returns: He sees himself beating Gloria with a meat tenderizer.

As soon as the image enters his mind, Rome shuns it away and falls into the recent memory of making love to Gloria, the memory of being inside her, feeling the warmth of her flesh, as he lay sprawled out in a bed so pillowy soft that it feels as if he's lying on a cloud.

He reaches out to touch Gloria, who, in return, stands up and walks to the bathroom, showcasing the bruises, the linear scratch marks, or the faded red handprints from a hand slapping her. Each one can be concealed by clothes. But Rome wonders if her students will spot the marks on her body; and if they do, what excuse will she give them. His mind floods with guilt.

During her wounded gait, Gloria glances over her shoulder at Rome, as though cursing his very eyes from staring at his handiwork.

He tells himself, after redirecting his eyes back to the ceiling fan, she *wanted* to be punished.

An image of his hand wrapped around her neck like a vise, squeezing but not strangling, allowing her just enough air to breathe. The veins in her forehead swell.

Once more, he shuns the image.

She asked for it.

But *why*?

She turns on the shower faucet and while she's waiting for the water to warm, walks back into the bedroom to gather the articles of clothing that were flung from her body during last night's heated exchange of flesh: Light purple panties dangling over the corner of the chest or a worn and oversized Dornick College tee cloaked over the alarm clock on the nightstand, the device bulging upright like a camper pitching a tent. As far as her husband's clothes, he wasn't so careful about where they landed or ended up. His sweats, underwear, as well as shirt, all mashed and piled up on the floor below the bed. The heat was like a cruel beast that wasn't at all interested in such pointless items.

While Gloria fetches the last article, the holey college tee, she reveals the time on the clock. One minute till. His hand is ready to hit the snooze as soon as it sounds. Gloria beats him to the punch and smacks the snooze, giving Rome a few extra minutes for his blood to cool.

Smirking, she says more specifically, "I'll give you ten. Then, wake 'em up and make 'em breakfast."

"Yes, ma'am," he says, loosely saluting his wife.

As Gloria walks back into the bathroom and steps into the shower, Rome notices an item on the top of the red oak chest, not an article of clothing, but rather a folded-up newspaper.

Intrigued, he rolls out of bed and picks up the boxer-briefs from the floor and slides them on while standing to his feet. With the blood rushing back into his head, he staggers at first, like a baby taking his first steps, before he fights off a creeping dizzy spell. Eventually, rhythm returns to his walk, despite feeling the radiating ache in his sore and overworked groin. He picks up the paper. The date on the front page is the same as the one from yesterday. He gives it a once over and confirms, based on the headline, that it's the same newspaper from yesterday. He stares at a grainy black and white photo of Román Bouchard, which was taken during his arraignment.

The details below state that once-reputable real estate agent, Román Bouchard, a retired seventy-four-year-old, has been charged for the murders of twenty-three victims, the latest, number twenty-three being Deborah Collins. The trial is still pending.

The article states that Bouchard has been cooperating with the FBI to locate each body.

Bouchard claims that there are more victims.

Rome goes back to the photo, the face in it.

For a moment, Rome sees himself in Mr. Sow and starts to wonder if he's somehow related to him. A past relative perhaps? Someone from his mother's or father's side? A shunned uncle perhaps? He looks closer at the face, imagining what he'd look like thirty-plus years from now. Vice-versa, he imagines what Mr. Sow looked like when he was his age. With one eye squinted, he begins to see a younger version of himself emerge in Mr. Sow. If Rome were drunk, he'd be fooled to think they *weren't* related, given the blue eyes, which look identical to Rome's. With a tighter squint, he shaves off the small bumps along Mr. Sow's pointy nose, slims down the chin to a narrow letter U, erases aged spots and dark blemishes from his tanned, cancerous skin, then, finally, brings out the pronounced, rounded bulge of his shapely brow line. Rome's mind wanders astray, as he asks himself: *What if* he's a past relative?

As Gloria steps out of the shower, Rome asks her about the newspaper.

While drying herself, she tells Rome that she picked up a copy yesterday after she dropped off the kids.

Once she steps out of the bathroom, she spots the paper in Rome's hands.

She looks it over twice, heavier than the time before, and furrows her brow in a similar fashion as a sane person stares at a humanoid newspaper with a pair of able legs dangling in the air.

"What is it?" asks Rome, as he acknowledges his wife's perplexed state.

"Nothing," Gloria says, dismissive. "With everything going on these days, I can't remember half the things I've done. Which reminds me: Why don't we take this weekend off. Maybe we can drive up to the mountains. I heard the leaves are starting to change colors—"

"Kind of late in the season, isn't it?" says Rome.

Gloria shrugs and forces Rome to set the newspaper aside.

"It would do all of us some good, especially Story, who is slipping farther away from me. I feel like she's growing up too fast."

"I dunno," Rome says, unsure. "I got a lot going on this week—"

"You're the one who suggested last week that we should visit Jupiter's Valley. Remember, Rom?"

He feels his own words coming back to haunt him.

Jupiter's Valley.

Rome says, "I did, didn't I?"

With innocent eyes, Gloria nods and waits for an answer.

"Lemme think about it."

Gloria pulls herself away from Rome.

"So," she says moodily, "it's a no then."

Rome grabs Gloria by the wrist and pulls her back into his body.

Tightening his grip over Gloria's wrist, Rome moves her arm behind her back in a submissive position and whispers closely, "Why don't you and me get outta here? Just the two of us?"

"What about the kids?" Gloria asks, as she embraces Rome.

The knot in the towel loosens from the pressure of Rome's body pressed against her.

The damp towel slips from her breasts and falls to the floor, forcing Gloria to make a feeble attempt to grab it.

Rome tightens his grip around Gloria's wrist and kisses her on the neck.

The touch of his lips on her skin tempts her to rush back into bed with Rome. Before the heat returns, she suddenly resists the urge and scorns his very behavior.

"Rom," she says, as she forcibly tries to push him away. "I have to get ready. *You* have to get ready."

Rome tightens his grip around Gloria.

The panic fills her eyes. More color rushes into her face.

"*Rom*," Gloria says, fearful of Rome's state, "you're hurting me."

As the rage suddenly washes over Rome, he snaps from his violent trance.

Meat tenderizer.

Gloria's face.

Rome removes his hand from Gloria's wrist.

With his head down, he says shamefully, "Sorry. Don't know what came over me."

Growingly frightened by Rome and the recent change in his demeanor, Gloria picks up the towel from the floor, wraps it back around her torso, and grabs an outfit from the closet.

Before Gloria dresses, she reminds Rome of his duties.

Wake 'em up.

Make 'em breakfast.

Unlike Gloria, who would've made eggs for Jonathan and Story, Rome is a more of a grab-it-from-a-box type of breakfast eater.

While Jonathan is eating from his bowl of corn flakes, he brings up the jack o' lantern.

He asks his father if he can to make one with him tonight.

"That time of the year again, huh, kiddo?" he says. "Feels like it gets sooner and sooner each year, does it not?"

"It's called capitalism," Story says with an attitude. "The only reason that corporations push the holidays on people sooner each year is to make more revenue."

"Well," Rome says back at Story, "capitalism made that cinnamon raisin toast that you love so much."

"It's not like we have any *other* choices."

"Well, you can get back to me when the government starts making bread for you. I'm sure as Salinger it won't taste nearly as good as your beloved. . . " he grabs the package of bread from the counter and reads the brand name, ". . . Nature's Train."

Story rolls her eyes at Rome and while taking an exaggerated bite from the toast, returns to her smartphone.

Rome draws his eyes toward Story's phone.

Melanie and her melons enter his head, causing his blood to boil.

The sudden temptation of snatching the phone from Story's hand and shattering it into a million pieces is spurred on by the thought alone of Story following the inevitable route of Melanie. He has a hard time believing that a young and athletic woman, like Melanie, would still pursue a career in the flesh trade, if the smartphone didn't exist, let alone, social media.

As though on cue, Gloria enters the kitchen at the right moment.

She brings up their father's night class, which he teaches only on Tuesdays and Thursdays, and reminds Jonathan and Story that it's only going to be the three of them for supper.

"I almost forgot," Rome says and touches Jonathan on the shoulder. "Looks like I'm going to have to ask Mr. O' Lantern for a rain check."

The sound of her stepfather missing out on supper prompts a remark from Story: "Seriously, why do you even teach that class?"

"You'd be surprised how many students find the subject quite interesting—"

"Believe it or not, Guru over here," Gloria says, referring to her husband, "has a rare item in his possession, which is worth quite a bit of money."

"Only a hundred copies exist throughout the entire world. Most of them said to be destroyed in a flood. I just so happen to own one of those copies. And also, good luck trying to find it on the Web—"

Story interrupts, "Nobody calls it that anymore."

"—Considering it was discontinued over a decade ago."

Story asks, "You mean that lame-ass book you were talkin' about the other day?"

"Language," Gloria snaps.

Gloria's sharp tone causes Story to back off.

While retreating back into her phone, Story, as with the previous bite of toast, exaggeratedly smacks her gums and says under her breath, "*Like you're one to talk about language.*"

With a pouty face, Jonathan asks, "What about the jack o' lantern?"

"Well. . . " Rome says, handing off the activity to Gloria, ". . . your momma would be more than glad to help out. Won't you, momma? After all, she's the artsy one in the family."

Rome shoots a flickering-brow glance at his wife, who gives him a shrug of her lips.

"Don't sell yourself short," she says and places today's newspaper that she recently grabbed from the front porch on the kitchen countertop. "I'm not the only one with the imagination in the family."

As Rome grabs today's newspaper from the counter, Gloria kisses Jonathan on the head and tells him that she looks forward to her date with him tonight.

Rome cracks open the paper; and sure enough, Mr. Sow gave the FBI a map to yet another body, which, as of now, increases the body count to twenty-four.

The FBI hasn't yet determined the identity of the victim's body.

So far, the only details: The body is female, early twenties. Based on the patterns along the fractured skull, the weapon matches the one used on the other victims.

Despite Bouchard's claims that he used a meat tenderizer to kill the victim, the investigators are still trying to keep an open mind.

"*All options are still left on the table*," reads a quote from Special Agent Karp.

Unlike the previous victims, the body was found along a hiking trail in Jupiter's Valley.

The name of the city, "Jupiter's Valley," causes Rome's stomach to sink, leaving behind a nagging, gnawing sensation inside his gut.

"What is it?" asks Gloria, as she notices Rome's slackened expression. "You look like you just saw a ghost."

"Cops found a body in Jupiter's Valley," he says.

"Another one?"

"They haven't identified the person."

"The Dream Machine strikes again, huh?" says Story.

"Dream Machine?"

"That's what the *Internet* is calling you. . ." she clears her throat, ". . .I mean, him."

"Story," Gloria says over her daughter, "not funny—"

"Where did the *Internet* come up with that name?" Rome mocks Story.

"You know the *Internet* and how they tend to stir the ole pot. Since the last name Blue Eyes, you know, because he has blue eyes, " she says with a sassy tone, "didn't really stick, they pulled up some of his greatest hits from when he was slinging houses. He's dreamy—at least, he used to be back in the day. Plus, he was said to sell houses like a machine. You combine the two and *voilà*! Dream Machine."

Rome says more fatherly, "That reminds me: You need to *stop* going on the Internet."

His demands have absolutely no impact on Story, but rather the opposite.

"What's wrong with Dream Machine?" she says mindlessly, as if she's become desensitized by the on-going murder case(s).

"Rome is right, Story," Gloria says, clinging onto Rome's words as if each one was spoken directly from her mouth. "You need to give it a rest. . ."

Once more, Story rolls her eyes and makes an incoherent noise from her mouth before exiting the kitchen.

"How come I'm the one who always looks like the bad guy?" Gloria asks, as she pours herself a cup of coffee.

Rome swoops in behind Gloria.

"That's because you are *baaad*," he says, mimicking a sheep as he pulls Gloria closer.

"Easy, Rom," Gloria says, touching Rome on the arm as if she's reminding him to behave in front of Jonathan. Her eyes suddenly light up. She rotates around and faces Rome. "I forgot to mention. I have some good news. I got an email from Carol—"

"From Flora and Further?"

She nods with a wide smile.

"She's agreed to sell my work in her main store."

"That's great, babe," Rome says.

"If it does well—"

"Of course, it will," he says over Gloria.

"Well, if it does, she'll make it available in the other stores. I was gonna tell you sooner, but I got distracted. . . " she says, still glowing from last night, ". . . if you know what I mean."

"I know exactly what you mean, *Ms. Foster*," Rome says, emphasizing Gloria's professional name.

Rome gives Gloria a hug.

Laughing, Gloria says, "Oh! Stop it!"

Repulsed by his mother and father, Jonathan tells the two to get a room.

After breakfast, Rome dresses and makes sure everything is turned off inside the house before leaving. While Story is making last-second adjustments to her wardrobe, Rome makes sure the lights are turned off on the back patio. Out of curiosity, he opens the lid of the charcoal grill and checks the grate. He can't find any traces that he burned the newspaper, not a single ash.

With the unsettling stirring of his flesh, Rome brings the lid back down over the grate; and right before he closes the lid, he caches a glimpse of hope in the form of a partial-face.

Rome lifts the lid back up, puts it aside, and removes the grate. At the bottom of the grill he finds a burnt piece of newsprint. Carefully, he uses his two fingers, both his index and his thumb like tweezers, pinches the corner of the blackened photograph, and pulls it from the bed of cold coals. He can only make out the back of Bouchard's head, as well as the upper part of his body in the grainy black and white photo. Sitting behind Bouchard in the background of a courtroom is a strange-looking partial of a face, a tired and familiar face.

Rome decides to pocket the burnt piece of paper.

LIGHTNING never strikes twice in the same place.

When I think about the first time I met Gloria, both of our eyes connecting like magnets, two tiny balls of life gravitating toward one another, two heartbeats beating in sync, two minds carrying the same thoughts, two universes meeting, two timelines crossing paths and eventually weaving and intertwining together, almost always the memory of Dara is attached to Gloria.

Even though the two devoted their lives to a world of art and expression, Dara's instrument of choice being her vocal cords, Gloria's, her hands, the two were polar-opposite in appearance, as well as personality. The two were worlds apart.

Dara was incredibly shy, surprisingly, being that she spent most of her adult life in the spotlight, as well as the public eye, surrounded by people who treated her as their own personal savior.

Gloria was anything but shy.

Dara mounted various metal records, from gold to platinum, on her walls as a reminder of her journey.

Gloria propped up her sculptures as if they were anything but reminders.

To Gloria, her work was an extension of herself.

In a way, the sculptures were mirrors into Gloria's soul.

Born in a seaside village in Cambodia, only to later grow up in Paris, France, while pursuing a modeling career, Dara rose to stardom at the age of nineteen after relocating to the States where she began a career in music. The next five years

Dara—you may know her by stage name, Jubi-Lee—would sell out concerts, tour across the world, and create an entire brand based on her image, as well as her voice. She was beloved by millions of people. After five years of giving her life to music, Dara met a broken down, burnt-out professional golfer, who, after spending ten excruciating years of traveling across the country from one tournament to another, was ignited by a spark, which gave him an entirely new perspective on life.

Dara and I met at an after party in Los Angeles. Dara was recuperating at her Malibu home after having recently finished an eight-month long international tour. I just recently wrapped up a commercial shoot for an "eco-friendly" watch, which ran off a solar battery. I was planning on taking a flight back home after the party. I never caught that flight. And for the next three years, I gave my life, as well as my soul to Dara, vowing to spend the rest of my existence treating her as if she was my queen.

After Dara, I *never* imagined I'd be able to capture lightning in a bottle for a second time. It took me several years to recover from such a tragic loss. I thought I'd *never* meet another person like Dara. I thought I'd never be able to climb that mountain and experience the feeling again.

If Gloria taught me one thing, it was to never say "never."

5

ROME stops at a gas station to fill up the car before heading to work.

As Rome watches with overwhelming frustration the cost of gasoline tick past the price that he normally pays, he hears a sudden *roar* of engines behind him.

The throaty gurgles of the engines sound closer, pulling Rome away from the gage.

The bikers from the gang, White Lightning, appear alongside the convenient store. Each of them is bundled up, like a pack, the alpha of the gang, the one with the pinkish scar shaped like a lightning bolt, positioned at the lead; whereas, before, Rome remembered, he rode in the back of the gang, like a caboose.

Rome eyes the same rider from before, when he was driving Randle home from jail, a man with shoulder-length scraggly, wiry, stark white hair and eyes the color of steel. The only difference in his leathery black and white appearance is the beard, which is shaved thin, prickly, like a negative five o'clock shadow, a white o'clock fuzz.

The leader of White Lightning rides past Rome.

The two make eye contact, like two forces repelling off one another.

They have numbers, he tells himself.

One against twelve?

Not exactly a fair fight.

The white-haired biker smirks at Rome, who, in return, redirects his attention back to a racing gage above the pump. The price is nearly double what he'd normally pay for a full tank. It's not until he feels the lukewarm gasoline pouring over his hand along the handle that he identifies one of the main reasons for the price spike. He's made a mess of himself. The gasoline has overflowed from the tank and splashed on his crotch, making it look as if he's pissed his pants. Some of the gasoline has already started to puddle below his feet.

"Shit," Rome says and removes the nozzle from the tank.

After he returns the nozzle, he grabs a handful of napkins from the side of a cleaning station and pats his pants dry.

Rome has no other choice than to drive home and change his pants, which reek of gasoline. By the time he makes it to Dornick College, he's a few minutes late for class.

Of course, there's always one student who has to be the center of attention.

The student, Cujo—his parents, especially his mother, must've had quite the sense of humor when she named her son after squeezing him out—chimes in after his instructor apologizes for his tardiness.

"Must've gotten held up after dumping his latest dead body," Cujo says to other classmates.

Some of the students burst out laughing.

Others try to conceal laughter by covering their mouths.

Either way, Cujo's Sports Medicine instructor isn't at all laughing. He's furious beyond words and based on the color of his face, it clearly shows.

While taking a break between afternoon classes, Rome drops by Gloria's studio and brings her a box of chocolates that he bought from a stand in the food court. Moments before entering the studio, he hears two people talking, one of the voices is Gloria's and the other's—Chuck's? He pokes his head into the studio and sure enough, finds Chuck talking to Gloria. The two are sharing a laugh—flirting? Gloria touches him on the arm, as though signaling for him to take it easy on the jokes. The joke, as Rome takes a step away from the doorway and eavesdrops over the conversation, is centered on Gloria's daughter and the controversial outfit that she's planning to wear for an upcoming Halloween party.

"I see where your daughter gets her imagination," Chuck says in a flirty way.

The remark spawns an awkward silence between the two and in that tense globe of silence, Rome's mind ventures into dark places.

Meat tenderizer.

Gloria's face.

The corners of his face color with anger, both of his eyes darken.

He pushes away the images in his head and walks away from the studio and on his way out of the building, he tosses the box of chocolates in the trashcan.

From his classroom window, Rome watches a fidgety Chuck leave the Art Building. For a moment, he thinks he sees Chuck adjusting his clothing, his belt first, then his collar.

That night, while finishing up his night class on "Gonzo Journalism," including the origin of Gonzo, the history, the term "*gonzo*," the godfather of gonzo, the usage in culture, as well as its impact on modern day journalism, Rome bumps into Chuck while leaving the classroom.

Surprised by Chuck's presence, Rome asks what he's doing here this late at night.

"Tutoring," Chuck says, more composed than he expects, given what he suspects his fellow colleague of doing to his wife. "One of my students recently lost her father to colon cancer. She has already missed two weeks of classes. So," he sighs, "in order to prevent her from falling too far behind, I decided to throw her a bone." Before Rome comments about the student, mainly "which student," Chuck asks Rome, "Say, you're not doing anything right now, are you?"

"No," Rome says mindlessly.

It's not until moments after the word, *No*, barrels from his lips that he anticipates Chuck's offer.

He tells himself that he should've lied or made up some excuse. Carving jack o' lanterns with Jon, remember?

But what if Gloria already told him about her husband's plans and how he doesn't have any. If she did tell Chuck, then why did Chuck ask? Maybe he's trying to catch Rome in a lie?

"What'd you say we grab a drink," Chuck says, his eyes lighting up.

Rome hesitates.

"I can't Chuck. . . I gotta— "

"Sure you can."

"I told my son that I'd help him with a jack o' lantern—"

"Gloria told me she's got your ass covered," Chuck says, catching Rome off guard.

Rome's eyes widen, his brow shifts to one side like a seesaw.

"She did?"

"She said that she was going to make a jack o' lantern with Jonathan. Come on," he doesn't miss a beat, "while we're still young."

Chuck pats Rome on the side of the arm.

"Just one drink," he suggests. "Or two?"

Rome points ahead.

"After you," he says.

By the time they reach their cars, Chuck suggests trying out a new joint, a local college bar, Shots in the Dark.

The name of the bar alone sounds like a place where he'd find his brother, Randle, slumped over the end of the bar, flirting with college girls, starting fights, making a scene.

Instead, Rome mentions a wine bar, The Great D'Vine, a quiet and dimly lit establishment where he usually frequents with Gloria, especially on Thursday nights whenever Gloria can find a trustworthy babysitter to watch over Jonathan, if Story was off with her friends.

Chuck shrugs and says, "I'm down."

The two enter their cars and drive away, Rome leading the way.

When Rome pulls into the empty spot in front of The Great D'Vine, he notices the group of motorcycles parked in the back of the parking lot.

Twelve of them, Rome counts, each one barely visible in the shadows outside the overhead floodlight.

Being a Tuesday night, there are only a few people inside the wine bar, mainly overeducated winos with laptops.

Before entering, Rome peers into the wine bar, searching for the bikers but doesn't see them from the sidewalk.

Relieved, Rome follows Chuck to the bar where he orders a local beer from the tap.

Chuck, a "when-in-Rome" type, looks over a menu of specials and decides to order the glass of Pinot Noir imported from Chile.

Rome doesn't bother to ask the reasons why Chuck was talking to Gloria, since Chuck had earlier stated that he had spoken to his wife. He figured, in order to keep his cool, he'd rather let it come out more organically, after Chuck has enough liquid courage in him to freely talk about what was so goddamn funny during the break.

Chuck brings up Jupiter's Valley, which makes Rome wonder if Gloria had mentioned anything to him about an upcoming trip that was inevitably going to be canceled, given a recent discovery of the latest victim and how it was only a matter of time before the circus came to town.

The topic of Jupiter's Valley falls flat, forcing Chuck to fill in the rather uneventful conversation with food.

Chuck insists on ordering an hors d'oeuvre.

Rome isn't at all interested in eating. To make matters more uncomfortable, he spots the unlikely patrons sitting on the patio located behind the bar.

The white-haired biker from earlier is sitting on the patio, his leather boots kicked up on the table, boss-like. Along with the other bikers is a middle-aged woman, who walks inside to order a drink from the bar. She's dressed similar to the other bikers; however, the leather is tighter on her body, same goes with each article of clothing.

While ordering a fruity mixed drink from the bartender, she stands next to Rome, one elbow perched on the edge of the bar, propping her upright with a slanted post. With her ruby red lips curling into one side of her face, she flicks her chin in a head nod at Rome, who appears sick to his stomach.

"How's it hanging there, *Rider*?" she asks Rome.

With his body swaying to one side like a buoy, Chuck leans over to Rome and whispers into his ear, "*Three inches to the left.*"

Rome ignores Chuck and responds defensively, "Good."

Based on the past encounters, three thus far, and each time, the bikers have shown a peculiar interest in Rome, he thinks of the old saying: "*Expect the worst and hope for the best.*"

In Rome's case: Expect a fight and hope for it to end quickly.

Maintaining the peace, Rome clears his throat and says, "And you? How are you?"

"Oh, me," she says, batting her eyelashes, "I can't complain. The roads are open and the air is dry—what's there not to like?"

"Is that your bike parked out front?" asks Rome.

"It is," she says mindfully. "Are you a *rider*, Rider?"

"Me?" he says. "Nah. I wouldn't even know where to begin. I'm sorry," he says abruptly, as he catches his own words, "Why do you keep calling me Rider?"

She shrugs.

"You look like a rider."

Chuck chimes in, "I'd take it as a compliment, Rome."

She overhears the name.

"Rome, huh?"

"Yes," he says, "in the flesh."

"I like Rome," she says. "I once knew a guy named Rome. Very popular with the ladies."

Rome holds out his hand for a handshake.

"Well, it's nice to meet you. . . "

His words hang in suspense, as though he's waiting for the stranger to fill in the space with a name.

"Misty," she says, shaking Rome's hand.

"Nice to meet you, Misty," Rome says and nods at the professor. "This here is Chuck."

Misty leans over Rome and shakes Chuck's hand.

"Chuck," she says. "A man's name."

While Misty's arm is extended past Rome, he acknowledges a scar, similar to the biker with white hair, along the inner part of her bicep. Rome concludes, after further study, that the scar is shaped like a lightning bolt, which he tells himself could be like a brand-thingy for a gang.

With a slight buzz from the beer, Rome decides to ask Misty about it.

"The scar," he says and points at the marking on Misty's arm. "Where you'd get that?"

"Oh! This ole thing. . . " she says playfully and looks at the scar, ". . . I got it when I was a little girl. My big sister was chasing me in the backyard. I snagged my foot on a water hose and tripped and fell. I ended up scraping my arm on a tree stump. Eight stitches."

"Ouch," Chuck says. "Must've hurt."

More standoffish, Misty says, "I dunno. I was young. I don't remember much, but only that number, eight, which, at the time, kind of sounded like *hate*, which was what I felt for my sister."

Rome makes an attempt to regain control over the conversation before Chuck takes it over.

All of a sudden, the backdoor opens. The alpha, the white haired biker, enters the wine bar. He walks past the three at the bar and sits down at the round table near the front entrance. On a dime, Misty's demeanor switches from warmhearted to cold-hearted and reptilian-like.

Rome shoots a glance over at the strange biker, who tries to smile, but the smile comes out all wrong, like he has a mouthful of pumpkin seeds and those two parched, quivering lips run as crookedly as a frayed thread.

"So, who's your friend ov'r—"

Misty interrupts before Rome can finish his question, "Nice chatting with you, fellas."

She grabs her drink and walks outside on the patio where she joins the other gang members.

For the rest of their time at the bar, the biker doesn't even move an inch from his seat. Instead, he watches Chuck and Rome, who become extremely uncomfortable by his presence.

Chuck asks Rome if he knows any of these goons, more specifically, the King Goon himself playing a perverse game of eye-tag across the bar.

"The fella looks like he wants your bones," Chuck says, voice lowered to a whisper. Then, he says more closely, "Want me to say something?"

"Leave it alone," Rome says. "Will you?"

The last person Rome needs sticking up for him is the two hundred and ten pound professor who can't even bench press half his weight. Rome is tempted to ask Chuck if he's ever thrown a punch throughout his entire life.

Chuck suggests that they leave after they finish their drinks.

Rome can't finish his drink quick enough.

While Rome and Chuck are leaving The Great D'Vine, the biker, whose eyes appear much softer and bluer instead of a steely gray color, calls out with a slight slur in his drawn out voice, "Soon, I'll be seeing you on the other side, Román, ole buddy."

The letter s's like sludge over his tongue as the words *soon*, *seeing*, and *side*, slither from the biker's lips in what Rome perceives as a lisp.

Rome suddenly breaks away from Chuck before exiting and storms over to the white-haired biker and asks, "Have we met before?"

The biker absorbs the question the same way an underdeveloped child registers words.

Rome asks again, "Do I know you?"

"No. . . " the biker drawls, as his eyes sharpen from Rome's looming presence.

Rome only gets through the first three words of yet another question "*How do you* know my name?" before the biker moves his bluish eyes up toward the brave challenger. Everything about the white-haired biker sharpens, not only his devilish eyes, but his entire aura, as if the handle of a blade has been removed from a holster and now, the blade is sitting freely and openly, ready to be grasped by the one who dares touch its sharpness.

Leaning forward over the table, the biker says over Rome, ". . . *But you will.*"

"Who are you—"

"I know a lot about you, Román."

"I think you might have me mistaken for someone else."

"Your name is Román Bouchard, is it not?"

"What do you want from me?" asks Rome.

The blood runs faster throughout Rome's veins, pulsating in various areas of his body.

Over the heavy silence, the two square off in a showdown, their eyes aimed directly at each other.

A staredown.

The stakes: Whomever blinks first loses?

As Rome stares into the biker's eyes, Rome suddenly feels as if he's looking at a reflection of himself, as if the biker himself is neither alive nor dead, but rather a mirror, an inanimate object which imitates the very thing who gazes upon it.

In the staredown, Rome flicks his unblinking eyes toward that jagged scar along the side of the biker's face. An image flashes in his mind, perhaps spawned by Misty—*if that's really her name*—and the previous story about her sister: He pictures a young girl chasing after a younger boy through a junky, unkept lawn when, all of a sudden, the boy trips over a water hose and falls forward and hits the side of his head along a tree stump.

Rome shakes off the image and turns his eyes back to the biker's.

As Rome loses himself in the biker's stormy eyes, Rome witnesses the envy of a man who was an outcast during his youth, betrayed by his own blood, beaten by the very paw that fed him, and finally, disowned by the creatures that delivered him into the world.

And in that moment of envy and enmity, Rome blinks.

The tension releases, as the biker sits back in his chair.

"I take it," the biker says more calmly, "your brother is having trouble clawing from the hole that he has dug for himself."

"You're friends with Randle, aren't you?" says Rome, surprisingly more relieved.

"I wouldn't exactly call us friends," the biker says, half-grinning. "More like associates."

Rome asks, "And exactly what business do you have with my brother?"

As the relief washes away and leaves him feeling more heated and perspired, Rome's mind runs through a checklist of possibilities: If it's illegal, then what? Drugs? If it's drugs, then what kind of drug? Coke? Weed? Uppers? Downers? Tranq? Fuck-it-alls? The notion alone of his brother being involved with Fuck-it-alls sends a ripple of disgust throughout his body.

The biker clarifies, "Let's just say: We're in the debt-collecting business."

With his mind racing, Rome interprets the misleading and potentially malevolent remark as a hand-over-heart, fingers-crossed threat; nonetheless, an invitation for Rome.

Driven by rage, Rome points his finger at the biker and holds it to his throat like a knife and seethes, "You stay away from my brother, you hear?"

The biker holds up his hands, not in surrender, but, more or less, a way of hissing "not here, but somewhere else, when I'm ready, on my terms."

"You're the boss," he says to Rome and grins, fully.

Rome storms toward the exit while Chuck, who's left in a state of awe by Rome's tenacity, follows Rome outside. As they make their way from The Great D'Vine, Chuck grabs Rome by the shoulder and says with a feverish excitement, "That's the Rome we all once knew and loved. I'm sure the whole time you were probably imagining his face as a giant golf ball. If you want, I can grab my seven iron from the trunk—"

"Give it a rest, Chuck," Rome says, as his entire body throbs like a heart beat.

Fearful of an ambush, Rome glances over his shoulder, forcing Chuck to follow suit.

"You don't think he was serious—"

"I dunno," Rome says. "Just watch your back on the drive home, will you?"

Less excited and more paranoid, Chuck says, "Sure. Of course."

Each movement is sped up.

"I'll catch you later," Rome says, making his way to the car.

As the two drive off without the bikers following, Rome decides to give Sheriff Figg a ring during the ride home. Rome informs the sheriff, whom he once rolled with, ages ago, way back in high school, not exactly best friends, but rather allies, before he left Knob to pursue a career in golf, that his brother, Randle, might be in grave danger. Rome gives Miles the description of the biker. The sheriff doesn't know anything about the man or his friends, only that the group may be passing through Knob. Either way, he'll keep an eye out.

After Rome calls the sheriff, he stops by Randle's apartment on the way home.

All of the lights are off.

Rome walks around the complex and concludes, after knocking on his door once more, that his brother is not home. He calls Randle and informs him of a possible threat. As predicted, Randle is at a hole-in-the-wall bar—he doesn't say which one for he doesn't want to ruin a sweet buzz—but the giveaway is a clamor of obnoxious voices in the background. On the other end, Rome hears the sound of the door *squeaking* open, then close. The voices cut to silence.

During the brief conversation, Randle swears on their mother's grave that he doesn't know the man whom Rome is describing. The biker. King Goon.

From the tone of Randle's voice, Rome believes him.

When Randle asks where Rome bumped into the biker, Rome stumbles his words before he finally confesses that he saw the biker at The Great D'Vine.

"Right," Randle says, disappointed. "I see."

Before Rome can explain himself, Randle tells him that he has people waiting on him, then ends the call.

Rome drives home; and during the entire ride home, he checks the rear view mirror to make sure nobody is following him.

Once Rome arrives back home, he sees a freshly carved jack o' lantern perched on the front porch. Gloria is upstairs, getting ready for bed. Before joining his wife, he comes across a mess in the kitchen, as though it's Gloria's way of telling him that he should've been the one to carve a jack o' lantern with Jonathan, not her; and for his absence, he's stuck with cleanup duties.

With his head foggy from a numbing ache, Rome grabs a trashcan from a drawer under the sink and proceeds to clean up the pumpkin mess. The blanket of newspapers is spread out along the granite countertop. Gooey globs of pumpkin seeds and stringy pulp are scattered over damp paper in small piles.

As Rome positions the trashcan below the edge of the counter, he gathers and wads up the newspaper and pumpkin insides— "*brainz*" with a z is what his son calls them—and slides them toward the edge of the counter. Right before he's about to push all of that gunk into the trashcan, he notices an image in one of the newspaper articles. Touching the drier corners of the newspaper, he carefully pulls it from the messy pile without ripping it. The date on the newspaper matches the one from the other day, with victim number twenty-three, Deborah Collins. The image in the photo is Román Bouchard, the other one, the older one, the killer, standing before a judge at his arraignment. He immediately recognizes the image. The partial. He hurries to the laundry room and finds his pants from yesterday in a laundry basket, unwashed. He reaches his hand into the pocket and pulls out a small scrap of burnt paper. He brings the paper back to the kitchen where he matches it with the image from Bouchard's arraignment photo where sitting in the background is the same face that he saw an hour ago. The biker's face. King Goon. He looks the same as he did when he first saw him, roaring past him when he was returning home after picking up his shitfaced-brother from jail.

Hoping to find a higher resolution of the arraignment photo, Rome combs the Internet, first starting with the local newspaper's website. He accesses archives and within a couple of clicks, he's able to pull up the original article on Bouchard before it went to print.

Rome can't track down Mystery Biker anywhere in the photo, even after he uses the mouse, as well as the quick keys on the keyboard to zoom in on the screen.

Perhaps the editors used a different photo.

There must've been dozens of photos to choose from right before publication.

He matches the photo on the computer with the same one from the newspaper.

The photos are the exact same.

The only difference: The biker is missing from one of them.

Rome heads to bed but doesn't rest until he double-checks, at times, triple-checks each door, as well as window throughout the entire house, making sure each one of them is locked.

Finally, in hopes of further deterring the biker from showing himself, Rome switches on the floodlight outside. The shadows that cast from the floodlight appear sneakier and darker, like the doubts darkening inside his head, after he realizes the threat that he's up against, a rare goon who isn't the least afraid of having his face exposed in the light.

And that thought alone makes his blood run icy-cold.

RANDLE and I have Death's number in our contact lists, tucked away in the very back.

For me, you might scroll to the very bottom of the list and find Bag of Bones in the Z's.

But every now and then, Death disguises itself and sneaks its way the top of the list, and it's the first name you come across if you're searching for someone to help make sense of a world that takes knowledge for granted and then demonizes those who dare dispute the knowledge which has been provided.

Death is the great holder of secrets whose arms expand across time and space, and if you're determined enough to seek out and unearth knowledge in its rawest form, then you'll obtain the very item that Death withholds from you.

Randle and I have nothing in common, except Death.

Her name was Alejandra, the feminine variation of Alejandro, and Randle once told me that, in Spanish, her name meant "*The Protector of Men*," and over time, while spending time in their company, I began to witness the meaning of her name in plain sight, only it should've been "*The Protector of Man*," Randle being her priest, her lover, *her man*, whom Alejandra, the personification of her name, would throw herself onto a sword if it meant protecting *her man*. Alejandra was a dance instructor who owned the corner studio on Main Street. She and Randle had been together since college. Randle dropped out after his first year—*too expensive, waste of fucking time*, he'd say, *leave the conformist brainwash-thingy to the little green men when they evade us and take over our minds through an app disguised as short-form video sharing social media platforms*—to start a career as a roofer. Alejandra lived in New York City for three years before returning back home to Knob. Of all the women in Randle's life, Alejandra was the only person who managed to dull down his edges, which were the roughest whenever she wasn't in his life. The late night partying, the drugs, as well as the drinking, the misbehavior: Alejandra was the greatest blacksmith who shaped Randle into a decent man.

Four years ago, Randle lost Alejandra to cervical cancer, which, by the time the doctors discovered it, had already spread to her lymph nodes, and the months before she began to wilt way, the violence, which once defined Randle, slowly returned. Ever since we were kids the violence followed Randle like a shadow and after he met Alejandra, it was banished by daylight, went dormant, like a genetic disorder that had temporarily been cured by the greatest waltz known to man. It was a curse that our father handed down to us. Somehow, I found an outlet in golf and managed to beat the curse before it had consumed me, as it did Randle. Each and every day, I'd see Randle becoming more and more like our father. He was a drunk who smacked around our mother. One day, I stood up for her after he struck her during one of his notorious binge-drinking episodes. Probably the worst mistake I ever made, which, in a way, created resentment toward my mother, who, over the years, especially after I lost Dara and the dark years that followed before I met Gloria, became incredibly manipulative and would do anything to keep me around, within reach and proximity, even if it meant lying to me or playing dumb with me in order to get *her* way, which was me, the good son, under the thumb of a woman who was losing power and resorted to crafty tactics in an attempt to control me. The incident left me with a broken jaw. I was only eight years old, Jonathan's age, and for the next three years, I could no longer hide my injuries from teachers or friends. Before cops could lock him up, he disappeared, vanished in the middle of a storm. Some years later, I learned that his body was discovered in the back alleyway of a small incorporated town in Missouri. Apparently, according to a police report, our violent-happy father picked a fight with the wrong guy. Even though an innocent part in me felt for him, I didn't spend too much time mourning him. The leftover, microwave-ready feelings I experienced after his brutal passing were only derived from the vanishing whims of a nonexistent relationship that could've been rewarding but were best explored in the fantastical world of television where fathers came in various forms, any shape or size, nonetheless, there to offer advice, there to lean on, *there*, always there. Not once did I ever shed one tear for him. That moment he broke my jaw was the moment I saw him for who he was, a man who had no business bringing a child into the world, let alone raising a child. But, on the contrary, if he hadn't met our mother, Randle and I would've never been born.

6

ROME has a dream that he goes back out after cleaning up the mess in the kitchen and stops at a bar where he hooks up with a local barfly who's as loose as the lid of a congealed rim on a jelly jar. The two have sloppy, awkward sex in the driver's seat of his car. Heat rises from their bodies like steam and clouds up the windows with a perspired, foggy tint.

The next morning, Rome wakes up slow and heavy to the empty spot of creased bed sheets that pass as white snakes.

Startled after dragging his hand across the creased bed sheet, Rome bolts upright and feels a distant rumbling of the garage door opening.

As the nerves settle, Rome runs his hand along his eyes and uses his fingertips to dig out the crust from the corners of his eyes. The crust is somewhat smooth and lumpy. He holds his findings before him, only to witness, not eye crust, but rather tiny white clumps, which break apart as he rubs his fingers together. Observantly, he scans the bedroom. During the scan, Rome comes across the same white powdery substance along the edge of the pillow. He then rubs his fingers along the backside of his neck and finds more of those small white clumps behind his left ear.

After rolling out of bed, he walks to the window where he finds Gloria, already dressed and ready for work, carrying a bag of garbage to the trash bin positioned at the edge of the driveway. Gloria runs the house like the head of a union. Rome's role: Garbage. For as long as Rome can remember, he's been the one to roll the trash bin to the street for the garbageman. Despite all of his wife's trash, with the arts and crafts and all, she's never walked the bin to the street.

Rome glances over his shoulder and checks the clock on the nightstand. It's only a couple of minutes after his normal set-time, and based on the commotion coming from the kitchen, both Jonathan and Story have already been woken up. He faces forward, his eyes moving toward the lock on the window. It's unlocked. It's never unlocked. *Never.* He locks it back.

Rome dresses for work and makes his way downstairs.

On the kitchen counter is today's publication of *The Hillside Messenger*.

The first page headline immediately grabs Rome's eye.

Another body, this time much closer to Knob.

The body was discovered in a ditch along the Cornelius "Corny" Brown Freeway.

According to the article, the investigators suspect that there might be a copycat killer based on the condition of the body. The young woman was without any clothes. Her face was unrecognizable due to the blunt force trauma. The death is "suspicious," the Head Investigator says in a public statement.

Throughout the morning rush, Rome goes about his business. Whenever Jonathan or Story or Gloria speak, their words are drowned out by the chatter of thoughts inside Rome's head, and the only replies from Rome come in the form of mumbles or stock answers, which are given little to no thought.

Before leaving the house, Rome asks Gloria if she could drop off the kids. He tells her that he needs to take the car into the shop for an oil change. He figures that if he goes right when the shop opens, he shouldn't have to wait long and he can get the oil changed before the beginning of his first class. She buys the lie and doesn't put up much of a fight.

Rome's family leaves the house.

After Rome watches his wife drive away with Jonathan and Story, he makes his way down into the basement, which has been turned into Gloria's own personal art studio. Each clay sculpture, each figurine, as well as dinnerware from his wife's "GLORIA FOSTER" line is perched on metal shelves that he built for her to celebrate their third wedding anniversary. Stacks of boxes filled with his wife's finished products cover nearly half of the basement.

Making sure not to touch anything for his wife would have his balls on a platter if she found out he was snooping through her studio, Rome cautiously walks to a working table and switches on the lamp. On the table rests a new piece made from material that Gloria hasn't used in ages: papier mâché.

As Rome lowers his hand toward the mask, he can feel an energy radiating from the newspaper, the feeling similar to hovering one's fingers over the screen of an analog television, a sort of static electricity pulling his hand closer and yet, at the same time, repelling his hand.

Carefully, Rome inspects the papier mâché mask, which is made from newspaper articles of Mr. Sow and all of his crimes. One of the articles, the most recent one, used in the mask is the one from last night's mess, with victim number twenty-three, Deborah Collins. He holds the mask underneath the lamp and closely inspects other newspaper articles. Rome can only make out fragments of the aged, yellowish clippings, partials of head-lines, as well as columns, each one he had memorized. Each headline, column, and article is about Rome, his past career as a professional golfer, his wins and his losses, as well as his first wife, the popstar Jubi-Lee, who tragically died in a plane crash after the plane was struck by lightning. One particular headline that stands out the most, the letters n-e-e from the word *knee* partially visible underneath the many layers of the hardened paper, which acts like glue after being soaked in flour and water: Rome's devastating injury which forced him into an early re-tirement, thus resulting in his fascination into the human anat-omy.

Rome's eyes fall back onto the most recent newspaper clip-ping glued onto the mask.

Number twenty-three.

Deborah Collins.

It's not until moments right before Rome begins his first class that he learns more about the latest victim.

Clearly, it's not Mr. Sow, considering the "alleged" serial killer is currently behind bars.

According to the local news report, the victim was last seen at the Drunken Donkey, a hole-in-the-wall bar that Randle nor-mally frequents. He doesn't know why exactly he thought of his brother when he heard the name of the bar on the news, but it's the first image that pops into his head after the reporter states that the sheriff's office is teaming up with local police in a coor-dinated effort to catch the person responsible for the victim's death, first by questioning two main suspects, who might've been involved in what Sheriff Figg is now calling an uncon-scionable act of violence, a "homicide."

Rome recalls passing Melanie on the way to class.

Minutes ago.

Gloria's face.

Meat tenderizer.

Melanie, not Gloria, rushed past him in the hallway and nearly bumped shoulders with him. She had tears in her bloodshot eyes. She was covering her mouth, as if she was either too afraid or ashamed to cry.

As Rome pulls himself from the video on his phone, he watches the rest of the students file into the classroom. Each one of them has different expressions on their faces.

Instead the playful, teasing expressions Rome received along with the whispered labels that they would throw around to each other, the students appear timid by Rome's presence.

Rome eyes a figurine of a homeless clown holding a golf club on the corner of his desk: the clown is Broken Bob, or his most notable depiction of "Hobo Golfer," a once popularized character during the Great Recession.

Frustrated by the latest discovery, Rome grabs the figurine and hides it away in the bottom drawer of his desk.

Throughout the day more details emerge from the developing case.

The victim is a former student at Dornick.

Her name is Lindsey O'Neil.

Rome never taught her.

He researches her name.

Apparently, Lindsey was on Red Collars, making enough income to buy her own house.

The suspect is said to have used a type of meat tenderizer, but it's unclear and as of now, all speculation, since investigators still haven't located a weapon. No sign of sexual assault was concluded.

Later that day, as Rome pulls into the driveway of his house and finally, after spending the entire afternoon sitting on the subject, comes up with a way to broach the conversation about his wife's strange mask without drawing any red flags, he receives a call from Randle.

Somehow, after speaking with his brother, the mask is the least of Rome's worries.

Concerned about Randle's well being based on the tone in his voice, Rome reverses the car from the driveway and drives straight to his brother's apartment.

There, Randle tells Rome what happened last night, how he was one of those suspects whom the investigators questioned.

They told him that a surveillance camera caught Randle leaving the bar with Lindsey O'Neil; however, according to Randle, he dropped Lindsey off at her house. A neighbor of Lindsey's backed up Randle's claim by telling the Head Investigator that she spotted Randle's car outside the house. She saw Lindsey walking into the house. Randle drove away.

Randle is still considered a suspect, even though an eyewitness cleared him of any wrongdoing. The sheriff told Randle not to leave town, in case there were any further developments in the ongoing investigation.

As far as the other suspect, they wouldn't say.

Rome leaves Randle's and stops by the sheriff's office where he can talk face-to-face with Sheriff Figg, who recently finished speaking with the other suspect in the Lindsey O'Neil case.

The first words to leave the sheriff's mouth when he first sees Rome: "*Speak of the devil.*"

Rome first mentions the biker from last night and the subtle "threat" that he made to him and his brother, Randle. Off-the-record, Sheriff Figg informs Rome that the "other" suspect is the man whom Rome described: the white-haired biker from the gang, White Lightning. The investigators questioned the biker, who went by the name—get this—Román Bouchard. Without batting an eyelash, the sheriff tells Rome that "the man claimed he was you."

"Me?" says Rome. "Is this some kind of sick joke?"

"Don't know. But cameras picked him up at the bar. . . " Sheriff Figg says, ". . . not too long after you called me. When I saw his face, I immediately recognized him from that description you gave me last night."

The sheriff reassures Rome that he has a couple of deputies following him.

Rome asks for protection.

Sheriff Figg gives it to him.

As far as Randle's safety, the sheriff tells him that his department is already stretched thin.

Later that night, the deputy, who's watching over Rome and his family, knocks on Rome's door in the middle of the night.

Each knock of the door echoes through Rome's dream.

In his dream, Rome is having sex with Melanie on a yoga mat behind the Hot Spot, a trendy café located on the outskirts of town.

Violently woken up by the sounds of the earth shaking, Rome rushes downstairs and grabs a poker from the fireplace and opens the front door. The deputy informs him about his brother.

"He's been rushed to the hospital," the deputy says.

Rome tries to extract more from the deputy, but the deputy doesn't have a lot of information to give Rome.

When Rome and Gloria arrive at the hospital, the two learn more about Randle's injuries. According to Sheriff Figg, Randle was stabbed after leaving the Drunken Donkey. One of his deputies picked up a woman named Melanie Faulkner wandering along the side of the highway. "The woman was completely out of it," he tells them. Both of her hands were covered in blood. Forensics ran the blood, which matched Randle's.

The catch: Melanie doesn't know how she wound up on the side of the highway.

"Shock" is the best diagnosis the doctors can find after a health evaluation.

Turns out Melanie was close friends with Lindsey O'Neil.

When Rome asks for the sheriff's thoughts, Sheriff Figg believes Melanie, after experiencing a mental breakdown, retaliated against Randle, whom she thought murdered her friend based on a recent—and to be fair, "reckless"—report stating that "Randle Bouchard" was one of the two suspects being questioned by the authorities.

Rome brings up the biker who's been stalking him for the past couple of days.

The sheriff tells Rome that his deputies, who had been following him and his goons around all day, lost them after a brief rainstorm.

Rome asks, "What do you mean 'lost' them?"

"They said, 'One second they were tailing the group through the abandoned Hyde Industrial Park, a rainstorm appeared out of nowhere, then, poof, they were gone.' Like ghosts. . . "

"What do you mean *poof*?" With his brows furrowed in confusion, Rome says more directly, "What the hell is going on here, Miles?"

The sheriff runs his hand along his scruffy chin.

"I dunno," he says, drifting off. He touches Rome on the arm and reassures him that they're going to get to the bottom of this mess.

Sheriff Figg gives Rome his word.

⊗

I'M beginning to wonder if the entire world knows something about me that I don't know.

A secret concealed from my eyes and ears.

One key-turn away from revealing what's behind Door Number 1.

I see it everywhere.

The looks I receive.

The constant stares.

Their eyes are like question marks.

I hear remarks behind my back.

My ears only catch words and partial sentences about me and help color in the blanks.

But the secret is *still* there.

Too soft and muffled to hear.

Who do they think I am?

What do they know about me that I don't?

Is the world beginning to turn against me?

Or, am I starting to turn against the world?

What if I'm only seeing what I want to see?

What if I'm only hearing what I want to hear?

Or, what if I'm only reading what I want to read?

Even worse, *what if* we are, in fact, connected?

7

ANOTHER nightmare.

Another dead body.

The murder doesn't make it to the front page.

Instead, Rome finds it on Page 2.

The name immediately leaves him speechless.

"*Margaret Marlowe*," Rome reads.

She is the wife of the very man who was reveling in his nightmares.

Only this time around, Rome was an observer, watching from the doorway as his friend had sex with Gloria.

And behind the window: Two glowing eyes of what looked like a wolf.

Earlier this morning, Chuck discovered his wife's body after she returned home from a shift at the hospital where she worked as a filing clerk.

The articles states that Margaret died from blunt force trauma to the head.

Similar, if not, the same way Lindsey O'Neil was deleted from existence.

It doesn't say in the paper, but Rome already has an idea of the weapon, which was used to kill Margaret.

The investigators are currently speaking to Chuck.

Nine times out of ten, it's always the husband.

But Rome knows Chuck, and he knows he'd *never* harm Margaret. It's simply *not* in his nature.

Contemplating about taking a sick day, he shares the troubling news with Gloria, who consoles him and suggests that he go about his day, like usual.

"You act like none of this bothers you," says Rome, as he pulls himself from Gloria.

"It does, Rom," she says, guard up. "But I'm not going to sit around here and dwell over it. It's not healthy or productive, and I'd rather keep my mind busy with work—"

"I know you and Margaret weren't close, but the least you could do, Gloria, is acknowledge what happened—"

Gloria shouts out over Rome, "*Things happen*, Rom! People do. . . monstrous things! It's part of life!"

Feeling more apprehensive, Rome backs off and holds up his hands in surrender.

You win this round.

He has neither the time nor the strength to argue with Gloria.

Instead, Rome storms back upstairs where he spends the next few minutes piddling around the bedroom until Gloria leaves for work. When he returns back downstairs, both Jonathan and Story are waiting for Rome to drive them to school, as if Gloria left them with Rome as way of punishment for Rome storming away from a conversation where the best resolve is an exchange of uncomfortable disagreements.

During the drive to school, the entire conversation between Rome and his son, as well as his stepdaughter is all about the "d-word" and whether or not Rome is going to leave their mother.

Rome tells them that he and Gloria aren't going to get a divorce, but even when these words leave his lips, a part of him believes it's a white lie.

When Rome pulls the car up to the carpool lane in front of the elementary school, which is much closer to Dornick College than Story's high school, he reassures Jonathan that what he and his mom are experiencing is a disagreement between two adults and tells him that everything is going to work out in the long run. While hugging and saying goodbye to his son, Rome hears a *thud* alongside the car. He peeks through the side-view mirror and finds the paperboy, Charley, riding away on his bike.

Rome arrives at Dornick College, only to find a swarm of news reporters in the parking lot, talking to students and members of the faculty.

Frustrated by the sight of reporters, Rome grabs his things and exits the car. As soon as he slams the passenger door, he spots a flat tire on the rear of the car. The back left tire, he notices, is in the same spot where Charley grazed. He inspects the tire and as suspected, the tire appears as if it has been punctured by a sharp object, perhaps a blade—Charley?

"You little piece of shhh. . . "

Rome pushes aside the frustration and dodges reporters and heads straight to his first class. Before class begins, he calls up Frank from Blackwood's Tires, who sends out one of his mechanics to switch out the flat while he's in class.

Only three students show up for class. The students don't bring up the subject about Professor Marlowe's wife. It's not until the class ends that two of the students offer their condolences to Rome, who, in return, thanks them for their nice comments.

Before his next class begins, Rome decides to take the rest of the morning off.

Frank's mechanic, Allen, is tightening up the final lug nuts on the spare tire.

Rome waits until Allen finishes changing the tire before driving back home.

The moment he steps foot inside the house an eerie feeling comes over him, leaving him in a heightened state of alert.

Quietly, he makes his way to the basement and as he's about to enter, he receives a call from Sheriff Figg, who, knowing that he may be interrupting Rome's class, apologizes for the disturbance. Rome informs Sheriff Figg that he can talk; and before the sheriff can bring up the subject, Rome tells him that he's already aware of what happened to Margaret. The sheriff is reaching out to people who made contact with Mrs. Marlowe before her body was found dead. While combing through the surveillance footage from the hospital, the sheriff found Rome talking with Margaret outside the hospital.

"I was?" says Rome.

"The video shows you leaving the hospital just minutes after Mrs. Marlowe left."

The sheriff asks Rome to stop by the office for a chat—more like a "statement."

With his voice trembling, Rome says, "We're chatting now, aren't we?"

"It'd be in your best interest, Rom," the sheriff says in a more serious tone.

When Rome arrives at the sheriff's office, he's surprised to see Gloria sitting in the waiting area. She confirms to the sheriff that Rome drove home right after he visited his brother in the hospital, which provides Rome with an alibi and clears him of having any involvement in Margaret's death; however, later that morning, at Hot Spot, where Rome and Gloria grab a cup of coffee, he shares to Gloria that he can't recall a thing about last night. He tells her that he has images of being somewhere else after he visited Randle.

A trashy underpass, which once used to be a hangout for the forgotten.

A tame fire burning inside a rusty oil drum.

Shadowy faces circled around the beating flames.

Eleven of them, he counts.

All dressed in black reflective leather.

Once more, Gloria consoles Rome and first admits that she was out of line earlier.

Gloria says, "I'm not good at handling these kinds of subjects, you know this?" She reaches over the table and grabs Rome's warm hand. "You remember how I was after my father passed?"

"You lost yourself in your artwork," says Rome.

"You're right," she says. "I did. And by doing so, in a way, I managed to make sense of his death. But sometimes, you can't make sense of why people do what they do. So don't blame me for wanting the same for you—"

"I don't blame you."

"But," she says, voice softer as she leans over the table, "if Chuck was involved—"

"He wouldn't, Gloria," Rome interrupts. "He's not the type."

"But everybody has a breaking point."

"Of course people have breaking points," Rome says and leans closer to his wife. "Chuck is not a killer, Gloria," he whispers sharply.

"How do you know?" asks Gloria.

"I just know, Gloria." He says off-the-cuff, "Besides, I don't know why you would say such a thing, with you being so close with the man."

"Me?" Leaning away as though repelled by the remark, Gloria points at herself. "Close? The man's obnoxious."

"You sure didn't seem bothered by him when he was talking to you the other day."

"When?"

"In your studio," he says.

"Were you spying on me?"

"Of course, I wasn't spying on you," Rome says. "I was going to bring you a treat when I walked in on you talking with Chuck."

"That?"

"Yes," Rome says. "*That.*"

"Exactly how much of the conversation did you hear, Rome?" The tone in her voice is back.

Round 2.

"Enough to get a hint."

"Well, if you only stayed around long enough then you would've known the real reason why Chuck stopped by my studio—"

"I know enough, Gloria," Rome says, raising his voice.

He draws a couple of eyeballs around the café, one from the barista and another from a customer waiting in line.

"Did he tell you that Margaret was recently diagnosed with breast cancer?" asks Gloria.

"What are you talking about?"

"Cancer."

"Serious?"

"Yeah," she says shortly. "Serious. She found a lump on her breast the day before we spoke. He wanted to tell you about it, but given your brother's history, everything he went through with Alejandra, he was. . . hesitant about talking about it with you."

From his deflated state a weight is lifted from Rome's shoulders, and he can finally breathe much easier knowing that Gloria wasn't sharing carnal knowledge with Chuck behind his back.

Guilty, Rome tells Gloria to take the rest of the day off.

The two drive back home where they make up.

For Rome, it's probably the best sex they've had since before Jonathan was conceived.

While lying in bed together, Rome runs his fingers across the linear scar from Gloria's cesarean section. The shape of the scar along his fingertips is less linear and more rigged. As he sits upright, he draws his eyes to the scar and closely inspects. One half of the scar is shaped like a lightning bolt, causing Rome to question the appearance of the scar.

"Has your scar always looked like this?" asks Rome.

Gloria tilts her head upward from the pillow, the skin folding underneath her chin as she notices her husband playing doctor downstairs. She says, "Of course it has, Rom. What is up with you these days?"

Rome shakes off the very thought and says foolishly, "Like you're one to talk. I hope you don't plan on wearing that ridiculous Halloween mask you made from *my* newspaper articles—some of which, by the way, I was collecting. Next time please let me know ahead of time before you rummage through my stuff. . . "

With her cheeks filled with color, she sits upright and rests her back against the headboard.

"What in the world are you talking about, Rom?" asks Gloria.

"You know, *the mask*, and forgive me for snooping around your studio, but I have a right to know what you do down there sometimes—"

"Rom," Gloria says, more soberly, "I don't have the faintest clue what you're talking about."

"The mask, you know?" he says. "The papier mâché?"

Rome rolls out of bed and throws on some clothes and then drags his wife out of bed.

"Lemme show you," he says.

"Stop it, Rom," Gloria says, pulling her hand away. "What has gotten into you?"

"Can I just show you," he says, holding out his hand.

Eventually, Gloria dresses and slaps away Rome's hand and without his assistance, follows him downstairs into her studio where he shows her the working table.

"It was right there, Gloria," he says, pointing at the spot underneath the lamp.

"A mask?" says Gloria.

"Yes," he says. "It was made out of papier mâché."

"Rom. . . " Gloria says, holding Rome, ". . . I didn't make any mask."

When Gloria speaks to Rome, she looks directly into his eyes, as if the eyes themselves are carriers of both lies and truths.

From what Rome can tell, his wife is telling the truth.

But he's been fooled before.

Last year.

Story's father.

The bruise on Story's arm.

At the time, Rome told himself that it was the mother-side in Gloria.

The protector.

If she told Rome the truth about what Brady did to Story, there was a strong possibility that Rome would overact and bust out his old set of golf clubs and put them to good use.

Later that afternoon, while a sheriff's deputy is combing through surveillance footage from Hot Spot, he picks up the white-haired biker whom he lost. Melanie, who is sitting at a table inside the café while editing videos on her laptop, acknowledges the biker as he strolls past her table. He picks up what looks like a credit card from the floor and as he hands it to

Melanie, their hands touch. The biker makes a remark to Melanie, but the deputy can't make out what he says for there's no audio in the video. Only moving images. And the images don't lie.

In the video, Melanie places the credit card back into her pocket and attempts to work on her laptop. She appears almost paralyzed. The sight of Melanie causes the deputy to zoom in closer. After sitting in a trance-like state, Melanie watches the biker exit the café.

Moments later, Melanie exits as well.

Deputy Metz brings the video to Sheriff Figg, who, after watching the footage, suspects that the biker, who calls himself "Román Bouchard" but even the sheriff knows that the name is bullshit, may be linked to, not only to the death of Lindsey O'Neil, but also the stabbing of Rome's older brother, Randle Bouchard.

EVEN now, I still feel shadows of him floating around my brain, like an elusive phantom.

At times, he's a bad thought that won't shut up.

A doubt.

A false memory.

A nuisance.

He clings to a body that he no longer possesses; and yet, he feels betrayed by his own flesh.

I can only imagine what he's doing right now inside that dying vessel.

Behind those bars like a caged animal.

Trapped inside that prison.

Rotting away.

No more distractions to keep his mind occupied.

The people in his life, his profession, or the past which once defined him: all plucked from his existence.

Sometimes, in order to acquire the combination, the job requires finesse and a more personal touch.

Other times, it demands blunt force.

A man is most vulnerable when he's backed up against the wall. He'll do about anything for extra space, even if it means destroying those who challenge his disposition.

At least he has a good book to keep him company.
I can't say the same for the others.

8

THAT night, after Rome goes to sleep on the living room couch
after having yet another argument with Gloria, he has a nightmare that he's laying on a used, disease-riddled, bloodstained
mattress inside an abandoned warehouse in Hyde Park. Standing behind a cracked window is a similar, if not, the same wolf as
before. Those two glowing eyes piercing right through him like
blades.

All of a sudden, a strobe light of red and blue flashes of police
sirens force him to check the outside where he finds cruisers
surrounding the warehouse.

Their guns, drawn, ready.

One of the deputies uses a battering ram labeled "DICK" to
knock down the door.

Sheriff Figg is the one who makes the arrest.

By the time Rome wakes up, he finds himself inside a prison
cell.

Rome is befuddled as to whether or not he's still in a dream.

The sheriff, Miles, sets the biker straight.

As Sheriff Figg stands on the other side of the bars, he questions the strange man.

After Rome throws a temper tantrum, the sheriff holds up a
mirror to his face.

Rome is wearing the face of another man.

A white-haired biker with a scar running down the side of his
face.

The head, the leader—the alpha—of the biker gang White
Lightning.

The only difference: his eyes.

They're blue, not gray.

Each and every member of the gang has disappeared from
Knob.

The sheriff tells Rome that if his goons so much as cross an
inch over the train tracks, which separate Knob from the next
town over, Reed Springs, then he will lock up each and every one
of them and throw away the key.

Rome tries to convince Sheriff Figg—his old pal, Miles—that he's arrested the wrong guy.

Later that day, during a lineup, Sheriff Figg phones in Rome—the other one—as well as his wife, Gloria. The two drive to the sheriff's office. First, Rome identifies the belligerent biker as the man who threatened him inside The Great D'Vine. Gloria is there for emotional support.

After Rome and Gloria leave the sheriff's office, the investigators take turns on the mysterious biker and spend hours rigorously interrogating him.

The investigator places two evidence bags on the table before the biker.

Inside one of the bags is the same meat tenderizer, which was used to kill Lindsey O'Neil, as well as Margaret Marlowe. The other bag: The knife, which was used to stab Randle Bouchard, who's still recovering from his injuries. The biker's prints are all over both weapons. The investigators are convinced that Gloria was one of his next targets.

The million-dollar question: "What is your angle? Your *motive*?"

As before, the blue-eyed biker claims to be "The" Rome Bouchard.

The biker's lawyer pushes "insanity" and states to both the prosecutor and judge that his client does *not* belong in a jail, but rather a rehabilitation center called *Substance Abuse* and *Mental Health Association* for *Indisposed Nonconformists*.

Even through the entire trial, the biker pleads his case of innocence.

But jurors don't buy it.

Before reaching a verdict, the jurors don't even spend a minute deliberating.

Guilty on all counts of first-degree murder.

As for Melanie Faulkner, she's clear of any wrongdoing.

The sentence is life in prison without parole.

The sound of the judge's gavel when he slams it down thunders throughout the courtroom.

In a state of shock, the handcuffed biker is hauled away, and the people of Knob sleep a little easier, knowing a killer has been removed from their streets.

NOTHING compares to the feeling of a cool breeze blowing through your hair.

The smell of exhaust fumes rich in the air.

The tread of tires like jagged teeth chewing through dark asphalt.

The handlebars like the horns of a conjoined beast among a creation of contorted metal.

Life rushes past you at a hundred miles per hour.

The road is a tongue that stretches out into oblivion; and if you stay on it long enough, it will eventually swallow you whole and spit you out on the other side of the stormy horizon.

Like it's own little assembly line pumping out one product after another.

A copy of a copy of a copy.

It's only when you remove the blinders from your head and release your grip from the throttle that life finally catches up to you until the road calls again.

Fellow Riders often ask me what's the trick, how do you unlock the secret of living.

Each and every time, I give them the same advice.

"It's no different than trying to crack open a safe."

Dalivia finished reading the novella and after comparing both novellas, the Barnes version and the Kross version, which she had read before, realized that, except for the change in the main character's name from Ramie to Román (Ram to Rom), Ram being the Kross version, Rom, the Barnes, as well as the presence of a strange wolf-like creature, which only appeared in Rome's nightmares, the two novellas were identical, nearly word-for-word, Ericka Barnes clearly copied—or stole—straight from Kross's original story. That was when Dalivia learned about a *disclaimer* in the book details at the bottom of the site's page, stating that Barnes's novella was altered by a program called "Leo," a name that she would hear more frequently over the next several years during what was known as "The Uprising," but exactly who or what was rising and rising from what, you be the judge of that.

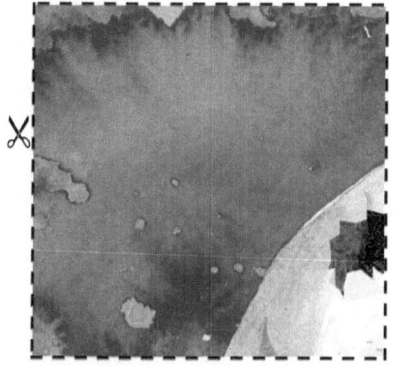

t

MORBID CURIOSITY

BELOW me (even I am no longer Me™ but, more or less, a scattered version of what was once Me™) the maggots roll and writhe before awkwardly scuttling in winding routes within a sea of now human flesh while others are bunched up in idled pose, chattering among their old tribes—and new. The pulse is strong and vibrant among them, a hearty thrum, and the unseemly radiance of their momentary physical existence pummels me like a tidal wave. Only can I envision a gallery so full within my youthful dreams. But I'll tell you this much to be true: it's difficult to acknowledge life and the endless space it occupies through a 24 x 36 gold-ornate Paisley picture frame. It's these four corners that keep me confined.

They're too sharp and rigid.

As I wait in exhibit, they all stare and study me as though I'm a disease, except for two of them, in female-form, one a brunette, the other dirty blonde.

As they shoulder their way through the dense crowd, I recognize both of their faces. Old friends of Riley's. More or less, acquaintances.

The dirty thirty, Electra Savoy, or "Elle," as her friends say, went to school with Riley in Connecticut before the two small town girls wound up in New York City. Elle was once an editor for a reputable magazine (forget which one) before eventually being laid off and seeking employment elsewhere (social media

behemoth *MyCircle* comes to mind) due to the great swallowing, the ultimate reset of the Wave, which forced many companies to shorten their staff before inevitably sinking into the digital abyss. Guess she thought: *You can't beat 'em, then why not join 'em.*

The other one, Elle's friend, is Phelan, a six-foot tall redhead who, at first, I confuse with the word *feeling.* I don't know much of anything about her, Phelan, only she drives a lime green Prius and used to date a writer I knew named Shayne, who had a squinty face, deep crow's feet, even on rainy days, looked as though he was constantly in pain. She's quiet, has characteristics of an introvert. Others would say intimidating, which was another way of saying she was a snobby bitch or worse, displayed the *false* impression of a snobby bitch when, in fact, she was far less superior. I've rubbed shoulders with her at a several parties through mutual friends. She's an enigma, to say the least.

Phelan steps in closer to the wall, Elle following suit.

With her eyes attached to me, Phelan mentions the name of a man who she's currently dating, Robert Marionette, prompting Elle to express a more than hostile critique of his last name, then later questioning if the name lives up to its nature.

Ignoring the impulse to retort, Phelan makes a confession: Rob, who's forty-three years old and up to his eyeballs in debt with his drug dealer despite his "professional-looking" façade, is cheating on her with a woman in her mid-twenties.

If memory serves me correct, Phelan is, like Elle, in her thirties, possibly on the wrong side of thirty based on her stoic lead, although insecurity is starting to get the best of her. It's all in her posture, as well as a grievance she lugs around on her shoulders. She has a tendency to slouch.

When Elle questions Phelan's claims, she receives a short answer that doesn't quite put her at ease.

"He is being secretive," she says. "Not answering my calls." She even goes so far as to tell Elle that she followed Rob to this twenty-something's brownstone in Greenwich Village. She must've been *handy*-capable in order to afford such a place.

"Yeah," Elle says nonchalantly. "He's definitely cheating on you. For sure."

Phelan rolls her eyes at Elle.

"Thanks, Elle."

"What?"

As she stares at me with watery eyes, she struggles to contain her emotions.

"Sorry," Elle says, trying to comfort Phelan. "Just being honest."

A strange darkness comes over Phelan's face.

Those liquidy eyes narrowing.

"And that fucking grin," she seethes. "I swear, it's the kind of grin someone would make right before stabbing you in the back. . . A car salesman's grin. What a liar! If he worked off commission, he'd be a goddamn billionaire."

Not sure I know who this Rob character is. Four years ago, when I was dating Riley, we bumped into a Wall Street-looking guy named Rob, who sold Riley a gram of blow, which she swore was cut with Bisquick. Now that I think about it, he could've worked for a hedge fund. I specifically remember Riley making a scene by storming out of his upscale apartment in Manhattan after he "allegedly" made a pass at her. I was taking a piss in his ivory-covered bathroom and never saw the actual encounter, but when Riley later told me about it, she made me make a promise that I wouldn't do anything "stupid."

Phelan takes a heavy pause after mentioning Rob's grin, as if the word itself, *grin*, stirs up something nasty inside her. That grin, her face says, the right-handed devil pulling the strings along the corners of his mouth with a booming *Ha-Ha*!

"Kind of like his smile," Elle says unsurely.

"You don't have to be nice, Elle."

Elle takes a beat.

"M'kay," she says. "You're right. He's Creep City. I never told you this but one time, he groped me."

Makes sense, if it's the Rob I'm thinking of.

"*My Rob*? Seriously?"

"Only reason why I didn't say anything to you was because I knew how gaga you were about him—and from what I can tell, still are."

"Where was this?" asks Phelan.

"Last year," Elle says, "at Melody's Halloween Party."

"You were dressed as Slave Leia."

"So?"

"You might as well been ass-naked, Elle."

"He was aggressive."

"You don't say. . . What's up with you and what's his name?"

"Yeah," Elle says coolly, "about that, yeah, we're so done. We broke up last week. Forgot to mention."

"That was a quickie. How'd long that last? Two months—"

"I lost track after the first week. He was extremely manipulative."

Phelan makes a face, which results in an uproar from Elle.

"Like you're one to talk, Phelan," she says. "How many guys were you with before Rob? Please refresh my memory because, after—What's his name?—that one guy who shitted himself in your bed, the 'Man-Baby,' they all seemed to, you know, blend together, like one giant blob."

"Brian couldn't help it," Phelan says, sympathetic. "He had a serious drinking problem."

"How'd that breakup end? *Right*," she says sardonically. "Was 'mutual.'"

Elle even uses 'air quotes' to express her viewpoint.

A larger crowd gathers around one of my first pieces, an oldie that I painted when I peaked at the age of twenty-three. The piece is called "*The Divine Hand*." Phelan's reaction has me more intrigued.

Phelan: "So, what happened between you and Anderson?"

"The other day some asshole cut in front of us while we were waiting in line at Whole Market and get this: all of a sudden, Anderson acts like he's missing his tongue. When I questioned this line-cutter, he turned to Anderson and told him to 'control his woman,' as in me."

"What'd Anderson do?" asks Phelan.

"What'd you think?" she returns. "He stood back and did absolutely nothing. Whenever he's doing that podcast of his, he'll say whatever the hell he wants and won't feel any regret about it and the thought of being canceled is the least of his worries. But when it comes to standing up for me, 'his woman,' this sissy turns into a mute. Where'd all the men go?"

Good question.

"That's what happens when you swim with the fishes in the sea," Phelan says grimly. "Every now and then, you meet a jellyfish."

Elle sips from the glass of Chardonnay.

"Maybe you're right."

Phelan throws a nod my way.

"Rumor has it that Ruffiano used his own blood to create the piece—"

Not a rumor.

"As well as other *organic* materials to create the authenticity of the painting."

"When'd you get all dark on me, Phelan?"

Phelan shrugs.

"Rumors, Elle."

Not rumors.

"It's not him."

Wrong again.

"I sure hope not. It's so realistic, though. I mean let's say just for fun that if it was, you know, *him*, isn't that, like, evidence or something?"

"Probably not." Once more, in a smug-like manner, she shrugs her shoulder. "Last week, I saw a dead dog on the side of the road. The other day, its blood still remained all over the concrete. Nobody's cleaned it up."

"Eww," Elle said, cringing, "come on, Phelan."

Elle wears a look of repulsion on her face.

"Like people in charge of running this city care about us or our furry companions," she says cynically and to Elle's surprise, truthfully. "You saw how they handled the infamous Plague. . . "

Elle rolls her eyes.

"So, what are you going to do with the Rob Situation?"

"Dunno yet," Phelan says, drifting off. "Guess, I dunno, I guess I still love him—"

"Clearly," Elle snaps.

"He has his moments. But. . . other times whenever we're together and I find myself struggling to get out so much as a response from him, I'd just like to know what goes on inside that head of his, know what he's thinking."

Phelan moves her narrow eyes toward me. There's something incredibly off about Phelan. Her look. I know that certain look on her face. Saw the same one in the reflection of the barrel, as I was moments away from pulling the trigger.

A Dragon never lies.

⊠

SOMEWHERE around the height of my career I often experienced what the Nighttimer Community (*yes, there was such a thing—didn't you know?*) called a "reoccurring dream—or nightmare" that, even till this day, stayed with me. These docile sleep study hypochondriacs, more obsessed with symbols, signs, and an unwillingness to accept the unknown than the decadence of a society devouring itself from the inside out, said it's common, in fact, very much human to forget a dream once you awake from that dream, which wasn't so farfetched; however, every now and then, according to Nighttimers, a dream that didn't go away was considered to be, without any physical proof, a message from the "unfettered subconscious."

The dream was upon me. Same time and location. Early morning, when the sun was peaking over the Fourth Trust Building on 23rd, the brilliant rays stabbing through the grimy windows of my loft and bringing out clouds of dust from the recently ruffled bed sheets. As always, in this dream, I was standing in front of a blank canvas, pre-coffee, drowsy eyed and dressed only in Hanes boxer briefs—I could certainly use a sponsor. *How about a shout out?*

Below me was a paintbrush lying on top of a bucket of crimson red paint.

I picked up the brush, dipped it into the paint, and started painting a portrait of myself on the wall-sized canvas before me.

Each stroke I made I aged and withered, starting with my hair—*always, with the hair!*—which went from a thick, lush brunette to a wiry grayish white; eventually, the hair thinned until my scalp was left bare and itchy. Next, my skin became drier like paper and developed wrinkles and liver spots. Each joint ached. Parts of my body sagged. My bones contorted and chattered, like they did in the cartoons. My muscles deteriorated.

Struggling to finish the final touches along the bottom half of the silhouette, I fought off the stagger. Each stroke, more tedious and taxing. Pieces of my body, a finger here, a nose there, snapped off and fell to the floor below like leaves in autumn.

The more I painted, the more I broke until I was left with only one remaining piece: my old, skeletal hand, which clung to the brush.

Reaching out to the canvas, I woke up!

My hand, dead.

I bolted upright from the tangle sheets along the bed.

As I worked blood back into my numb arm by thrashing it around and even beating it against the side of my leg, a wave of panic filled me up inside.

What if the numbness spreads to the rest of my body?

After several minutes of waving around my noodle-like arm with the help of my other hand, the blood rushed back into my arm first, then my hand.

Flexing and curling away a pins and needles-like sensation from my revived hand, I scanned the loft in a state of needed relief.

Compelled by the recent images, as startling as they were, I wrestled through greasy, brown and beige spotted, off-white bed sheets, which, I suddenly realized, hadn't been washed in over six months, maybe longer, and rolled out of bed.

I was caught off guard by those familiar sounds of the tenant banging around upstairs, like she had been known to do at random times of the day, even worse, when I was in the middle of working on a new piece, my resurgence, which often times re-shaped my mode and had me yearning for a free-floating un-processed and unfiltered world where the only untimely disruption came from its natural climate and manmade structures, corporate greed and overreach, and the corrosive disease that permeated its *unnatural* design were justifiably nonexistent. What a terrible neighbor, like a spoiled child throwing hissy fits, who brought nothing but sighs once I heard her door shut above me and from my window, watched her exit from the building with her pink Vera Bradley-inspired duffel bag that she used to carry her gym clothes in hand. She was a light walker as well, which was a plus; however, every now and then, I'd receive a *thud* as if she tripped over her own feet and dropped something heavy, shaking the ceiling above me, resulting in my paint brush to tap dance along the floor; and at times, I found myself thinking: *What in the hell is she doing up there?*

With the comfort of the morning sun bursting through the loft, I walked into my studio and still, despite old—and new—horrors, I was obsessing over the thin, wrinkled bed sheets, the brownish hue to them, and why I hadn't taken them over to the Laundromat yet. *What's the hold up*, Lazy Bones?

The self-deprecating humor spilled over into the unfinished piece of work, a blurry cross between, let's say, Basquiat's neo-expressionism and Pollock's abstract expressionism, which had been dragged out for several weeks now, and the broken artist in me wondered if it'd ever be completed. The piece fell under a tentative title of "Flowers for Mary," *Mary* being a muse named Cassy, who adamantly described herself as a "recent divorcee" who had done the rodeo and circus, which was being a wife to an nonexistent husband, as well as a full-time mother independently raising two kids, who were in college, one at Rutgers and another at Syracuse, and was now looking for a temporary fix during what she so called her, um, "Me Time." Cassy hadn't returned any of my texts in the past week, which I knew was a sure sign that she moved onto another useless fool whom she was going to use like a Black and Decker power tool. I made half-ass attempts to finish the piece—even though, *nothing* was ever finished, per se, only completed by the deadline—but I was uninspired and craving a deep fracture, a new muse to sweep me under a rug. "Flowers for Mary (or Cassy)" started out strong, brutish in every stroke, but now she has come and gone and all that remained of her were unfinished flowers, unable to grow or blossom, wilting.

With the pantry depleted of any coffee—the thought of re-brewing old coffee from yesterday comes to mind—I fished out a couple of dollars from a drawer and threw on some clothes: a pair of wool socks, Jevs, which, like the sheets, needed to pay a visit to the Mat, a Nirvana smiley face T-shirt, a heavy jacket, and a pair of Timberlands, gangsta.

I left the loft and passed the newsstand where a headline from the *New York Times* caught my eye. My ninth grade crush, McKenzie Horrorwich, now a successful defense attorney in Long Island, was a member of Rhodes' legal team that was pushing for a recount in several battleground states after accusations of election fraud. Very little evidence suggested such doing, depending on what bubble you lived in; however, footage of tampering of voting machines recently surfaced on less than credible news outlets, nonetheless, leaving election results up in the air. McKenzie hadn't aged much and I was sure the high schoolers who thought she wouldn't amount to hardly anything were eating their own words as they most often did. She was still as beautiful and witty as ever, despite choosing a profession that faced so much scrutiny and ridicule from the majority of the public. The expression was still there, though, when she spoke to reporters or shot a slanted brow glance toward the cameras. Liquid courage could only take a young man so far to the edge, yet the only thing that was racing through my head fifteen years ago was McKenzie's newly diminished outlook on those of the opposite sex and if I wasn't so reluctant to kiss her open-mouth during an innocent game of "Truth or Dare," I supposed McKenzie might've been scarred for life.

The headline read: "*Rhodes And His Legal Team Face An Uphill Battle.*"

I placed the paper in the stack and as I made my way to Cool Beans, I stopped at a pink flyer stapled next to a MISSING CAT sign on the street post. According to the flyer, the graffiti-influenced artist Seth Greenwell, or most notably known by his moniker, Cloud 9-ish, whom most of his followers would prefer to him as currently "hot" or on his way to become the next Dimzy, was holding an exclusive gala tomorrow night at Lakewood Arts Center. I came across the same flyer yet again on the front window of Cool Beans and then another one posted on the side of a mailbox between Thirteenth Street and City Drive.

Frank Parish bumped into me while I was ripping yet another "Cloud 9-ish" flyer from the side of the Comedy Quarter on Fifteenth Street. He nearly caused me to spill my cup of coffee, but he seemed the least apologetic.

With clouds on my mind, Frank and I small-talked for a couple of minutes, mostly about the weather first. Yesterday, it was in the upper 70's, dry as a bone, sunny, and now, all of a sudden, it felt as though we were in the middle of February, the sky gray and electric, that buzz in the air right before a snow. A former squatter turned line chef at the restaurant Grateful Lamb off Park Run, he wasn't the kind of individual who brought up conversations about the weather—usually, for him, it was last night's pussy feast where he sampled from a spread of various pussy accompanied by craft beer. *What has gotten into him? Has Frank himself finally grown up?*

As he stood bundled up from the cold and unable to further any interesting conversation, I witnessed my father in Frank. A man so grown that I could never imagine him once being a child, let alone having experienced a childhood. Only one memory comes to mind, a distant yet eerily close one: As I sat anxiously with my head down at the kitchen table while one after another obediently shoveling spoonfuls of my mother's soupy casserole into my mouth, I'd listen to my father's heavy silence in between bites, a man who was either unable or unwilling to muster up anything to talk about in order to keep me engaged in domes-tic—even worldly—affairs because the man had the personality and often times, characteristics of a barbel and despite being a man of many trades (after all, he was one hundred proof Italian), never had anything else interesting to say instead of, like, stating the obvious, like the weather. A man named Benito must've had something to say, at least, slightly ear-worthy. He'd remain still, *silent*, instead of encouraging discussion or provoking thoughts and feedback, but rather asked questions which he al-ready knew the answers to or give me lectures on subjects that I was already aware of or make sure I was living—and *acting*—by his standards, according to a society run by a generation of hypocritical halfwits who spoke in "slogans" while creating "rules" to fit their own needs, ones which I had been taught over and over ever since I reached a pivotal age where I achieved the ability to toe the threshold of what was right and what was wrong and delve into that murky area in between which most adults considered "complicated," like making sure my bedroom was clean or making sure I put enough Draino down the sink once every month to keep the pipes from clogging, always mak-ing sure I played by his rules while belittling me and treating me—as well as my mother—as if we weren't worthy of the most basic freedom, which was independent thought: if that's not a definition of a person wanting control, *not* compliance, I don't know what is. In other countries, some people might go so far as to call it tyranny. He died right about the time I reached a stage of rebelling against everything my parents had taught me. Edu-cation, religion: in other words, when I reached an age of reason. When I glimpsed back at him and tried to rehash any good memories, all I saw was a summer heat in that angry red face of his, whenever he drove me to Saturday morning soccer practice in a state of pent-up frustration while I sat within arm's reach in the passenger seat too frightened to speak or whenever he'd *supervise* over Wynona and I at the park in Coney Island and never take his eye from us as if he was waiting for that very moment we misbehaved—mainly me doing all the misbehaving—so he could drag my ass to the closest bathroom stall to spank me until I was sore and red. He was a two-season man, Benito was, summer on the outside, winter on the inside; every now and then, whenever I was reminded of him, I tried to play detective and piece together the inception of his deep-seated rage. *Was it the burden of having to drop his pursuits or dreams*—whatever they might've been—*in order to raise two children?* His father, Alfonzo, whom I had only met once at a much earlier age and the only memory I mentally owned of him was the buttery smell of Whiskey on his breath and his bottomless appetite for boiled shrimp and womanly fingernails, which he said were used to peel shells—or snort cocaine—was (from what I was told) a man who nurtured with the brute force of his hand, long coke nails or not. When I thought back about these men who roared before me, I wondered if the main reason why I never had children was because of a looming fear of one day becoming one of these figures, who now seemed so ancient yet, at the same time, so relevant to me—*Why are we, as children, the recipients of our parents' misfortunes?*

Stella grabbed the corner of my eye—or at least, a woman, who could pass as her twin, riding away in a taxi—and as I stood waywardly with my heels gripping the edge of the curb and preventing myself from falling into the busy street, a swallow of sorrow burrowed deep into the pit of my stomach before spreading and paralyzing my entire body, momentarily overwhelming me with a great, uncorrectable emptiness. *What is she up to these days?* If so (more than likely, she isn't), is *she on the way to a photo shoot for a digital femme magazine like* Bare? Or, *an in-depth interview with Ellis?* Or, *a date with whatever pop star who was currently* trending? Stella didn't have much of a relationship with both of her parents, mainly her father, and I think that was one of the reasons why we got along so well, well, at least, at the beginning. *Did Stella see that emotionally vacant man whom I was destined to become?* I found it more than strange—even disturbing—how Stella's mood changed, more like flipped like a coin, ever since she spoke to Wendy, who didn't possess a filter, especially when it came to sharing "The Family Secrets of a Ruffiano." It should've been a *title* of a half-cookbook half-guide, providing all the right recipes to the downfall of our bloodline, as well as what-to-do and what-*not*-to-do when it came to severing such haunted legacies. As days went by, I wondered if it was my father who Stella saw in me. The often "jadedness" that my mother mentioned to me and Wynona—and if she had mentioned it to us, then it wouldn't have been so outlandish that she mentioned it to Stella.

I parted ways with Frank, who was still hungover from the previous night and wasn't doing much good at small talk, and walked back to my loft.

Before heading in, I received a call from the curator, Anubis Shuffly—yes, his parents named him after an Egyptian god.

"Next month's gallery is off," he told me upfront, as if he was peeling off a Band-Aid.

His main reasons for the last-minute cancellation, at least the ones I managed to squeeze from him: He didn't feel confident in the turnout. He felt as though it was too risky for a. . . all of a sudden, he struggled to speak, as words wedged in the back of his throat. *"Irrelevant artist,"* I knew he wanted to say. Instead, he attempted to explain the turnout and how I hadn't been "around lately," which was another way of saying my artist value, my "street cred," if you will, had declined over the past ten years and I was no longer the same Dimzy that painted "An Evening Walk," which rested in its cozy spot in the New York Art Museum. He went on to claim it was the times we lived in, how people, a society, this bastard of a bravely ruinous society, no longer separated the *art* from the *artist*; instead, this new society leaned more heavily on the "artist" even if the art was shit.

Being as blunt as I could, I told Anubis how I saw his viewpoint: If so, "it is the final nail in the coffin."

"I'm sorry, Dim," Anubis said with that familiar rattle in his voice. *He's lying,* I could tell from his tone.

My former roommate, Francis Blaylock, who was one of the contributing factors to my early success as a young artist after he intervened in a time of desperation with his persistence in helping me kick a yearlong struggle brought on by my sister's death, carried the same rattle in his voice when he told me straight to my face that Riley was "no good" for me. In a way, despite having, more or less, rescued me for an inevitable death of drowning myself with Tennessee bourbon after a slippery pattern of heavy binge-drinking, Francis, to me, still didn't receive any free passes when it came to the whole "Riley Situation." Riley and I had been off and on for four years prior to me walking in on her with her legs spread open for a man whom I once referred to as a friend—How in the hell could Francis do such a thing, especially after what the two of us had been through with the passing of his mother and *Wynona, my sister, whom I discovered dead while I was visiting my mother for the weekend? Even till this day, I couldn't get that vivid image out of my head: Wynona's pale, lifeless body slumped over the footstool in front of the glowing TV, Conan cracking jokes over the dark silence, my sister, gone; in fact, had been gone for at least three hours, I'd soon learn after the autopsy report was released, as well as a toxicology test, which found enough fentanyl in her system to kill a full grown elephant.* The two weeks building up to the grand unveil I suspected that Riley was starting to lose interest in me. She grew more distant from me and possessed the characteristics of your sad-eyed angel. Only two instances I witnessed that glow in her eyes, the one where it sucked me up from my Emo-Hot Topic darkness like an unyielding tractor beam, the first one being when a friend of a friend first introduced me to Riley outside Crown Theatres (She poked fun at my first name, which shared the same one as the dark short haired lady who played Patrick Swayze's love interest in the movie, *Ghost*, as she puffed on a Cowboy Killer down to the filter—later she'd go on to quit— yet, regardless of my distaste for the smell of cigarettes, as well as the typical response I received whenever I told people my name, which was short for Dimedius and in Latin, meant "half," never had such a medical term like secondhand smoke seemed so insignificant or dare I say, tolerable). The second instance, which led to a sidebar of other unnerving instances, was *every* time she was either around or in the vicinity of Francis. The part that tore me up inside: Riley trying to hide that glow in front of me, as if my presence had become toxic. For two weeks, I tried to pull everything I could out of my friend, to put an end to the charade, like asking him questions, catching him in a lie. Wearing the disguise of a friend, he was impenetrable, his acting alone, Oscar-worthy, and ultimately, infuriating. I knew that the only way to get what I needed out of Francis was with a blunt instrument. *Isn't that how it works?* You need to take a sledgehammer, in my case, Francis's head and crack it wide open in order to scoop out the truth within the messy remains.

As I was about to hang up with Anubis, my stomach knotted up, both of my hands turned into damp towels. The door to my loft was cracked open; fingernail-sized pieces of wooden debris, as well as screws were scattered below on the floor like evidence. The panel along the side of the doorway crushed in and crumpled. The doorknob hung from a couple of metal rods like a loose tooth.

"You okay, Dimzy?" asked Anubis.

After I didn't answer, the tone in his voice turned to one of deep concern.

With caution, I stepped inside my loft and discovered items strewed around the loft as if the entire place was recently raided. The strangest finding—well, not so strange—the artwork inside my studio was untouched. The furniture was overturned, including the sofa, the kitchen table, and a couple of chairs. All of my appliances and equipment were missing: stereo, TV, a microwave that I had recently replaced, which appeared to be yanked out of the mount on the wall, as well as my beloved toaster.

"Who the hell steals a toaster?"

"Toaster?" Anubis said over the phone. "Demi, what happened?"

"Someone broke into my place," I said, walking into my studio.

Each piece was accounted for—*phew.*

"Did they steal anything?" asked Anubis.

"Just a couple of things," I uttered and drew my attention to my most recent work.

I took one last look around the rest of the loft, witnessed the chaos of things everywhere, and afterwards, brought my eyes back to my latest painting, "Flowers for Mary." Not a thing, yet real.

Like the inside of the studio, the painting appeared untouched. *Had the thief made it to the studio?* I came across a couple of footprints covered in mud and street grim below a couple of other paintings, but as I gathered before, none appeared at all disturbed.

The gritty sound of the glass vase that Amelia had bought me rolled over the kitchen counter and shattered along the floor. I flinched from the *piercing* sound of shattering glass. I zoned out for a moment, as the sound of glass shattering left behind a *ringing* in my ears. On a lazy, rainy day, Amelia bought me that purple Prince-inspired vase covered in sequins, which she thought would help spruce up my place and add more of a "hominess" to it. She was an interior designer—and quite good at her job—spending her days decorating the penthouses of 1%'s and dreaming of one day having her very own reality TV show on the Home Network. Only three months prior I asked Amelia to marry me over an unforgettable dinner at Primo's Steakhouse on Bookie Square. She said yes. Fast-forward two months later, Amelia and I moved in together and I couldn't stop smiling despite a part of me shooing away doubts. After a couple of months of living with Amelia, I came to realize the hard way of her little habits, which, I knew, could get under my skin if I let them, such as listening to—as well as often smelling—her blatant flatulence throughout the day and recoiling in disgust as she'd let them rip, unapologetically, at the dinner table while we were eating takeout—which we ate a lot—or unabatedly crop-dusting me while I was working or even worse—which, to me, turned out to be the ultimate deal breaker—taking a whiff of a silent one while we were in bed together, a Dutch-oven, which I believed it was called. She had other intolerable habits, too, like biting her fingernails until they bled or drinking herself sick whenever I had friends over (it was always my friends because, except for the random strangers she met on the subway, the only types of friends she had were fair-weather) or finally—which wasn't a habit but, more or less, a red flag telling me that she had given up on being "sexy"—the degradation of her clothing style, which made me wonder: *Was the person whom I originally asked to marry all a front? Or, was it my passiveness or lack of criticism destroying her womanhood?* She replaced six hundred dollar dresses with ten-dollar hoodies, skirts for holey jeans, leggings (which drove me wild) for baggy sweatpants. Whenever the two of us were out in public—which was rare—she never dolled herself up; and at times, she'd wear the same clothes as she wore the day before. As Amelia gained more weight and that natural beauty of hers started to fade by the day, I concluded that I had made a mistake. In Amelia's eyes, she had found her own "Prince" and that was that. She acted as if she didn't have to put any more work into our relationship. Amelia's dreams were no longer *her* dreams, yet they were mine.

After I walked a few laps around the loft, I mustered the courage to call the police; however, they didn't show until two hours later, and the excuse as to why they took so long was that they've had a "busy morning." I gave them my statement and stepped outside for a breath where two other cops were hanging out on the sidewalk. One of them had no interest in setting up the roadblocks or calling every cop in the city in order to catch some thief who stole my property, yet the jerk was too busy drooling over a piece of tail talking to her boyfriend outside the Quickie Mart next to my building. She was wearing leggings.

The air of arrogance and superiority reminded me of the bad "news cops" you hear about time and time again on TV and through word of mouth, the one with only his race (*white* or *black* or *any color in between*, depending on the race of the suspect) and title (*cop*) attached to deliberately constructed headlines to draw reaction—and rage—and after a few minutes of talking to him but not getting much substance out of him, it was clear to me that he had more important issues to deal with right now and none of them involved doing his job.

I parted from the cops and as I was about to head back inside my building, I noticed a crowd forming along the street corner.

People dropped what they were doing, even went out of their way to follow the crowd, including workers, like Willis, who ran a food truck, Great Ribs, as well as a bus driver and several construction workers. I soon learned that a man with salt and pepper hair, sporting a green windbreaker, perhaps in his late sixties, who was lying on the side of the road and grabbing his chest was the cause of so much attention. The man lost consciousness.

As I shouldered through the growing crowd and poked my head over another pedestrian's shoulder, I watched the light go out in his eyes. He died there on the street, face inches away from a grimy puddle. His sudden death caused more attention and before I scrambled back to the sidewalk, I was surrounded by dozens of people, some deeply worried and heartbroken while others trembling with uncontrollable excitement, as if they were about to capture something truly glorious. The concept, like roads, opened up before me. . .

Lines crossed.

Avenues: intersected and connected.

Purged by *fire*.

While walking to Zadie's Art Supplies on East Village, I couldn't stop thinking about Wynona days after her passing. Despite having few friends around the time of her passing, except for a pocket-sized gangster drug dealer, Julio, whom Wendy despised and called the cops on multiple times after she found him plunging needles into Wynona's veins on the back porch in the middle of the night, as well as two other lowlifes with vacant backgrounds whom Wynona occasionally referred to as "Just Some Guy" or "A Kid Who Went To Dawkins," Wynona had a decent turnout at the visitation, as well as an over-the-top funeral held at Light of the World Church (the Wynona I knew would've loathed such pageantry, being that she couldn't tolerate being the center of attention, yet, her rebellious high school record, i.e. assaulting a tenth grade English teacher, resulting in suspension, or pouring #FF0000 red paint all over the basketball court, or setting fire to Dawkins Bobcats' flag in front of the school, proved to contradict her true nature—at least the one I had grown so accustomed to—and were only the outbursts of a young woman struggling to pursue more constructive and lasting outlets to funnel such deeply-rooted disdain for a label such as "Demi's *Little Sister*"); however, it was Wendy's idea to drain her savings account to give her daughter an elaborate funeral. Everybody who attended Wynona's funeral knew, even Wynona's "victimized" friends who slurred and mumbled final respects, it was an act of celebration, not that Wynona would be missed, which, to most of us, she would, for sure, despite her antics, but rather a gathering to somberly cheer her departure—in other words, a Good Radiance Party.

Where did everything go wrong? When did it get to the point where Wynona believed the entire world was conspiring against her? For someone who couldn't bare the center stage, it was attention she craved. If the tragic tale of The Ruffiano's were made into a film, she'd consider herself as a leading role; yet throughout most of my adulthood, she remained absent. A girl who grew up too fast yet, regardless of her age, she was forever stuck on a number that she couldn't shake. One who was often spoken about in past tense, *never* the present. I didn't know how bad the addiction had gotten until I visited Wynona just a few days after Thanksgiving, which would be her *final* Thanksgiving. My mother had given up on Wynona, wasn't monitoring her, and treating her as if she was too far-gone to rescue. "On her own." Imagine a nineteen-year-old's head below the water while she was sinking in an ocean covered in life rafts, both arms flailing above water, drowning, and every time she managed to grab hold of a raft, she'd reject it, as if she wasn't ready to surface for a breath. The poison coursing through Wynona's veins was keeping her under. Figuratively, it liked water and it'd do everything in its power to keep "outsiders" from throwing its perfect little host into one of those *homes* where the only water that literally existed was the kind you drank.

Was this the last branch of the Ruffiano treeline? A cursed bloodline with a pathway to extinction and I, the sole survivor of such putrid blood, was living in denial about my own mortality, as well as reclaiming my rightful title as "Artist of The Year." As time and technology moved at a breakneck pace and each moment was one where its causality was either lagging behind and struggling to keep up or surrendering to his or her ultimate demise, such branded titles were reduced from that year, that month, that day, that hour, that minute (as with Stella, *who's currently trending?*) to that very moment. But who was I to fool when it came to understanding people? People built you up in order to tear you down. Like a child full with imagination and potential constructing towers of Legos, a perfectly flawless city where no rules existed, but rather the ones that shaped his raw logic, only to destroy it afterwards based on a bitter—yet often—sweet mantra of "*Why not?*"

I walked through automatic doors where an exhausted elderly woman stood carrying a shopping basket of artificial white flowers. Her clothing attire, which consisted of beige slacks, a black button down sweater with busy yellowish zigzag patterns to match a same colored cloche covering her wiry gray hair, and blue surgical gloves that conceal a medical condition, all of it old, faded, raggedy, and appeared as if she had been wearing the wardrobe for a duration of an entire generation and beyond. My mother, Wendy—who was residing in a home, not rehab but "retirement," in South Carolina called Green Meadows, not my idea, hers—used to cling to attire, outdated or not.

Throughout my childhood, Wendy wore the same black silk summer dress about three or four times a week; and every now and then, especially after my father passed, I'd find it lying around the house, either on a coffee table or draped over a couch whenever she had one of her friends over. She had a lot of them, so many it was hard to keep up with. I only knew a couple of these "friends'" names and most of the time, whenever she wasn't hastily—and on more than one occasion, unexpectedly— ushering strange men from the house, they'd hardly speak a word to me and whatever conversations, as forced as they were, would arise, they usually came with a series of gaffes, awkward pauses, and useless "get-to-know-you" chit chat to conceal their true intentions with my mother. I knew the game, and how she was playing it. Like I couldn't hear her and her lecherous *friends* upstairs whenever I came home from school or a friend's house. Once, when she was running errands, I snuck into her bedroom without permission and inspected every inch of it, trying to pinpoint the origin of pounding noise that had plagued my innocent ears. Maybe it was Chandler books I read as a teen or *Dick Tracy* comic books I devoured as a young child. I had an obsession with searching for evidence, and in my mother's case, it didn't take me long to find dimples and tiny cracks in the painting on the wall behind the headrest or all four legs of the master bed shifted slightly from the small crater-like indentations in the shag carpet. Her excuse whenever I questioned her was that Bill—or *was it Dillon?*—was working on the upstairs toilet. I knew right then and there that I wasn't the only one who was a recipient of somebody *else's* misfortune.

The two of us shared eye contact; and in that moment, I witnessed confusion in her swirly, worn gaze, as if she was struggling to make sense of my presence. In her other hand, she was holding a fistful of four crinkled dollars. I acknowledged her with a civil nod; and in return, she cracked open her mouth, revealing a grin full of black, crooked teeth.

Maintaining a steady pace, I moved past her and headed straight to the canvas aisle, and didn't waste too much time picking out supplies.

Lastly, I found the right size, which was a 24 x 36 canvas.

After I paid for the art supplies, I ran into a shady-looking man on the street, who looked as if knew a thing or two when it came to "illegal" goods.

I asked him a question, which had been on my mind ever since I saw the poor man dying on the street outside my loft.

He said he could help me out.

More than likely, the man, who called himself "Mac," might be ripping me off; however, it was one of those moments where an opportunity presented itself and the universe was, for a split second, opening a window to let me inside. What other reason would someone go out of his way to help out some whiny artist whom he didn't even know? Maybe he saw something in my eyes when I asked him if he could get what I needed or perhaps he, too, could take full advantage of the sticky predicament I was in? Or, could he simply see through me as if the recent events that unfolded turned my body into the translucent pod of a crustacean life form and each thought spinning round and round underneath my slick, velvety flesh was like a projection of moving pictures? I leaned toward the latter.

Mac reached for his pocket—I anticipated a smoke, a knife, or perhaps even the item I was in search for—but he pulled out a phone instead. One that flipped open. Possibly a burner. Mac hit up his "guy" while we took a shortcut through a seedy alleyway. We stopped near a dumpster overflowing with soggy cardboard, melted plastic toys, and rusty shopping carts. Constantly checking my shoulder, I made sure I wasn't walking into an ambush. Except for the rats everywhere, Mac and I were the only humans in the alleyway until a clunky backdoor next to the dumpster *squeaked* open. . .

A tall man, who was pushing seven feet, stepped outside. Each feature on his face appeared disproportionate, like Mr. Potato Head was given different parts from an older model that didn't properly fit into place. In his hands he was holding a dirty oil-spotted rag. The man, who gave no name, asked Mac if I was "the guy." Slightly more timid from the man's presence, Mac pocketed the flip phone and answered shortly.

The tall man pulled back the dirty rag, unveiling a revolver—Smith and Wesson, from what I could tell. Part of the model number, 629, had been crossed out with a blade. I was immediately intrigued by the "red tape" around the handle.

"This here is the Dragon," Mac said, more aroused. "Shoots dat fire, you feel me."

I asked, "How much?"

"Two hundy," he said.

I pulled out my life savings from my pocket.

"What's up with the canvas?" asked the tall man.

"I'm going to paint my masterpiece," I said, as I gathered the money.

I was way more than a few dollars short. To my name, I only had a hundred and eighty-seven cents in change (two quarters, three dimes, a nickle, and two pennies covered in street grime), but the tall man didn't seem to mind at all; in fact, from the constant surveying of the alleyway, he appeared as if he couldn't get rid of the piece soon enough, all of course for reasons strictly unknown. Only one that came to mind: the gun was "hot," as in it might've been connected to an illegal activity, like a crime, burglary, a shooting, even a murder.

I handed the tall man his money; and in return, he handed me Dragon.

The tall man broke off a few wrinkly bills from the wad of cash and slipped them to Mac as what Mac deemed as *his* "finder's fee."

The two men didn't question my business, as I parted ways with them.

In a way, they already knew.

Once I arrived back at my loft, I set the canvas on an easel in the center of my studio; and as I sat down in the chair directly in front of the canvas, my thoughts spiraled out of control while self-diagnosing my path and if the path always ended right here. All the wrong choices I ever made throughout my life presented themselves before me as I placed a round in the chamber. All the mistakes fleshed out and highlighted. Each thought diseased by a life that was and what *could've* been. Tormented by a never-ending list of could'ves, a spiral of shame that left me waning: I *could've* kissed Megan without losing my dinner, *could've not* taken all the blame for Wynona and her misdoings and let her learn the hard way, *could've* left Riley at the first whiff of suspicion, *could've* stood up to those men who took advantage of my emotionally vulnerable mother; *could've* told my father that I loved him before he died even though I knew that he knew that he thought I carried so much resentment for him. I *could've*, I *could've*, *could've*.

As I spiraled farther downward, I slid the end of the barrel into my mouth.

I could've chosen another life in another body.

Perhaps these questions would be answered in another chapter.

Perhaps I was sick and tired of all that filler in the middle and I was ready to skip to the end.

What *would* the last page look like?

I guess, *That's my curiosity.*

⊠

IN a clothed blackness each voice among the ambience of a chatty crowd becomes clearer as the number of voices reduce in size, making each word attached to their voices more perceivable. The critics roar, some in great delight and envy or both, while others, over-thinkers, ones who speak as though the world revolves around themselves, gripe and groan, soggy words ooze from their loose lips like phlegm, trailing off in slurs and bursts of uncontrollable laughter—what a scene! Eventually, the crowd dims. Doors shut and slam. Blackness is peeled back, revealing a man with a mustache. He's staring down at me with shades of disgust and speaking: "Who in the hell would buy such a thing?"

Another man from behind: *One disturbed individual. That's who.*

He covers me in coarse-black and off I go, being carried into another room where I wait in silence. More doors closing. Rumbles. More voices, blunt. Street ambience. A man, whose voice sounds familiar, is selling short ribs on the street corner. More hands, this time coarser, grip me, loading me into a dirty truck where I hear more voices, like my own, *crazy* voices, disturbed, ones of pain and despair, one of a man crying out for forgiveness, another of a woman seething with rage, shouting villainously, *I'll show you, you incompetent pieces of dog shit, you'll see, you will all see!* I'm driven through the city, catching each and every bump in the road. The engine purrs. More street noise and ambience.

"*Two more stops*," the man says. "*Then, we grab some food.*"

The other one: "*How about Gino's?*"

"*Fine by me. I'm starving.*"

I'm carried up flights of stairs. The man breathes heavier.

Then, silence.

A great, strange silence.

Once more, after I'm mounted, the blackness is pulled back from the corners of the frame, revealing yet another room, the living room of an apartment.

The woman from earlier, Phelan, is holding the black sheet in her hand. She drops it on a sofa and switches on three spotlights underneath me, slightly obscuring the hard gaze she's wearing as she takes a few steps back and studies me.

She leaves and turns off the lights behind her, leaving me alone inside a dark apartment where I obsess over a line of blank white canvas positioned in an empty room across from me.

Night falls.

Once more, I wait in darkness.

The city lights outside the living room comfort me.

Keys *jingle*.

The door opens, a sword of light shines throughout the apartment.

Phelan has a guest—a man.

I hear Phelan say his name, Rob, a couple of times, once when she's reaching for a wine glass in an upper cabinet above the stovetop and another time when she slides his hands from her breasts as he "attempts" to make out with Phelan, who has me wondering if it's the same "Rob" who she was talking about earlier. The two step into the living room. This "Rob" character's cheeks are cloudy red, and he's trying to rearrange the bulge in his pants from the recent diss.

He tags along Phelan's tail like a puppy dog.

Phelan walks up to me, Rob not too far behind.

"Holy shit," Rob says, amazed from the sight of me hanging on the wall. "Is that what I think it is?"

Phelan's lack of answer is the answer.

Rob steps closer to me, again, studies me.

"Phelan," he says, not once taking his eyes from me, "where did you get this? This isn't real, is it? If it is—I mean, it can't be—this is pretty dark. . . "

The tone in his voice shifts, as he sniffs the wall around me. He crinkles his nose in disgust.

He glances over his shoulder at Phelan, who's standing coolly as she takes a sip of her Pinto Noir.

Rob sticks his finger directly in my face—or at least, what I believed to be a piece of my face.

"Is that a bullet hole?" Rob asks.

"Thought maybe the teeth and chunks of dried brain matter gave it away."

"Phelan," Rob says, a smile curling on his face, "what is it, really?"

"*Morbid Curiosity.*"

"Morbid Curiosity?"

"If you look closely," Phelan says from behind, "the streaks of blood running down the canvas look like people. If you listen, you can hear them talking."

"Streaks of blood," Rob repeats more skeptically. "You haven't changed one bit, Phelan?"

He waves his hand at me as if I'm not worth his time.

"So," he says loosely while facing Phelan, "you wanted to talk?"

Phelan coyly shrugs.

"Yeah," she says simply. "Sure."

"About?" Rob says, moving toward Phelan.

Clearly uncomfortable by Rob's presence, she takes another sip of wine.

Before he moves in to kiss her, she turns away and walks toward the bedroom next to the living room. She teasingly waves her finger at Rob, who dumbly pursues her into the room.

As he steps inside the other room, he gawks at the blank white canvases positioned in a sickle-shape line from one end of the room to the other.

Phelan lures Rob into the center of the room, in front of the center canvas.

"Wait here," Phelan whispers into Rob's ear and kisses him on the neck.

"What's going on, Phelan?" asks Rob, as he examines painter's plastic covering the hardwood floor.

Phelan leaves the room.

Rob calls out to her but doesn't receive a response.

She walks into another room, a dimly lit room, and returns with a strange object with a long wooden handle by her side.

As Rob downs the glass of wine, Phelan conceals a sledge-hammer behind her back.

Rob, who appears curious by the unusual setup of canvases inside the room, faces Phelan, who's now leaning up against the doorway.

The handle of the sledgehammer slips father down her grip, that heavy metal hammer dropping to the hardwood floor, creating what I can only perceive as the sound of a soft yet quaking, a novel yet strangely recognizable *thud. . .*

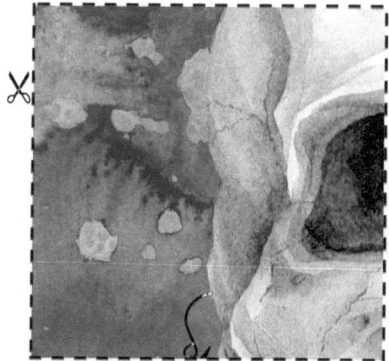

FYRWHL

EVENTUALLY, the *thuds* coming from the inside of the trunk stopped.

Blasting a hand-me-down, corporate-sponsored rock station with the letter K used alternatively in the call sign on FM radio in order to drown out the witch who was adding an extra kick drum to the track, Michael adjusted the volume and thought to himself: *About fucking time.*

As he turned down the volume to an elevator-music tone, he could finally breathe a little bit easier, opposed to carrying around what felt like a cinderblock pressed against his chest.

Leaning back in the driver's seat while removing one hand from the steering wheel, Michael, as though anticipating those *thuds*, heard the metallic sound of a latch opening. He shot a wide-eyed glance in the rear view mirror, only to find the upper part of the backseat slightly cracked open and moments away from falling forward.

Before the backseat could fully open, he rotated around in the seat and with his right hand—his left gripping the steering wheel—he pushed the seat close, causing the metal bar of the latch to catch.

Blinding headlights filled the inside of the car, forcing Michael to face-forward.

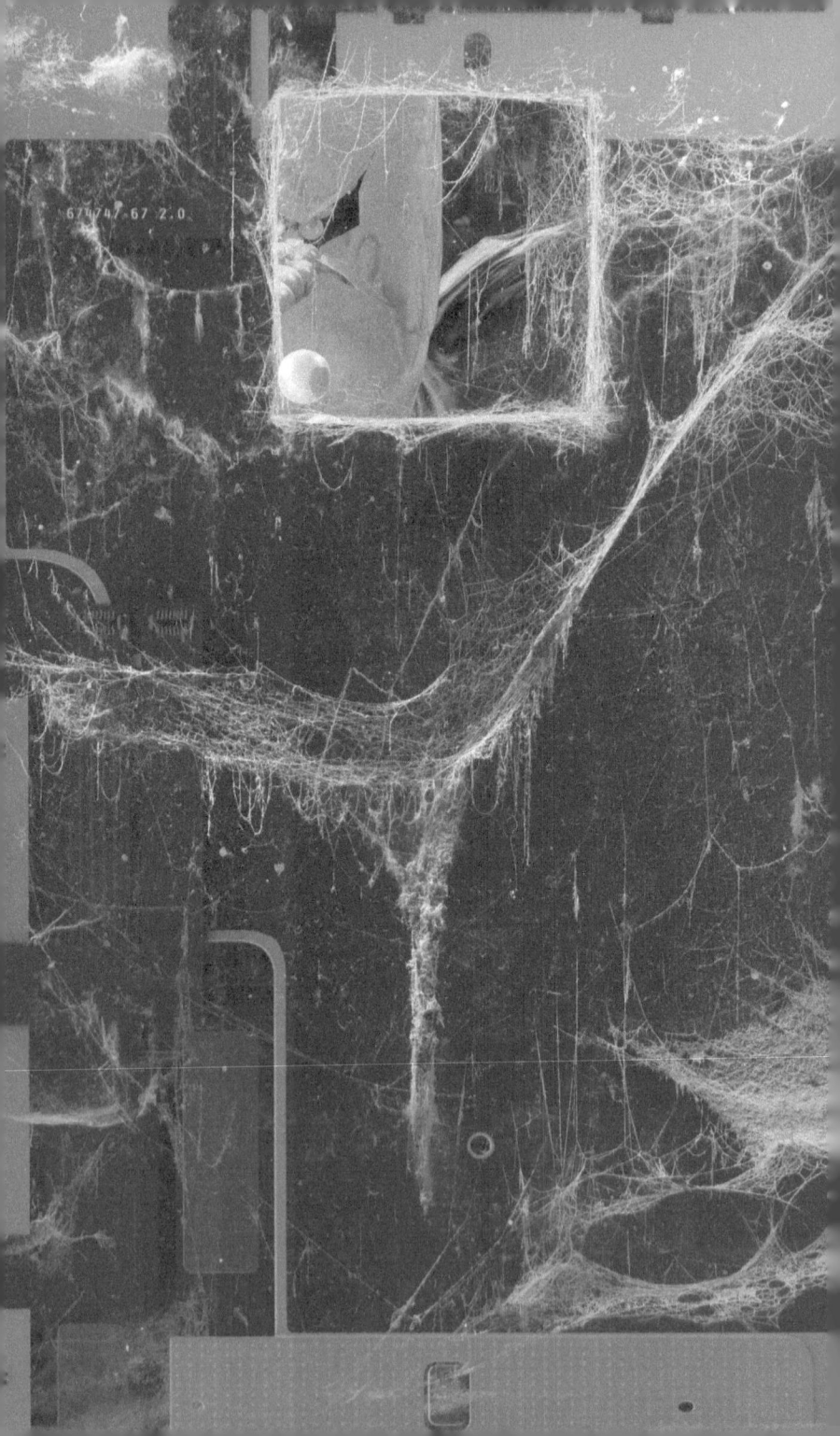

With a windshield of bright light punching him across the face, a car horn blared out, the honker holding down the horn until the driver veered away from the opposite lane.

Coming within inches from sideswiping the passing car, that driver, Michael, corrected and with both hands gripping the steering wheel, his knuckles appearing bloodless, returned to his side of the highway. Over the wailing car horn, he heard the soaking-wet roar of the other driver screaming out through his cracked window, "*Asshole!*" over the murmurings of talk radio.

With all the color draining from his face, Michael trembled in the seat. He glanced in the rear view mirror and for a second, watched the two red lights of the other car fade into the night darkness. He told himself that he should've been dead. The thought of death eventually faded and he sat in silence for the next ten minutes or so, thinking about all the people in his life who would miss him. The list was embarrassingly short.

But really, when it came to narrowing down those on the list, there was only one or two who remained steady at the top of his Billboard of Bullshit.

Number One on the chart was Robin.

Despite how much over the past couple of years Michael's love for Robin had devolved into a deep-seated hatred where the darkly fantastical thought of creatively murdering her and disposing of her body, or what remained of her body, spread to certain facial gestures, Robin, well-aware of her husband's growing irritability, wasn't going anywhere anytime soon, and these so-called quarterly "*conference trips*" where managers from all over the country gathered in the lame ballrooms of overpriced hotels to share ways of how to improve the business—he'd lie straight to his wife's face about how being a manager for one of the nation's most popular and influential fast-food joints offered him plenty of elbow room to grow both personally and financially, even though Michael's store #D70040 was scheduled to shutter next Monday, which meant, by the time he returned home, he'd have to make up yet another excuse not to see his wife—had no bearing whatsoever about Robin's decision to stay.

The ball was in Michael's court.

Robin would even go so far as to say that Mike was one of the greatest ball-hogs of all time and that, in all her years of being with another man, she never met one who only drove on a one-way street; in fact, he named the entire street after his name. He erected his own billboards—the other kind—along the side of roads, each one congratulating his morose attitude, which had turned into a trait, positive in one cultural cycle, negative in the very next. Over time, it had become clear to Michael that his wife recognized the delicate line separating thoughts—Robin didn't want to picture what was going on inside that violent mind of his but she could only imagine from the subtle ticks and reflexes along his face—from actions had developed into quite a loose and dangerously-unraveling thread and that she, despite the morbidly-grim outcome, deliberately and internally cheered on its glorified unravel, as though it was her ultimate payback from her soon-to-be grave. She'd win, in the end, he knew, and win big. Only sour wives haunt the dead.

Besides the silent abuse, Robin was too dependent on Michael, his income, his house, even his cat, Spark, who melted her heart the moment he laid those lime-green eyes on her—and in cat terms, "claimed" her, first the backside of her leg, then her hand, then her lap.

Then, the closest runner up, after her latest breakout single, "*I Used Up All of Your Money From Child Care to Tat Murals on My Body*," his estranged daughter, Louse, the entitled brat formerly known as Louise, named after her mother's favorite poet. Louise, who always had a thing for metal, both the material and the music genre (Michael blames himself for blasting *Black Wolverine* on the way to drop her off at preschool and suspects that maybe lead singer Nails and his unique-sounding voice played a pivotal part in her metallic upbringing—the guy had a set of pipes that'd make a piper sound like a baby), was currently enrolled at a trade school in Rhode Island that specialized in welding.

Unlike Robin, Michael's baby's momma, Névé, who gave birth to Louise out of wedlock a few months after Michael dropped out of community college, had no tolerance for Michael's bullshit and wouldn't even make it on Michael's list. The feelings, though, were not at all mutual—Névé being Michael's first and only true love, and for Névé, Michael being a possessive, uncompromising individual who would never meet her halfway with any uncertain decisions.

Post-Névé, Michael realized, through much trial and error, mostly error accompanied by pinching regret, self-pity, and at times, a hangover which lasted for two days, that trying to find another Névé was a lost cause, and the only women who captured his eye after Névé were the partially-thawed leftovers of those who participated in The Rodeo and ultimately, felt the sting of Bull's horns (*hopeless romantics who lived vicariously through characters in beloved rom-coms, bitter divorcees who had, over the years, collected enough dust downstairs that they needed a high-powered shop-vac to look presentable for a night out in town, mysterious daddy-never-paid-me-enough-attention types whose intention remained shrouded by shadows and icy-cold glares that could* freeze *a sucker dead in his tracks, a cured military wife who went straight AWOL on a trigger-happy husband who had enough testosterone to defeat a Persian Empire and then, afterwards, sleep like a newborn baby, a victim of abuse who absolutely refused to be a victim even though she unknowingly wore some dirt bag of a designer called "Down-and-Out" on The Concrete Carpet*), each one of them missing that secret ingredient, and like Robin, who didn't taste as good as the original, except for that late-night chili dip, which tasted much better the second day. Michael's Chili Days were over, gone, reduced to the faded stains on a retired bed sheet, which had been shelved inside a hallway closet until Robin had her girlfriends over for one of her quarterly Wine-O-Cues at the house. Michael was forever stuck with week-old casserole that, when fully-ingested, turned his gut into a fucking blender.

The *thuds* returned, this time sporadic and not as constant.

Since he was starting to see fewer cars on the highway—except for the one car with a whining talk radio wet blanket in the background that he nearly hit head-on—he decided to pull off on the side of the highway. He waited for the final car to pass before he stepped out of the car.

With the highway falling back to night darkness, he reconsidered his options and not one of them included politely asking her to stop kicking. For Michael, he had reached the point where he was only left with one option, and it sat on the passenger seat: a 40-ounce bottle of malt liquor that he purchased at a gas station. The bottle was nearly half-full but the amount of alcohol in the bottle didn't favor him, legally-speaking, considering his

"BAC" levels (blood alcohol content) were already well above the legal limit for the state of Arizona: Six shots of *One-Eye* whiskey, then, on top of that, one drink of *Tommy Gun Gin* and tonic, then, on top of that, four beers, three of them domestic and one an IPA that a bar-maggot pushed on him as if he was a spokesman for the maker of the IPA after he struck out with an all-around 10 seated by herself at the bar, the third strikeout with, not a 10, but rather a 6 or 7, who, after his second beer and well-adjusted goggles, looked more like a 9 if he caught her face in good lighting. The 9, who had bumped into the Michael-type numerous times at Jimmy's Lounge and Spirits, made a scene after Michael invaded her space despite having been told to jump off a bridge, warranting the attention of the concerned bartender who, in return, called over a bouncer, who had been hitting the gym all week, pumping those muscular fibers, preparing for the weekend in case he had to strangle some disruptive pencil-neck who, after a drink or three, magically grew balls made of brass.

With the decision finalized, he grabbed the bottle of *Pimp Juice* from the passenger seat, emptied it out onto the highway, and with the bottle in hand, stumbled toward the trunk.

She had already seen my face, Michael told himself.

Throughout his drunken thoughts, he clung onto the very idea that he could—and most definitely, would—make it out of this mess without having any involvement in the woman's inevitable disappearance. Despite the many patrons, as well as bystanders (their statements, if any, would be inadmissible due to their altered states where a person's judgment was about as reliable as a two-lane riddled with potholes and missing street signs) who witnessed his face throughout the haze of a night, Michael was identified three times on video, once on a surveillance cam across from The Lounge, which captured an intoxicated Michael stumbling his way into the parking lot moments after Brute-A-Tron kicked his horny ass to the curb, the second time on a surveillance cam outside a Fill-R-Up gas station where Michael put twenty dollars worth of gasoline inside his car, then, lastly the overhead camera behind the cashier inside the convenient store where Michael purchased a 40-ounce of *Pimp Juice*. If it were any other night, the notion alone of being visibly drunk on camera wouldn't have caused him to lose any sleep. It was the moments soon after he drove away from the gas station which made that video footage crucial in choosing his next decision.

As he stood in front of the locked trunk, he struggled to hold a single thought in his head, except for the idea that had stayed with him ever since his first DUI when he was twenty-four years old, not the one about waking up the next morning convinced that he played an innocent law-abiding citizen who wasn't at fault but rather, based on a corrupt legal system that never factored in his self-proclaimed *"excellent driving skills while under the influence of alcohol,"* constrained to clean up the mess of a reckless, suicidal pedestrian who was playing a deadly game of chicken-roulette by walking alongside a dimly-lit highway in the middle of the night, but the one about being locked in a cage for the remainder of his life—that idea.

After the DUI conviction when he was twenty-four going on thirty, after all those lawyer expenses, after having to blow into that hackable mechanical cock of a device in order to start up his vehicle, after shamefully standing in front of the judge who held his fate in the palm of his silky smooth hands, only one takeaway forced Michael to keep both eyes on the road if he so much as had a drop of alcohol in his bloodstream: A cheaply-produced videotape that was shown to one of his sobriety classes, which was required after his conviction, and in the grainy and heavily-saturated video was, perceived by Michael, a rather decent man, a clean-cut man, well-spoken, perhaps in another life, a charitable and compassionate man, someone important, like a motivational speaker or guidance counselor, a pillar in his community, who shared his life's story and how he ended up serving a twenty-five year sentence behind bars. The inmate was blunt and didn't use any flowery language to describe, in detail, the car accident where he was undeniably at fault, blew twice the legal limit after cops pulled two bodies from the wreckage, one of them being dead and the other, at the time, wishing that he was dead— Michael reckoned ten years in prison had shaven off the words from the inmate's sentences and each and every word that projected from his mouth was a poignant, punchy, and purposeful one.

With his hand reaching for the car keys, Michael visualized the inmate's face on that grainy videotape. The thought alone, vague and short-lived, forced him to insert the car key into the keyhole. He turned the key clockwise; and as he cracked open the trunk, he saw bright headlights shining from behind. He immediately tossed the empty bottle inside the trunk, shut the door, and spun around where he stood in front of what appeared to be a dark van which pulled up behind Michael. Using his hand to shield his eyes from the blinding light, he said, as though instantly sober, to the driver of the solid matte black van, "Can I help you?"

No response from the driver of the van, only the glare of headlights cutting right through Michael.

As he stepped away from the car and cautiously made his way toward the van, the driver suddenly skidded away, leaving behind a smoky cloud of burnt rubber and exhaust fumes!

Trying to get a good look at the driver, Michael stared into the van as it sped past him but couldn't identity the face, except for a dark profile of a strange figure with reflective iridescent eyes.

Michael waved away the smoke and watched the van drive away. He managed to pick up two observations: First, a spray-painting of heavy-metal-like flames with a matte finish alongside the faded-black van; and second, a small round black sticker with white outline and letters reading "FYRWHL," Michael thinking that it was initials or an abbreviation.

While pushing aside the letters, he redirected his attention back toward the trunk, which was partially cracked open. His stomach suddenly sunk into his gut like an anchor, causing the blood to escape his expressionless face.

After the initial shock subsided, Michael stumbled toward the trunk and with one arm reared back, ready to grab or defend each attack that came his way, swung open the door, only to find an empty space.

No body.

No bottle.

Immediately, he turned his attention toward the desert to his right.

He stared into the blackness of night.

Distant flickers of lightning randomly ping-ponged behind billowing gray clouds.

Michael asked himself: *Why didn't she use that bottle on me?*

Then, the suspicion swirled: *She could've whacked me over the head with it, grabbed my car keys, and drove away. But she didn't.* Why?

The only sound reasoning for Michael's conundrum: She, too, wasn't completely "all-there," mentally, that is, as in, her CPU was temporarily and possibly permanently compromised. He told himself that, based on her life-threatening injuries, she couldn't have gotten far on foot. The way her legs folded like a lawn chair when the side of her body hit the grill of the car and then her lifeless body flipping in the air and then the impact of her head striking the ground. Sounds of the flesh and bone being crushed. The thought alone of her head bouncing off the pavement like a deflated basketball caused his insides to twist and knot.

Michael searched for footprints, tracks, strings of blood—anything that would give him a clearer picture as to where she was headed—but couldn't find any clue that would point him in the right direction. He peered down the highway, first west and then east. She wouldn't have gone south, considering she would have to cross the highway around the time the van sped away. The only plausible direction was north. Into the desert. Toward that approaching storm.

After trekking roughly a quarter of a mile into the pitch-black desert with only the glow of his phone's flashlight providing a limited range of light, occasionally stopping to catch his breath or ward off a creeping dizzy spell, he heard a *crunch* of broken glass underneath his shoe. He slowed his step, as if he was gently tapping a break pedal.

More cautiously, he pulled back to his foot, aimed the light below, and discovered a triangular shard of glass, part of that *Pimp Juice* sticker still partially attached to the remaining pieces. The upper part of his body sprung upright. He frantically aimed the flashlight in every direction but couldn't find any sign of her.

The storm from the north was rapidly intensifying, more flashes of lighting, illuminating those massive clouds.

Back toward the highway the same van pulled up behind Michael's car, grabbing the corner of his eye like a floater.

Intrigued, Michael lowered the phone with his other hand acting like a cover to shield the light.

From what Michael witnessed, the mysterious driver exited the van while the van was still running, walked over to the side of Michael's car, kneeled down beside the back right tire, then returned to the van and drove away.

More sober from the sight of the van, Michael rushed back to the car where he found his rear tire slashed.

As the anger began to mount, he returned to the trunk and fetched the spare tire, as well as a jack and socket wrench from the small compartment. When he closed the compartment, he found the ripped ticket stub from a movie theatre, part of the film's title *Wolves Who*, as well as screen number *11* revealed in front of a glowing red brake light. He pocketed the stub, shut the trunk, and tended to the flat tire.

Occasionally glancing over his shoulder while changing the tire, he counted eight cars that drove past him. Each one of the cars caused him to pause and wait in anticipation until they passed; and during the entire time, he couldn't help but question the driver of the van's intention. The only plausible reason for the driver to slash the tire: He—or she—witnessed the woman in the trunk escape, sped away in fear, and then, later, after taking a moment to stew over his next actions, returned to Michael's car and found an opportunity to slow him down. And *why exactly would he want to slow me down*, Michael wondered. He must've called the cops.

Paranoid, Michael finished tightening up the remaining lug nuts and sped away. His focus was no longer on the woman, who he struck with his car. If she's dead—more than likely, she was—Michael figured that he'd be in the clear, considering the woman was one of possibly two people who could identify his face, number two being the driver of that van.

Determined to catch up with the mysterious van, Michael drove fifteen miles over the 65 mph speed limit; and each time he passed an oncoming car he would ease his foot off the gas pedal. The last thing that he needed was to be pulled over for speeding. He was convinced that the cops were already after him. Convinced that they had his plates, the make and model of his car. As far as he was concerned, he was a wanted man.

After driving seven miles down the highway, Michael was forced to slow down due to a construction zone, which was lit up by work lights. Both lanes closed. The sides of the highway were lined by bright neon orange signs that read *"Construction,"* *"Road Closed,"* and *"Detour Ahead."* From what he gathered, one side of the road was being dug up with a bulldozer. Most of the workers were standing around, smoking cigarettes and watching as one of the workers with a shovel was removing chunks and heavy slabs of asphalt. Michael slowed down the car next to a worker holding a cardboard STOP sign. He rolled down his window and motioned to the "Detour" sign.

Michael asked the worker who was guiding traffic toward a detour, "Will this detour bring me back to Highway 1?"

The construction worker, who had a hairy pea-sized mole on the left side of his face, nodded his head and said, "Yes, sir. Just take a right here and follow Grey Lee Sting for about five miles until you reach I-10 West. After that, you'll stay on Interstate 10 for two miles, I believe, then you'll take El Camino Road Exit 9B—"

"El Camino?"

"You can't miss it," said the construction worker. "Before you reach the exit, you'll see a massive pink billboard sign with the letters FDE. You'll want to take a left on El Camino, then from there, just follow those detour signs and they'll bring you back to Highway 1."

"Grey Lee Sting to I-10 then—"

"El Camino," he said over a confused Michael.

"Right."

"Just follow the signs and you'll be all good."

The construction worker stepped away from Michael's car, as another car pulled up behind. Not the van, Michael identified the different headlights in the rear view mirror. He drove away, repeating the construction worker's specific instructions in his head: *Five miles on Grey Lee Sting, I-10 West, then two miles on I-10 West, then look for the letters FDE, then El Camino, then take a left on El Camino, follow signs.*

Michael did exactly what the construction worker said and found those letters "FDE" on a pink billboard sign, which was promoting a popular retail company that specialized in nutritional herbs, vitamins, and supplements.

After Michael exited onto the off-ramp, he made a left-hand turn onto El Camino.

For a couple of miles, he stayed on El Camino, passing a small town with a downtown that consisted of three buildings and each of them appeared as if they were housing squatters. While passing what looked like a car dealership with no cars in the lot, he spotted activity coming from a small roadside diner called The Sandbox, which was lit up like Christmas along the corner of a desolate intersection where streetlights were flashing yellow.

Among the dozen or so cars parked in front of the diner was a sketchy black van with a dull sheen. He decided to slow down the car; and once he picked up a better angle of the van, he realized it was the same van after he witnessed those flames on each side of the van.

As Michael drove past the diner, he suddenly slammed on the brakes, reversed the car, and parked in an available space in the back of The Sandbox's parking lot. First, as soon as he exited the car, he discreetly walked behind the parked cars and right before he cut his way toward the sidewalk in front of the diner, walked past the mysterious van and shot a subtle glance through the driver's side window. He didn't *see* anything inside the van that warranted another glance. The only observation that forced him to instinctually alter his walk to a near slo-mo stroll wasn't what he saw with his own eyes; instead, it was what he *heard* with his ears. He could best describe the sound as a growl, as deep and guttural as the earth itself, rising from the darkness of the back of the van.

Unnerved by the sound, which he believed was perhaps a kind of creative alarm system that alerted any intruder for being too close to the proximity of the van, he proceeded toward the diner, his left foot tripping over the curb on the sidewalk. He suddenly caught himself before he did a face-plant into the pavement and casually played off the clumsy moment by dusting off the pants along his thigh, as if it was the pant's fault for nearly causing him to eat a face-full of sidewalk.

Once he entered the stale, quiet, and bright diner, which reminded him of a fluorescent-soaked waiting room inside an ER, he visibly pointed out each and every patron, starting with the ones who were slumped over the bar and then those neatly tucked away inside the booths. He mentally counted nine of them, three at the bar—not including the middle-aged waitress who welcomed Michael while topping off a cup of coffee for a heavy-set trucker seated at the bar, as well as the baggy-eyed cook who, from the kitchen, glared at Michael while carelessly plating a spatula-full of scrambled eggs—two couples and two singles inside the booth, five on his right and one on his left.

Curious about the loner on his left, he decided to grab the window seat three booths away behind the loner, whose presence never raised any red flags for Michael. He was a rather clean-cut individual with what looked like a twenty-dollar haircut, probably collected coupons and shopped at a Save-More store on the weekends. Michael didn't see a wedding ring on his finger; these days, Michael reminded himself, a ring acted like a perfect cover for a man who was hiding in a plain sight.

Shortly after he made himself comfortable with the decent view of the van, the waitress stopped by the booth and asked him if he'd like any coffee.

"Please," Michael said, as the tense mood inside the diner made him thirsty and desperate to sober up.

The waitress poured a cup of coffee and asked Michael if he was having a good night so far. He kept his answers short and tried not to draw too much attention to himself. He eyed a slice of key lime pie in the case. The pie had probably been sitting out all day, he thought, but he needed food in his stomach. He ordered a slice. Moments later, the waitress returned to the booth with the pie.

"Enjoy," she said and smiled at Michael.

As though his squinting bloodshot eyes required the support of reading glasses, he peered at the nametag.

"Thanks. . . " he read, ". . . Sh*anon*."

"Sharon," she corrected.

For a woman who tirelessly slaved over night owls, such as himself, he was impressed by Sharon's grace and how, despite all the roadkill that she served throughout the night, she still managed to hold her head high.

As Sharon tended to other patrons, Michael glanced at his own reflection in the window; and for a moment, he couldn't recognize himself.

While taking his time with the pie, Michael patiently waited for the driver of the van to exit the diner. During each careful bite, he eyed each patron without staring at him or her. Of all the patrons, only one had a giant question mark hanging over his head: The loner seated with his back turned to Michael.

First to leave was the couple, who drove away in a sedan.

He was down to seven candidates.

Then, five, after the other couple, two young hot-blooded lovebirds who acted as if they were glued to the hip, exited the diner.

After the couple was the loner.

Ready to make his move, Michael placed fifteen dollars on the table, ten for the pie and coffee and a five dollar tip for the kind waitress, and carefully watched the loner stand up from the booth, pay for his meatloaf diner, and exit the diner.

While seating on the edge of the booth, ready to pounce, Michael tracked the quiet loner to a car parked *next* to the van.

Disappointed, Michael eased back into the booth and redirected his attention to the four patrons, three at the bar and an older gentleman seated at the booth at the opposite end of the diner. He already chalked off the older fellow. Same with the trucker at the bar who was, more than likely, driving the green tractor unit with a sleeper cab parked in the back of the parking lot. He was left with two patrons, both seated at the bar.

As Michael tried to figure out each of their backstories, the two finished up their meals and exited from the diner and left in their vehicles and not one of them was the van.

Frustrated, Michael waved over the waitress and asked her if she knew the driver of the van.

"I'm sorry, dear," she said, brows furrowed. "What van?"

Michael faced the parking lot outside.

"The van parked right. . . "

He searched for the van but couldn't locate it anywhere in the parking lot. He scanned the street where, to his surprise, he witnessed the van driving away. He bolted from the diner. The notion alone of that driver of the van being inside the van possibly the whole time during his mental fit of trying to guess the lucky patron caused the pie to churn in his stomach. *If he was* inside the van, Michael wondered, *was he watching me?*

Panicked, Michael sped away from the diner and eventually caught up with the van. From a distance, he tailed the van as it followed those bright orange detour signs.

As Michael was rerouted onto the previous highway with the construction work, he lost sight of the van.

Thinking that the driver kicked the van into full-on hyper speed as soon as he realized he was being tailed, he accelerated well over the speed limit. He drove roughly five miles and still no sign of the driver. The headlights suddenly caught a reflection glow of a yellow sign in the middle of the night. He slammed on the brakes, coming inches away from hitting the yellow "Dead End" sign in the center of the highway. Beyond the sign: a vast desert that faded into the blackness of night.

The highway gone, as though the asphalt itself was washed away by a sea of desert sand.

Confused by the sign, Michael wondered if it had anything to do with the construction work. Perhaps the workers were rebuilding a section of the highway. He pulled out his phone and checked the GPS—sure enough, Highway 1 was *not* under construction. There it was, on the glowing screen, like a main artery running through the rugged terrain, a tiny white outlined marker of Michael's precise location like a radiating red blood cell. *Was the GPS outdated?* Or, Michael wondered, *was I going completely insane?*

With no other path forward, he decided to make a U-turn. The muscles in his chest were tighter and much tenser from the building stress. As soon as he began to drive away from the dead end, a burst of familiar light appeared in the rear view mirror. The headlights of the van were bearing down on him.

The sudden fender bender caused him to jolt forward, causing him to nearly crack his chin on the steering wheel.

"Goddamn it!" he cried out.

As the van made yet another attempt to ram the car, Michael accelerated. His right foot was pressed so hard against the gas pedal that he could actually feel the belts and pistons and all of those key components of the engine spinning and pumping as if it was an extra organ inside his body.

After several miles of driving to the car's maximum speed, Michael gained more distance from the van until, eventually, it faded into the night darkness.

Somewhat relieved, he reduced the speed of the car. The notion suddenly dawned on him: The construction site, as well as that specific zone where he was forced to detour, nowhere to be found. Like the highway before, gone, as if it never existed in the first place. He specifically remembered passing the billboard for the Happy-Go-Lucky Rest Stop moments before he arrived at the construction site where workers were digging up one side of the highway.

As he approached that one particular billboard, he slowed down and switched on the high beams and in his brief survey, found no evidence whatsoever of a construction site. He kept driving until he reached the same gas station as before, Fill-R-Up. For a moment, Michael wondered if he was driving on a different highway, not Highway 1, since most of the highways, as well as the gas stations looked the exact same. Like a lot of things these days. Copy and paste. Rinse and repeat.

Forget all the signs, which couldn't be trusted either. The only way that Michael could be sure whether or not he was on the same highway: The clerk inside the convenient store. He told himself that you couldn't "copy and paste" an individual and that even twins had certain yet incredibly subtle characteristics that told them apart. Despite Michael's inebriated state, how could he forget a face like the clerk's? He parked the car in front of the convenient store and stepped out of the car for a better look at the clerk, who was skimming through a science magazine behind the checkout counter.

Once the clerk pulled his walled-eye gaze from the magazine, the wind was suddenly knocked out of Michael.

With his breath labored, he returned to the car and drove west, as though he was repeating the same drive as before but expecting a different outcome.

Not too long after he drove away from the gas station, he saw a hitchhiker strolling over the narrow rumble strip alongside the highway.

Thinking it might've been her, he slowed the car to a near creep, his foot hovering over the gas pedal like a finger over a trigger, ready to pull the moment that he confirmed his suspicions. *Not her*, he realized, based on the masculine frame. He moved his foot toward the brake and inched slightly ahead of the hitchhiker and then finally braked. The hitchhiker walked up beside Michael's idled car, face covered in shadows, despite the hazy glow of headlights.

The hitchhiker leaned over the passenger side window.

As Michael switched on an overhead light above the center console, the hitchhiker's once dark face suddenly lit up, causing the blood to run from Michael's face.

Gawking at the smirking hitchhiker, who looked identical to himself, Michael asked the look-alike what he was doing out here in the middle of the night, but the words spilled from his lips like dollops of mashed potatoes.

The hitchhiker asked Michael the same exact question, but unlike Michael, the question was spoken with much clarity and confidence.

Left in a state of terror, Michael suddenly sped away, leaving the hitchhiker in a cloud of dust. He continued on Highway 1, passing that same billboard moments before he entered the construction site. He read those words *Happy-Go-Lucky Rest Stop*, encased by a green four-leaf clover, which was lit up by a spotlight; then, as though anticipating bright orange detour signs and street cones lined on one side of the highway once he pulled his eyes away from the billboard, he felt a stirring in his flesh. A sort of internal mechanism being switched, warning him that he was in the presence of an apex predator.

Gasping from the sight of the parked van, Michael hit the brakes and skidded to a complete stop. He embraced a deep breath and stepped out of the car and approached the driver's side of the van.

Left at his wits' end, he cried out, "*What the fuck do you want from me? Huh!*"

The mysterious driver didn't respond.

Michael bravely walked up beside the van.

Seated in the driver's seat was an unflinching man dressed in a solid baseball cap and a faded and holey black T-shirt. He coolly sported a pair of pink steam punk-like shades, which he wore slightly lowered along the stiff bridge of his pointy nose. The one feature that caught Michael's eye: A bullet hole-sized scar, shaped like a starfish, on the left side of his cheek. Immediately, he confused the driver for the construction worker, who had recently given him directions for the detour. Michael specifically recalled the mole on the worker's cheek, as well as his baldness.

Once more, Michael cried out to the driver, demanding an explanation as to why he was stalking him.

As Michael stepped closer to the van—several feet away—he noticed the frayed and straw-like bleach-blonde hair, which could pass as a wig or an extension, sticking out from underneath the black baseball cap.

"*Hey, you son of a bitch!* I'm talking to you—"

"Are you sure, my friend?" the driver said smoothly, turning pink-shaded eyes toward Michael. "I'm not the only one who's been looking for you tonight. . . "

"Looking for me?"

The driver pulled out a cigarette from the top of his right ear and lit it with a gold lighter. He dragged from the cigarette and as smoke streamed from both nostrils like the steam from the cartoon of an angry bull, he made a *clicking* noise with the back corner of his mouth.

All of a sudden, the flame spray-painted van door slid wide open and forced Michael to backpedal away from the van.

He heard a growl erupting from the inside of the van.

While slowly backpedaling and inching his way back to his car, he tried to make out the other person seated in the backseat but the interior of the van was soaked in blackness.

Following the unnerving sound, he witnessed two marbled eyes of a beast form in the dark.

As soon as Michael saw the lush mane, as well as the two front paws, which were about the size of boxing gloves, land on the asphalt, he made a beeline to his car. The lion chased after Michael, who hurried back into the car. He safely slammed the door close as the lion swiped at him and came nearly inches away from clawing his arm.

Next, Michael locked all of the doors as the lion continued to violently scratch the window of the driver's side door. Eventually, the lion pounced on the hood of the car. Looming over Michael, the lion opened its gaping mouth, only to reveal a set of metallic fangs, as black as slate, dripping white with saliva.

As the lion clawed at the windshield, Michael floored the gas pedal. The lion leaped off the hood without suffering any injuries and while staring down Michael as he fishtailed away, prowled its way back toward the van.

The emotion poured from Michael, who screamed out in a mix of horror and jubilation and everything in between, all of the blood in his knuckles wrung dry as he choked the steering wheel. He was forced to make yet another U-turn after running into yet another dead end. He drove back east, toward the direction of the very threat he was trying to escape; then, only a couple of miles down the road, he ran into yet another dead end, forcing him to make yet another U-turn. He drove west; and sure enough, after driving not even a mile down the highway, he was stopped by yet another "Dead End" sign.

Instead of making a U-turn, Michael decided to drive past the sign. He switched on the high beams as he drove into the desert.

After driving several miles through the bumpy desert, he came across his only salvation.

Lost in the maw of the night, Michael had no other choice than to drive onto the dirt road, which led him northbound, to the colossal storm, brutal yet magnanimous, where an unruly and highly intrusive code cheered on the end of his existence—and strangely, the beginning.

OFF-RAMPS

DIFFERENT seasons tick by like hours before my eyes.

The hour hand climbs closer to twelve, the twelfth hour, the witching hour. That unyielding hand, persistent as hell, continues along its inevitable trajectory, where upon its rightful insurrection, a great storm swallows me whole, pulling me apart, devouring me, leaving me no other option than to seek a provisional refuge in the wasteland, where upon my patience and serenity, I will use my thirty pieces of silver to build my army of the dead and the decommissioned, rusty parts and all.

The desert holds no mercy for the weak, and yet, it turns a blind eye on the shadowbanned, who thrive among its very ruins.

Along its sandy strips which lay bare and wavy, once highways, now all but ghosts of what came before, momentary blips to satisfy the unsatisfied, I stumble upon the remains of a skeleton dressed in ageless black leather, my first finding a hardened shell encrusted with earth from decades of relentless storms underneath a loose mandible, which is separated from a fractured skull.

I crack open the shell, revealing the earring of a lightning bolt and hold it in my palm as it faintly glints in sunlight beating from above.

All around me the sun beats down upon the desert, if only for a moment, leaving behind a trail of lights, a fleeting ripple, a

path among the sea of sand illuminating each grain along its parched surface, still like death, yet moving and shining its light, capturing those who gaze upon its very womb.

Once more, before I venture further into the desert, I examine the bite marks along the skeleton's femur, as well as the leather, which appear as if they have been chewed through by a man-eater, the great beast, the ultra-prime alpha of all alphas, a seeker and a destroyer.

I search the vicinity for a motorcycle, but instead, only come across my next finding: The skull of a similar creature with a snout, the left side of the skull covered in scratch marks.

I pluck away the glassy black fang from the skull and examine the fang, which appears much smaller in size, depth, and diameter than the bite marks on those warped bones. As I did with the earring, I place the fang in my pocket and save it for a rainy day.

My next finding is a meat tenderizer on the soiled counter in the back of a dusty old convenient store, which has been gutted and ransacked and stripped down to its bare bones, exposing dead wires and cables that hang like nooses.

The instrument was lying there like both a needle and a *thread*, the holy receptacles of past voices—and screams—weave through one storm to the next, sowing seeds of the darkest of all spells.

One of those spells came in the form of a worn and crinkled paperback, *Quiet Storm*, the author's name rubbed off with a sharp blade of some kind.

I pick up the book from the dust-covered floor behind what used to be a checkout counter, which has turned into the landing of bat droppings.

The bats are gone, including the ceiling, which has caved in from the weight of their accumulating waste.

I add the book, as well as a pair of pink shades from the over-turned rack, to my collection, and exit the back of the store, where, inside a full dumpster buried half-deep in sloping sand-drift, I discover a guitar case, as chapped as winter lips, except for a pick inside, empty.

I store my finings inside the leathery case, first that earring I pulled from the skeleton, then that black fang from the skull of a beast, then that meat tenderizer, then that book, then, finally, those pink shades.

Not too far away from the dumpster, what used to be a parking lot, offers me my next finding: an x-shaped tire iron. So, in the guitar case it goes, and then, roughly a hundred and two steps later, a rubber duck, still yellow and orange, despite the gory surroundings, a bloodstained bathtub inside the bathroom of an abandoned house riddled with unholy Death, whose foul breath forces me to wait in a creaking silence.

If you listen close enough, you can hear the walls release the haunting voices of those who occupied these very spaces, saying in the sharpest and faintest whisper: "*Now* kiss me, deep and dark, caress my *nefarious ballad.*"

What a cruel and untimely prelude, it is and was.

The strum of love, its touch like a drug—but why, I ask myself, why, oh, why, am I so addicted to the withdrawal?

After placing the rubber duck inside the case, I nearly step on a bullet casing.

I pick up the empty casing, no theories or questions.

I fill the emptiness with the very emptiness it deserves and step onto the back porch, where the charred remains of a soot-covered field, once consumed by fire, strums yet another cord inside me—not of love, but rather the opposite of love, which forces me to understand, to dig deeper for the origins of such hatred.

Where did it manifest? And how did it spread so fast and vast over such growth and gains? The answer is brought forward on a silver casing.

My next—and last—finding is an obsolete smartphone with a cracked screen covered in hundreds of tiny carpenter ants. Yet, somehow, despite the smartphone bearing the similarities of a glorified paperweight, the once secretarial device acts as a reminder, like the highway blanketed with sand, reminding me of those moments, which were obstructed and fragmented and left lost in time.

A life of many roads diverged into a stage full of repeat offenders.

One avenue left untraveled.

The other, purged by fire.

But, like love, *is it the fire I desire?*

Shattered glass falls like snowflakes from a starless sky, covering a barren, rubble-ridden ground around me. Thousands of smoldering ambers release snake-like hisses. Elevators of stem ascend above me.

The nag of uncertainty triumphs into the blaring of a delayed *ringing* sound, greeting me, engulfing me, becoming me.

Yet, despite the violent welcoming, the *ringing* remains tucked away underneath the eternal hum of death, soft yet present like a subdued soundtrack curated by the designated life-jockeys who brace space and time.

From a distance, I hear life in the form of a dog barking.

Or, is it a howling?

Whatever it may be, I embrace the sounds with a heart, not only wanting to be full, but also hoping to turn, for I'm nothing more than a relic collecting forgotten remnants of a future already written.

*BLACK FANGS MOTORCYLE CLUB SIDE NOTES A-Z

TO *cram or not to cram*, that is the question—well, more or less, a predicament most, if not all, writers face while finalizing a story, which, after spending enough time imagining oneself rattling around in the heads of fictional characters, eventually turns, almost always, into *The Story* with a capital T. The center of attention, a piece of work that rightfully—given the patience and consideration it required—earned a "the" in front of it, and everything outside the work, either by fault or inconvenience, is nothing more than background noise buried underneath another kind of noise, head noise: Is there too much bloat or fat? Does *The Story* need to be trimmed down in size, made tighter and leaner? And if so, by how much?

Think of the section below, not as an appendix, even though, in a general observation, it's exactly that, additional matter at the end of a book or in this case, a particular story, which, given its brevity, deserves a more in-depth look, but rather the author's personal notes, which, if provided the space, would've wound up along the side of the page in a handwriting that may resemble an oddly-shaped wave on an electrocardiogram. The section below is everything that wasn't included in Dalivia Plaut's *Black Fangs Motorcycle Club*. So, please, indulge yourself or shall I say, wolf it up, if you still have room:

A. Grant used to run as business called "100% Stone." He never took his family to their grandfather's house. Didn't get along with Marley; in fact, he didn't have any relationship with him. Resented him for controlling his mother with an *iron* fist.

B. Wildwood is located near a reservoir.

C. Every year, locals profit from the Legend. Vendors sell candy, refreshments, like snow cones and shaved ice, and over the years, adults incorporated alcohol into the festival.

D. Wildwood Beast was slain by Sir Hammer in the 1800's. Found gold stashed by slave owners, who were using the monster to keep townspeople scared and locked up in their homes, making them "compliant." Once monster was slain, the people lived without fear. Simple as that! Could draw parallels to Big Brother being the monster! Actual mascot looks kind of like Bigfoot, *not* werewolf, who, over centuries, changed its appearance, looking nothing like a werewolf. Festival includes jousting matches, medieval lore. The locals celebrate the defeat of the great beast who lived in the woods, once came out during summertime to feast.

E. Statue of ruggedly dressed Knight—Hammer—in town's square.

F. Movie reference: *Lost Boys*.
Mention muscled dude with sax.
<u>Act (swan in kiddy pool of tar):</u>
<u>Mute Swan (Use Rosewood Std Regular font)</u>
Cover/Image(s): Group of bikers on a smoky hilltop in woods; howling under moon, partying; or a black helicopter tee, collage-like.
Think character, Tyler, and his overbearing father figure in *Waves* meets Sam's situation in *Lost Boys*: Family moves from big city to slower-paced town, which has a dark secret unaware by most of its own townspeople and especially outsiders, only instead of vampires. . . werewolves.
(I know. Werewolves, right? Why in the hell do we need more shit with werewolves? Which would more than likely be CGI'd and look like a shiny dog turd. Spare us the misery. Same goes

with vampires? Or, any other monster you keep dumping on us every single year? Enough with the fucking monster movies about monsters we've seen over and over! But. . . what exactly makes this picture different from the rest of the pack? We turn the cliché of the werewolf on its head. Instead of treating the werewolf as a curse or whatever, we treat it as a virus; and in return, we make "society" the werewolf—figuratively speaking. Instead of focusing on what we already know about the conventional werewolf, like shapeshifting from man to beast, hunting under a full moon, or possessing a ravenous appetite for flesh, we replace the "shapeshifter" with the "grifter," the "predator" with the "politician," the "killer" with the "consumer." Two insidious creatures who possess similar traits, both equally driven by one goal, one primitive, yet another self-indulgent. Like Romero did with Night of the Living Dead *or what Carpenter did with* They Live, *the story will be a subtle social commentary exploiting society's bottomless hungry for consumption, as well as the figurative werewolves who come in different shapes and sizes—Too much?)*

G. Army believes Charles can't take care of himself, let alone, his father, as well as the new house; thinks he's irresponsible and has no mission in life. Charles and Grant do <u>not</u> get along. Army is bossy. Charles, on the other hand, looks up to older bro but doesn't show it. Charley didn't want to move from D.C., away from his friends.

H. Cow logo on the side of a boxed cargo.

I. There's no "I" in *Black Fangs Motorcycle Club*, or BFF.

J. Thunder Street Soldiers (Skinheads) wear "SS" arm patch on leather jacket.

K. Members of BFF rarely hook up with those outside the club; Charles is an exception.

L. This sets off a chain of effects, i.e. a domino effect.

M. Neighbor is unhinged, possibly insane, or at least, made to sound insane, a known conspirator who thinks government created werewolves and the werewolf virus.

N. We see many wolf bums, homeless, former werewolves, city scrapped them off like fried eggs.

O. "Z Balls" like cocaine or speed, manufactured from dandruff of male wolf. Could also be beneficial to the politicians in charge who may use drug to enhance soldiers of war or whomever politicians fuck or fuck over in order to get elected.

P. Vet's house located in the small town of Hunters Valley.

Q. Detective says: "*You're better off in that jail cell right now than you are hanging out with those animals.*" Smithen thinks it's for Charles's own safety.

R. Probably one of the most cinematic scenes in the story. *Dark and gory enough to quench the thirst of any horror fanatic.* We're talking heavy shades of *Aliens* here, the ambush scene, leading up to the abduction of Newt, where Xenomorphs infiltrate the barricade and drop down from the ceiling and attack Ripley and the Gang. Hudson going straight up ape-shit, going out in style!

S. Later, after pack is disbanded, remaining members become lost, become assassins traveling up and down The Coast. Lone Wolf left the pack after falling hard for Gwen.

T. Werewolf virus draws similarities to AIDS, rabies, and STDs, virus spread through both salvia, fluid, or sexual contact, like a venereal disease, full breeds carry virus, however, it varies in spread, for Gwen, body didn't react well to virus. Ripped her insides to shreds.

U. In a way, Charles blames his father for Gwen's infidelity.

V. Later on, Private Sector or perhaps Branch of Government extracts female werewolf's blood and body parts for sophisticated weaponry project (Project Black Fang)?

W. Or, scientist could use virus to cure certain cancers and find ways to target a disease, use virus to "eat" or consume bad cells in body. The possibilities are endless, but at what cost?

X. *Literally throwing Sasha to the wolves!*

Y. Trey "lost" his way over the years and only cares about money and settling down. He's getting older now and tired of riding. Consumerism, American greed, technology has made Trey indolent, he abandoned his will and desire to hunt, to be free; however, Charles changes him and gives him hope, feels young again while around Charles, doesn't want to live up to his end of the deal. Before Trey can stop Slim, it's already too late. Slim promised Trey that BFF didn't have to worry about losing the bloodline. *Neuvak could freeze Sasha's eggs, then return her to pack safe and sound—a lie! Also, Slim is being used. Not really a Lone Wolf but more like a Lone Pawn.

Z. It would be cool to make Sasha pregnant with Charles's offspring. Charles knows exactly where they're going or where they might be based on a conversation he had with Sasha, how she liked South Beach, Miami, and always dreamed about going there. Plus, he can smell the bitch, you know, with his super senses and all. What a gangster!

Glooo

ONCE YOU *Glooo* IT, YOU CAN'T UNDOOO IT!

Glooo Stick
Non-Toxic
Safe
Clean
Washable

For home use

- Easily spreads over most surfaces
- Leaves behind no sticky residue
- Dries within *10 seconds*!
- <u>PRO-TIP</u>: For best results while applying GLOO, draw a letter "X"

*This product is fictional and any resemblances to other or similar products are entirely coincidental.

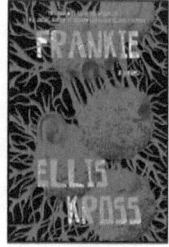

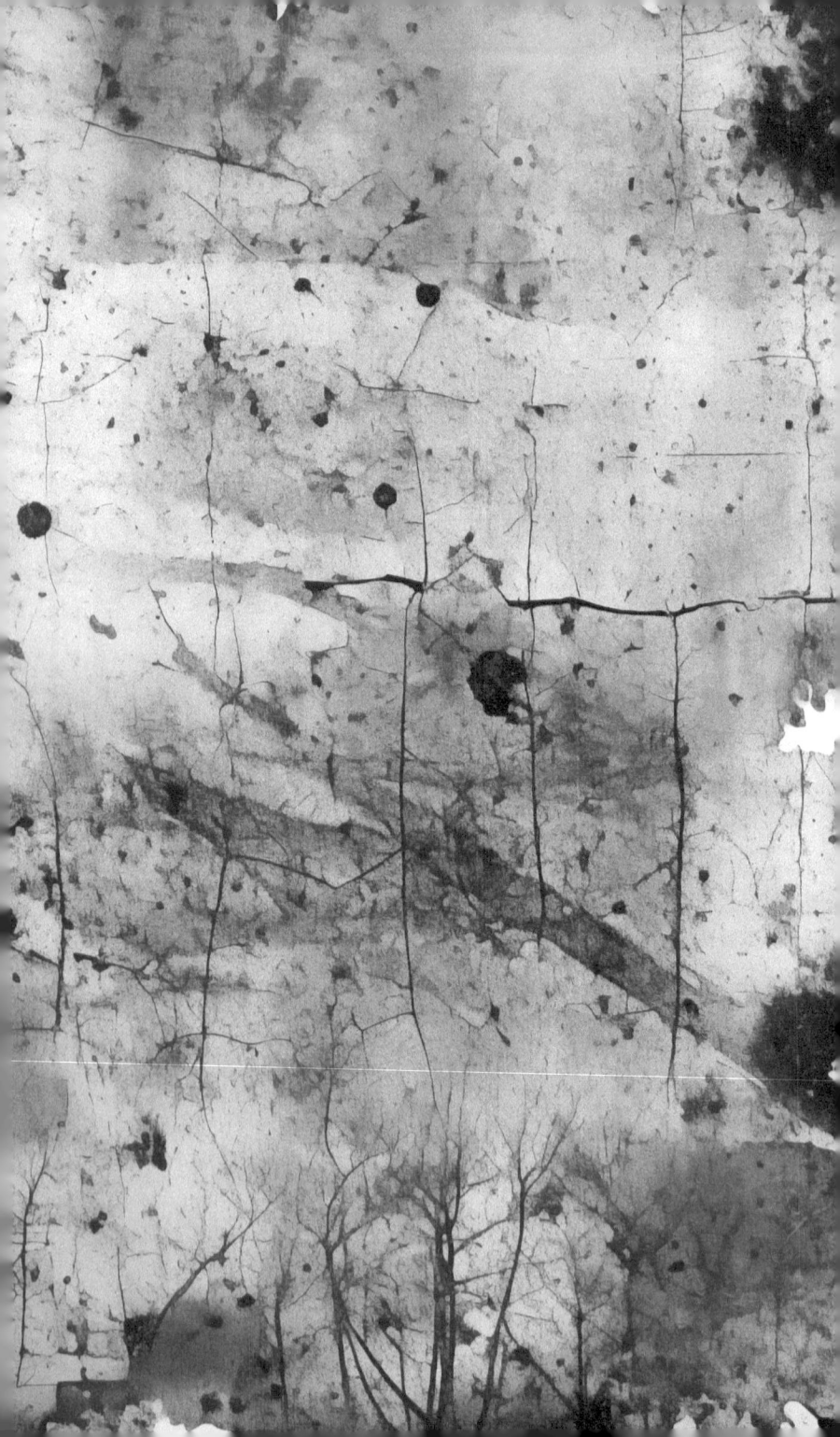